BLACK
and
BLUE

FRANK F.
WEBER

Front and back cover photo: Trisha Spencer of Xsperience Photography
Cover Design: J. M. Kurtz Libby
Cover Art Graphics: J. M. Kurtz Libby

Represented by Krista Soukup, Blue Cottage Agency

Published in partnership with BookBaby
7905 N. Crescent Blvd.
Pennsauken, NJ 08110

And

The Story Laboratory www.writeeditdesignlab.com
Published by Moon Finder Press
500 Park Avenue
P.O. Box 496, Pierz, MN 56364

I am dedicating this book to my partner, best friend, lover and wife, Brenda. Your presence makes every day of my life an enraptured treasure. I ended Chapter 21 with a thought you gave me: *The world doesn't spin on love, but love makes every moment on earth better.*

I would like to thank my editor, Tiffany Lundgren Madson, for the incredible work she did with this book. Her guidance with writing, her help getting me get in contact with the right people, and her creative insight was invaluable to the development of this book. I can't thank you enough, Tiffany! You're amazing!

Frank F. Weber, True Crime mysteries
(Jon Frederick series) include:

Murder Book (2017)
The I-94 Murders (2018)
Last Call (2019)
Lying Close (2020)
Burning Bridges (2021)
Black and Blue (2022)

I feel a tremendous sense of gratitude toward all of the great Americans, and friends of America, who shared the insights that begin each chapter.

Pay attention to the name in bold at the beginning of each chapter, as the chapter is told from this character's perspective.

Minneapolis

Minnesota

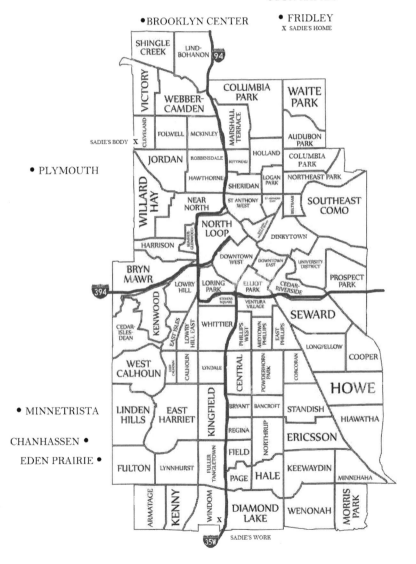

- ELK RIVER
- NOWTHEN
- ANDOVER
- COON RAPIDS
- BROOKLYN CENTER
- FRIDLEY
  X SADIE'S HOME
- PLYMOUTH
- MINNETRISTA
- CHANHASSEN
- EDEN PRAIRIE
- LAKEVILLE

SHINGLE CREEK
LIND-BOHANON
94
VICTORY
WEBBER-CAMDEN
COLUMBIA PARK
WAITE PARK
CLEVELAND
FOLWELL
MCKINLEY
MARSHALL TERRACE
AUDUBON PARK
SADIE'S BODY X
JORDAN
ROBBINSDALE
BOTTINEAU
HOLLAND
COLUMBIA PARK
HAWTHORNE
LOGAN PARK
NORTHEAST PARK
SHERIDAN
WILLARD HAY
NEAR NORTH
ST ANTHONY WEST
ST ANTHONY EAST
BELTRAMI
SOUTHEAST COMO
NORTH LOOP
SUMNER-GLENWOOD
DINKYTOWN
HARRISON
DOWNTOWN WEST
DOWNTOWN EAST
UNIVERSITY DISTRICT
BRYN MAWR
394
LOWRY HILL
LORING PARK
ELLIOT PARK
CEDAR-RIVERSIDE
PROSPECT PARK
KENWOOD
STEVENS SQUARE
VENTURA VILLAGE
SEWARD
CEDAR-ISLES-DEAN
EAST ISLES
LOWRY HILL EAST
WHITTIER
PHILLIPS WEST
MIDTOWN PHILLIPS
EAST PHILLIPS
LONGFELLOW
COOPER
WEST CALHOUN
EAST CALHOUN
CALHOUN
LYNDALE
CENTRAL
POWDERHORN PARK
CORCORAN
HOWE
LINDEN HILLS
EAST HARRIET
KINGFIELD
BRYANT
BANCROFT
STANDISH
HIAWATHA
REGINA
NORTHRUP
ERICSSON
FIELD
FULTON
LYNNHURST
FULLER TANGLETOWN
PAGE
HALE
KEEWAYDIN
MINNEHAHA
ARMATAGE
KENNY
WINDOM
X
WENONAH
MORRIS PARK
DIAMOND LAKE
35W
SADIE'S WORK

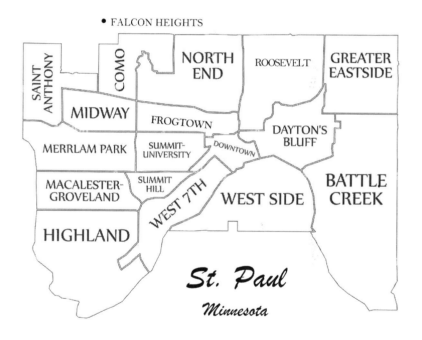

• LINO LAKES

STILLWATER •

• FALCON HEIGHTS

SAINT ANTHONY

COMO

NORTH END

ROOSEVELT

GREATER EASTSIDE

MIDWAY

FROGTOWN

DAYTON'S BLUFF

MERRLAM PARK

SUMMIT-UNIVERSITY

DOWNTOWN

MACALESTER-GROVELAND

SUMMIT HILL

WEST 7TH

WEST SIDE

BATTLE CREEK

HIGHLAND

St. Paul

Minnesota

List of Characters

1

*"The greatest lie ever told about
love is that it sets you free."*
—ZADIE SMITH

2013

XAVIER "ZAVE" WILLIAMS

4:25 A.M., FRIDAY, JULY 5,
CUB FOODS, NICOLLET AVE,
WINDOM NEIGHBORHOOD, MINNEAPOLIS

Don't tell me I speak *too white*. That comment is like finger-nails on a chalkboard to me. Did Martin Luther King Jr., Malcolm X, or Shirley Chisolm speak too white? Do Melvin Carter, Robyne Robinson, or Ilhan Omar speak too white? They have a message for all of America and in 1795, our government decided everyone should speak English. German Americans, who still to this day are the largest ethnic group in the U.S., asked if the laws could also be printed in German, too, so they could understand them. They were denied. English Americans constitute 8% of the U.S. population, with the highest concentrations in Maine and Utah. Still, 96% of the U.S. Presidents are of English ancestry. English is the language of money. If you want to change America, you need to be fluent in English. Former slave, Frederick Douglas, told Black America this back in 1845.

The money game is played in a variety of ways. Let me give you an example: Your English vocabulary is predictive of your intelligence. This research led me to question how we measure intelligence. Intelligence tests are designed to predict your likelihood of success in school—nothing else— with English being one of the main subjects. So, you become "gifted" by being raised in a predominantly English-speaking home, and that success leads to scholarships, jobs, and money.

I don't speak too white. I speak too *"money,"* at times. Keep in mind that African Americans, German Americans, Mexican Americans, Scandinavian Americans, Native Americans, Irish Americans, and Asian Americans have all been criticized for the way they talk in America. Like all of these groups, when I'm with my friends, I speak differently—a language I call *American.* My parents drilled it into my head that, if I wanted to be successful, I had to write and speak in the language of *money.* In his later years, John Steinbeck wrote how he mourned the loss of dialect he used to enjoy when he traveled the U.S. Well John, the cause was literacy, and we're all being taught to read and write the same way.

THE FIRST TIME I MET SADIE SULLIVAN WAS after the end of a late-night Independence Day shift with the Minneapolis Police Department. I had just finished patrolling the Freedom from Pants parade. The underwear bike ride began in Northeast Minneapolis and ended at Powderhorn Park, where participants cooled off in the lake. It was the "Minnesota nice" spin to avoiding the naked rides that occurred in over fifty cities. I personally didn't see any pleasure in riding a bicycle naked. People respected the dress code, and it was a relatively peaceful event.

Tired and hungry, I stopped at the grocery store to pick up eggs for breakfast. As I exited aisle seven and turned to dairy, there knelt a weeping Cub Foods employee. Hopeless tears streamed down the cheeks of a beautiful brunette.

I was tired and honestly, not in the mood to deal with drama, particularly from a teenager. I looked up and down the aisle for someone I could send to help this poor creature. Where were the Tuskagee Airmen when you needed them? Hell, I'd have even settled for the Rescue Rangers. *Sigh.* I was the only customer in the store.

A white person might have said, "It can't be that bad." But as an African American, I knew better, so asked, "How bad is it?"

Her eyes remained glued to the floor. Through her tears, she blathered, "I'm engaged—but I think I'm making a mistake. A big mistake." She slowly raised her focus from my feet to my eyes, and then remarked, "Oh, crap."

I helped her to a standing position. "How old are you?"

"Nineteen." With concern, she asked, "You don't know him, do you?"

There were only 350,000 African Americans in Minnesota; of course, I would know him. "What's his name?"

"Bobby Long." She begged, "Please—*please* don't say anything."

I gave her the best smile I could muster. "I don't know Bobby Long and I promise, if I ever run into him, I'll never tell him you're having second thoughts." Okay, not a crisis; I could move on.

But she wasn't about to let me. She stepped in front of me and shook my hand, "I'm Sadie." Her long black hair suggested an Italian gene pool; dark eyebrows highlighted mesmerizing, large hazel eyes.

"I'm Xavier—my friends call me Zave." While my intentions were altruistic, I initially had that weird sensation black men got when they were alone, talking to a white woman— like I was *doing something wrong.* I hated that feeling. It immediately brought to conscious the story Dad had told me about his grandfather, Gabriel. One Sunday afternoon, when he was playing with his daughters on a homemade swing in the front yard of his Mississippi home, two white men walked right up on the yard and shot him dead—because he had married a white woman. I closed my eyes for a second. The script racists shove down your throat was, *walk away and no trouble.* I wasn't walking away from this distressed young woman.

She clumsily wiped away tears with the sleeve of her red Cub Foods pullover and began rambling in true Minnesota dialect, "Geeze, how do you ever know—ya know? He's a great provider—treats my daughter well. And it's not like I bring anything to the table, aside from a pretty awesome wild rice and wild mushroom soup. I think it's hard for a man to be with a woman who had a child at fifteen." She sheepishly glanced up, "Did I say that out loud?"

I smiled. I could have said, "I'm sorry, I just need to get some sleep," and politely continued shopping, but I didn't. Gut instinct on relationships was what made me the miserable lonely man I was today. Still, there was an innocence about her that made me want to tell her it would all be okay.

Sadie went on, "At times, he's just so disconnected. Bobby doesn't *get* me. And the anger in his eyes . . ."

My thinking immediately went into cop mode. "Is he abusive?"

She quickly picked up on the change in dynamic and became defensive. "No—never. He's a good man. Look, I'm sorry for bothering you. Just having a bad morning."

I had my chance. I could've let her scurry away, but I didn't. I said, "Hey, just give me minute. So, where did you meet the brother?"

Sadie smiled, "He isn't black—not that it would be an issue."

Confused, I asked, "Why did you ask if I knew him?"

"He's a cop." Chagrined, she added, "I don't want to humiliate him in front of the entire force. Honestly, he's a great guy. *I'm* the problem—second guessing everything."

"I don't know that you're second guessing everything. You seem to be questioning a major decision. One you can't afford to be wrong about." It was hard for partners of cops to talk about domestic abuse, as a charge had the potential to cost him his job. I asked, "Is he the jealous type?"

Aware of the direction I was headed, she skirted the question. "He doesn't hit me, if that's what you're asking. Bobby says I send out *signals* to guys." She looked around. "Maybe I do."

Wanting to cheer her up, I teased, "Do you mean like gang signs?" I made some goofy gestures with my hands—not actual gang signs—and she started laughing. I had given her *nala*, an African word that refers to the first drink of water in a desert. It's sometimes translated to mean *gift*.

Her eyes shimmered with mischief, as she added to the levity, "I do use jazz hands whenever he asks me something intimate." She shook her hands by her face and smiled, "Do you think that might be an issue?"

I could have educated her on the history of *jazz hands*, but she wasn't being malicious—another time. I let it go.

After an awkward silence, she said, "You know what? I was just being nice and there's nothing wrong with that. Bobby's just going to have to get used to it." Sadie put her hand on my shoulder for a second and said, "Thank you for your kindness, Zave. Now, I need to get back to work and to let you get about your business," and she was gone.

I didn't want her to leave. Some guy named Bobby was coming home to Sadie, who was in trouble for being too nice. I was coming home to graveyard stew. (Three eggs, a half a cup of milk, a couple pickled jalapeno slices and black pepper—nuked for three and a half minutes.) It was what my dad made when he came home from a late night of plowing snow—after Mom stopped getting up for him. And I'd probably fall asleep on the couch before I finished eating it. But it was just as well. The last thing I needed was to be flirting with a teenager engaged to a white cop.

12:30 P.M., TUESDAY, AUGUST 27, 2013
LU'S SANDWICHES, 2624 NICOLLET AVENUE SOUTH
CALHOUN ISLES NEIGHBORHOOD, MINNEAPOLIS

"SADIE" MEANT *PRINCESS* IN HEBREW. I WAS enamored by the combination of her innocence and beauty. Over the next several weeks, Cub became my favorite place to shop and each short interaction we shared seemed to get a little more intimate, even if it was just a flirty smile. *What the hell was I doing?* Finally, I talked her into meeting me for a sandwich at Lu's.

It was the last time I'd see Sadie Sullivan alive. Did I have regrets? Every day.

I ordered the Vietnamese meatball Banh mi sandwich, which was amazing. Sadie went with the mock duck vegetarian sandwich. I had made up my mind—if Sadie maintained her engagement, today would be the last time I'd see her. I would not interfere with a marriage. I hated the man my mom had an affair with. I would not be that guy.

I teased Sadie, "So . . . getting married in ten days."

"Yeah." She set down her sandwich. "It's coming up so fast." With apprehension, she softly added, "No going back, now. Got the hall rented—bought the dress."

"I bought a pair of Lebron Witness basketball shoes, but it doesn't mean I have to play in the NBA. Sadie, you're not going to prom, here. You're talking about marriage—the rest of your life."

Internally, she appeared to be nervously processing a myriad of concerns, but verbally covered them with distractions. "My sisters are excited to be bridesmaids. And at my request, Bobby is letting my older brother, Liam, be the best man. Liam tells everybody that he's my protector, but the truth is, more often than not, I'm the one talking him off the ledge. My mom has worked so hard to make my wedding perfect. And my daughter's so proud to be the flower girl. Like I said, it's a done deal, now." She wasn't elated. Nauseated would've been a better description.

I tried my best. "It's your call. If this is what you want, I wish you the best. But if that's your choice, I won't be seeing you again."

She gasped, "Not at *all*?"

"No. My mom's affair ruined our family. I won't be part of destroying a marriage."

Sadie frowned, "I'm not looking for an affair. How about being a friend?" When I didn't respond, she commented, "It must have been a hard divorce."

"They never divorced, but depression wore on my dad, like water eroding a rock. Every time I asked if they were getting divorced, they'd say, *I don't know.* I will never do that to my kids. The answer is a hard *no* until you know with certainty. There's nothing worse than living in depressive ambiguity."

Sadie started, "Who am I to say—" So soft, I could barely make out the words, she suggested, "Maybe it would be easier for your dad if you'd stop referring to it as the event that ruined your family. Life is hard—and people make mistakes. My dad had an affair and they divorced, but I still love him, and we can still laugh together."

After an uncomfortable silence, she asked, "Is that why you're not married? I mean, look at you. Handsome—strong as a soldier—smart as a whip."

"I'm only twenty-five years old." I caught her gazing into my eyes and restated, "Not ready."

She raised an eyebrow. "Is anyone ever ready?"

"I hope so. I plan to marry someday."

With jittery hands, Sadie stirred her tea. "I imagine you've got a line waiting for you."

Talk about the pot calling the kettle black. I immediately deprecated myself for the idiom. The saying only worked if you assumed that black was undesirable.

She continued, "I worry that this is my one chance. What if no one else asks?"

Part of me wanted to say, *what if I asked?* Sadie didn't have a clue how precious her genuine kindness and humble beauty were to me. I was infatuated with her. I wanted to sweep her off her feet and carry her through a vine-covered trellis into a peaceful sanctuary, reserved only for us. But she was damn young and naïve. Even if she agreed, I'd feel like I was taking advantage of her. I sat back, "Girl, you're only nineteen years old. You could get a decent guy to propose to you three times a year."

"Don't say that. I have nothing. My mom was a single parent of five and I lived at home, sharing a bedroom, until the day I was proposed to. I've lived with Bobby, since."

"So, you still share a bedroom." I suggested, "Maybe you need to be on your own for a bit." I bitterly reminded myself, *look how happy I am.*

She brushed away the thought. "Too scary."

"Where's your daughter at?"

Ashamed, she looked down at her plate, as if the duck would help her escape. Maybe a real duck could have helped her flee, but this duck just *mocked* her. Sadie admitted, "Mom's friends helped me adopt her out to a couple at our church. It's an open adoption, so I get Abby every other Saturday, plus I babysit for them. That's why I work early mornings—so I can be with her when they need a sitter in the afternoon."

"You're amazing." I couldn't help grinning. She was truly a down to earth, loving mother.

Embarrassed by the compliment, she avoided eye contact as she explained, "Realistically, I couldn't afford a child. I was fifteen and I had nothing." She searched my face for disapproval over her sinful indiscretion.

I put my hand over hers, "Hey, I'm no one to judge. I could've fathered a kid at fifteen. It's only by the luck of the draw I didn't. And I wouldn't have been in a position to parent then, either."

Her hazel eyes warmed in appreciation, revealing a ring of shimmering gold between the emerald green and the mahogany brown concentric circles in her eyes. She said, "I always anticipate being judged harshly when I admit that. And your opinion is important to me." She flipped her hand under my palm and squeezed. Neither of us let go, our sandwiches all but forgotten.

In fond appreciation, Sadie said, "Thank you." She added, "The cycle keeps repeating itself. My mom married an immature guy, who fathered five kids in seven years, and then cheated on her. She kicked him out. Mom had to go to the county for support and, when my dad fell behind in his child support, the county took away his driver's license. After that, he could never afford to keep up on child support, because now he couldn't get to work. Then I come along and, just on the other side of puberty, had a child with an older guy, locking me into poverty, too. My guy insisted I keep the baby, even though he only worked part time and all his money went to chronic."

Chronic was a form of weed so potent that the THC crystals were in plain sight.

She continued, "When I asked how we'd manage, he kept saying, 'We'll find a way,' but offered nothing. So, I adopted Abby out and he dumped me. Said he couldn't forgive me."

"He sounds like a piece of work."

Sadie smiled, "He's all right—always made me smile—at least until I was pregnant. Then he just made me cry. But I don't blame him. I believed that somehow, I was immune to the risk I was taking. There's a reason post coital prayer isn't listed as a form of birth control." She swiped a lock of hair behind her ear. "In the end, I had sex with him because I was afraid he'd leave me if I didn't. Ultimately, he left me because I did."

I ended a relationship in high school after we had sex. *Man, was I an ass.* I imagined Lachelle hated me now. She should. But Sadie always gave people the benefit of the doubt, no matter how hurtful their decisions were to her. Her compassion was admirable.

Seeming lost in thought, Sadie looked at our hands; her light complexion contrasted against mine. She considered, "I don't imagine your friends would be wild about you sitting here with a white girl. I've been reading about interracial relationships online and people claim black men being with white women isn't good for the culture—that it goes back to slavery and men desiring what was denied."

I pulled my hand away. "Sadie, I don't give a damn what people online say. When it's right for me, I'll know it, and the friends I want will respect my decision. Do you think I'm not capable of seeing beyond race?"

She grabbed my hand again. "I'm sorry—I don't know what I'm talking about. I didn't mean to be insulting. I just think you're so together. Why would you bother with me?"

I pulled away again, reluctantly, and said, "You're a gem Sadie, but this is where I say goodbye and wish you a happy life."

"I wish I would be more like you."

I wish you would too, Sadie.

And then she said something I would never forget. She locked my eyes with hers and told me, "I know I'm weak, compared to you, but I think vulnerability is the best expression of courage. I put myself out there because people need love—and hugs. Even the hardest, most difficult people need affection. I embarrass myself all the time—just ask my sisters—but I'm also a great friend."

Unfortunately, I wasn't. If I couldn't have all of her, I wanted none of her. Finished eating, we stepped out on to the sidewalk of busy Nicollet Avenue.

I said, "I guess this is goodbye."

Sadie reached to me and said, "You look like you could use a hug."

I squeezed her tight. When she turned to face me, I kissed her.

She kissed me back for a moment and, with her hand on my chest, gently pushed me back. She implored, "I wish I would have met you six months ago."

I tried optimistically to offer, "We met now."

Sadly, she redirected her eyes to a passing car. "Windows of opportunity close, Zave. Mine has." Keeping her hand on my chest, she attempted to comfort me, "You're a good man and you'll make a lucky woman very happy." Trying to lighten it up, she added, "It would be easier if she was black."

"I don't want easy. I want right."

Sadie smiled and gave me one last peck on the cheek. "She will be." As she walked away, she turned and gave me a devil-may-care smile. "I meant right—not easy."

2

*"You may not control all the events that happen to you,
but you can decide not to be reduced by them."*
—MAYA ANGELOU

2021

CHEYENNE SCHMIDT

10:20 P.M., THURSDAY, JUNE 10
(PRESENT DAY)
BUREAU OF CRIMINAL APPREHENSION, 1430 MARYLAND
AVENUE EAST, ROOSEVELT NEIGHBORHOOD, ST. PAUL

I found myself sitting in an interrogation room across from a polite, thirty-something investigator, who had introduced himself as Jon Frederick. He was a lean, athletic man a little over six feet tall. In his untucked burgundy shirt, black jeans, and black tennis shoes, he struck me more as a guy I'd meet at a concert rather than an investigator. Jon had coffee brown hair and compassionate, sky-blue eyes, which made pouring out my answers easy.

I repeated his question. "You want to know how I met Xavier Williams?"

"Yes."

"It was eight years ago, back in 2013 . . ."

2013

I'D BEEN DRIVING FOR TEN MINUTES BUT MY CAR hadn't even considered cooling down. The year 2013 would go on record as the hottest August in the history of Minneapolis. With the stale, suffocating humidity, 93 degrees in Minneapolis was like 110, anywhere else. It had to be even 50 degrees hotter inside my car. I wore a sweatsuit over my lingerie and my body was starting to itch like crazy. I decided to stop for gas, just to have a breath of fresh air—or at least *fresher* air. I didn't dare have the windows open, as I didn't want to have to redo my hair.

After my parents divorced, Mom moved us from the tourist destination of Stillwater to one of the poorest school districts in the state—Brooklyn Center. My mom was always more invested in parenting my brothers and I think she kind of resented me—like I was the one who cost her the marriage. I knew it was sick, but I missed my dad. We were two families when we were together—me and Dad, Mom and the boys. After I reported that he touched me, it was just me. I thought the touch was the price I paid for his kindness. I didn't miss what he did. I missed having an ally. We were close. Then he was gone, and I had nobody.

Moving in high school was hard because everybody already established their cliques. I remembered the word *pheromones* because I wondered if it applied to me. *A substance released by an animal that effects the behavior of other members of the species.* I expelled the powerful scent of *needy*. Guys always wanted to hang with me, which only made things worse with the girls. It was the girls who called me a whore, slut, stupid, and THOT-girl (That Ho Over There). Girls who didn't even know my name got all judgy. It would seem like you had to do something wrong but you just had to be different, or new. So, I latched onto a guy for security. Then I wasn't a threat. Everybody was happy—well, everyone but me.

Just a little over two months ago, I graduated from Park Center High School. We were allowed to use our laptops to take notes. I knew all the tricks. I sat my cell phone in the middle of my laptop screen during class, so it would look like I was paying attention. If I got called on, my patented answer was a playfully shy, "I can't think when everyone's looking at me." I made it a point to sit next to brainiacs. For a little friendship, they would make their test answers visible to me. The girls were no different than the boys. My boyfriend would write papers for me, but they weren't exactly free. The fallout was that I bombed the college entrance tests. And then my guy told me he could get me a job. So, tonight, I needed to be dancing by eight at the Spearmint Rhino Gentlemen's Club. I was wearing sweats over my lingerie because I didn't like dressing in the strip club—it was grody.

I took the West Broadway exit off I-94 and pulled into the Winner Gas Station. The place looked like a *winner*, all right, next to the Salvation Army and Merwin Liquors. I hopped out of my microwave on wheels, slid in my credit card, and began filling.

Suddenly, a big black man was standing right next to me, asking, "Hey, can you give me a ride? I'm hotter than a stolen tamale." He smiled big, showing a big old gap in his front teeth.

Where the hell did he even come from? Like a dementor, he appeared out of nowhere in a sweat-stained t-shirt.

I swallowed hard and came up with, "I'm sorry—I can't. I'm already running late for work."

He pressed me, "Where do you work?" He eyeballed my face and overdone makeup.

"On Hennepin—at a market."

He begged, "Aw, c'mon then. I'm right on the way. Just pull over on 94 and I'll run the rest of the way. It won't cost you a minute."

Ignoring him, I stared at the dollars clicking away on the pump. I decided to skip a total fill.

He was right on my tail when I made my way back to the driver's side door, whining, "You're just gonna let a brother have a heat stroke? So that's how it is."

Feeling guilty, I gave in. "Fine, hop in. But I can only take you a few blocks. They're waiting for me."

This dude filled up the passenger seat in my Chevy Cavalier so there was even less air in my small car. He had to be over six feet tall.

He asked, "They let you work in sweats?"

"I watch the gas pumps." *What a stupid answer. Why would I be stopping for gas if I worked at a gas station?*

He nodded with a smile and dragged out, "Aight."

I started driving back toward I-94 when he leaned into me and pointed, "Sista, pull in there and I'll get out."

We'd only gone a block, but I was relieved to get rid of him.

As I turned left, he pointed to the darkened back of a business. "Right there. I can go in the back door."

I mindlessly followed directions before I realized I was parking behind a closed store.

I'd no sooner got the car in Park when suddenly, his hand was on the back of my head, pounding my face against the steering wheel.

Dazed, I tried pushing away, but he was so powerful.

He was out of his seatbelt and pulled my sweatshirt partway over my head, my face still covered, and arms stuck in the sleeves. He twisted the fabric so tight I felt like I was suffocating in a straitjacket. My terror grew as I lost my sense of sight. "Do you want to get beat to death, or you just gonna agree to suck me off?"

I managed to grunt, "Let—go!" I squirmed out of my shirt so I could see again and pulled my arms free.

He spat, "I like this red bra a lot. Stupid bitch—lyin' to me? I know you a stripper." He yanked at my sweatpants. "Let's see what's downtown."

"Stop—just stop!" I slapped uselessly at his hands.

He jeered, "I don't mind a fight, dolly. But if you're gonna make it hard, I'm having you every way you can imagine."

And from that point on, it was a brawl. I scratched and he hit. My right arm was too close to his body to get any leverage. His blows struck like a jackhammer.

His fist blasted into my stomach with such force it felt like I was hit by a cannon ball. With the wind knocked out of me, I whimpered and gasped as I tried to catch my breath. A punch to my head rocked my brain and I felt consciousness slipping away.

He pushed my bra up and I could feel his mouth on my breast. When he started to pull his pants down, I willed myself to find the door handle. I jerked the door open and, holding my sweatshirt beneath me, lunged onto the tar. I slipped my sweatshirt back on—*a stupid waste of time. I should've just took off.*

He was out of the car before I could get to my feet and was now standing over me.

I tried crawling away, but he grabbed the neck of my sweatshirt and began dragging me backwards like a bag of trash toward the darkness. The fabric cut into my throat. I grabbed a fistful of the front of the sweatshirt and pulled some slack. "HELLLP!" I screamed so loud I peed my pants.

Headlights soon lit us up.

He turned his back to the lights and let go.

I scrambled to my feet and ran toward the lights, pulling my shirt back down and tugging my pants completely up. While I couldn't make out a face, the streetlight reflected off the woman's white hair.

The older woman pulled away.

I remembered pleading, "Come on. Give me a break!" Now what? *Where was that dirtball who attacked me?* I glanced back at my car. I needed my car, but it was completely dark around it.

Hell with it. I ran toward the traffic on Broadway.

Squad car lights flashed on and turned toward me.

I knelt on the hot tar and broke down.

The officer ran to my side and asked, "What happened?"

And that's when I met Zave Williams. Caramel eyes and eyelashes even a vain woman wouldn't mess with. The young officer was careful with me. In a smooth voice, he softly asked, "Who attacked you?"

"I don't know."

"What did he look like?"

"You."

He squinted, "Black?"

"Yeah. But bigger. Over six feet." I thought for a second and then it occurred to me, "Like Forest Whitaker without the lazy eye." And it was too bad—I liked Forest.

The officer helped me to my feet and said, "I'm Xavier. I'm gonna help you to the squad car, so you can cool down a little, and call for assistance."

He thought I was sweating through my pants. I was too embarrassed to say I had peed myself. "I'll just sit in the back." Despite the adrenaline rush, my body was shaking.

Once Xavier was off the scanner, he drove me to my still-running car, shut it off, locked it, and handed me the key. He said, "We're going to head over to Hennepin County Medical Center. It's only about two and a half miles from here."

I moaned, "I have to get to work."

In a serious but tender voice, he made it clear, "I need to investigate a crime, here. I'll call your employer."

"No—I'll call." Xavier was easy on the eyes, and I was hoping I wouldn't have to tell him I was a stripper. I clarified, "I'll call from the hospital."

He asked, "Any type of DNA involved?"

"He didn't get off, if that's what you mean."

I found myself getting lost in his caring brown eyes; his gentleness almost made me cry. He was thin and fit, and I felt safe with him. He continued with his questioning, "Any saliva or blood?"

"He had his mouth here—on my bare breast." I pointed, as if he needed some guidance to its location. I was being so stupid.

Xavier very politely didn't crack a smile. Instead, he told me, "That should give us the DNA we need . . ."

3

*"The greatness of a man is not in how much
wealth he acquires, but in his integrity and his
ability to affect those around him positively."*
—Bob Marley

2013

XAVIER "ZAVE" WILLIAMS

10:45 P.M., WEDNESDAY, AUGUST 28
HENNEPIN COUNTY MEDICAL CENTER,
730 SOUTH 8TH STREET,
ELLIOT PARK NEIGHBORHOOD, MINNEAPOLIS

With all the resources we had access to, you'd think it would be impossible to get by with a crime in a city—witnesses, cameras, fingerprints, DNA, cellphone tracking, and associates willing to turn a killer over to cut a deal. Still this year, half of the Minneapolis homicides were unsolved. You'd think getting away with murder was the result of careful planning, but most of the time it was dumb luck. Occasionally, the luck turned in our direction and we got a break on a case as random as the crime. We were about to get one.

After the DNA was collected and Cheyenne Schmidt had showered, I had her sit down with a sketch artist. With her dark hair splayed over the shoulder of her blue scrubs, Cheyenne was resting in a hospital bed as we waited for one of her friends to bring her clothes. She looked years younger and vulnerable without all the makeup, her eyes wide and doe-like. Her physical similarities to Sadie shot a pang of guilt to my very core. I shook the thought free, for now, and focused on getting a description of her attacker.

I was comfortable working with Lauren Herald, and she wasn't hard to look at, either. Lauren was a couple years older than I—a leggy blonde with a perky nose and a ready smile. Her long, wavy hair wasn't fussy but flowed simply down her back, working with all her natural beauty. She was from a small, northern Minnesota town—probably explained the wholesome look. There was no makeup on her tanned face, which was appropriate for the circumstance. Honestly, she didn't need makeup. Her arctic blue eyes could light up a room.

She looked the part of an artist, wearing a long, tie-dyed skirt with a sleeveless denim blouse knotted at her slim waist. Her huge hoop earrings could have doubled as bracelets and were all the jewelry she seemed to need. She wore what I liked to call Jesus sandals, all straps across her foot and wrapping around her ankles. Despite the flower child look, Lauren was all business on the job and the victims were always satisfied with her work.

Cheyenne suggested Lauren draw Forest Whitaker and she would point out the differences.

Lauren was a talented artist; we soon had a charcoal sketch.

Cheyenne pointed out, "My attacker's face was rounder."

Lauren softly teased, "Even rounder than Forest's?"

"Yes."

She redrew it.

Cheyenne added, "And he had lines on his forehead."

As she watched Lauren do her magic, she added, "And he didn't have a lazy eye."

Lauren erased and replaced the eye.

Cheyenne corrected her, "The eyes still aren't right. Forest has friendly, inviting eyes. This guy had dark, piercing eyes."

Lauren worked her illustrative wizardry and, after some minor adjustments were made to the eyes and mouth, Cheyenne stated, "That's him."

I asked Cheyenne, "Have you ever met him before?"

"No. I have no idea who he is—but that's him."

She was about to say something but stopped herself.

I quickly followed up. "What?"

She looked away. "Nothing."

"Tell me. I want to catch this guy. I need everything you know about him."

"He knew I was a stripper." She studied my reaction. "I don't remember him. There are so many guys who come in and out of the club every night. I know I never danced for him."

Without emotion, I said, "Thank you. That's helpful." I could go to the club with the picture and see if any of the bartenders recognized him. I waited for Lauren to hand me the picture, but she just held it and stared at it. She worried one of her hoops, oblivious to my waiting on her.

What was going on with Lauren? Finally, I reached for the drawing and said, "I'll take it to the station and have it distributed."

She wouldn't let go of it.

I asked, "What is it?"

"I *know* this guy. His mother lives in my neighborhood. She's always yelling at him, but he seems to handle it—even expect it." After a moment she said, "His name's Ray Fury . . . "

3:45 P.M., THURSDAY, AUGUST 29
1249 FREMONT AVENUE,
NEAR NORTH NEIGHBORHOOD, MINNEAPOLIS

AS AN OFFICER FAMILIAR WITH THIS AREA, I should've recognized the sketch. I'd seen "Flamin'" Ray Fury box at Northside. I didn't expect to see him in this context.

I spent last night and most of today talking to people in Hawthorne and near North Minneapolis, to see if someone could direct me to Ray. He was avoiding home. Word on the street was he was friendly with the Gangster Disciples.

You didn't solve cases in the office. I cruised Lyndale and Lowry Avenue North, through the Hawthorne neighborhood. Hawthorne was the most dangerous 'hood in Minneapolis. It was where I worked and was raised. My mom was a social worker in this community. Dad worked road construction in the summer and plowed for the city in the winter. They both volunteered for a program called Appetite for Change, teaching people the benefits of growing your own produce. The compassion they shared with the community was drained by the time they reached home. But they loved me and my brother. In all fairness, the lack of progressive change in law enforcement in Minneapolis exhausted all of us. Perhaps the boarded windows on the pictures of houses for sale in Hawthorne were the best indicator of our sorry state.

I turned onto North Dupont and cut over to Freemont. I cruised by the backside of the prison release program. A small child stood on the sidewalk, unaccompanied, so I pulled my squad over. When I got out, a mother came running out of the house to quickly scoop the boy up. She gave me an angry look, suggesting I mind my own business. *Bad parenting is my business.*

This was the neighborhood where Ray Fury was raised. Quiet, decent people, barely surviving, sprinkled with desperate young men trying to make a quick buck. Ray had made something of himself. He was a legitimate boxer. But his size and strength made him a desired commodity by every gang banger in the area who wanted to squeeze money out of somebody. Ray had earned his side money as muscle for the Disciples since he was fifteen.

I walked the block. Cautious eyes followed as people tried to discern who I was looking for. At one point, I wanted to make a fortune and start a business here, offering black Americans good paying jobs. But after realizing that was almost impossible, I became a cop thinking at the very least, maybe I could keep some from being shot.

I saw a large man fitting Ray's description rushing into a worn-down rambler, five houses down. I sprinted back to my car and called for backup. I then drove to the house, skidded to a stop, and ran to the door.

Four bulked-up brothers filed out and, with arms crossed, blocked the entrance. All bore the Star of David tattoo. These brothers weren't Jewish. It was a symbol of the Gangster Disciples. Honestly, I was scared. Life and death meant so little to these men. They all thought they were invincible.

Back in Chicago, Larry Hoover, leader of the Supreme Gangsters, and David Barksdale, leader of the Black Disciples, combined forces to create the Black Gangster Disciple Nation. The Black Stone Rangers ordered a hit on Barksdale and shot him seven times, but he survived. Two years later, when Barksdale and Hoover were leaving a bar, he was shot again, with M-14 rifles. Barksdale died of kidney failure, at age twenty-seven, following the shooting. His wife was murdered three years later and their child years after. Hoover was now serving a 200-year sentence for drug conspiracy, extortion, and running a criminal enterprise, after it was determined he ordered a hit on a nineteen-year-old. And that's *thug life*. Money for a little bit and then death or prison. That brief moment of power is alluring. I wanted it myself, at one time. The Disciples were now the largest gang in Minneapolis.

I kept my cool as I told the gang, "I'm not looking for trouble. I just need to talk to Flamin' Ray."

My wretched uneasiness was sweet nectar to their toxic machismo, so they puffed up and stepped closer. The shortest of the crew stood about five foot six, not counting his four inches of afro. He sneered, revealing gold grillz that probably cost as much as my car. "No one here by that name."

"What's your name?"

"They call me the Fox."

Like Erwin Rommel? The Nazi general? He did spend a considerable amount of time in Africa. I contemplated my next move.

Fox turned to a thin, athletic man at his side and said, "Dreads, talk to him."

Dreads' nickname was obvious; his ropes of waxy hair were pulled into a nappy ponytail at the back of his head. He was only a couple years older than I, but a hardened, veteran gang member. His eyes were flat and lazy as he looked over my uniform and disparaged me. "Workin' for the man, now. Doin' the white boys' dirty work."

Dreads and I had history. Back when I was fourteen, I had friends who were gang members and I wanted in. They had money and status and I was nothing. Just a basketball player. Looking back, I had one saving grace—a letter jacket.

I went to a gang party and Dreads stopped me at the door. He asked my friends, "What is he doing here?"

They assured him, "No worries—he's cool."

Dreads angrily said to me, "Dissipate. You're a baller and if you lose your eligibility we're going to lose to Cooper. Can't have that. I don't wanna see you here again." Beating our cross-town rival was bigger than winning the state tournament. I left, secretly relieved.

Now, a decade and change later, I was again at Dreads' mercy to allow me entrance. My uniform had changed, and he wore his even harder demeanor like a badge in itself. I said calmly, "Stop trippin'. Just give me a look inside. They're coming for Ray. I'd be doing you a favor by walking out with him."

Fox stepped closer. "No can do—'less you got yourself a search warrant."

"One will be delivered." I got on my radio and said, "Officer Williams at twelve forty-nine Fremont Avenue North.

Spotted Ray Fury walking into a house. I am going to need a search warrant . . . "

Dreads reminded me, "The only reason you're a cop is because we protected you. Don't forget that. You lost your swag, man. You even walk like a white boy."

The group all laughed.

A squad car came to a screeching halt in front of the house and white police officer, Dan Baker, hopped out. Danny was always the first to my side when I needed backup, which was much appreciated. He knew not to always draw his gun, but his hand was right on it as he stalked toward us, asking, "Is there a problem?"

This simple gesture amped up the tension in my adversaries and the laughing ended. The situation now had the potential to end badly.

Fox jeered, "Look, cookies and cream. You're in over your head, here. Just walk away."

Another banger stepped out of the house and nodded to Fox.

Fox gave the moment some thought, and then told me, "I'm feelin' particularly generous today. Go in and have a look. Just don't trash the place."

Dan and I carefully stepped by the gang and into the house. Videogame controllers sat on the couch and open bottles of Modelo Negra on the floor. A beer first brewed in Mexico by Austrian immigrants. A weight bench was pushed against the wall. With guns drawn, we made one careful turn after another, as we traversed down the hall into each bedroom. There was no sign of Fury.

We holstered our guns and stepped back onto the front porch. I thanked the men for allowing the search.

They laughed at me, in their most condescending manner.

I knew they'd likely helped Fury escape but still, I was polite. I'd be dealing with them again.

Fox warned, "Don't come back. I can't guarantee what'll happen next time. You hear me?"

Dan remarked, "If I wanted a guarantee, I'd buy a toaster."

Feeling disrespected, Fox took a step toward him.

I bumped Dan and said, "We're done, here."

Dan eyeballed Fox, and then commented to me as we left, "You sure it was Fury?"

"No, not a hundred percent—but pretty sure." I looked back to make sure no one pulled a weapon. All was good.

Dan asked, "What do you want to do now?"

Trying to be a decent cop was exhausting. "Let's get out of here. Stop for one?"

"Do you want to try Indeed Brewing? Mexican Honey Lager—a friend in need is a friend indeed."

I countered, "Luce Line has the perfect pilsner. Tastes like a breath of fresh air on the north shore."

"Loose lips sink ships. Sounds good." He looked at his watch. "Let me clock out and I'll be there."

8:45 P.M.
LUCE LINE BREWING,
12901 16TH AVENUE NORTH, PLYMOUTH

DANNY AND I SAT AT THE LONG DARK BAR, enjoying a tall, cold glass of the Piedmont Pilsner. He asked, "How do you like working with Lauren Herald—sketch artist extraordinaire?" Before I had a chance to respond, he said, "She once gave me a glacial stare that damn near froze me in my tracks." He snorted, "Dresses all hippy like—peace and love and shit. I tell ya what, there was no peace or love in that look."

My eyes slowly made their way to him, as I questioned, "What did you say to her?"

He shrugged, "I just told her, 'Your license should be suspended for driving all these guys crazy.'"

"Don't be dissin' on Lauren. She's one of my favorite people and beyond talented. Once, when we were both waiting outside a courtroom to testify, I watched her create a reductive charcoal drawing of Jimi Hendrix that was ridiculous."

Danny asked, "What the hell is a redactive drawing?"

"Re*ductive*. She covered the paper with charcoal, and then drew the picture with her eraser."

"Lauren's a woman with a secret."

"Please don't say that you think she's a lesbian because she doesn't succumb to your cheesy lines."

Danny started laughing. "I don't think she's the stereotype hardened, cold lesbian. As a matter of fact, I'd argue that hetero folks are more often hardened and cold. I'm just sayin', if someone seems too good to be true, they usually are." He challenged me, "Give me your best pickup line. Maybe I can give you a pointer or three."

The last thing I needed was dating advice from a guy I'd never seen on a date. I teased, "Your teeth are like the stars. They come out at night."

He laughed, "That's not a pickup line. That's a death sentence." He looked past me and jutted his chin over my shoulder. "Check out those two."

I turned to see a voluptuous, dark woman of Latino descent and her African American friend—both in their mid-twenties—walking directly toward us. The Latina woman had a knowing smile, like she was privy to clandestine information about me.

As the black woman fluttered long eyelashes, she said so casually it almost seemed tiresome, "Hi Zave."

Lachelle was a blast from my past. She was once my dream girl—maybe still was—a strong, black woman with smoldering chestnut eyes. Her satiny black hair was smoothed free of curl and captured in a ponytail.

When they attempted to slide by, Dan decided he wasn't going to let them off the hook. He exclaimed, "Hey, wait a minute. What am I—furniture?"

Lachelle stopped and said politely, "I'm sorry. I'm Lachelle and this is my friend, Marita."

Lachelle was straight up pretty, while Marita's beauty was intriguing. Her facial features and straight black hair appeared South American; she had caramel brown skin and—woah, one crystal blue and one bottle green eye—both glowing like exotic gemstones against her darker complexion. As a kid, I had a friend with heterochromia. I thought it was so cool, while all she cared about was what she would put on her driver's license when that day came.

Dan studied Marita and remarked, "You must be a magician, because when I look at you, all my troubles disappear." His cheesy line didn't seem to concern either of the women.

Marita paused, as if she was trying to figure Dan out. Unfortunately, this was fodder for his continued efforts. He tried again, "I was feeling a little off today, but my dear, you've turned me on."

Danny was so damn embarrassing.

Lachelle looked into my eyes as she responded to Dan, "Maybe another time. We were just leaving."

I wasn't sure what she wanted me to do.

Relentless, Dan took out a card and handed it to Marita, "If you're ever stranded and need help, give me a call."

She smiled, "Thank you," and the two left.

Danny watched their swaying backsides until the door closed behind them. He turned to me and laughed. "Okay, I may have struck out, but that's why I have a lot of cards." He took a large swallow of beer and suggested, "You, my man, have a story to tell me."

"You caught that, huh?"

"Hard to miss that deer-in-the-headlights look you were rockin'. You got so pale, we were damn near twins."

I shook my head. "I was with Lachelle in high school. Stupid teen stuff."

He waggled his eyebrows. "*With* her—in the biblical sense?"

"We were both big into sports in school and we flirted. One hot, summer night it got heavier than either of us anticipated. And I made her a promise I never meant to keep."

"You told her you'd love her forever."

"No. She told me she loved me. I didn't know how I felt, and I didn't want to lie, so I said, 'You will always be—special to me.'"

Dan groaned loudly, "That's like slapping her with a cold fish. What the hell does that mean? Special, like special ed?"

"No, she took it to mean, 'I love you, too.' Honestly, I *did*. But instead of telling her, I got all weird when I saw her after that. I was so embarrassed around her. And then her dad died. I didn't know what to do. I was fifteen. I thought I'd give her some time to grieve. Last I heard she was headed off to college somewhere along the east coast."

"Healthy grieving involves talking about it."

I scrubbed a hand over the top of my head, the awkward emotions all coming up again. "I didn't go to the wake. Just vanished. I was such an arrogant ass. I thought I was either going to play in the NBA or be President of the United States, so I couldn't get a reputation for being putty in a girl's hands. I acted all distant and cool, and let my friends dictate my free time. And," I snapped my fingers, "we were done."

Dan commented, "Lachelle still has feelings for you."

"Maybe, but they aren't good."

"She's pretty—still takes care of herself."

"That she is . . ."

4

"I refuse to accept the view that mankind is so tragically bound to the starless midnight of racism and war that the bright daybreak of peace and brotherhood can never become a reality . . . I believe that unarmed truth and unconditional love will have the final word."
—MARTIN LUTHER KING JR.

2021

JON FREDERICK

11:15 A.M., THURSDAY JUNE 10,
BUREAU OF CRIMINAL APPREHENSION, 1430 MARYLAND
AVENUE EAST ROOSEVELT NEIGHBORHOOD, ST. PAUL

Back in 2013, I didn't know any better than Zave that, in 2021, we'd be working together investigating Sadie Sullivan's murder, and eventually I'd be in the position of investigating Zave.

8:45 P.M., SATURDAY, AUGUST 31, 2013
(7 YEARS AGO)
MARSHALL STREET,
NORTHEAST MINNEAPOLIS ARTS DISTRICT

I STEPPED INTO THE BEDROOM TO SEE JADA Anderson's smooth sepia toned skin from the backside. With a blissful smile of model-white teeth, she peeked over her shoulder and teased, "You know better than to enter a woman's bedroom when she's dressing."

I commented, "Obviously, I don't."

She shooed me out, handing me a pile of clothing, "Put your tux on and meet me on the rooftop."

Jada had been to a homicide scene this morning and, as an aspiring investigator, my curiosity was killing me. "Do you mind if I look over your crime scene photos while I'm waiting for you to get ready?" She'd mentioned that she wanted me to render an opinion on the pictures. A young mother named Sadie Sullivan was found murdered and partially undressed, in a wooded area within the city limits of Minneapolis.

Jada waved her index finger back and forth as a warning. "Nuh-uh. Absolutely no work tonight! Would you mind bringing the food up with you?"

I had already worn the tux last night, to the WCCO gala at Aria in Minneapolis. Aria was a large, exposed-brick venue featuring thirty-foot ceilings. Second-story balconies overlooked the audience, crystal chandeliers dripped from the ceiling, and pop art accents highlighted the halls. Jada helped organize the fundraiser for research into pediatric illnesses. She managed to land numerous local professional athletes and celebrities. Jada elegantly greeted guests and thanked donors, while I stood by quietly, supporting her and running errands. Honestly, she had little time for me at the event, but it wasn't purposeful, and I understood. After wearing the tux all night, I'd hoped to be done with it, but Jada promised I wouldn't be in it long, tonight.

I carried the jambalaya with jalapeno cornbread and warm brownie batter dessert, which I'd picked up at Stella's, to the rooftop of her apartment complex. A small table covered with a white tablecloth waited with three large, lit candles. The flames flickered slightly with gentle gusts of the summer breeze.

Jada and I had dated for four years, in a committed and loving relationship. We were both intent on our career paths with employers who progressively demanded more of us, which meant less time together. Jada worked as a reporter and followed stories whenever an opportunity arose. I worked for the Bureau of Criminal Apprehension and, as a rookie, was stuck performing late-night and weekend surveillance.

Alicia Keys' *No One* played on a Beats Pill by the table. As Alicia belted out, "No one can get in the way of what I feel for you," I had to believe this was going to be a good night. Jada had that Alicia Keys beauty—a swan-like neck, flawless caramel skin, brown eyes that shimmered like syrup—luscious.

The door opened to the rooftop.

Jada stepped out wearing a bright, white wedding dress with a plunging V-neck and lace flowing over each shoulder—simple but elegant. I didn't know what I was expecting, but it wasn't this. I didn't know what to say. I loved Jada, but I wasn't ready for the altar.

Chivalry overrode my confusion—*when in doubt be polite.* I stood and assisted her to her seat.

Picking up on my reticence, she said, "I appreciate that you had my back at Aria—all night. I heard the guy comment to you that you were my *whipped boy*, and watched you graciously ignore it and move on." Her eyes met mine, "It meant a lot that you would swallow your pride and let the night be just about me."

"It wasn't worthy of a reply." Despite our racial differences, people were, by and large, kind and respectful to us. But there was always that five percent that had to share their microaggressions. I could make a difference in this world, or waste all my energy on someone who was never going to change. I preferred the former.

Jada continued, "I know how you ruminate on things. You'd obviously feel better if we were officially committed to each other and I respect that you've held back—knowing I don't know if I'm ready. I love where we're at. I bought this wedding dress, so you know that, before I'd risk losing you, I'd marry you."

Unsure how to respond, I simply offered, "I'd like to be married in a church."

"I wouldn't make your family go to Chicago. We could have it here in Minneapolis. But your friend, Serena, won't be invited. I've seen the way she looks at you."

The comment surprised me. Serena and I were high school friends who hadn't had anything but a passing conversation since the last girl I dated in high school disappeared. But that was another story.

I told Jada, "You don't have to worry about Serena. I still haven't been forgiven back home for something I didn't do."

Jada sardonically smiled, "That's what it's like for a black American in a store."

I loved Jada and, while it was weird to have a night with a lover in her future wedding dress, I couldn't envision this ending badly. Honestly, I wasn't ready to marry, either. I had an unresolved question we needed to address, but for damn sure wasn't bringing it up tonight.

Following dinner, we slow-danced on the roof, her graceful fingers feathering through the back of my hair, as she looked into my eyes. We were so synchronously connected, when Jada kissed me, I felt her warmth—her love—through my entire body. Time froze. At that moment, I was the luckiest man on earth.

With a graceful turn of her head, she guided my eyes to the Minneapolis lights below. "This is our city. Our future . . . "

9:05 A.M., SEPTEMBER 1, 2013

I WOKE UP WITH A SMILE, STARING AT A HALF empty bottle of champagne abandoned on the nightstand. I slipped my boxers on and found a t-shirt. Knowing Jada could be sleeping for a couple more hours, I brushed my teeth and decided to take a look at her pictures from the murder scene.

I opened up the photos on Jada's laptop and started scrolling through a file titled, "Sadie Sullivan Homicide." A picture of Sadie's abandoned truck captured my interest. It was the sole vehicle in the parking lot by the tennis courts. A close-up revealed the truck had been driven with the seatbelt still fastened. The seatbelt melded against the seat suggesting it had been sat on by the driver. I wrote on the notepad by the computer, *Pic 16—Cop?*

Another shot showed Sadie lying on the ground, partially dressed. Her shirt had been removed and her jeans were open but hadn't been pulled down. She was wearing a black bra and the lace of matching underwear peeked out of her unfastened jeans—both undisturbed. Sadie's body was positioned like a centerfold. Her knees were bent, and her legs were immodestly spread open. Her arms seemed to rest comfortably back on each side of her head, in relaxed anticipation.

People didn't fall to the ground with their legs spread. The body was posed, to make her appear seductive. Had a sexual assault started and then stopped? Or had the killer partially undressed her to make it look like a sexual assault? If she had been groped, her bra and underwear wouldn't be perfectly in place. I needed to think about that.

There were no gunshot wounds and no bloody incisions from a knife. Strangulation marks ringed her neck; part of her cloth belt was torn and lying on the ground next to her body. The killer was strong and angry. I zoomed in and made a note that the woven pattern on the belt was similar to the pattern of bruising on Sadie's neck. I scrolled back to picture 18. The remainder of the belt was lying on the ground just outside of the truck. If her belt was the murder weapon, Sadie wasn't murdered where her body rested. Only half the belt was there.

Sadie was a pretty young woman. I hated that we lived

in a world where misogynist men destroyed women like her. I feared that, someday, something similar could happen to Jada.

Curiously, the killer had started a sward of grass on fire, parallel to Sadie's body, but it had gone out without doing damage. The killer obviously wasn't a farmer, as he would have known that green grass wasn't going to burn. That trivia didn't significantly reduce the suspect list in Minneapolis. My mind calculated scenarios furiously as I processed the pictures. The killer took time to pose the body and started a fire, but then fled before the fire spread; someone must have interrupted his efforts to first create and then destroy his fantasy scene. Her killer either believed all women were whores or that she specifically was, hence the need to publicly humiliate her.

One picture showed some Busch beer cans lying on the ground, about twenty feet from the body. It would be interesting to see whose DNA was found on the cans.

Jada had made a short video of the body being loaded into the coroner's vehicle. I clicked *Play* and watched. As Sadie was loaded onto the gurney, one of the paramedics slipped. Still Sadie's body remained stiff. It was creepy to watch. Sadie's muscles were frozen solid, suggesting the period of rigor mortis was in full force. Rigor mortis usually set in two hours after death, making the muscles rigid. About eight hours later, the muscles are rock solid. If Jada was at the scene at 8:00 a.m. yesterday, as she said, Sadie had been dead since sometime before midnight the previous evening.

I would later find out that, last night, when I held Jada and we gazed out at the city, Elizabeth Erickson was being raped by the same man who had sex with Sadie Sullivan before she died. Poor Elizabeth was in a dark alley, less than a mile away.

SLEEP STILL IN HER EYES, JADA STROLLED OUT of the bedroom in white pajama pants and a white muscle shirt. She kissed me and sat across the table. "You should've seen Sadie's family when they arrived at the scene. They were inconsolable in their grief. I've experienced that agony with too many of my brothers and sisters. The harrowing anguish of losing a child transcends race."

She gave me a long look, punctuated with a heavy sigh. "Please close that laptop. I don't want to think about poor Sadie this morning." Jada leaned forward on her elbows, rubbed her eyes, and grinned. "I'm a little embarrassed about the wedding dress shocker. It seemed like a great idea for a second. I think you got the point."

I took a deep breath and grinned. "I did." As I closed the laptop, I said, "Okay. I'm going to take a risk, too."

Uncertain, she quipped, "Johnny, be good."

"Your fundraiser for babies has my mind racing. I want children."

Jada quickly stood up and anxiously searched for a task. She began making coffee. With her back to me, she said, "I'm not having children. I want to be a national news anchor, which means I have to be out there for every hard-hitting story. I don't have time."

"What if I would take full responsibility for raising the child? I would arrange daycare when I couldn't be there."

Jada spun back to me. "I can't. Even in the twenty-first century, people still aren't forgiving of a woman who doesn't dote on her kids. If I was a guy, no one would question it."

Disappointed, but not surprised, I sighed. "Okay."

She asked softly, "So, what does this mean?"

"You're not going to need the wedding dress." I rubbed my forehead. It was definitely bad luck to see your bride in her wedding dress before the wedding. "I know we were both gung-ho about our careers when we started, but honestly, I think it means more to me to be a father than an investigator."

Jada turned her back to me and poured her coffee. "Then you're going to have to find somebody else."

"I know." I went to her and tried to kiss her; she turned her cheek to my lips. I gave her a chaste peck, politely gathered my items, and left. I was a logical man. There was nothing more to be said. The line had been drawn. We both stood alone, on opposing sides.

That moment wasn't the end for us, but it was the beginning of the end. We were both too busy to dedicate time to looking for partners, so we continued to meet that late-night niche for each other. It ended any talk of a future together and, with that, we lost the sense of naïve hope lovers share. Our relationship was terminal; mornings together brought a quiet sadness. We were still each other's *plus one*, for friends' weddings and events, but after Christmas, we agreed to go our own ways.

2013

2:30 P.M. SATURDAY, DECEMBER 28

CHRISTMAS HAD PASSED WITHOUT THE TIDE turning. Honestly, there were moments Jada and I laughed hard and reveled in each other's company. I tried to convince myself I didn't need children, but my undeniable desire to parent always resurfaced. I could've given up my desire to live in the country, to be with her, but this was a deal breaker.

I remembered leaving Jada's apartment for the last time. The flame was out; we now had to let go. We agreed it was best to start out the new year single.

Calvin Harris, an elderly black man, worked the desk in Jada's apartment building. He always got a good-natured jab in at me before I left, but it never stung because he had a good heart. We would always end up laughing. More than anything, the dialogue referenced the stupidity of racism.

Calvin pretended to be mad at me as he saw me coming. He cracked, "Slummin' fuckin' cracker."

I responded, "I take offense to the word *slumming*. Whose stock do you think is higher at this point—Jada's or mine?"

He sat back and grinned. "Well, there's no doubt Jada's the rocket between the two of you."

"And that's my point. *Cracker* I can accept. I did come from white trash. And there *had* been fucking."

Calvin laughed.

I asked, "What do I owe you for the psychological assessment?"

"I'll put it on your tab."

My phone played *Vaporize*—my friend, Clay's ringtone. I silenced it and waited to take the call outside.

Calvin asked, "What was that?"

"Amos Lee."

"It's not enough you got the best jobs, you just gotta have everything we have. Our music—" he glanced down at my tennis shoes, "our shoes. Even our Jada."

I said, "Amos Lee looks pretty white, but I believe he's mixed race. And great music is just great music."

"Mixed race means *black* in the U.S."

I glanced down at my shoes. "I think Michael Jordan is fine with me buying his shoes. And," I added, "Jada just dumped me, so Happy New Year!"

Calvin looked a little disappointed. His tone softened uncharacteristically. "I'm going to miss you. You haven't even heard some of my best stuff, yet. There are single white women in this apartment. You don't have to pluck our rose."

With a sad smile and wave goodbye, I commented, "Jada is a rose in any garden."

5

"America never was America to me.
And yet I swear this oath—
America will be!"
—LANGSTON HUGHES

2014

XAVIER "ZAVE" WILLIAMS

4:15 P.M., WEDNESDAY, AUGUST 11
4ᵀᴴ PRECINCT, 1925 PLYMOUTH AVENUE NORTH,
NEAR NORTH MINNEAPOLIS

Rumor had it Ray Fury fled to Chicago in January but had now returned to Minneapolis. Walking the beat gave me my first solid lead to his whereabouts. By following the thread of talking to someone's "friend of a friend," I discovered Fury was staying with his cousin in an apartment complex across from East Phillips Park in Minneapolis.

Pleased with my work, Minneapolis Fourth Precinct Police Chief, Brent Collier, invited me to attend a meeting before Ray Fury's no-knock warrant was executed. Collier had taken some heat for always finding the killing of black civilians as justified by police officers. No-knock home invasions had fallen under scrutiny recently, because of the number of innocent people being killed during SWAT raids. This year,

African American men were twice as likely to be shot by police officers as white men. And God forbid, if you were mentally ill *and* black, you were sixteen times more likely to be shot.

When I arrived at the Fourth Precinct, a private meeting involving only police administration had just ended. They had information about the case we lowly officers weren't privy to.

We packed into a room and Medical Examiner, Dr. Amaya Ho, stepped in front to address us. "We know from DNA evidence that we are in pursuit of a serial rapist. You need to understand, Ray Fury has crimes more serious than the sexual assault of Cheyenne Schmidt."

Flamin' Ray was what was referred to as a "known product" by the police, meaning his name had come up numerous times in complaints.

Dr. Ho continued, "When you confront him, it's important to know that Fury was a heavyweight Golden Gloves boxer. The DNA in the Schmidt assault has been matched to additional assaults. His first was the sexual assault of a twelve-year-old girl."

I couldn't help wondering why we were mustering the troops. Fury had to be suspected of something major.

A slide flashed on the wall of the young victim. There were numerous bite marks about her face. It was disturbing to see the blood-red indentations of teeth in the girl's smooth, white cheeks.

"In 2011, Fury broke into a home in the Hawthorne neighborhood. He attacked a girl of European descent, whose parents were gone for the night. Fury pinned her down and pushed his penis into her mouth. When she bit him, he proceeded to rape her vaginally and bit her face numerous times while doing so. It was dark, so she was unable to identify him; however, the DNA in this twelve-year-old is a match with the Cheyenne Schmidt case."

Dr. Ho turned to Chief Collier and said, "You can shut the slide off."

He let the picture linger and my anger with Fury escalated. I imagined every officer in the room felt the same.

Dr. Ho glanced back at the slide and, when she realized it was still on, stared daggers at Chief Collier.

He changed the slide. The second picture was of an adult woman who was severely beaten.

Dr. Ho said, "Elizabeth Erickson was assaulted August 31, 2013, walking home from the Dangerous Man Brewing Company on Thirteenth Avenue, in Minneapolis."

This was right across the river from the Hawthorne area, where Cheyenne was assaulted—it wasn't even a mile away.

Dr. Ho continued, "Elizabeth was raped and left in an empty parking lot behind the Grain Belt bottling house. She was unable to identify the attacker; however, the DNA from her attacker is also a match to Ray Fury."

Collier nodded for her to go on, but she closed her folder and stated, "I'm done." Good old Doc Amaya was worried about Brent firing up the troops before the raid.

The chief took over the screen, now displaying a picture of a Caucasian woman with one eye swollen completely shut. The left side of her face surrounding her eye was a painful shade of deep purple.

Collier said, "Fury was accused of raping an intellectually disabled adult woman in 2010; however, he claimed she said it was rape because she was white, and she didn't want to admit she had sex with a black man."

Someone asked, "How did she get the black eye?"

"He said she made a racial slur to him after they had sex, so he hit her," Collier explained. "Fury was acquitted of all charges."

There was a murmur among the officers.

I didn't like Fury, but I found myself looking about the room at the waspish officers and realized I was the only one who considered that, maybe, Ray was acquitted because he was innocent. There'd been too many times the story wasn't exactly right.

The screen now flashed a black and white shot of Ray Fury in the boxing ring, standing over an opponent he had just knocked out. Collier added, "Be careful," and then gave everyone their assignments.

The photo of the twelve-year-old girl's ravaged face returned to the screen.

I was nervous as hell that someone who simply *looked* like Fury could get caught in this net and seriously hurt. Back in 1999, plain-clothed police officers were looking for a serial rapist when they came across Amadou Diallo, a 23-year-old Guinean immigrant, standing in front of his apartment complex. They asked him to identify himself, so he reached for his billfold. An officer shouted, "Gun!" and the officers fired 41 shots, killing Amadou. He had been working a variety of odd jobs to raise money to attend college, hoping to one day be a computer programmer. Amadou didn't have a gun, yet officers were acquitted on all charges.

At this very moment, Ferguson, Missouri, was burning. An 18-year-old African American, Michael Brown Jr., had stolen Swisher Sweet cigarillos from a convenience store two nights ago. I remember chewing on the plastic tips of those candy-like cigars as an adolescent. I might even have shoplifted a pack myself. When the police arrived to arrest him, a scuffle occurred between Brown and a white police officer. Brown ran, but he stopped in his tracks after the officer fired at his back. The officer said unarmed Michael ran at him and he had to shoot him. Michael's accomplice stated Michael turned and raised his hands in surrender and the officer shot him to death. The officer wasn't charged. In Ferguson, 25 buildings had burned as a result of the riots and many more were looted.

I didn't ever want that for Minneapolis—but c'mon, we had to stop shooting brothers. The officer fired twelve shots at an unarmed man, hitting Michael six times.

I prayed to God we wouldn't create anything similar with our adrenaline-infused officers.

What did they have on Ray Fury? It was unusual to get the troops this riled up. Something was going on that was bigger than the rape cases. The room quickly emptied and we rolled out to the Phillips neighborhood in Minneapolis.

4:45 P.M.
EAST 22ND STREET, PHILLIPS NEIGHBORHOOD,
MINNEAPOLIS

WHEN WE ARRIVED AT THE TWENTY-SECOND Street apartment complex, Chief Collier allowed me to lead the crew through the door. Taking into account that Fury was a trained fighter, and knowing how hyped up the crew was, this would be a challenge. As a black man in a racist system, I always wondered how I was being manipulated when I was put in charge. In this case, I assumed the chief's motivation was that it would be less of a political ordeal if Fury was shot by a black cop.

I made my way to the front door, backed up by officers with the battering ram at the ready. I stood to the side, and yelled, "Police!" Before waiting for a response, my colleagues rammed the door and it smashed open. We waited, guns out, but there was no movement in the apartment.

I eased inside, followed closely by a second officer. We immediately spotted a large, four-foot square cardboard box in the living room that once housed a recliner. I heard nothing beyond my heart hammering in my ears. Suddenly, the box moved slightly.

Dan Baker stood by me and, until he spoke, I was relieved to have a friend at my side. He said under his breath, "When we're done, we can count the number of bullets fired by the holes in the box."

I raised my hand, "Hold off." I heard whispering inside the box and it tipped slightly.

A black boy about five years old inched out from underneath the box. I waved him toward me.

With terror-stricken eyes, he looked at me, and then down the row of the other officers, who were all white. He ran to me. This simple choice reminded me of why I became an officer. I scooped him into my arms and carried him to the door.

The boy realized I was about to hand him off and pointed to a female officer.

I complied with his silent request and returned to the living room.

Someone was still in that box; I could tell by the way it slowly came to a rest back on the floor.

I spoke to the box, "Fury, come out. It's the only way you're getting out of here alive. Lift it up—slow and easy."

Officers slid by me to quick search the rest of the house. After coming up empty-handed, they returned to my side. The box sat stubbornly still; I was staring so intently at it, I was sure I could've moved it by sheer force of will.

We now had eight officers in the apartment, with guns aimed at the box.

I announced, "Man, I've seen you fight and I know you don't give up. But this is the moment where the fight has ended. The ten-count is up. I'm giving you a chance to fight another day."

Finally, the box slowly rose off the floor, revealing the bent legs of an adult man. I hoped to hell Fury wasn't going to try something stupid. He eased the box aside and unfolded himself. There he stood, Flamin' Ray Fury, unarmed.

I yelled, "Don't shoot!"

Collier was soon in the apartment and, as Fury was cuffed, said, "Ray Fury, you are under arrest for the rape and murder of Sadie Sullivan."

There was the missing piece. He had raped and killed a fellow officer's fiancée.

Ray knew the drill. He dropped to his knees and laced his fingers behind his head.

Dan was on him in a hot second; he pulled Fury's hands down and cuffed them behind his back, while I kept my gun trained on him. I continued to silently beg him not to make a sudden grab for something as I recited the Miranda.

Fury was hauled to a squad car without incident.

I knew I didn't know Sadie well enough to love her, but it sure felt like I did. Far be it from me to have ever told her—or anybody, for that matter. Her personality was so soft—so accepting and loving—like the perfect pillow to rest your head on. She was a compassionate mother; even if she didn't keep her child, Sadie lived for her daughter. *And what did she die for?*

My failure to tell her how much I admired her altruistic love for her daughter was like a snakebite that left unleashed and foul venom running amuck inside me. Ray Fury was a first-class ass. Would I have handled his arrest different if I'd have known he raped and killed Sadie? I hoped not.

8:35 P.M.
CLIFF N NORM'S BAR,
2024 NORTH WASHINGTON AVENUE, MINNEAPOLIS

I PRIDED MYSELF IN BEING A CONNOISSEUR of beer. I didn't drink a lot, but I liked to try different brews. Like sports, it gave me something else to think about on a bad day. Cliff N Norm's had Cory's Kölsch on tap, brewed over at Alloy Brewing Company in Coon Rapids.

I was pleased with Fury's peaceful arrest but couldn't shake my sadness over the thought of Sadie being raped and strangled to death. The undeserved violence she endured was tragic, but the loss of her gentle kindness was worse.

Danny swung into the pub and plopped tiredly next to me at the bar. He ordered a glass of Truth Twister Double IPA, brewed at Luce Line Brewing Company in Plymouth.

After we clunked our beers together over a successful arrest, he narrowed his eyes at me. "Did you honestly think I was going to open fire on that box without knowing who was in it?" When I didn't say anything, he said, "I drove truck before I got into law enforcement. The rule of thumb is to never drive over a box, because kids love crawling into them."

I reminded him, "If you intended the comment as a joke, it was too real to be funny to me."

"I'm sorry, and I mean that." Danny grimaced, "The smartass comments help me relax, but I might relax my way right out of a job." He shook the thought away and said, "Man, that Fury is a piece of shit. Raped and bit up a twelve-year-old girl."

I agreed, "It's disgusting. And poor Sadie."

It wasn't lost on me that we skipped over the stripper and the alcoholic who were raped. We judged all the time—even when we were trying to be compassionate.

I asked him, "Did you know her fiancé, Bobby Long?"

Danny stared at his hazy glass of pale ale and said, "Nah—not really."

There seemed to be more to the story, but he and I didn't push each other to talk about things if we weren't ready. I let it go.

He looked up. "I saw you at Sadie's funeral."

"I thought you didn't know Bobby."

"He's a cop. We need to support each other—*code blue*."

"Code blue is what they say when there's a medical emergency in a hospital. If you're talking about the *blue code*, it refers to the blue wall of silence that keeps officers from reporting on other officers." The hair stood on the back of my neck. It infuriated me when cops looked the other way while a colleague was abusive. In all fairness, I wasn't sure that Dan knew the implications of what he'd said.

He dismissed the correction. "Whatever. So, how well did *you* know Sadie?"

"What makes you think I knew her?"

"We make a living reading peoples' expressions. I saw the way Bobby spoke to you. He was questioning you."

Dan was observant; I'd give him that. "Bobby wanted to know how I knew Sadie and I told him I knew her from Cub. He asked if I'd ever been to his house, and I told him I hadn't. Then I ended the conversation. I didn't go there to be interrogated."

"I think you gotta cut Bobby a little slack, there. He had a dead fiancée and all they knew at the time was her body had DNA from an African American male on it. Now they know it was Fury."

"Why'd he ask if I'd been to the house? Wasn't her body found by Plymouth Creek?"

Danny tried to give Bobby the benefit of a doubt. "Maybe he thought the rapist had been in their house. He was dealing with a lot. I think his frustration was forgivable."

I thought out loud, "Do you think it's a little weird Sadie was buried in her wedding dress?"

Offended, Dan said, "She was proud of the fact that she paid off her dress before the wedding. Why shouldn't she get to wear it?"

"Chill. I don't have a problem with it; I've just never seen it." I gave him my best cop stare. "For a guy who attended the wedding just to support Bobby, you seem to know a lot about the case."

"I worked in the same precinct as Bobby. We all wanted to solve it for him." Danny shook his head and took a large gulp of beer, maybe to stop his mouth from motoring. "Man, they were only *days* away from their wedding."

My thoughts were interrupted by Lachelle and Marita walking into the pub.

I glared over at Dan, and he shrugged. "I hope you don't mind that I called them."

Like I had a choice.

We spent the next hour catching up. Lachelle was a physical therapist and Marita was an accountant for a realty company. Lachelle and I eventually broke off into our own conversation. We caught up on old friends from school and when that topic grew tired, she asked me, flat out, "Why did you ghost me?"

Unprepared, I decided to wing it. "I was fifteen. I didn't know what to do with the flood of emotions that hit me when you were around. And then your dad died." The words felt empty; he didn't just *die*. Lachelle's father had just purchased his dream family vehicle, a Chevy Tahoe. He'd made a trip to Uptown Minneapolis and some gang members decided to carjack it. When he resisted, they shot and killed him.

Lachelle said bitterly, "You told me, 'He should've just let the vehicle go.'"

He should have, but it was the wrong thing to say at the time. "I felt bad for what you lost. I'm sorry. I didn't know what to say. When I saw how mad I made you, I decided to just stay away."

"Zave, we had just made love for the first time. And then I come home to find my dad was murdered. I was upset, but I didn't think I'd be ghosted from *you*, of all people."

I rubbed my eyes. "I know. I was just young and dumb." I didn't know how to explain it. "What do you say to a girl you've made love with for the first time, when she comes home and finds out her dad is dead? I still don't have an answer."

Frustrated with my ignorance, Lachelle closed her eyes in fury for a second and said, "How about, *I love you?* You didn't even come to his wake or the funeral."

She was right. I scrambled for an explanation. "I hate wakes, but I know I should've gone." I actually did go to the funeral, but I stayed way in the back, so she wouldn't see me. I was horrified at the thought that I'd be asked to sit up front with the family. Looking back, it was a ridiculous fear. I didn't know her father. They wouldn't have put me in that position.

Lachelle scolded, spiteful, "You got what you wanted, and you were done with me. Can you at least be honest with me?"

That wasn't true, but I couldn't find the right words.

She slammed what was left of her drink and set the glass hard on the counter. With that, she got up and left the bar.

Danny and Marita silently observed me. I tried to explain, "It wasn't like that."

Marita interrupted, "I need to go." She gave me a knowing smile. "It's okay, Zave. You were just kids."

She left and I watched her rush to catch up with Lachelle outside. They were a contrasting pair, both striking in their own ways. Lachelle was athletic and quietly graceful, straight-backed, and held her head defensively high. Marita was thicker and had curves for days; she owned and moved every inch of her softer body with pride, oozing sensuality. As the heavy bar door slowly swung shut, I thought, *Women are better friends than men. I can't visualize any guy rushing to my side to make sure I was okay.*

Danny continued to study me.

I finally barked, "What!?"

He watched Lachelle and Marita disappear around the corner, huddled in friendship, then looked hard at me. "How many people do you talk to in a day?"

"I don't know—dozens. I make it a point to talk to everybody. Even the most difficult people that nobody talks to." I bragged, "And those connections found us Ray Fury."

"Yeah," Dan chided. "Kudos to you. Is there anybody you love?"

What the hell has got into Dan? I loved my family, but as for lovers, I hadn't met the right person yet. "Outside of family—no."

He was serious. "You never take it to the next level, do you? You're kind and respectful, but don't you dare let that conversation get too deep. God forbid, someone gets to know the real Zave."

I deserved some credit for my efforts to be a friend to the neighborhood I worked in. The only thing worse than being alone was being asked to think about it. I ignored him and took a swallow of beer.

Danny seemed to know exactly what I was thinking. "You're great for the community, but is it good for you?"

I directed my focus to the television screen. Angry protesters in Ferguson were chanting, "Hands up. Don't shoot!" My blood boiled at the loss of life—over shoplifting.

Dan pointed to the TV. "People have threatened to kill the cop's pregnant wife."

I emphatically stated, "No *charges*, though? How do you explain shooting an unarmed man six times?"

Dan argued, "I'm not defending him. I'm just sayin' we don't really know. We weren't there. You know how fast we make life and death decisions. The entire police encounter, from beginning to end, was ninety seconds long."

"Isn't that even more of an argument against shooting?" I turned to the bartender, "Is the Twins game on?"

He turned it on. The Twins were tied two-two in the ninth inning. Jon Schaeffer was on third base and Brian Dozier was on second. St. Paul native, Joe Mauer, was at the plate. Joe was the only catcher to lead the league in hitting.

Dan commented, "C'mon Joe. Give us some good news." After Joe took strike two, Dan swore under his breath, "Dammit. He takes too many pitches."

I nudged him, "Don't lose hope, man. Mauer's the best two-strike hitter in baseball."

As the words left my mouth, Joe waited patiently on a curveball and drove it up the gap between left and center. The Twins took the lead four to two. The Astros had the last bat. Stillwater native, Glen Perkins, came in to close the game for the Twins. Glen had the pleasure of getting the save in this year's all-star game, at Target field, in front of a sold-out crowd of his home fans. Tonight, Perkins retired the side in order and the Twins were victorious.

For a moment, a couple of hometown boys shut off the pounding in my head. Dan and I clinked our glasses together again, in celebration. And *that* was why we watched. On a bad night, a win was still something.

It wasn't long before concerns about racism crept back. There were fewer Black players in pro baseball last year than there'd been since 1953—*sixty years ago*. The decline was attributed to the shutting down of many inner-city youth baseball programs. If you wanted your kids to play basketball, they only needed sneakers. Football provided the uniform. But baseball often required the purchase of a glove, a bat, spikes, and a uniform.

In the background, Dan was saying, "You know Perkins married author Alicia Weber . . ."

6

"I have learned over the years that when one's mind is made up, this diminishes fear; knowing what must be done does away with fear."
—ROSA PARKS

2017

JADA ANDERSON

10:30 P.M., THURSDAY, APRIL 13
SOUTH WASHINGTON AVENUE, DOWNTOWN EAST
NEIGHBORHOOD MINNEAPOLIS

I hadn't thought about Sadie Sullivan's murder for a year. Ray Fury, an imposing heavyweight boxer, had been convicted for raping and murdering her. There was no more news to cover about the case—at least until the appeal. A brief encounter with Jon Frederick led to the first chink in the armor of what was sold to me, and the rest of the public, as a solid case against Fury.

Jon texted me at 10:00 p.m. and asked if I'd been in his apartment. The call seemed a little impudent and audacious, being we broke up over three years ago. The truth was, I *had* been in his apartment, but how could he have known? It was a bitterly cold night; still, I ventured over to explain myself. *I've got to learn to let go of that boy.*

I smoothed my hair into a ponytail and selected a scarlet cotton top to wear with my blue jeans and Chuck Taylors. I initially left two buttons open but, on a whim, unbuttoned a third. I put on my wool pea coat and ventured over to Jon's.

Damn—no parking in front of his apartment complex. This forced me to park behind it, in one of the sketchiest places in Minneapolis. There were no streetlights, businesses, or even houses providing any type of illumination back there—just a pitch-black parking lot. Jon always told me to call before I got out of my car if I had to park there. Of course, I never did.

I loved being a newscaster, but it was unsettling. Because of my work, I knew one of Ray's alleged victims was brutally raped right down the river from my apartment. Fury had a pending court date on that rape, which I planned on covering. I cautiously looked around after exiting my car. The darkness reminded me of being at the bottom of the Soudan mine with the lights off. I couldn't see my hand in front of my face. I fumbled to activate the flashlight on my phone.

I swore I heard the baritone throat clearing of a desperate man approaching.

I broke into a full sprint, my phone's light dancing in front of me, toward the lights of the apartment complex.

When I reached the front of the building, I bent and dropped my hands to my knees to catch my breath, gulping in the cold winter air. My blood was still racing, but it was finally safe to look back.

There was no sign of life on my trail. A graveyard of abandoned cars lined the streets, reminiscent of catacombs that had released their spirits for the night. Was it a killer, a homeless man, or just my imagination? Whisps of steam rose from the manhole covers like phantoms haunting the desolate neighborhood.

I made up my mind I was just going to tell Jon the truth. I had one glass of wine too many a couple nights ago and wrote him a letter, declaring I still loved him. I asked—okay, embarrassingly *begged*—if he would be willing to take me back now that he had his child. Jon had fathered a child with Serena Bell, but they had recently separated.

I convinced myself I had to drop the letter in the mail that drunken night. In the light of day, the letter was a bad idea. Fortunately, I still had my key to his apartment, and I knew where Jon kept the key to his mailbox. So, I retrieved that letter before he had the chance to open it.

Tonight, on my mission of truth, I rode the elevator to his fifteenth-floor apartment.

The door opened and my heart melted. Just over thirty years old, Jon was as lean and strong as ever. When his soft blue eyes met mine, my first words were a flat out lie, "You do remember that I returned my key three years ago."

Jon ran a hand through his hair and apologized, "I'm sorry for calling so late. I just can't make sense of it."

I cupped my hands in front of my mouth and blew warm air into them. I peered about the spotless apartment. How on earth did he know someone had been inside?

I teased, "You could've just said you were lonely."

He gestured toward the countertop and said, "My extra set of keys was sitting on the counter. And the toaster's plugged in."

I grinned nervously, realizing I had taken his extra set of keys off the hook to get to his mail key. And, while I checked out what Jon is eating these days, I had absent-mindedly plugged the toaster in.

I commented, "And you have to unplug your toaster because your mom bought you one with a light on it, so it burns electricity anytime it's plugged in. God forbid, you'd waste electricity." I raised an eyebrow and changed the subject. "Remember why we used to call each other late at night?"

He was momentarily jolted into silence.

Amused by his awkwardness, I winked and commented, "You could at least offer me a beer. It's so cold, I thought about asking a cop to Tase me, just to warm up."

Jon went to the fridge and retrieved a cold Surly Furious. He rinsed off the top of the can and poured it into a glass. He carefully made certain the beer was the appropriate, untampered color before he handed it to me. I should've told him it was just me and that no one was trying to poison him, but it was getting to the point of being entertaining. I'd mess with him a little longer.

After he closed the refrigerator door, Jon reopened it and grabbed another Surly for himself, and repeated the process.

I sipped, "Mmmm, lots of hops," and then rambled on about work. During the course of the conversation, I followed him into the kitchen and leaned a hip against the countertop next to where he was standing. He didn't back away from the intrusion into his space. I maintained the conversation, as if I hadn't noticed.

Jon finally stepped back and circled around me to the kitchen table, placing his phone on its polished surface and eyeing it expectantly. He pulled out a chair and I joined him. I picked up his cellphone and scrolled through his recent calls.

He gave me his *what the hell are you doing* look.

Contrite over invading his privacy, I said, "I'm sorry. It's the reporter in me. Serena's not calling, but you're waiting for her to change her mind—ruminating over everything you could've done differently." I set the phone down and, with one finger, slid it back across the table. I asked, "What are you going to do?"

"Work obsessively and make enough money so I can build a house close to my daughter." He raised his beer in a toast and took a drink.

Concerned, I reminded him, "You're a great investigator, Jon. Don't throw that away."

"The only time I'm happy is when I'm with her . . ."

The realization that I didn't belong there settled over me like a weighted blanket of regret. I took a large swallow of beer and stood up. I picked up my jacket and reluctantly said, "I should go." I threw him an apologetic but expectant grimace, "I had to park in the back."

Jon threw on his favorite, beat-up juniper green field jacket and walked me out to my car.

I asked him, "Remember the Sadie Sullivan murder?"

He searched his memory. "Is that the one you showed me pictures of?"

"Yes." I said, "Sadie was raped and murdered by a guy named Ray Fury. He was convicted for First Degree Murder a couple years ago. He's got an attorney and they're appealing the conviction." I stopped walking. "I've always wondered, why did you write 'cop' by the picture of the truck?"

Jon stuffed his hands in his pockets as he scrounged around in his brain, recalling photos from a scene he looked at four years ago. With the loads of information in that head of his, it was a wonder he could find anything, but he always did. Finally, the lightbulb went on. "The seat belt was buckled but appeared to be sat on by the driver. Cops do this all the time, so they can exit the car quickly and can avoid the unpleasant dinging from the unfastened belt."

"That's odd. Her fiancé was a cop." I shook the thought away and said, "They had DNA evidence on Fury indicating he had raped her. And he claims he never knew her. It's a closed case. Fury's doing life in prison." The revelation bothered me, but I continued, "You had another note on the video of the medical examiner loading Sadie's body at 8:00 a.m. that said something like, *Died before midnight.* What was that about?"

"It takes a couple hours for rigor mortis to start, and then it takes six to eight hours to set. If they loaded the body around 8:00 a.m. Sadie must have died before midnight. Her body was rock solid."

"Sadie was still home with her fiancé at midnight. It was determined that Ray Fury had raped her after she left home at 3:00 a.m., to go to work at Cub Foods. Sadie had showered with her fiancé just before leaving the house, so the DNA had to be introduced after that."

Jon looked lost in thought as we continued the walk to my car. He finally responded, "Well, if Amaya Ho was the medical examiner, I'm sure she had good reasons to support her conclusions. She knows more about the science of the evidence than I do."

When we arrived at my car, I lightly kissed his cheek, and said, "Give me one real hug before I go."

Even though it was freezing, I opened my jacket and invited him in.

He opened his in return and we held each other.

I closed my eyes and snuggled into the warmth of his body. For a minute, we were back dancing on the rooftop. But the moment passed and, with melancholic thoughts of what could have been, I finally pulled away.

I asked, "Do you ever think about us?"

Jon glanced around the dark parking lot and frankly said, "No. I wanted children—you didn't. There was nothing to resolve."

I chuckled at his blunt answer. That was Jon—so logical. I'd been second guessing the idea of not having children, recently. My aspiration to be a national news anchor seemed so far out of reach now. But I had lost Jon. I'd seen that old flame burning in Jon for years—but had protectively denied it. And now Serena had his baby. I wiped away a tear and shared, "It's been a tough week."

Jon said softly, "I haven't been great with coming up with solutions lately, but I'll listen."

My brain knew we were over, but my heart wanted to cry. I nodded in appreciation of his offer, quietly got in my car, and pulled away while Jon stood politely on the street and watched. I was glad I retrieved the letter. Jon loved Serena.

7

"What kind of a man wants a woman today that cannot hold a conversation?"
—MALCOM X

2017

XAVIER WILLIAMS

2:30 P.M., FRIDAY, JUNE 30,
HENNEPIN COUNTY GOVERNMENT CENTER,
300 SOUTH 6TH STREET DOWNTOWN WEST
NEIGHBORHOOD, MINNEAPOLIS

It'd been a terrible week for the Sullivan family. Sadie's older brother, Liam, put a gun to his head and took his life on Monday. In his suicide note, he blamed himself for not protecting her. Today, Sadie's mom and three surviving sisters buried another family member. I'd never been particularly good at dealing with death, but I forced myself to go to Liam's funeral. Bobby Long stood with the family and sadly placed his hand on Liam's casket before it was lowered to the ground. For the first time, I truly saw grief in his eyes. The question was, *What does he do with it?* When he spotted me in the cemetery, his mourning quickly turned to hate, as if somehow, I was responsible for the tragedy. Maybe it was simply that my race was a reminder. *Imagine if I looked at Bobby with the hatred I have for what terrible white people have done to my brothers and sisters.*

But I hated Ray Fury, too. He had done so much damage. What was justice for a man who raped and murdered a loving young mother, who was the pride and joy of her family?

As for me, I was so busy trying to make the world kinder, Dan thought I didn't have time for my own life. Maybe he was right.

After the burial, I went to Fury's hearing involving his rape of Elizabeth Erickson. He was finally being charged with one of the sexual assaults. The prosecutor, Paul Tierney, took this step after Fury's appeal of his murder conviction started to gain momentum. A popular metro reporter, Jada Anderson, had been interviewed by both the St. Paul Pioneer Press and the Minneapolis Tribune, questioning the selective attention investigators gave to Fury in this case. The reason he hadn't been charged for his previous rapes was that he was already sentenced to life in prison. The prosecutor thought it was better not to put the victims through a court hearing if it was unnecessary.

The Honorable Judge Saul Tyson was ruling on today's rape case. Flamin' Ray Fury sat next to his attorney in an ill-fitting brown suit and tie. The jacket's seams strained in complaint across his broad back. Ray's hair was clipped into a neat fade and the edges of his goatee were crisp as a razor's edge. I imagined he'd made a quick outfit change from his prison-issued jumpsuit in the secure meeting room just outside of the courtroom. Fury opted out of using a jury and elected to have the judge rule on his case, instead. This seemed like a bad direction for a black American to take with an elderly white judge. It made me wonder if his attorney was working at a legal technicality.

When I looked around the courtroom, I saw Cheyenne Schmidt paying careful attention to how the victim was being handled. She wore a casual midi dress, but too much makeup for a courtroom.

Wanting to give her some support, I sat next to Cheyenne and whispered, "Are you okay?"

Failing to even look my way, she silently stared straight ahead at the witness.

A scruffy looking, fortyish bartender from the Dangerous Man Brewing Company was on the stand.

I was familiar with Fury's middle-aged attorney. Margaret Brown had helped some decent poverty-ridden individuals, but also helped terrible people escape consequences. I guess I'd categorize her as a great attorney, but a questionable person.

Margaret asked the witness, "Are you familiar with Elizabeth Erickson?"

The bearded man stated, "She has been in our taproom a number of times."

"A large number?"

He remarked, "Any number is large, if you write it big enough."

Margaret showed no glimmer of humor. She flatly asked, "More than ten?"

"Yes."

She repeated, "More than twenty?"

"Yes."

Paul Tierncy, a silver-haired prosecutor in his sixties, objected. "Irrelevant. It's been established she was a patron of the taproom."

The elderly judge concurred. "Sustained."

Fury's defense attorney smiled. "Okay. On the evening of August 31, 2013, how much did Elizabeth Erickson have to drink?"

"She had three glasses of beer."

"It was four years ago. How could you possibly remember?"

"She paid by credit card and her beers were itemized on her bill."

"She was drinking by herself?"

The bartender obviously felt some compassion for Elizabeth when he softly said, "She almost always drinks by herself."

"What did she drink?"

"Liza likes the Belgium Golden Strong."

"Is that one of your higher alcohol beers?"

"Yeah. Three of those and you'll love your mother-in-law."

Judge Tyson wasn't about to have his courtroom turned into a comedy routine. He directed the witness, "Just answer the question."

"Was she drinking before she arrived at the taproom?"

Uncertain, the witness responded, "I wouldn't know."

"Wouldn't you say it's probable, by her appearance?"

Tierney stated, "Objection. He already answered the question."

Judge Tyson tiredly agreed, "Sustained."

Margaret continued, "When she left, was she in any shape to drive home? If she was by herself, she didn't have a ride."

Tierney objected once again, but the defense attorney argued, "This is an assessment that bartenders are asked daily to make at work."

The judge ruled, "I'll allow the question."

The witness stated, "No, she wasn't. I made sure she wasn't driving before I allowed her to leave."

Margaret added, "So, it's safe to say she was intoxicated."

The bartender agreed, "Yes."

"But she could walk."

"Yes. I offered to call someone, but she said she was okay."

Margaret commented, "Didn't the patrons refer to her as Bottoms Up Betty?"

The side of the witness' mouth tugged against his efforts not to grin. "They did. But that wasn't just about her drinking."

The attorney pretended to be shocked by his response, but she obviously knew where this was going. "What else could the reference be for?"

"One night when she was drunk, someone had witnessed her getting it dog style in a truck in the parking lot and shared the story with all the bar patrons."

The prosecutor yelled, "Objection! Elizabeth isn't on trial, here."

I couldn't help thinking, *Oh, yes she is.*

Ray Fury busted out laughing.

I wanted to hit him so hard he'd be the first man on Mars. It seemed appropriate to launch Flamin' Ray Fury to the red planet. I searched the galley for Elizabeth Erickson and found her at the outside edge of a row. She glanced back at the courtroom door, pondering escaping this nightmare, but seemed to know this was no longer a possibility. Embarrassed, she stared straight down at the floor, like a small child who closes her eyes and hopes no one can see her.

The attorney asked, "Did you force Elizabeth to drink?"

"No. No one forced her to drink."

"She was intoxicated by her own doing, correct?"

"Yes."

Margaret drove it home with a dramatic gesture. "She picked up the glass and poured beer down her throat. No one else made her."

The bartender remarked, "That is generally how people drink."

"No more questions." The attorney smugly sat down.

Tierny stood up, "Ray Fury was also in the taproom on August 21, 2013, correct?"

The bartender nodded. "Yes."

"When did he leave?"

"It wasn't immediately after Liza left, but it wasn't long after."

"And you know with certainty it was Ray Fury?"

"Yeah. I card everybody."

Tierney stated, "No more questions."

Curiously, the defense attorney was given the opportunity to cross-examine him once more but elected not to. This was too easy. *What was she planning?*

Elizabeth Erickson was called to the stand. Her face was blanched with tension; she looked nervous enough to faint.

The bailiff directed her, "Please raise your right hand. Do you swear to tell the whole truth and nothing but the truth?"

With her hand in the air, she responded, "I do."

She sat on the witness stand and Judge Tyson directed, "State your name for the record."

"Elizabeth Erickson."

Tierney stepped forward, "Elizabeth, were you at the Dangerous Man Brewing Company on the night of August 31, 2013?"

She nodded but was quickly informed she must answer questions aloud. Elizabeth swallowed and said, "Yes."

"And it's been established you drank three strong beers, which were the equivalent to seven glasses of wine."

"Yes."

"Did you drink before you arrived at the taproom?"

"Just a sip. I was struggling with the loss of my husband. He died of a heart attack just a month earlier."

Tierney continued, "And Ray Fury was also in the bar."

"Honestly, I don't remember."

"Shortly after you left the taproom, you noticed a man following you. Is that correct?"

Elizabeth nodded again but caught herself. "Yes."

Tierney prompted, "And then what happened?"

She painfully looked down and stated, "I tried to run, but I stumbled and fell. I managed to get back on my feet and started walking. He yelled for me to stop, but I kept going. He caught up to me, dragged me behind a dumpster, and raped me."

The defense attorney stood up. "Objection! Her statement to the police indicated she walked by her own accord."

Judge Tyson cut her off. "The objection is overruled. Let her testify. You'll get your chance to cross-examine her."

Elizabeth argued, "I was drunk, and he knew I was drunk."

The judge reprimanded Elizabeth, "You can only speak when you are asked a question. You need to respect this."

She cowered as she feebly apologized, "I'm sorry."

The prosecutor asked, "At any time, did you indicate you were interested in having sex with Ray Fury?"

"No! For God's sake, no. He forced me."

With cool calmness, the prosecutor slowly raised a picture of Elizabeth's battered face. Paul slowly turned so everyone could see the gruesome beating she had taken. Her left eye was dark purple and completely swollen shut. He stopped and held the picture in front of the judge as he asked, "Elizabeth, is this what your face looked like after Ray Fury was done with you?"

Elizabeth acknowledged, "Yes."

"And you know, with one hundred percent certainty, the man who raped you was Ray Fury."

"I didn't at the time. I didn't when the police interviewed me that night because I'd never met him before. When I saw him again, I knew he was the guy."

Tierney asked, "Did you ever speak to Ray Fury outside of the time he was raping you?"

"No."

"So, you couldn't have consented. Just to clarify, you didn't speak to him in the taproom that night?"

"No. I don't remember him being there. And even if he was there, he isn't my type."

Tierney stated, "I'm not going to make you go through details of the rape, but can you give us a basic description of what happened?"

Elizabeth dropped her head as she spoke, "He ordered me to lie down, forced his penis into my vagina, and thrusted in me over and over until he was done."

"How did it end?"

"He stood over me, fists clenched, like he was going to finish beating me to death. I begged for my life, and he finally just left." Lost in a memory, she added, "And there I was—pummeled and defeated. Like trash he'd just discarded."

The prosecutor seemed pleased with her closing comments. He said, "I don't have any more questions. Thank you, Elizabeth. I understand this has been hard for you."

Margaret Brown stood up and strolled toward the witness. "Elizabeth, let's get something clear about that picture of your bruised face right off the bat. You stated in the complaint that you fell and hit your head, before Ray had any contact with you."

Elizabeth interjected, "I was running from him."

Margaret studied her curiously. "But he hadn't threatened you. He hadn't even spoken to you. That is what you said."

When Elizabeth didn't respond, Margaret added, "The bruising on your face came from that fall."

In almost a whisper, Elizabeth started, "Some of it—"

Margaret cut her off. "Maybe all of it. Elizabeth, they call you Betty sometimes, right?"

She attempted to bravely face the attorney. A little embarrassed by the question, she said, "Yes, some do."

"Have you had any drinks today?"

"No." Elizabeth was shaking, likely because she *was* sober.

"When you said Ray isn't your type, Betty, were you referring to his race? You had already judged him because he was black."

Startled, Elizabeth said, "No. I meant he's scary—dangerous."

Attempting to appear aghast, Margaret replied, "Are you aware that, other than a case that's currently under appeal, Raymond Fury has never been convicted for hurting anybody?"

Elizabeth weakly shook her head *no*.

Margaret turned and faced the galley, "How many times have you been ticketed for Driving While Intoxicated?"

"Three."

"You're the one who sounds dangerous. You stumble and mutilate your face. You've driven home drunk, endangering the lives of others numerous times."

The prosecutor said, "Objection. The defense attorney is testifying."

Margaret said, "Let me reword it. You've put yourself in dangerous situations numerous times. Is that accurate?"

"Yes."

"And nobody made you. You did so by your own choice."

Elizabeth gazed back down, "Yes."

"Have you ever blacked out before?"

The prosecutor stated, "Objection. Irrelevant."

The judge stated, "I'll allow it."

"Yes."

"Is it possible you could have blacked out for a moment and told Ray you wanted to have sex that night?"

"No."

"How do you know?"

"Because I remember what happened."

"I thought you said you were mentally incapacitated."

"I was. I could barely walk. I was slurring my words."

"Do you feel your level of intoxication clouded your reasoning?"

"Yes."

Margaret adjusted an earring. "When you said Ray dragged you, you basically meant he took your hand and led you to a private place?"

"I didn't know what I was doing."

"But he didn't knock you out and drag you, did he— *Betty?*" She again chastised her with the nickname as if she directly spat it at her.

Elizabeth softly answered, "No—he didn't drag me."

"You walked to where the two of you had sex and, as you said, you were difficult to understand, right?"

Elizabeth reluctantly admitted, "Yes."

Margaret Brown made direct eye contact with her. "Who removed your clothes?"

"I took my clothes off." She weakly pointed at Fury, "But he told me to. He scared the hell out of me."

"Do you always take your clothes off when you're scared?"

The prosecutor stood and shouted, "Objection!"

Margaret turned to the judge, "I'm merely trying to establish why she took her clothes off. It's important to our defense."

The judge pondered for a moment and ruled, "I'll allow it."

Elizabeth said, "I was afraid. I did as I was told."

"So, you walked with him to a private area and took your clothes off. If you were so afraid, why didn't you just run?"

"I was drunk. I'd just tried that and fell flat on my face."

"Did you physically fight him? Did you hit him, or scratch him, or bite him?"

"No, but I told him—"

Margaret cut her off, "Just answer the question. Did you physically fight him?"

"No. He would have—"

The defense attorney again interrupted, "It's a yes or no question. Please, just answer the question—because you don't really know what he would have done."

Elizabeth conceded, "I didn't fight him. The toxicology report indicated I was twice the legal limit of intoxication."

"Are you saying this was the bartender's fault?"

"No. I wasn't that drunk when I left the taproom. I was mad when he asked if I needed a ride, so I left. I had a pint of Absolut vodka in my coat pocket so, after I left the bar, I took a few hits. And then I just felt sad and started walking home."

Margaret asked, "Do you feel you were mentally incapacitated due to your level of intoxication?"

"Yes." Elizabeth admitted, "I didn't know what I was doing. He knew I was in bad shape."

"And if you wouldn't have been mentally incapacitated, you would have handled it differently."

"Yes."

"You would have made it clear to Ray that you didn't want to have sex—by saying something understandable, or by running, correct?"

"Yes—but it doesn't make any difference, because I was stumbling drunk."

Margaret interjected, "We don't use layman's terms in our statutes. I believe the term is mentally incapacitated—correct?"

Elizabeth sat up straighter. "Yes. I was mentally incapacitated."

"Did anyone force you to drink alcohol that night?"

She admitted, "No."

"And you testified that you hadn't spoken to Ray, before having sex with him, so he couldn't have forced you to drink, correct?"

"Ray didn't force me to drink. But—"

Margaret cut her off, "You already answered the question."

The prosecutor interjected, "Objection. She keeps interrupting the witness. Let her finish answering the question."

The judge asked Elizabeth, "Did you have anything more to say pertaining to Ray not forcing you to drink?"

Elizabeth shook her head, "I guess not."

The defense attorney abruptly stopped. "No more questions. Thank you for your helpful testimony, Betty."

The judge turned to Tierney and asked, "Do you wish to redirect?"

Paul pondered and then said, "What was your blood alcohol level?"

Margaret quickly interrupted, "That isn't a question appropriate for redirect."

She was right. If the question wasn't part of her direct testimony, you couldn't redirect her on it.

The judge ruled, "Objection sustained."

Paul rescinded, "I have no further questions, Your Honor."

The judge turned to Margaret, "Do you have witnesses you wish to call for the defense?"

Margaret smirked. "That won't be necessary."

I had a bad feeling about this. The defense attorney was entirely too confident. I decided to stay and listen to the closing arguments from both sides.

During his closing arguments, the prosecutor pointed out, "We have witnesses that place Ray Fury with the victim. DNA testing has demonstrated Ray Fury's sperm was in the victim's vagina. Elizabeth was mentally incapacitated, as indicated by her level of intoxication, demonstrated by both witnesses and her toxicology report after the assault. This is an open and shut case of sexual assault."

And then the defense attorney dropped the bombshell. "Ray Fury is accused of taking advantage of Elizabeth Erickson while she was mentally incapacitated. He is accused of a violation of Minnesota Statute 609.341. Under the statute, 'mentally incapacitated' means that a person was under the influence of alcohol, a narcotic, anesthetic, or another substance, administered to that person without the person's agreement, so the person lacked the judgment to give a reasoned consent to sexual contact." She put the definition on a screen in the courtroom. Margaret pointed out the portion in bold, ADMINISTERED TO A PERSON WITHOUT THE PERSON'S AGREEMENT. "By the statute's definition, Elizabeth Erickson does not meet the criteria for mental incapacitation, as she readily agreed to consume all of the alcohol, which led to her intoxicated state."

Everyone in the courtroom leaned forward to read the statute.

The Honorable Judge Saul Tyson called for a thirty-minute recess, to consider the information at hand.

4:00 P.M.

WHEN WE RETURNED, JUDGE TYSON RELUCTANTLY stated, "Based on the statute, I am going to have to find Ray Fury not guilty of Criminal Sexual Conduct. According to the statute, her state of intoxication could not leave her mentally incapacitated because she self-administered the alcohol."

Prosecutor Paul Tierney interjected, "Your honor. If you make this ruling, you will make every intoxicated person a target for a rapist."

The judge turned to the prosecutor. "Then you might want to get to work rewriting the statute. While it makes common sense that the term 'mentally incapacitated' would include any sexual assault victim who was intoxicated, whether they drank voluntarily or involuntarily, that isn't what the *law states*," he emphasized. "The meaning is clear, and my task is to apply the meaning of the law, rather than what I wish the law should be."[1]

I was furious. Cheyenne stood up and hurried out of the courtroom.

It would be difficult to get Cheyenne to testify against Fury, after she'd witnessed what Elizabeth went through.

Lauren Herald was sitting right behind me. She tapped my shoulder and said, "This same idiotic reasoning could be used to argue a person chooses to go to sleep; therefore, a rapist shouldn't be prosecuted for sexually abusing a sleeping person."

---

1. On September 15, 2021, the Minnesota State Legislature changed the statute to include individuals intoxicated by their own choice into the category of mentally incapacitated, to provide intoxicated people protection from sexual predators.

Ray Fury had now been acquitted twice for sexually abusing women he left physically battered. My only salvation was he was serving a life sentence for murder. As long as that ruling stayed in place, Fury remained locked up.

6:30 P.M.

GRAIN BELT APARTMENTS,

1215 MARSHALL STREET,

NORTHEAST SHERIDAN, MINNEAPOLIS

WHEN MY SHIFT ENDED, I MADE IT MY MISSION to find Elizabeth Erickson. I drove to her apartment complex and knocked on the door. Elizabeth was a resident in the community I swore to serve and protect. It wasn't good enough for me to say, *Life sucks. Get over it and move on.* Even though the murder rate gets all the publicity, the suicide rate for women Elizabeth's age is more than double the homicide rate. I wanted her to be okay and this was a hard blow to recover from. I stayed in uniform so she would clearly know I was a police officer.

Elizabeth answered the door with a drink in her hand and sarcastically asked, "What now? Are you going to arrest me for being raped?"

"No, I'm not." I stood uncomfortably in the doorway. "I just wanted you to know that I'm sorry for the way this all played out, Elizabeth."

She waved me in, and I joined her at the kitchen table. "Call me Liza. Only people making fun of me call me Betty and I'm only Elizabeth in court."

"My dad always said, 'It's not what they call you, it's what you answer to that matters.' So, how about if you don't answer to Betty, anymore?"

"I won't." She asked, "Do you want a drink?"

"No, thank you. I'm Xavier—*my* friends call me Zave and you feel free to do so, too." I said, "I'm still angry about court.

I can't imagine how you feel. Those asses asked you to testify, to help keep our community safe, and then tore you apart. I don't want to leave you apart."

"Why do you care?" She toasted her glass in the air, "I'm drinking, so I guess I'm open game for sex—according to Judge Tyson."

I sighed, "I'm tired of all the carnage. I guess I'd like to see someone who wasn't left destroyed. You're better than Ray Fury. He shouldn't get to destroy you."

Liza set down her drink. "You're serious."

"Serious as sin. I want you to be okay."

"Why bother? I'm a sinking ship. Jack and I used to go to the pub every weekend. Jack was a decade older than me, but honestly—he was my lighthouse. I've been a lost soul, since he passed. After three DWIs, I decided I'm walking to the bar. That didn't play out so great for me though, did it?"

"You're not going to find what you need in a bar. If you'd like, I'll go with you to Fairview Recovery Services tomorrow. You could use some new friends." I fumbled for words and was beginning to question why I even bothered this poor woman. I suggested, "I was kind of hoping you'd give treatment a shot."

I expected her to argue, but she didn't. Instead, she walked to her window and gazed out. "We were already talking about cutting back on our drinking before he died. When Jack died—I just kept on." After a moment, she responded, "Okay." Liza glanced back at me, "What time are you going to pick me up?"

It was clear she was going to get drunk tonight. "How about high noon? Can you promise me you'll be here, alive?"

She joined me at the table. "Yes. Thank you, Zave. You're alright."

9:00 P.M.
ANGRY INCH BREWING COMPANY,
20841 HOLYOKE AVENUE, LAKEVILLE

I FELT LIKE DRINKING TONIGHT, TOO. THE BAD guys won today. When I felt like I was losing, I kept trying to do something positive until some good happened. Hopefully, Liza would answer the door tomorrow. I called Dan Baker and he said he'd join me for one.

Angry Inch had some creative names for their beers. I passed on the Therapy Session Pale Ale and the Samoan Kisses Stout, and instead ordered Love Potion #208.

Dan came walking in with Marita. He ordered the True Confessions while Marita went with the Ménage à Trois.

I told them, "It pisses me off that Liza was raped and then basically told it was her fault."

After I vented about today's events, Marita said, "I invited Lachelle, but she was busy."

I gave her a half-smile, "That's fine. I think Lachelle and I are done talking." I wasn't in the mood to deal with her tonight, anyway.

Dan said, "The bottom line is Ray Fury isn't getting out of prison."

"His appeal is going forward, and it makes me nervous as hell. He's walked away from two sexual assault charges, and he's got a good attorney."

Dan looked like he wanted to say something, but instead avoided eye contact with me.

A catchy reggaeton song with Caribbean lyrics began playing over the sound system.

Oblivious to my concerns, Marita enthusiastically said, "Do you believe *Despacito* is the number one song in the U.S. right now? Having a song entirely in Spanish, at number one, is like having an African American president."

I had to respond, "Not *quite* like having an African American President."

Marita argued, "It is, if music is more important to you than politics." She stood by our table and danced in slow motion, swaying her substantial hips as the women do in the *Despacito* video. She was alluring.

I asked, "What does *Despacito* even mean?"

Marita smiled seductively as she purred, "Slow and gentle."

Dan remarked wryly, "It's the second most played video online—right behind Baby Shark."

Watching her didn't feel right. She was with my friend. I focused on Dan, "You have something to say to me. I'd like to know what it is."

Dan didn't appear to be particularly interested in Marita's seductive dance. He casually turned to me, "Do *you* think Fury killed Sadie?"

"Yes, I do."

He frowned, "Me, too—but not as strongly as I once did. I don't know if it means anything, but I know something crazy about Sadie's fiancé."

I waited.

He said, "I stopped back at the funeral parlor to check on Bobby after Sadie's wake. I walked in and he was standing over her casket. He hadn't heard me come in. He grumbled to Sadie's dead body, 'You got what you deserved.'"

"Did you ever tell anybody that?"

"No—hell no. We all say things we don't mean, at times. I know that better than anybody. He was under a lot of stress. Maybe he was thinking she shouldn't have offered to give him a ride?"

"*Did* she offer to give him a ride?"

"That's the theory, but no one really knows. It was proposed that she stopped at the Winner gas station."

The same place where Fury approached Cheyenne. I asked, "Don't they have it on video?"

"The cameras weren't working," he said with disgust. "I don't know if they ever do."

"They must have her credit card on record."

"No." He paused, "They said she always paid cash."

"Dan—it was three in the morning. If she stopped, she had to pay by credit card. It's closed by eleven."

Not wanting to argue, he responded, "Yeah—I don't know."

Honestly, I could see Sadie stopping to help someone who appeared stranded.

Feeling ignored, Marita rejoined us at the table. I pulled my eyes away from the way her low-cut dress revealed an alley that left little to the imagination. The green and blue pattern of it pulled the colors of her eyes to life. To call her exotic would be an understatement.

I wasn't sure what to think of Bobby's remark. Sadie was raped and murdered, and her fiancé was angry at her for it. Her brother was buried today. This had really been a shitty day.

Dan's phone buzzed and he stepped away. When he returned, he said, "I'm sorry, but I need to help somebody out. Would you mind giving Marita a ride home?"

"No problem."

After he left, Marita glanced over at me and asked, "Do you want to grab a bite?" I *thought* she was talking about food, but the way she purred it had me wondering.

I was hungry but wasn't sure if I should eat with Dan's date. She read my mind. "You know, Dan and I aren't together. We're friends."

As I finished my beer, I texted Dan, "Mind if I grab some food with Marita?"

He texted back, "No problem. Marita and I aren't a thing."

10:45 P.M.
LYNDALE AVENUE EAST,
NORTH LOOP NEIGHBORHOOD, MINNEAPOLIS

MARITA AND I ENJOYED SOME KILLER SANDWICHES at Revival on Nicollet Avenue. I went with the fried chicken thigh sandwich—Tennessee hot, while Marita had the vegetarian beet Rueben. I was now driving her back to her home in the North Loop.

Marita was sweet and funny. She laughed, "Everyone tells you to follow your dreams. Me, I just find out where they're going and promise I'll catch up with them later."

I had to admit I was drawn into her sexy vibes, and I was tired of being alone. When I pulled up to her apartment, she invited me in. I wasn't sure if she had completely convinced me she and Dan were just friends, or if I just wanted to believe it. I do remember I was on the verge of going in.

And then Marita purred, "We could watch a porno; I've got some juicy flicks that would curl your toes."

It was the cold shower I needed. "I think I'll pass."

It wasn't that I was opposed to seeing a naked woman. There were few things better in life—as a matter of fact, at the moment, I couldn't think of any.

She quickly backtracked, "I'm sorry. Please pretend I never said that. It was going so well. I just figured you'd probably like that—as an ice breaker." She pouted, "Now you're thinking I'm some sort of creep."

"Why do I seem like I'd like that?"

"Danny says some of the guys call you X at work."

"They call me X because my name is Xavier. And I don't respond to X. X is what people write when they can't spell their names. I could accept just about any other letter as a nickname, except N."

"Dan says you're never with a woman for long. The cops refer to your dates as *X and his one-night sex*. I assumed the relationship piece isn't your focus."

I detested the picture people had of me. I stayed out of the mindless gossip, so they made up their own stories about me. For me, Marita's desire to watch porn was a deal breaker. It was analogous to having the best gourmet meal right in front of you, and then watching someone else eat it.

"Look," I said. "I'm not going to pretend I'm all buttoned up, because I'm not. It's just not my deal."

Trying to be optimistic, she blurted, "That's great! It's not really my deal, either."

She wasn't getting out of my car without an explanation. I blew out a long exhale. "Here's my thinking. A great night with a woman, to me, is one where we're in rhythm with each other. We're discovering who we are. I'm learning what she wants and she's learning what I want. It's pleasant and seamless."

She interrupted, "I felt it. Didn't you?"

"I did. And then you stopped us and wanted to go watch porn. I have no desire to be with someone who's not in the moment."

Marita demurred, "I can be in the moment."

I restlessly fiddled with my car keys. "That's great."

She raised her eyebrows. "But you're not coming in."

"Marita, I wish you the best. I just can't trust where your brain's going to be when we're getting intimate. Sorry."

8

"When you have police officers who abuse citizens, you erode public confidence in law enforcement. That makes the job of good police officers unsafe."
—Mary Frances Berry

2017

BOBBY LONG

11:45 P.M., SATURDAY, APRIL 8,
WEST MINNEHAHA AVENUE,
FROGTOWN NEIGHBORHOOD, ST. PAUL

It's sixty degrees—a nice, warm April night—and Frogtown is hopping. I've already had to deal with a store theft and a disorderly conduct. While I diligently collected evidence, dirtballs taunted me with profanity and insults, just because I'm a cop. Yesterday, I had to deal with a murder-suicide on Van Buren Avenue in the Midway neighborhood. We'd already been to the home twelve times for domestic calls; each time, we separated the couple and offered her help. The next weekend, they were back together, drunk, and of course, fighting. He finally killed her, and then killed himself. You need thick skin to do this work.

I miss Sadie. Have you ever met someone who was always kind? No matter what anyone threw at her, she was gracious and accepting. When I was in high school, I thought I could make a relationship work with a lot of different women. I was a starting lineman on the best football team in the state. Small for tackle, but tenacious in my efforts to help the team. A year out of high school, no one cared. Worse, the people who knew football resented my success. At our ten-year reunion, I was sitting with some old teammates at Fat Pants Brewery, and some cocky young buck referred to us as "has-beens." I seethed over it and suggested to the punk we have a conversation outside, but the guys held me back. Told me it wasn't worth it.

I'm still a force to be reckoned with and the years have added wisdom. As I get older, I realize I had a shot with one person, maybe two, and that was it. Sadie was my shot at happiness. I haven't had a decent conversation with a woman, since. Nobody cared like Sadie did. Nobody listened like Sadie. I have to admit, since her death, I've stopped caring. That part of me died with her.

I'm sitting in my squad car watching a woman trip over her own feet, as she leaves the Nickel Joint Sports Bar. She's going to struggle with driving. She manages to start her car and heads down Blair Avenue. When she turns on Kent Street, she weaves so far to the right she almost hits a pedestrian on the curb. The innocent bystander manages to rush out of the way.

I hit the lights and she pulls into the St. Agnes Church parking lot. When I approach her car, she sits silent. She knows she's in trouble. Despite her intoxication, she puts her hands on the steering wheel. I guess that's a good sign.

"You could've killed somebody. Can I see your license?"

She hands it over and starts crying. "Please, give me a break. I was out celebrating with friends. I'm an in-home worker and I have families who depend on me. If I lose my license, I lose my job. I didn't mean to get that drunk."

"I'll make a note of it." Her license reads: Merri Raye Collins. Eyes blue, five feet four inches, 135 pounds. Honestly, you could probably add at least ten more pounds to that estimate.

"Okay, misspelled Mary, you should've called a cab."

"Try getting a cab to come out here."

She has a point. I tell her, "I'm going to give you a breath-alyzer and then I have a feeling we're headed to the station."

"Please, I'll do anything." She pleads, "*Anything.*"

I grin. "Anything?"

She goes mute.

I tell her, "Think about what you're saying, Merri."

When she doesn't respond, I order, "Get out of the car!"

She softly tells me, "I have someone at home who cares about me, who will come and get me."

"Yeah, that's not going to happen. You almost killed an innocent bystander. There's gotta be consequences, or next weekend, you *will* kill someone." I decide to mess with her, "Being it's a Friday night, we won't have a free cell for you. Most likely you'll be in a community cell, with addicts and abusers. You might be the only white woman in there." The truth is, while most men in prison are black, most women in prison are white.

Merri's weeping as she stumbles out of her car.

I drag her to the back seat of the squad car and push her in.

She continues to plead, "Please, give me a break. I'm a good person. I'll lose everything I went to school for."

I sit in the squad and begin driving. "At this moment, everything you went to school for *is* lost. I'm going to give you a second to think about it and maybe get it all back."

She repeats, "I'll do anything. I'll go to treatment."

I inform her, "The mandatory jail time isn't the worst of it. Between fines and increased insurance, this is going to cost you upwards of three thousand dollars—closer to ten. Plus, you'll lose your license and maybe your job."

I drive her to the darkness of the community garden on Dale Street and pull her out of the back seat.

Merri stumbles in front of me. "What are you doing?"

"Like I said, there are consequences. If you want a break, I need to get something in return. I haven't been laid in forever, but I'm not going to make you do that. Get on your knees in front of me and I'll let you walk away. No night in the tank with killers and addicts."

"Please—I swear, I'll never drink again."

"Now, that's a decision you can make tomorrow. Right now, you've got a decision you need to make *tonight*."

She can't seem to make the decision.

The choice is obvious. "This is a three-thousand-dollar blow job. It erases jail time and allows you to retain your license. Your call. You asked for a break. Here it is. How bad do you want to keep your job?"

We both know what's going to happen. I push her down to her knees and undo my uniform slacks. She can't say she didn't ask for it. I laugh as I recite, "Mary, Mary, quite contrary, what does your garden see? Silver bells and cockleshells and a pretty maid on her knees."

When she fails to take initiative, I help her get started. With some guidance from my hand on the back of her head, she begins working it.

9

"Not everything that is faced can be changed,
but nothing can be changed until it's faced."
—JAMES BALDWIN

2017

BOBBY LONG

8:25 P.M., JULY 21
ENGLEWOOD AVENUE, FROGTOWN, ST. PAUL

A call for a domestic comes over the scanner from Englewood. The complainant reported a brawl between a married couple, Miles and Piper Perry. According to a neighbor, at one point, Miles was on the front lawn kneeling over Piper, punching her in the face.

I'm the first officer to arrive on the scene and I can hear them yelling as I approach the house.

A man's voice bellows, "How the hell are we going to pay our rent? How am I going to get to work?"

I yell, "Police!"

I hear a crash and when I enter, I see broken glass on the floor behind the man. She'd thrown a glass at him.

They are ten feet apart, so I step between them and direct them, "Calm down. You're Miles and Piper?"

They both nod affirmatively, sparks of anger flying between the two.

Miles has a couple of days' growth of a dark brown beard and drunk, glassy eyes. He holds up a hand missing his ring and pinky fingers and explains, "She took what was left of my workman's comp settlement and blew it at the casino—six thousand dollars. How dare you?"

I glance back at Piper who is now defiantly flipping him off. She's a firecracker—red hair and all attitude—scrawny in comparison to Miles' six feet of dough, ponch spilling out over his belt.

I warn her, "Knock it off. We need to take it down a notch, here."

Miles yells at me, "Ask her who she was with!"

Piper taunts him, "I was with Ben, and you know what? He's got a big dick! There, are you happy? Is that what you want to hear?"

He steps toward her. It takes all my strength to hold him at bay.

An officer bursts into the home and joins me. The two of us manage to slam Miles against the wall. We press him back, each holding an arm, until he stops resisting. At that point, I need to catch my breath.

When I glance back at Piper, she's mouthing to Miles, "Eff-you!" Little shit.

Miles' right arm breaks free of mine and swings wildly. The officer hangs on tight and the result is the flailing arm smacks my colleague in the face. I recover and help him pin Miles to the floor, face down. I press my forearm against the back of his fat neck, while my partner pulls his arms back and cuffs him. Miles has a gun tucked in the back of his jeans. When I remove the gun, I notice the safety is off and it's loaded.

Two more officers arrive at the scene and Miles is hauled out of the home. I am about to apologize to the officer for letting the arm get free, when he turns and barks, "We'll deal with Miles. You get a statement from her. Think you can manage that?"

The slow boil starting, I nod and watch them leave.

Piper bobs her head to swing a lock of ginger hair out of her face, walks to the counter, and takes a large pull from the bottle of Jack Daniels. She mutters, "That was *intense.*"

I take the bottle from her and set it back down on the counter. "I'm going to take you to the station and get a statement. You can drink all you want when that's done."

10:45 P.M.

CONCRETE PRODUCTS, 781 HUBBARD AVENUE,

WEST FROGTOWN, ST PAUL

AS I DRIVE PIPER BACK HOME FROM THE STATION, she asks, "Why do guys need to control women? When I moved in he said we'd share our money, so half that money was mine. And he knows my friend is transgender and *definitely* has no interest in me."

Instead of turning toward Englewood, I take Avon Street North. This self-centered bitch grates on me. Miles received the financial settlement from his employer because his fingers were crushed at work. What right does she have to any of his money?

She asks, "Where are you going?"

"I thought a short drive, before you return home, would calm your nerves."

Piper sighs, "I'm exhausted." She closes her eyes. "He had no reason to punch me in the face over it. My cheeks feel like they're on fire."

I pull the squad to a stop in the dirt parking lot at the concrete yard. The large plant had been abandoned for the night. It's easy to hide my car between the parked cement trucks.

I open the door and help her out. "Are you finally feeling relaxed?"

Confused, she asks, "What are we doing?" She looks nervously off into the darkness that surrounds us. "I'm ready to go home."

"We'll see." I laugh as I say, "Piper Perry poked a peck of pickled peckers. Ever hear that one before?"

She says lethargically, "Yeah. About a hundred times."

"You made my life miserable tonight." I slide out my gun and put it to her head. "Time to pay the piper—Piper. Take off your clothes and lay down in the dirt."

Piper's eyes bug. "What?" I stare her down and watch reality register across her battered face. I feel myself getting hard seeing her realize my true power. She begs, "Please— I'm sorry—just take me home."

"It's a little too late for an apology. If you can give me a good lay, you're going home. If you can't? Well, maybe Piper was distraught and just went for a walk and shot herself. Your call." When she hesitates, I say, "If you knew how little your life means to me at this moment . . ." I press the barrel against her temple. "This isn't a negotiation. In ten seconds, you'll be lying on the ground—either naked or dead."

Defeated, she quickly undresses and lowers herself onto the gravel. Just how I like 'em.

11:50 P.M.
ENGLEWOOD AVENUE, FROGTOWN, ST. PAUL

I'M ALONE IN MY SQUAD ONCE AGAIN. PIPER HAD nothing to say when I brought her home. I studied her blank stare and told her, "If you call the police, I promise to catch you when you least expect it and punish you accordingly."

Piper had no sassy comeback.

I left her on the couch, walked her bottle of Jack Daniels over to her, and left.

Piper could've got me killed by continuing to provoke

her armed and abusive husband. I flipped the script. I avoided getting shot and collected a reward. There are consequences for disrespecting authority.

A call comes over the scanner. "We have a reported ten-eighty at one-one-ten on Englewood Avenue in St. Paul."

That unbelievable bitch. A ten-eighty is a sexual assault.

I immediately respond, "I'm in the area. I'll take the call." I hit the lights and speed to the address.

The operator asks, "Aren't you waiting for backup?"

"Not necessary. Known product. History of crying wolf." Piper Perry had called the police on me.

When I pull up in front of the house, I am pleased to see no other officers have arrived. I get back on the scanner. "Ten twenty-two for the call on Englewood."

The operator asks, "Are you sure you want officers to disregard the call?"

"Yes. The alleged victim is Piper Perry. I'm talking to her right now. Piper was assaulted by her husband, Miles, earlier. He's in custody and she's telling me she just had a nightmare. She's sorry for the call."

"Can I speak to her?"

I should've seen that coming. "Negative. She's stepped into the bathroom."

"Okay."

I walk to the house and knock on the door. I step to the side, so she won't see me, and shout, "Police!"

When Piper opens the door, I rush her and put the barrel of my gun to her head. I kick the door shut behind me. "No wonder Miles beats you. You just don't listen."

I walk her to the couch. "Pick up your phone."

She fumbles to grab it off the floor, but finally has it in hand.

"You're gonna get a call from a dispatcher in a minute, asking if everything's okay. And you're going to say, 'Everything's okay. I just had a bad dream.'"

The call comes, as anticipated.

Piper stutters, "I—I'm okay. Jus—just a bad dream."

She thinks she'll be smart and leave the phone on, but I take it from her and end the call. I toss the phone on the floor and direct her, "Walk me to your bedroom."

"What are you going to do?"

With my gun to the back of her head, I tell her, "Blow your brains out, if you don't follow directions."

We walk to her bedroom. "Strip and put your clothes in a pile on the floor."

She does as she's told.

"We're going to do this again and we'll see if you're capable of learning."

She starts crying, but quietly lays down on the bed. I undo my belt. Back to business . . .

AFTER I'M FINISHED, I NO LONGER NEED A GUN. Thoroughly conquered, she silently complies when I walk Piper to the bathroom and order her run a bath. Once in the tub, I tell her, "Wash yourself thoroughly." I gloat over my victory as she obeys. My opponent has been annihilated. "I need to do a little laundry. I've been told women love a guy who does laundry. Is that true?" When she doesn't respond, I tell her, "I'll be right back, dear."

I strip the sheets off her bed and pick her clothes up off the floor. I find the washing machine, toss in the bedding and clothing, add a bottle of bleach, and start it. Any DNA will dissolve with that potency of detergent. When I return to the bathroom, Piper resumes washing herself.

"Good girl." I smile, "Lesson learned," and depart.

10

"If you are silent about your pain,
they'll kill you and say you enjoyed it."
—Zora Neale Hurston

2017

PIPER PERRY

1:25 A.M., JULY 22
ENGLEWOOD AVENUE, FROGTOWN, ST. PAUL

When I heard my front door close, I dragged myself out of the bathtub. My body was so sore it hurt to stand; I felt like I'd been torn inside out. I dried myself off and sat on the closed toilet considering my options. I'd been punched in the face, raped in a gravel parking lot, and then raped again at gunpoint in my own bed.

Okay—I fucked up. I blew six thousand dollars we couldn't afford to lose, at a casino. My fantasy with the money I won— Miles and I would fly away to Cancun for a week, and I'd still have enough to return every cent I'd taken. Pull a C3PO. In Star Wars, C3PO responded to every sticky situation by angling his gold metal head and saying, "We're doomed." Then he took off. It had been a hard year for us, with Miles getting laid off. What was the saying, *When the going gets tough, the tough get going?*

Unfortunately, C3PO, like me, never seemed to get far. My eyes welled up as I considered the price I paid for my stupidity.

I gingerly inspected my bruised cheeks with my fingertips—they felt like they were an inch thick. Miles shouldn't have hit me, but I'll forgive him. We were both a little ADHD and we didn't always make good choices in the spur of the moment. But we understood each other. I shouldn't have taunted him, but I hated it when he did that big man shit.

Miles and I would be okay, but he was the least of my problems. What the hell was I going to do with that cop? What was going to keep him from coming back? There only was one thing to do. I limped to the living room and found my phone on the floor.

I dialed 911 and the operator stated, "What is the nature of your emergency?"

"I've been raped twice. How about if this time you don't send the same fucking cop to my house who raped me the first time."

The operator paused, and then assured me, "This time it's not going out over the scanner. I will call a female officer personally to respond. Please give me your address."

"You've sent officers here twice tonight—but here it is again—one-ten Englewood in St. Paul."

"Please stay on the line while I make the private call."

I'd been so violated; I hadn't even considered that I was now standing in my living room naked. "Yeah, I should probably set my phone down for a moment and get dressed."

When I headed back to my bedroom, I heard the wash machine running. That pig thought he was so smart by having me bathe while he washed my bedding and clothing. He knew exactly how to get away with it. My word against his. Who were they going to believe?

Still, I wasn't giving him the satisfaction of kowtowing to his demands. I pulled a t-shirt and underwear out of my dresser and, for the first time, noticed my bag of clothes was still sitting in the corner. I smiled as much as I could through swollen lips. *Dumb ass.* He didn't realize I wasn't wearing the same clothes when he came back for round two. I had already put them in a bag, as I was advised by dispatch, to give to the police.

After dressing, I heard a car pull up. Two female officers, one white and one black, were walking to my home. They looked like they meant business. *Time for some justice.*

11

"You don't lose if you get knocked down.
You lose if you stay down."
—MUHAMMAD ALI

2017

JON FREDERICK

2:30 P.M., THURSDAY, AUGUST 10
BUREAU OF CRIMINAL APPREHENSION OFFICE
1430 MARYLAND AVENUE EAST, ROOSEVELT, ST PAUL

T he Bureau of Criminal Apprehension in Minnesota investigated all officer-involved crimes. BCA Investigator Sean Reynolds requested I sit in on his interview with police officer, Bobby Long. Our supervisor insisted both an African American investigator and a white investigator were present, which led to my invite. Sean was our best investigator. There were rumors that Bobby Long was a racist, so it wasn't certain he'd open up to Sean.

As we were about to step into the meeting, Sean took a call. I patiently waited for his return.

Sean's style of dress reminded me of an old-school FBI agent. Black jacket, slacks, and tie, with a white button-down dress shirt. He was clean cut, with a tight, short afro.

Sean strolled back and said, "Jada needs to talk to me tonight. You still involved with her?"

"No, Serena and I are back together for good. I'm accepting the transfer to the Brainerd office so I can live with her and my daughter again."

"I can never keep track." Sean directed, "Okay, I appreciate your willingness to sit in, but let me run the interview."

"No problem."

The last couple of years hadn't been kind to Bobby. Only in his late twenties, his body was taking the shape of Porky Pig—all bulbous, with pink skin and sparse hair. Going into the interview, I knew Bobby was the fiancé of Sadie Sullivan.

After we were all seated, Sean told Bobby, "There have been rumors about your conduct over the past couple months. What the hell happened with you, Bobby?"

Bobby whined, "You know what it's like working here. Last week, we had a couple of African American teens on their first date, shot by a couple of gang members in a case of mistaken identity. Life doesn't mean anything to these guys. And we're targets out there, in our uniforms. It's a jungle. You know it as well as I do."

I considered the history of racism Bobby overtly ignored. African Americans, like boxer Charles Tanner, for example, received a life sentence for possession of cocaine, when there was no equivalent sentence for a white person with no violent crimes.

Sean ignored Bobby's racist implications. "Let's start with Piper Perry."

Bobby puffed up, "Who's going to believe that lying bitch?"

"Hmm. Me, for one," Sean smiled coldly.

I liked the fact that, despite what Piper had been through, she never gave up. Every time she was knocked down, she found her way back to her feet, and came up swinging. When it came to the police, Piper knew Bobby Long was the exception, rather than the rule.

Bobby argued, "I dropped her off at home after she made her statement downtown about being beat by Miles, and I never saw her sorry ass again. And, by the way, she was a pain when I was trying to stop Miles from beating her. Damn near got me killed."

I asked, "You never had sex with her?"

"Never."

In a drawn-out fashion, Sean played his ace. "Thing is, Bobby, we have DNA evidence. You washed the wrong clothes. Piper had already changed before you went back for seconds."

The wheels spun in Bobby's head. I could see a madness come over him as the realization set in. Still convinced he could talk his way out of it, he offered, "Okay, she invited me in to have sex when I brought her home. I know I shouldn't have, but it'd been a while. It was all consenting. You gotta give me a break, here. I'm just a lonely public servant—working through my own personal tragedy. You must have heard about my fiancé, Sadie."

Sean was not one to be distracted. He asked, "So, you had sex at Piper's home?"

Attempting to appear contrite, Bobby said, "Yes."

We sat silent for a moment. Bobby was thinking fast, gears shifting into overdrive as his eyes flicked from one of us to the other. From numerous interviews, I could see he was trying to ascertain how much evidence we had. A neighbor noticed his squad car in front of Piper's home at the time she reported the rape occurred. Bobby was arrogant enough, he might still try to lie his way out of being arrested, simply because he thought he was smarter than Sean. I knew he wasn't. Sean took advantage of Bobby's underlying racism.

Bobby modified his story. "She'd been assaulted by her husband, earlier. And then she made a false report of an assault. They have a recording of her on a call from the dispatcher admitting she made a false report. Why would anybody believe her after that?"

I asked, "How do you know she admitted making a false report to a dispatcher?"

He again took a moment to consider his response. "I was there. I came over and saw that she was troubled and comforted her. One thing led to another."

Sean was painting Bobby into a corner, simply by pretending to be ignorant of all the evidence we had. "So, just to be clear, you never had sex with her at the concrete plant?"

"No—is that what she's claiming?"

Sean added, "As a matter of fact, she is. And here's what I find peculiar—the crime scene techs say the dirt on her clothes matches the gravel at the plant. And you only find that soil consistency at a concrete plant."

Bobby was pulling at straws now. "She could have dragged her clothes in the dirt, just to frame a cop."

Sean smiled, "I thought you might suggest that. So I considered it, until I saw your squad car pulling into the plant on the security camera. And additionally, your fingerprints are on her washing machine. All of the evidence is consistant with her story."

Bobby clamped his rubbery lips together. "I'm done talking."

I asked, "Did you kill Sadie Sullivan?"

Angry, he said, "Hell no! You can thank Ray Fury for all of this! Imagine the woman you loved being raped by a—"

He stopped himself and Sean curiously asked, "By a *what*, Bobby?"

He started over, "Imagine the woman you loved being raped." He hesitated, "Her murder went unsolved for over a year."

I made a note that he didn't say *Sadie's* murder. He didn't want to say her name.

Bobby squeezed his hand into a fist. "And then I had to go to work, every day, and am badgered by black gang bangers and I'm thinking—is he the one? It messed with my head." He stood up, "I'm done."

We stood, too, and Sean announced, "Bobby Long, you're under arrest for the rape of Piper Perry . . ."

12

*"I'm not concerned with your liking or disliking me.
All I ask is that you respect me as a human being."*
—JACKIE ROBINSON

2017

XAVIER "ZAVE" WILLIAMS

8:00 P.M., FRIDAY, AUGUST 25
WEST RIVER ROAD NORTH,
HAWTHORNE, MINNEAPOLIS

I stayed up to date on the prosecution of Bobby Long. He'd made bail and was awaiting trial. The rumor was he was trying to work out a plea deal with the prosecutor.

It was Friday night. I was young and single. My friends, Jamal and Kyrone, were supposed to stop over, and we were going out for a beer.

I was one of the few Minneapolis police officers who actually lived in Minneapolis. Nationwide, 40% of officers lived in the city they policed. In Minneapolis, only 5% did.

Dad called to check in and immediately challenged, "Date tonight?"

"Nah."

He fell into a familiar sad silence, before suggesting, "I hope this doesn't have anything do with your mom—"

I cut him off. "For God's sake, get over it. Mom's been committed to you for years and we all walk around like we've just taken a beating. If you're miserable today, it's on you."

I heard a knock at the door. "Dad, I got to go. I just can't keep living like we're cursed."

Dad said, "Alright. Love ya . . ."

I opened the door to find Lachelle, dressed in all black— blouse, jeans, and leather jacket.

Her first comment to me was abrasive. "Did you sleep with my best friend?" Suffice it to say, the magic we once had was long gone.

I didn't bed-hop, but to counter her rudeness, I responded, "I don't know. What's her name?"

"Marita."

"No, I didn't sleep with Marita. I did grab a sandwich with her. Is that okay?"

Lachelle's bravado dissipated, as if she used up all she had in her. In a tortured soft breath she asked, "Why are you so cold to me?"

I took a deep breath. "I'm sorry. I avoid you, because I know you're mad at me and I don't want to fight with you. I'm not sure what you want from me. Back when your dad died, I wish I would've told you he didn't deserve to die. He was a good man trying to protect what he'd earned, and I respect that. When my first effort angered you, I bailed, and I'm sorry for that."

She sighed. "I just want you to be sorry for brushing me off when I was in so much pain. The floor dropped out on my life. I *loved* you. I don't like being bitter about it. Help me let go of it. Everybody says you're such a nice guy. You're *not* a nice guy, though. When I really needed you, you left me hanging out there—all alone." Her brown eyes stared into mine.

I explained, "I get it. You're right. It wasn't until about a year later that it really sank in. I was a self-centered jerk. I didn't know what to say—but I know that's not an excuse. I could've just listened. I'm mad at myself for treating you so rotten." I closed my eyes for a second as I'd taken in the pain in hers, and asked, "What can I do?"

Attitude recharged, she sarcastically cracked, "Stop making excuses. Be miserable."

"I promise to do both." At the moment, both seemed easy. We had reached a truce. Lachelle turned on her heel and said, "I've said what I needed to say."

She was halfway out the door when I shouted, "Stop! Let me say this. When you see me laughing or talking to someone on the street, I don't want you ever to take it as a slight on you. The way I treated you changed me. I decided to make amends by trying to be a decent person every day to someone in need. So, if someone tells you I'm a nice guy, it's no snub of you, it's me trying to be better *because* of you."

Her tone softened and her appreciation caught my eyes. She held my gaze as she stepped back in and closed the door slowly, then moved closer. "You could offer me a hug."

I felt her entire body sigh as I held her.

She turned her face to mine and we kissed.

When our lips finally parted, I asked, "Anything else you needed to say?"

Lachelle's grin was timid, probably both of us wondering what that was about. "Why do you let the Vikings and the Wolves torment you? The Lynx is the only winning franchise in professional sports in Minnesota."

I cut in, "There is the Wild."

"Not for us. Name a black player on the Wild."

"Jordan Greenway."

Lachelle ignored me, "By the way, I had a hell of lot better chance playing in the WNBA than you had in the NBA . . ." Confidence restored, she pulled away from me and strutted back and forth, as she spoke.

She was right. I didn't dare say it, but there wasn't decent money in the WNBA. She was better off graduating from college. I guessed that was only if your dreams didn't matter. I stopped playing basketball in college when I came to the realization the coach didn't care if I graduated. He just wanted me to be eligible to play so he could get a better contract. Having a great basketball team was for him. Getting a degree was for me. Late nights studying began to affect my game performance and Coach ordered me to lighten my load. So, I did. I quit basketball.

When she realized I wasn't arguing, she teased, "When did you become such a pushover?" Lachelle pushed me back until I was seated on the couch. She joined me and I was soon enjoying her luscious taste once again.

Before I had a chance to process it all, my phone buzzed. I pulled it from my pocket and, seeing it was Lauren Herald, I answered.

Lauren said breathlessly, "Zave, there's an officer down in Hawthorne. You're going to want to head over here. I think it's Dan . . . "

10:15 P.M.
1249 FREMONT AVENUE,
NEAR NORTH NEIGHBORHOOD, MINNEAPOLIS

WHEN I ARRIVED, A BODY BAG WAS BEING zipped up in finality. I ran over and flashed my badge. Chief Brent Collier approached me and said, "It's Dan Baker. One lethal shot to the heart. He called over the radio, 'Ten nine-nine-nine,' shortly before he was shot."

A ten nine-nine-nine was an officer in distress.

Collier added, "There was no call over the radio. Dan was out of uniform. Any idea why he came here in the first place?"

Mute with shock, I shook my head.

He suggested, "Let's keep this as quiet as possible until we know why he was here. We don't want this all over the news as a cop shooting, if he was here buying drugs."

I found my voice and made it clear, "Dan wasn't here buying drugs." While I couldn't say I knew Dan well, I had never suspected he was using illegal drugs.

The chief studied me. "Why was he here? Our records indicate you've called from this address before."

"I called for help from this location back when we were looking for Ray Fury. By the time I was allowed in the house, Fury was gone. Dan was here with me." I remembered the warning Fox had given us about returning. "Who shot him?"

"We don't know yet."

"Is Fox here?"

He pointed toward the house. "Yeah, but nobody's saying anything."

When I turned and stalked in that direction, Collier warned at my back, "Don't do anything stupid!"

Fox stood on the front porch with his cronies, not as cocked up as he was the last time we met, but arms still crossed in defiance. He broke his silence. "We had nothin' to do with this, man."

Anger clouding my fear, I stepped in his face. "Why was Dan here?"

Even as he took a step back, Fox replied smugly, "You tell *me*. It's not like we invited him."

"So, you're tellin' me he wasn't shot by one of your gang-bangers? Bullshit!"

"No way. This cop-killing ain't on us. It was one shot—and it wasn't any of us—so we're talkin' about a rifle, man. You might wanna look at the Native Mob. The Vice Lords or Latin Kings woulda just sprayed us all with bullets from an automatic."

I told him, "You know we're going to be able to tell the distance that shot was fired from. If it came from one of you on the porch, there will be powder burns on Dan. You don't want to start out by lyin' to me."

Fox declared, "The truth will set us free, brother."

I WENT BACK TO MY SQUAD AND GRABBED MY flashlight. The Streamlight Stinger was small but lit up the area.

Chief Collier marched over, tight faced. "What are you doing?"

"I want to have a look around this neighborhood." There was a small, broken-down drug house across the street that had been boarded up and cordoned off with police tape.

Collier warned, "Watch your ass. We don't want to lose another soldier, here. It'll be easier to look for evidence in the light of day."

Ignoring him, I walked across the street to the small white house in the darkness. The windows were boarded, and the doors strung with tape—CRIME SCENE DO NOT CROSS—like morbid streamers celebrating Día de los Muertos (the Day of the Dead).

When I reached the back door, I turned the knob and it opened. I stepped in, shining the light in front of me. Roaches skittered across the floor. Despite my anger, my skin crawled. I walked across the sticky linoleum in the rundown kitchen. Half the cupboards were missing doors. I could see a sliver of light shining into the living room from the street and walked toward the window. The plywood on the outside didn't cover it completely, leaving a two-inch gap of open space on the side—the side facing Fox's home. It would be a difficult shot using a handgun, but an easy shot with a rifle.

I flashed my light on the matted carpet but didn't see a shell casing. And then I heard the creak of footsteps behind me. I turned quickly and my light caught the bottom half of a man racing toward the door. I dropped the Streamlight and took off after him, tackling him from behind, halfway out the door.

I was livid but doing my best to not do or say anything inappropriate. I sat on him and pulled his wrists back to cuff him.

He turned his face to the side yelling, "Get off me! I din't do nothin'.'"

It was Dreads.

Riled, I fought the urge to grind his face into the ground. I leaned into his ear as I used his body as leverage to push myself up, and asked, "Why? I just want to know why."

He gasped, "I swear, I don't know! I was standing right next to him when he was shot. I was expecting a volley of shots, so I took off."

As I yanked him to his feet, he continued, "Then I thought—runnin' makes me look guilty. I *helped* you," he stressed. "Thought maybe you'd help me. When I got close, I was gonna hide out until I saw you were here."

I marched him to my squad, as he pleaded, "*You* take me in, man. Don't let any of these cracker cops take me—I might not get there."

I brought Dreads to the Fourth Precinct. Since I wasn't an investigator, that was where my involvement with him ended.

12:35 A.M.
SATURDAY, AUGUST 26, MINNEAPOLIS

ON MY WAY HOME, CHIEF COLLIER CALLED and told me, "Dreads stated he was standing next to Dan when he heard the gunshot. He claims he doesn't know anything else about it. He's not giving us anything. I told the investigators to keep him overnight. Let's make the Disciples sweat a little over concerns that he's giving something up . . . "

I was furious at the Gangster Disciples. Dan wanted to make the world better. Always treated people with respect—even people who didn't deserve it. I needed to find out why he was shot. There was a crazy potential for this to turn into a war between the Disciples and the police.

12:45 A.M.

WEST RIVER ROAD NORTH,
HAWTHORNE, MINNEAPOLIS

WHEN I GOT HOME, MY PHONE CHIRPED WITH a message from Lauren: *Are you okay?*

I texted: *Not really. But thanks for caring.*

She texted back: *Call me—if you need to talk.*

I could've called Lachelle, but I didn't. I was afraid she'd take my anger personally and it would put us back to where we were before. I needed to vent, and Lauren was easier to talk to, at this moment. We had no history. I had nothing to lose.

I made the call to Lauren and, after our initial greetings, I asked, "How did you know about the shooting so fast?"

"A neighbor saw a man running from the scene. The responding officers called me right away to do a sketch. After I finished the sketch, someone from the neighborhood said the man was called Dreads."

"Did the witness see Dreads shoot Dan?"

"No. She just saw him running from the house after the shot was fired."

I exhaled my anger and told her, "I went along to inform Dan's parents. It was heartbreaking. His mom grabbed me and hugged me hard. She told me to be careful."

"How did you respond?"

"I told her Dan was always the first guy to back me up when I was in trouble. Both his parents said ever since Dan was little, he'd go out of his way to help others. He left truck driving because he wanted a chance to make the world better. He felt he had to be walking the streets, rather than hauling semi loads down them."

113

Lauren allowed some quiet, then said, "I didn't know Dan well. He seemed like one of the good ones. How'd you come to know him?"

"He transferred from the Third Precinct in St. Paul to ours. He was awkward, but funny. Just a nice guy . . ."

Somehow Lauren managed to keep me talking until I was finally able to fall asleep. It was easy to forget there were amazingly kind people in the world. I'd have to thank her for being there for me.

13

"Does anybody hear us pray for Michael Brown or Freddie Gray? Peace is more than the absence of war . . . Maybe we can finally say, enough is enough, it's time for love."
—Prince

2017

XAVIER "ZAVE" WILLIAMS

10:15 P.M., MONDAY, AUGUST 28
1249 FREMONT AVENUE, NEAR NORTH, MINNEAPOLIS

Wesley Washington "Dreads" was released today. There was no gun residue on his clothing or hands. We had no witnesses to the shooting and no weapon.

I drove back to the site of Dan's shooting. The disciples house had been torn apart by a couple of investigators, as they both took out their frustration and desperately looked for the murder weapon. The home was now taped off as a crime scene. Fox and a couple of his gang- banger friends were complaining to officers about the damage.

The officers were pissed and paid no attention to the whining.

Fox caught my eye and waved me over.

I hesitated but walked over. We weren't on the same side—I wanted truth and justice. He only wanted to cover his ass.

Fox said, "I'm tellin' you, man, we din't kill that cop."

"Explain to me how he died on your porch."

His shrewd eyes were in a constant scan mode of the area. "He came here looking for somebody, asking, 'Where is he? I'm not leaving without him,'" he gestured with big eyes and drama. "We had no idea who he was even *talkin'* about. There was a gunshot, and he was down. I don't know where the hell the shot came from, but it wasn't from us."

If he had nothing to do with the shooting, he was still squirrely and hiding something. But he looked scared, so I just nodded like I was buying into it. "Why was Dreads hiding in the house across the street?"

"We was standing there on the porch 'n Dreads was right next to that cop when he was blown away. We thought the shooter was gonna level all of us. What would you do if someone shot and killed the dude you're standing next to?"

I wasn't sure what to think. They called him the Fox because he was great at deceiving people. The police were going to put pressure on the gang, one by one, until somebody gave someone up.

10:45 P.M.
WEST RIVER ROAD NORTH,
HAWTHORNE, MINNEAPOLIS

I GOT A CALL FROM CHIEF COLLIER. "I NEED you to come in for gun residue testing. Wesley 'Dreads' Washington is dead. He was shot when he was walking from his car to his apartment in the Hawthorne neighborhood. There are no witnesses and it's such an impoverished neighborhood, no one has cameras."

"Do you honestly think a cop killed Dreads?"

"No. I think Fox sent a message to the Disciples that *no one talks to the police.* The Vice Lords did this same thing back in 1992, after they shot Officer Jerome Haaf. They executed the first gang member we interrogated as a message to the rest to remain silent. So now, we're going to have a hell of a time getting a statement from anyone. I want all the officers tested, so I can show beyond a reasonable doubt a cop isn't responsible for this."

"I'll be right in."

14

"It's about the journey—mine and yours—and
the lives we can touch, the legacy we can leave,
and the world we can change for the better."
—Tony Dungy

2021

XAVIER "ZAVE" WILLIAMS

9:15 P.M., WEDNESDAY, MARCH 31
WEST RIVER ROAD NORTH,
HAWTHORNE, MINNEAPOLIS

Eight years had passed since Sadie Sullivan was murdered. My brief time with her now felt more like a dream than a reality. I wanted to remember her. Sadie was a sweetheart. She put her life on hold just to enjoy time with her daughter and she was taken from us by some self-centered prick—and I didn't stop it. I became a cop to stop tragedies. It was miserable when I had to suffer through them.

Ray Fury was serving a life sentence in the Minnesota Correctional Facility in Lino Lakes. Bobby Long took a plea deal and agreed to serve six years in prison for the rape of Piper Perry but, with good time, he would soon be released after only serving four. I felt like a black man wouldn't have been offered that deal—at least not in 2017. With COVID, it was a lot harder to get people incarcerated today and much easier for them to get released.

I was still single. I wasn't sure if that was good or bad, or just where I needed to be. Being single had its advantages; it allowed me extended time to work investigations without feeling guilty.

Lachelle and I never did get together again, but I felt good about apologizing to her. Dan's death threw me for a loop; I didn't feel like talking to anybody outside of work, for months. I felt like I needed to be penitent and miserable when I talked to Lachelle, and I already spent too much time in that state. The consequence of *ghosting* her, again, was that she was now coolly polite when our paths crossed.

I ran into Marita the other day and we agreed to get together again. I was ambivalent about that, too.

Danny's funeral was the largest I'd ever attended. I appreciated the way officers came together, from all over the state, to respect a fallen officer. Police Chief Collier, who had recently retired, never officially called Dan's death an on-duty killing and that rubbed me raw. Dan was constantly asked to help officers out when he was off duty, and he always responded. The *blue* had cracked in the years. Rumors emerged, questioning Dan's sexual orientation. I thought it was a way for some guys to rationalize that his loss was less significant. I didn't know much about Dan's personal life beyond that he spent some time with Marita, and he helped others every time he had the opportunity. Personally, I couldn't have cared less if he was hetero, gay, bi, trans or pan. He was simply a good man.

Looking back, Dan might have been one of the cagiest guys I knew. No one suspected he was gay, because he was always trying to pick women up with these cheesy lines—lines that never worked. He wasn't insulting and everyone had a laugh. The rejection never bothered him because he never hoped the lines would get him anywhere.

I was now working as an investigator for the Minneapolis Police Department. We were one of three agencies in Minnesota connected to the National Integrated Ballistic Information Network (NIBIN). The other two were the Hennepin County Sherriff's Department and the BCA. The bullet that killed Dan was a Federal Fusion 150 grain soft point. It penetrated deep and mushroomed out as it went through the body, to ensure lethal force. It was a bullet that was specifically designed for deer hunting. Our ballistics expert told me the bullet was likely fired by a Browning X-Bolt Mountain Pro rifle, which ran upwards of $2000. Dreads was killed by a bullet from the same rifle. While I didn't see the Gangster Disciples buying high-end deer hunting rifles, it wouldn't have been beyond a gang to have them in their stash, having stolen them from home break-ins. I was beginning to believe the shot was fired by a rival gang, knowing the police would squeeze the Disciples after a cop killing. I'd looked for that rifle in every gang home raid, since, but still hadn't found it.

I worked with some great people of every race, and some who couldn't let go of their racist belligerence. There were two white investigators who always stopped talking about cases involving black perpetrators every time I entered the room, out of fear that I would somehow leak their information to the African American community. I finally asked them, "Do I need to stop talking to you when a suspect is white?" Sometimes, we needed to make the ridiculous obvious. The good news was Minneapolis had our first African American Police Chief, Medaria Arradondo.

Today was the third day of the Derek Chauvin trial in Minnesota. Chauvin was the white cop charged for kneeling on African American, George Floyd's neck until he was dead. Yesterday, a white firefighter, who happened upon the scene, testified that she asked the police officers to take George's pulse to see if he was responsive. When the officers failed to do anything, she called 911 for help. You shouldn't have to call for help when police officers are on the scene.

The Floyd killing deeply disturbed me. It was a punch in the gut for decent officers and made my "crossing the blue line" as a black man more difficult to justify. There had been too many of these tragedies. Still, I gave my colleagues credit for their willingness to testify against Chauvin.

15

"How far you go in life depends on your being tender with the young, compassionate with the aged, sympathetic with the striving, and tolerant of the weak and strong. Because someday in your life, you will have been all of these."
—George Washington Carver

2021

JON FREDERICK

8:30 A.M., FRIDAY, APRIL 8
PIERZ

Serena and I were now married and had two children. Serena had stayed home with the kids to protect them from the coronavirus; however, in February, she caught COVID. Since neither the kids nor I had it, Serena moved in with her parents to protect our children. Her parents had a walkout basement with a full bedroom and bathroom; they had her set up with a mini-fridge and necessities, so she could protect them, as well. This was hard on both of us, particularly because she initially thought I wasn't careful enough and somehow passed the virus onto her. Eventually, she learned she contracted COVID from a doctor's visit. We took a hit financially, during this time. Knowing the BCA was overburdened with organizing security for the Derek Chauvin trial, I had asked if they'd consider taking me back on a temporary basis.

I was reading a book about the wonders of Egypt with my six-year-old daughter, Nora. Sadly, many of the "world wonders" were built on the backs of slave labor. In Egypt, people died so a king could have a large mausoleum. While Nora and I shared that the pyramids and Sphinx were impressive, I reminded her that some things aren't worth having if you had to hurt others to get them. Both the White House and the Capital were built by slave labor, on land donated from Virginia and Maryland, which at the time were slave owning states.

Our discussion was interrupted by a call from Sean Reynolds. It was the first time we'd spoken directly for almost two years. Sean had fired me after I shared information with a victim's family on a case. I still felt it was the right decision. Families deserved honesty. I no longer had strong feelings about my termination, as Serena and I had a good year in private practice until she was struck with COVID. Sean informed me he had recently suffered a heart attack and I wished him well.

He said, "I have a favor to ask of you. I'll hire you back if you'll take on the investigation of the murder of Sadie Sullivan. Ray Fury's been convicted for raping and murdering her; however, Sadie's fiancé—you remember Bobby Long—now has a Crim Sex One conviction, and he was just released from incarceration."

With COVID running rampant in the prison system, there was a push to release prisoners with good behavior. Good intentions did not always equal good policy. Mandatory sentencing for DWI offenders meant that drunk driving offenders couldn't be released early, so sex offenders were, instead.

Sean added, "Jada's been on my case about reopening the investigation."

My former lover, Jada Anderson, now had a child with Sean and they were engaged to be married.

I told him, "I'd be happy to take over this case. When do you want me to start?"

"Monday. I'd like you to work with an African American officer. There's an advantage to having black and white investigators working this case. This time, we're getting a black investigator from the Minneapolis Homicide Unit."

"Is it Charlie Adams? I've heard he's outstanding."

Sean said, "No such luck. They're loaning us a young investigator named Xavier Williams." He added, "The first officer I asked for was a white officer named Dan Baker, but he was shot and killed four years ago at a Disciples home in Hawthorne."

As I mulled this over, he added, "And you'll want to talk to Jada. She has some information on the case."

Sean had a history of being a little paranoid about my interactions with Jada. I hesitated, "I'll make certain those exchanges are brief."

"Don't worry about it. Almost dying puts everything back in perspective. Jada's been here with me every minute. I'm over being jealous."

"I've been all about Serena since 2018 . . . "

WHEN I HUNG UP, MY BEAUTIFUL BRUNETTE wife approached with our two-year-old son, Jackson, in her arms. Nora was trailing close behind.

Nora was asking Serena, "Why do you wish you would have invented water beads?"

Serena smiled, "Because everybody in the world has them now."

Nora questioned, "Really, Mom? Do you think people in Egypt are playing with water beads?"

Serena smiled and turned to me, "What was the phone call about?"

"I'm back with the BCA, fulltime but temporarily. But I have to return to Minneapolis."

With mixed emotion, her green eyes glistened. "Okay. You've got work again and we've got medical coverage, but how much are you going to be home?"

"I don't know. I need to be in the BCA office Monday morning. I'll have a better idea then."

Nora asked worriedly, "Am I going to have to move again?"

I bent down. "No, honey. We are a family living in Pierz. I just have to go to Minneapolis for a few weeks to work. It will be during the week when you're at school."

Serena comforted Nora by pulling her close and reassuring her, "We are a family. We've been lucky that Dad's been home a lot, but now he needs to work away from home until we're back on our feet again."

Nora asked, "Aren't we on our feet, now?"

I hugged her. "You know that warrior training we've been doing?"

She beamed. I'd performed a variety of physical tasks over the winter and spring with the kids that involved climbing over objects and traipsing through the woods, to help them burn off energy. I'd also had Nora performing exercises, such as going from a summersault, to standing, and then firing a foam arrow at a target, just to make it all a little more dramatic.

I told her, "I just need to see if it really works."

Serena rolled her eyes and asked me, "Are you coming home Monday night?"

"I don't know. I'll pack for the week just in case."

She groaned, "Could this year get any more stressful?"

The answer was *yes*, but I elected not to respond.

16

"That's what Americans do when others are in need—we help. We give. We inspire."
—BARACK OBAMA

2021

JON FREDERICK

8:15 A.M., MONDAY, APRIL 12
BUREAU OF CRIMINAL APPREHENSION
1430 MARYLAND AVENUE EAST,
ROOSEVELT, ST. PAUL

Yesterday, twenty-year-old Daunte Wright was shot and killed in Brooklyn Center by Police Officer Kimberly Potter. While it wasn't related to our investigation, it was one more event that was going to hamper it. The ACLU suggested that Daunte was pulled over for having an air freshener dangling from his rearview mirror, although the truth was, he was pulled over for expired tabs. Once the officers checked his license, they realized Daunte had an outstanding warrant for having a handgun without a permit. He attempted to get back in his car and drive away. The officer reported she thought she grabbed her Taser, but instead fired her gun, killing him. The public didn't know this yet, but there were rumors Daunte shot a sixteen-year-old in the head, which I imagined escalated the nerves of the officer when he dove back into his car. The Minnesota Twins had called off their baseball game with Boston, out of respect for the victim's family. The Minnesota Wild and the Minnesota Timberwolves followed suit and cancelled their games as well.

Brooklyn Center businesses were looted, and squad cars were vandalized last night. Bullets were fired into some of the stores by angry rioters. The cities of Minneapolis and St. Paul issued a curfew for tonight and the National Guard was called in to prevent the mass destruction that occurred after George Floyd was killed. We didn't need another tragedy, especially while the Chauvin hearing was progressing. Xavier and I were going to get pulled away from the Sullivan investigation frequently to investigate shootings and to help provide security.

I felt badly for the people living in Brooklyn Center, as it was about to become ground zero for rioters. The Park Center school system was the poorest in the Twin Cities, with over 80% of the students living in poverty. The 40-degree weather may have been the biggest factor keeping more people from protesting tonight.

Eventually, it would come out that Brooklyn Center was founded by Earl Brown, a former member of the Ku Klux Klan. Earl went on to become the sheriff of Hennepin County and started the Minnesota State Highway Patrol. He testified in 1923 that he joined the Ku Klux Klan to be able to spy on them—there was a need for law enforcement to have a better understanding of the Klan. They began in Minnesota in 1921 and grew into 51 chapters, with 30,000 members in 1923. The Klan promoted intolerance for African Americans, as well as Catholics, and German and Jewish immigrants. The KKK viewed them all as *outsiders*. Today, there were no Klan chapters in Minnesota.

XAVIER WILLIAMS AND I MET IN THE BCA OFFICE in St. Paul. Our official headquarters was going to be in the library, where all the old law and statute books were shelved. I had requested a locking cabinet to keep interested investigators out of our evidence and it was provided.

I told Zave right off the bat, "Don't hesitate to call me on it if I'm coming across as rude. I'm task oriented. I don't spend a lot of time thinking about the best way to say something. I'm just focused on what needs to be done. That said, I'm pleased for the opportunity to work with you."

Zave smiled. "I don't mind direct. Let me ask you this— what do you think about Derek Chauvin?"

"What Chauvin did shames me as a white person, a law enforcement agent, and as an American. From the video, George looked like he was tweaking, so he wasn't going to respond coherently. A veteran officer has dealt with this a hundred times. George bought bananas with a counterfeit twenty-dollar bill and died for it. The store owner should've called the police. The police should have responded. But the way it was handled was unforgiveable."

Zave nodded in agreement.

I added, "Minneapolis is a nightmare. Shootings are sky-rocketing. Police intervention is down and people want to take away our guns. I don't support the looting; it's just more punishment leveled on innocent people."

Still pondering my thoughts, he responded, "I appreciate your honesty."

I shared, "Reporter Jada Anderson will be joining us. You should know that we used to date."

He laughed, "Everybody in law enforcement knows you and Jada used to date. You were the *it* couple, at every gala event."

"Jada was the master of ceremonies and I basically fol-lowed her around. I'm happily married to my wife, Serena, now, and Jada's engaged to Sean."

As if on cue, Jada breezed in and, out of respect, Zave and I both stood. Even though my heart was no longer invested, I was always struck by her fierce beauty. She walked easily on her heels like she was born in them; there was not so much as a wrinkle in her olive green, one-piece pantsuit. Considering her crazy schedule, she never looked disheveled or harried.

She shook hands with Zave and introduced herself, "I'm Jada Anderson, reporter." After giving him a once over, she turned to me, "You got yourself an athlete for a partner."

He smiled and simply said, "Zave Williams."

Jada leaned in and gave me a brief hug. We sat at a table and in typical Jada fashion, she got right down to business. "Sean was initially going to handle this investigation himself, four years ago, but the officer he planned on working with got shot and the case was set aside."

Zave asked, "Who was the officer?"

She said, "Dan Baker. He was Bobby Long's former partner."

Surprised, Zave quietly said, "The blue code."

I asked, "What?"

He shook his head, "It's probably nothing. Danny and I were talking about Bobby, and he casually mentioned the code of silence between officers. Dan told me that Bobby Long muttered to Sadie's body, in the funeral parlor, 'You got what you deserved.'"

I asked, "Did he say any more about Sadie's death?"

"No. I didn't even know he was Bobby's partner. I'd like to take another look into Dan's murder. We assumed it was gang-related, but nothing's come out of investigating it from that angle. What if his death was related to his working this investigation?"

I matter-of-factly told him, "I don't think Dan was shot by a gang member."

He curiously studied me. "What do you have that we didn't have?"

I showed him an x-ray of Dan Baker's chest with the bullet present. The shot hit just below his heart. It was lethal due to the mushrooming effect of the bullet. I then took out an x-ray of Wesley "Dreads" Williams and pointed to the bullet—in the exact same area. I told him, "This rifle was sited in at 100 yards."

Zave commented, "But the lethal shots came from fewer than twenty-five yards away. If it was sited in a hundred yards, wouldn't the bullet be higher, as siting adjusts for the bullet to drop with gravity."

I smiled, "You'd be right after fifty yards. But the scope sits on the rifle, so it's higher. It takes more than twenty-five yards to make up for the difference in height between the barrel and the scope. If it's within twenty-five yards, the shot is lower than where it's sited in."

Zave continued to study the picture. "You're right. The bullet's in the exact same location on both. Dan and Dreads' killer is a hunter. How the hell are they related? And are they related at all to Sadie's murder?"

"Those are the million-dollar questions. I don't know."

Jada interrupted our quiet deliberation. "I'm interested in a story on Ray Fury's conviction. I've spoken to him on the phone and have set up a series of interviews with him in prison. I'm willing to share everything I get from the interviews, if you're willing to share what you can, with me."

I assured Zave, "Jada can be trusted with keeping what we share confidential."

He smiled at Jada, "Okay. Welcome aboard." He asked her, "So, how does Fury explain his DNA being in Sadie?"

Jada explained, "He initially denied knowing Sadie. Now he's saying they had a consenting sexual relationship. A couple of her coworkers suspected Sadie was having an affair with an African American man. Sadie's cousin says she saw her flirting with Fury."

I said, "I'm going to check out Bobby Long by talking to people who knew him."

The evidence box rested on the table. When I opened it, Zave had the same frustrated look I had. I muttered, "What the hell?"

Inside the box were both pieces of the torn belt, beer cans, Sadie's clothing, and other miscellaneous items. Nothing was bagged.

I told Jada, "Whoever did this left the evidence, but removed all of the bags. This means everything in the evidence box is cross-contaminated." If Ray Fury's attorney found a way to get a retrial granted, there was no way a conviction could be achieved again with this evidence.

Jada looked in and said, "No wonder Sean had a heart attack when he pulled this from the evidence room."

I didn't bother to tell her that I retrieved the box.

Exasperated, Zave asked, "How did this happen?"

"That's a damn good question." I thought out loud, "Sean told me the belt had never been tested for DNA. The question is, now, is there any value to testing it?"

Zave said, "I think so. What if we find DNA evidence from someone else in the system? We won't be able to convict anyone, but at least we'll know—give us some direction."

"Okay. I'll have the belt sent over to the lab."

Jada said, "I'm sorry, but I have to go. I want to be at Sean's next doctor's appointment. It was such a shock seeing him almost die, after we'd committed to spending the rest of our lives together. It's scary."

I told Jada, "I understand. Family comes first. Zave and I will be meeting face-to-face every week and talking daily by phone. I'll invite you and if you can't make it, don't worry."

Zave asked, "We don't have to meet every day?"

I responded, "I'm not one for meeting for the sake of meeting. That's what drives me nuts about working for the state. We're not going to find any useful evidence in the conference room. We need to get out and talk to people." I turned to Jada and said, "Be careful. Both Ray Fury and Bobby Long are dangerous. Both are rapists, which adds an extra risk for you. In addition, Bobby's a racist."

After Jada left, Zave commented, "Sean wasn't in the evidence room when he had his heart attack."

"How do you know?"

He pointed to the evidence room attendance log that had been taped to the cover. "He isn't on the list."

We both shrugged as I said, "I don't know why he lied to Jada about it." It wasn't relevant to our case. Getting back to task, I said, "Zave, if you could look into Fury, it would be helpful. You said you're familiar with a couple of his rapes. The only rape he was ever convicted for was Sadie's."

"He's been acquitted twice, but he wasn't *innocent,*" he stressed. "There just wasn't enough to convict him. There are two additional victims who came forward. The only reason he wasn't charged with those rapes was because he already received a sentence for life without parole."

"Now that Fury's sentence is being challenged, we'll want to push forward to get those cases prosecuted. I'd also like to know if he threatened to kill any of his victims."

Zave nodded. "I'll check into it."

"If you end up putting in a late night and need to sleep in, just let me know and we'll catch up later. But let's talk, at least briefly, every day. This is a dangerous case. We already have one cop dead."

"Do you think Dan's murder is related to this investigation?"

"I don't know. It's too early to rule it out. Our best weapon is being informed so we need to communicate."

"Do you think Fury's guilty?"

"I'm skeptical. He was convicted and his DNA was in the victim, but I've seen evidence that raised doubts. How about you?"

Zave said, "I think he's guilty, but I'm open-minded and I'd like to know exactly how Sadie's last day played out. I'm familiar with a couple of Fury's rape cases. He's not a nice guy."

"Honestly, I don't know much about him."

17

*"Fear of something is at the root of hate for others
and hate within will eventually destroy the hater."*
—GEORGE WASHINGTON CARVER

2021

JON FREDERICK

11:00 A.M., TUESDAY, APRIL 13
MINNESOTA CORRECTIONAL FACILITY—RUSH CITY
7600 525th STREET, RUSH CITY

I respected Police Chief Medaria Arradondo, but I struggled
with his announcement that Minneapolis police would no
longer pull people over for minor offenses like expired tabs. I
get it. African American males were pulled over ridiculously
too often. What people didn't realize was that we often caught
radical white militia members on license issues. When Timothy McVeigh bombed the Federal building, he was caught
because of a license plate violation. Militias did not like giving
the government money, so their plates were typically not in
compliance with the law. Some were so arrogant they actually created their own license plates. Now we couldn't pull
them over in Minneapolis. How about if we allowed officers to
enforce the law and just got rid of cops who racially profiled?

After spending yesterday going through updated training videos for my return to work at the BCA, I decided to
spend my first day of real investigative work at the Minnesota
Correctional Facility in Rush City. I wanted to get an idea of
what Bobby Long was like in prison. I'd been informed by
the guards who knew Bobby that he had joined the Aryan
Cowboy Brotherhood while incarcerated. The FBI data on
white supremacists indicated that members of the Brotherhood with criminal charges were three times more likely to be
violent, in the future, than other militia members.

The guards directed me to a mangy-looking fellow nick-
named *Shovelhead*. The nickname was based on a type of
Harley Davidson motorcycle, called a Shovelhead, due to
the rocker heads having the appearance of an upside-down
coal shovel. The man's real name was Dave Smith. *Dave* was
the most common name among prisoners. This Dave was
serving time for sexually abusing his partner's daughters;
his sentence was a dozen-year commit, as two of the girls
were under the age of twelve. I was sure he gave his cohort
another story.

Shovelhead was a wiry character who looked like he just
woke up. His stringy dark hair jutted out in various directions
and his grubby beard had grown wildly down his neck. Dave
wore the standard, prison-assigned jumpsuit in dark green. He
had a tattoo of the Iron Cross on his right bicep. It was once
a military decoration in Prussia, but later worn by soldiers in
Nazi Germany. I remembered seeing the iron cross as a small
child, when I went with my grandfather to his friend's home. I
found it in a drawer when I was looking for something. When
I told Grandpa about it, he said, "Sometimes, people think
they're fighting to save their home and they later learn that
much more is at stake. Things so bad, you'd give up your home
if you could make them go away. We're not going to talk about
seeing that cross." I later came to realize the man kept the

cross to remind him that we could all be a part of something shameful if we weren't careful.

Shovelhead and I sat on flat, circular metal chairs, which were attached to the metal table in front of us. I'd never sat on a chair less comfortable. It was like sitting on a cinder block.

After introductions, Shovelhead asked, "What am I going to get out of this?"

"I don't know. I have to see if what you have to offer can contribute to a prosecution, first. Are you a member of the Aryan Cowboys?"

"I'm on the fringe."

Which basically meant no. You were either in or out. He hung around the gang.

He continued, "Bobby came to us looking for protection. You know the way cops are hated in here. I couldn't believe what he said. I wrote it down exactly, and the date and time. I can tell you just where he was when he said it and who-all was there. Maybe you can even look at old video and see him mouthing it, since it was in a common area. After Bobby said it, I thought, 'Holy shit, man! This is my ticket out of here.'"

He was dying for me to ask, crazed eyebrows dancing on his forehead in anticipation.

Acting bored, I finally asked, "What did he say?"

Shovelhead seemed to love hearing himself talk. "The Brand leader asked Bobby, 'What have you ever done to earn our protection?' Bobby told him, 'I murdered my nigger-loving fiancée.'"

18

*"For in the end, freedom is a personal and
lonely battle, and one faces down fears of today
so that those of tomorrow might be engaged."*
—ALICE WALKER

2021

JADA ANDERSON

2:30 P.M., TUESDAY, APRIL 13
MINNESOTA CORRECTIONAL FACILITY—LINO LAKES
7525 4ᵀᴴ AVENUE, LINO LAKES

I thought about cancelling my interview with Ray Fury out
of concern I could get COVID. Sean had been vaccinated
and told me I shouldn't cancel on his account. I'd also been
vaccinated, but the vaccination still wasn't available for my
little guy, Isaiah. I'd make sure I showered thoroughly and
changed clothes before I'd have contact with him. There'd
been over 4012 deaths from COVID in the Minnesota prison
system. The sergeant who escorted me to the interview room
told me the guards hadn't been vaccinated, but the prison psy-
chologists, who were working from home, had been. The best
off always managed to get services first.

After I was seated, Fury was escorted into the room, in
a dark green, prison-issued jumpsuit. The fact that he wasn't

wearing orange suggested the prison staff didn't view him as a high-risk offender. Ray stood about six feet two inches tall and was a solid, muscular man. I wondered how many innocent black men had spent their lives in cement and metal cages. Ray Fury, like all of us, deserved justice.

The guard asked, "Are you comfortable interviewing him without him being restrained?"

I said I was fine and the guard left us. I knew we were being observed on camera. I made myself as comfortable as I could, shifting around on the unforgiving metal chair and thumbing open my pocket-sized notebook.

Ray sat back in his seat like he owned the place and asked, "Can I take my mask off?"

"No."

Disappointed, he offered, "I'm fine with you taking yours off."

"I'll continue to wear it."

"Could you just take it off for a little bit? It's been years since I've seen a beautiful woman."

I thought about this. I tried to come into this interview open-minded, but he was already making me feel a little creeped out. Still, I wanted him to open up to me. I stepped as far back against the wall as I could and pulled the mask down for a moment. I held his gaze as his eyes traveled unabashedly over my face. When I could see he was working his way further south, that was enough. I snugged my mask back on, pinching the fabric tightly against the bridge of my nose, and returned to the table.

As I sat back down, Ray said, "You're even hotter than you are on TV."

I occasionally covered stories on Channel 5 News. I ignored the comment and asked, "Tell me a little about yourself."

Ray laced his fingers behind his head, the skin on his upper arms pulled tight across knots of muscle. He flexed one bicep at a time to a silent rhythm, as he shared his story. "My mama worked two jobs, so she was never home. The old man wasn't in the picture. I got a brother in Stillwater for armed robbery, but I'm sure you already know that. We were so poor, my brother and I used to take turns runnin' around the yard barkin' because we couldn't afford a dog." He chuckled to himself, and I appreciated his effort to lighten the mood.

He went on, more serious now, "Boxing was my life, and they took it away from me. But once I get out, I plan on making a comeback. I work out in my cell every day."

I warned, "Boxing has taken a hard hit in the last few years, with concerns about concussions and now COVID."

Disappointed, Ray's dancing biceps stilled, and he dropped his arms, elbows landing heavily on the chair's arms. He sat forward. "You gonna ask me if I killed Sadie?"

"Did you?"

"No, I didn't. I was convicted by an all-white jury."

That didn't necessarily make him innocent.

Ray added, "Those pigs have been trying to convict me for years. You think it's a coincidence that every charged victim is white? They accused me of raping a retarded girl. I even offered to take a lie detector test, but they just bulled ahead with the charges. Found not guilty every time."

"Except with Sadie."

He sternly repeated, "I didn't kill Sadie. Can't you see I was set up?"

I grimaced, "Why?"

"The hoes—" He stopped himself and tried to be considerate. "Sorry—what do you call the babes lookin' for an easy ride?"

"Slattern."

He gave up on trying to say it. "They worshipped me as a champion boxer—including Sadie. She would've done anything for me. How you think that sat with a redneck white boy?"

I'd seen the pathetic way some women hang around the athletes. "Why did you hit a disabled woman?"

His face flattened of all emotion. "There's words a black man can't tolerate from nobody."

"I'm not going to hit an intellectually disabled person over words."

"Well, you better than I am."

I asked, "Did you rape Sadie?"

"No." He looked away before finishing, pulling the stale cell air in through his nose. "I didn't have to. She was into me." He leered into my eyes and bluntly stated, "Fuck buddies. But 'cause her man was a white cop, we had to keep it on the downlow." Ray stopped himself, "Look, I know I ain't politically correct, but I'm not a killer. Only reason I'm in jail is because I didn't have enough money to keep me out. Sole reason."

It did seem his attorney could have raised reasonable doubt.

Ray told me, "Hell, I have a friend who'll swear Bobby Long pulled us over and warned me to stay away from her. Why didn't my public pretender find him?"

"Did you tell your attorney about him?"

He looked away. "I couldn't think straight at the time. You know what it's like comin' off steroids cold turkey?"

Withdrawal from any drug has the opposite of the effects of the drug. So, coming down from drugs that jack you up had to result in extreme fatigue.

When I didn't respond, he told me, "My life was on the line, and I couldn't keep my eyes open."

I believed him. "How did you meet Sadie?"

"At a gas station. We hit it off and she gave me her number."

"Where did you get together?"

"We had to be super careful. She warned me that Bobby was jealous. We'd meet at the store where she worked and go for a ride in the car."

I considered, "So you'd be on video at Cub Foods."

"I wish. It was eight years ago, now. All those videos are gone. My attorney checked."

"Did you ever go out to eat together?"

"Oh yeah, once, at Pizza Lucé's."

"Is there any record of this?"

"I paid cash, but my attorney found a witness who saw us there."

"Why didn't you come forward with this when you were charged?"

Ray looked away and harrumphed, "I told you, my mind was draggin'. I forgot about it until Saint Frannie brought it up. My attorney says a religious fanatic is the perfect witness for me."

That was certainly possible, but my skeptical reporter's brain wondered if St. Frannie might also be easy for an attorney to manipulate. I said, "Sadie Sullivan died on August 30, 2013. When was the last time you were with her?"

"We were together the Tuesday of that week. Had sex in the back seat of my car. I know it's not the politically correct thing to say, but she was a bit of a freak—liked it rough. No hittin' or nothin' like that. It's like she was working out her frustration and I was happy to oblige . . . "

19

*"Service is the rent you pay
for room on this earth."*
—Shirley Chisolm

2021

XAVIER "ZAVE" WILLIAMS

3:30 P.M., TUESDAY, APRIL 13
HENNEPIN COUNTY GOVERNMENT CENTER,
300 SOUTH 6TH STREET,
DOWNTOWN WEST, MINNEAPOLIS

I visited Hennepin County Prosecutor, Paul Tierney, to share the information I had on the Fury conviction.

Paul sat back behind his desk with a ridiculously priced Caribou coffee, taking in my concerns about Bobby Long's comment at the wake, along with the poor state of the evidence in the Fury case.

He rubbed his chin and pondered, "The statement from Dan Baker isn't admissible in court, now. He's dead and your comment about what he said is simply hearsay. It's not acceptable evidence."

"It doesn't change the fact that Long said it."

"I believe you. But people get angry with their partners for a multitude of reasons. Maybe Sadie was getting cold feet about the wedding—it doesn't mean he killed her. Have you ever said anything you regret?"

My comment to Lachelle after her father's death immediately came to mind. "Of course."

"There it is. Maybe she cheated on him—who the hell knows? We do know that a rapist had sex with her just before she died. We have DNA evidence. What more do you need?" Becoming agitated, Paul reorganized some papers on his desk as he spoke, "I can't believe how careless you guys were with the evidence box. Did it never occur to you that this case could be appealed?"

I had to bite my lip to keep from confronting his condescending attitude. When one cop messed up, we were all swept together.

Tierney continued his rant. "Fury's attorney, Margaret Brown, is a bulldog; she may find a way to get this verdict reversed." He tapped away at his laptop, then stopped and drilled the cool eyes of an overworked prosecutor into mine. "Are you trying to tell me you think he's innocent?"

"No. I don't buy his story of having a consenting relationship with Sadie. I knew her. She was a gentle and caring young woman. Where were Fury's witnesses when he was convicted? I'm skeptical of friends who appear as witnesses years later." I didn't bother to mention that Fury was friendly with the Gangster Disciples.

Paul commiserated, "I have a witness who is willing to testify that Ray bragged about raping Sadie. Ray said Sadie sobbed and under her breath she was praying, *it's in pardoning we are pardoned. And in dying we are born to eternal life.*"

The prayer of St. Francis.

Paul shared, "The guy even passed a polygraph indicating his statement is truthful. But I can't use him."

"Why not?"

"He won't risk being viewed as a jailhouse snitch without a reduced sentence. He's a pedophile and Margaret would make mincemeat out of him. There've been rumors that Fury's raped a number of black women in Hawthorne, but I can't get anybody to make a statement against him. And our white witnesses aren't exactly stellar citizens."

Sadie would have been a great witness against him. That might have cost Sadie her life.

It didn't seem to concern Paul that I had stopped responding. In all-business tones, he continued, "There is no doubt Fury's guilty, and I hate losing to Margaret. I'm going to prosecute Fury on the remaining rape, so she can't keep hollering that he's never been convicted for hurting anyone other than Sadie."

"There are two pending rape allegations," I reminded him.

"Not anymore. The statute of limitations has passed on his rape of the twelve-year-old, so Fury can no longer be prosecuted for it."[2] As I opened my mouth to protest, Paul held up a hand. "This isn't my fault. I wasn't the county prosecutor at the time they decided not to prosecute. That case was a slam-dunk conviction. They had his DNA. They had his teeth indentations on her face. Fury couldn't argue that the sex was consenting because the victim was only twelve. If I could, I would've put those pictures of his bite marks on that girl's face in front of a jury, and they would have sentenced Fury for as long as possible. But that's lost. I can't even use them in court, now."

"I thought there was no statute of limitations if there's DNA evidence."

Paul harrumphed, "There isn't anymore, but there was when that rape was charged. Now I need you to convince Cheyenne Schmidt to testify. Rumor is she's getting cold feet. I get her reluctance—you saw what Margaret did to

---

2. The Minnesota legislature lifted the statute of limitations on sex offenses on 9/15/2021, which means there is no longer a ticking clock for cases to be prosecuted.

Elizabeth Erickson on the stand, just because she was drunk. Margaret will have even more fun with a stripper. But we need a conviction."

"I'll talk to her. I did convince Elizabeth to get into a chemical dependency program. So far, so good."

It made me feel good that Liza was currently sober. You never knew how people were going to respond to offers for help. I anticipated she would be severely hungover or would refuse to leave with me. Instead, she told me she had one more drink after I left her that night, and then dumped all her liquor. She didn't even discuss drinking the next day. She talked about Jack all the way to the treatment facility.

It didn't feel much like Paul cared about Elizabeth Erickson's outcome. He unemotionally responded, "Good," and basically dismissed me.

20

2021

JON FREDERICK

5:30 P.M., TUESDAY, APRIL 13
PIERZ

I ended up finishing earlier than anticipated at Rush City, so I drove straight west to Pierz with the intention of surprising Serena and the kids. To my surprise, they weren't home. Nora and Jackson were left with my parents for the night. It was the first time they'd spent the night with Bill and Camille, and both Nora and my parents were excited about it. Jackson would've been fine leaving with me, but I didn't want to break up the planned event. Serena had left for her first shopping trip to the Mall of America since the pandemic hit over a year ago.

I played hard with my dynamic duo for a couple hours, and then headed back to where I was staying in Minneapolis.

Serena and I weren't firing on all cylinders and the friction between us bothered me. It wasn't like her to drop the kids for an overnight with anyone, and then take even a day trip without at least letting me know what she was doing. They always say married couples had periods like this; I just never thought it would happen to us. It frustrated me that she wasn't answering her phone, but I had a pretty good idea what occurred. She used the GPS on her phone for long trips and forgot that she should plug it in, so her phone eventually went dead.

8:30 P.M.

51ST STREET & WASHBURN AVENUE SOUTH,

FULTON AREA OF MINNEAPOLIS

DISAPPOINTED WITH MISSING SERENA AND getting more frustrated as I read into the Ray Fury conviction, I quit for the night and decided to shower off the depravity of my work.

There were so many holes in the investigation of Sadie Sullivan's homicide. Even though the case went unsolved for almost two years, they'd never searched Bobby Long's home—the home Sadie had left before her body was discovered. At the very least, this should have been done to rule out Long as a suspect. The prevalence of domestic abuse troubles me. Women were 15 times more likely to be killed by a man they know than a stranger. Most female murder victims were in romantic relationships with the men who killed them. I sometimes asked abusers, "Would you treat her this badly if you didn't love her?" I hate it. There's no excuse.

Bobby Long moved out of the house shortly after the murder and now, eight years later, it had been remodeled. All the carpeting had been torn out and destroyed. If Sadie had been stabbed or shot, we could still go back and see if blood seeped into the wood beneath the new flooring, but she was strangled. If there was ever any evidence, it was gone now.

21

"Be passionate and move forward with gusto every single hour of every single day until you reach your goal."
—AVA DUVERNAY

2021

SERENA FREDERICK

8:30 P.M., APRIL 13
51ST STREET & WASHBURN AVENUE SOUTH,
FULTON NEIGHBORHOOD MINNEAPOLIS

Jon and I had been out of sync since I had COVID two months ago. He was going to bury himself in a case, while I still was making up for my lost time with the kids. But our marriage was too precious to leave in this precarious state. He might've been able to shut out the tension with work, but I couldn't.

Jon told me last night that, after he worked late, he'd spend the night in Fulton as he needed to be up early. I checked our credit cards, and he wasn't staying at a hotel. *I know Jada Anderson helped Jon get his job back, but if he is staying with her, I swear . . .*

Now that I had my phone recharged, I followed the GPS tracking device on his phone to this address. I marched to the door and knocked. I prayed to God I would find another explanation.

It took him a minute to answer, and he seemed surprised. There he stood, bare-chested and barefoot, in jeans.

I asked, "Are you home alone?"

Jon smiled, "Yes."

"Do you always answer the door shirtless?"

"I saw it was you."

I walked by him and looked about the home. As I did a quick walk through, I asked, "Who in God's name are you staying with? It's a woman."

Still smiling, he said, "That's good detective work. I was about to shower. I washed up good and changed clothes before I played with the kids. But I was in prison today, so I'd prefer to shower before we hug."

"Are you going to answer my question?"

Jon responded, "When I told you I was staying in Fulton, I assumed you realized I was staying with Agnes."

Agnes Schraut was cantankerous eighty-year-old woman we both grew up around. I laughed, louder than intended, with relief. "You called Agnes late last night and asked if you could stay?"

"She told me I was welcome to stay if I ever needed a place."

Jon had asked Agnes look out for a criminal in this area years ago and, after she spotted the culprit, I helped her collect the reward money.

He continued, "Mia and Agnes are at some event tonight and should be home about nine."

I told him, "Go shower." I wanted a little time with Jon uninterrupted by Agnes' miserable banter.

I STEPPED INTO THE BATHROOM TO MAKE CERTAIN my *hurry and worry* didn't leave me looking haggard. I decided this was the best I was going to do, as a mother of two who was now, for the most part, parenting on my own. I undid my blouse and slipped off my bra.

Jon shut the shower off and I watched him pull his towel over the top of the shower rod.

When he stepped out, I was standing there waiting for him. We passionately kissed, and then I continued to caress and kiss his strong hard body.

I had descended to my knees. The door must not have latched when I closed it, as it slowly creaked back open. I wasn't concerned, as no one was home.

And then to my horror, I heard a throat clearing in the doorway.

Jon and I simultaneously turned to see Agnes, staring at us.

She sniffed and walked away, muttering, "The satisfaction doesn't come from looking at it."

I felt my cheeks burn with embarrassment.

Jon laughed as we both quickly dressed, giggling, and looking at each other like a couple of kids. I loved his face most when innocence took over his worry lines.

When we slinked out, guiltily, into the living room area, Agnes' personal care attendant, Mia Strock, entered the house. We were both familiar with Mia, as she had once interned with Jon; her living and working with Agnes was her penitence for her own mistakes.

Mia said, "I'm going to help Agnes get ready for bed and then I'll be on my way."

Agnes chided me, "Good to see you back on your feet again."

With genuine concern, Mia asked, "Were you sick?"

Jon stared hard at Agnes, a silent warning to her not to say more, as he responded, "Serena had COVID back in February."

Mia questioned, "Oh, I'm sorry to hear that. Did it affect your taste?"

Agnes gave me a wicked smile, "Apparently. And Jon looked down on her for a bit." She was enjoying my predicament way too much.

Jon politely responded, "I have the utmost respect for Serena. I would give my life for her."

Mia teased Agnes, "I've seen Jon with Serena. I'm afraid you might be mistaken. I know you hate being wrong."

Agnes quipped, "It's not a sensation I'm familiar with."

Before she could make another remark, I asked, "Would you mind if I stayed here with Jon tonight? I'll be gone before you're awake."

Agnes was tired and had run out of jabs. She said, "No problem. Don't mind me. Just do whatever it is the two of you do. I've never been much for romance. Poets say, *follow your heart.* Well, the heart ultimately attacks and kills its host, so it's not the most trusting organ."

Jon added, "It is the leading cause of death in the U.S." He smiled and took my hand, "But I think I'll follow my heart, anyway."

On that note, we retreated to the bedroom.

Jon took me in his arms and held me, as he asked, "Are you okay?"

I hugged him hard. COVID messed with my thyroid levels, which were already problematic. I rubbed tears away on his shoulder. "I'm sorry. I'm up and down. I don't even know why I'm crying. Right now, I'm jittery, panicky, and jealous, and I know it's all physical."

Jon stood strong. "I love you, Serena. It's hard enough not sleeping with you. I have to know we're okay. There will always be another case. I need *you.*"

I tugged at his shirt and he removed it.

He smiled, "I need to feel your skin against mine. Even if we just hug."

He stepped back as I undressed, and told me, "I will always love you. I am faithful and will be protective of you. Not to the point of denying you opportunities—but to minimize your hurt. Your presence heals me . . . "

11:30 P.M.

JON'S WARM BODY WAS SPOONED AGAINST MINE. Agnes aside, tonight was worth it. Jon and I had reestablished that *we* were the priority. We agreed that, once this case was resolved, we'd get our private investigative business rolling again. The pleasure was all mine. Well, a lot of it was mine.

The world doesn't spin on love, but love makes every moment on earth better.

22

"Everybody's at war with different things . . .
I'm at war with my own heart, sometimes."
—Tupac Shakur

2021

XAVIER "ZAVE" WILLIAMS

9:30 P.M., TUESDAY, APRIL 13
WEST RIVER ROAD NORTH,
HAWTHORNE, MINNEAPOLIS

Brooklyn Center Police Officer Kimberly Potter resigned today, after twenty-six years with the force. She grabbed her gun instead of her Taser and fired it. Her gun weighed thirty-four ounces and a Taser weighed eight. She should've felt the difference. I had to assume her adrenaline was racing to the point of not noticing. Another brother was dead, and I was heartsore. There would be no solace for the victim's family—an empty bedroom—an empty chair at the table— dead is from now on . . .

In 1995, the New York Times referred to Minneapolis as "the city of wakes," due to its high homicide rate. But then the rate declined, until 2020, and at this year's pace, we will break the record. A concoction of cheap heroin and meth, a gang war between the Highs and the Lows, and a lack of police officers all contributed to our sorry state. The Highs referred to the gangs on the north side of Minneapolis and the Lows were the gangs on the south side. All it took was a few online insults and they loaded their automatic weapons and headed to the streets. The violence resulted in Minneapolis being unable to replace police officers who left and COVID had weakened the force further.

Last night we had one squad car patrolling north Minneapolis, when there should've been eight, and we really needed fifteen. That one set of officers had to respond to shootings in three different areas. Everyone was frustrated. We had some bad cops, and we had some good cops making mistakes.

I lived in a modest little house in Hawthorne, just south of the North neighborhood. I grew up here and I wanted to make it better. This neighborhood was named after author Nathaniel Hawthorne. Nathaniel's grandfather was a judge who presided over the Salem Witch Trials and good ol' Nate attempted to dissociate himself from his granddad.

Ironically, Hawthorne's books were described as dark romanticism, which might've been a good description of this community. Housing covenants embedded in property deeds prevented black Americans from obtaining housing loans to live in certain areas, resulting in forced segregation. Half the Hawthorne neighborhood was African American in a state that was 7% black. Only 44% of adults in Hawthorne were employed, which was the worst rate in Minneapolis. We had to remind people that there were some great law enforcement officers, like Charlie Adams and his Blue Bloods, working hard at revitalizing North Minneapolis.

I'D INVITED MARITA PEREZ OVER FOR DINNER. I told her I needed to talk to her about Dan and she agreed to speak to me tonight, provided I buy her dinner from the 112 Eatery. The 112 had been shut down because of COVID and the riots, and it wasn't opening back up for two more weeks. I offered to buy at Spoon and Stable instead, and she was alright with that. I went with the Spaghetti Nero and Marita wanted the Grilled Venison. I wasn't in the mood to sit in a restaurant and Marita was fine with stopping over, so I promised to grab take-out.

I wasn't fooling anybody. I was lonely and she was interested.

I'd had this nagging shame over Sadie's death eating at me, lately. Was there something I could've said to her that would have changed her outcome? During our limited time together, I saw her as the naïve, struggling damsel, and myself as a relationship veteran. Eight years later, I was alone and depressed. I'd have loved to run into her today.

Marita was dazzling as always; her jeans wrapped around her full hips like a second skin. She wore an off-the-shoulder cream top showing off a throat and shoulders that looked just damn delicious.

Marita was engaging and more fun than I remembered. Dan had shared little more with her than he did with me. After we finished our gourmet meals, I had no more work questions for her. We sat together on the couch in the living room, discussing bad dates while sharing glasses of Red Axe Irish Ale. I'd heard good things about it, so I had a friend bring me a growler back from Moose Lake Brewing Company. Red Axe was an amber beer that went down like a smooth lager.

I said, "I brought a woman to Revival restaurant in Minneapolis and told her I liked the food and the people who worked there. She proceeded to pick at everything and everyone, just loud enough so they could hear. I was so embarrassed, at one point I asked, 'What's wrong with you?' I left a generous tip to compensate and when we got up to leave, she stepped back to pick it up. I told her if she touched that tip, I was going to arrest her. Needless to say, it was our last date."

Marita giggled. "That's not even close to mine. A guy brought me to a funeral on a first date, and then to his parents' house. I thought, *Okay, he wants me to meet his parents—that's fine*. Then I realized he *lived* with his parents. Even that I tolerated, thinking everyone hits tough times. After sharing only a few words his dad said, 'Okay, your mom and I will leave for a bit. How long is it going to take the two of you?'"

I busted out laughing.

Marita said, "I walked out the door and never looked back." She leaned in and kissed me.

I backed up a little. "I'm not turning you away, but I need to tell you I'm not ready for a steady relationship."

She gave me a wicked smile, her eyes locking with mine like some kind of voodoo spell was underway. "The story of your life, Zave." Her voice was smooth as glass when she added, "Let's go with what we're feeling right now."

I needed to get out of my head and just enjoy the moment and her spell was taking effect. It's all we had—moments . . .

AT ALMOST 10:00 P.M., I HEARD A KNOCK ON THE DOOR. I answered it, finding Lauren Herald standing at my door. What a pleasant surprise! But terrible timing. Lauren was like Jada—a classy woman I'd expect to find in the arms of some guy I'd despise.

Lauren peeked by me into the apartment, and I assumed she saw what I did—Marita clutching a pillow against her bare chest. Marita stared back at Lauren with only a challenge in her eyes.

Lauren immediately apologized. "I'm sorry. I wanted to see if you were interested in talking for a bit, but I see you're busy."

At that moment I realized my shirt had been unbuttoned and my consumption of ale had gotten the better of me. The best I could do was suggest, "Another time," and she walked away.

10:45 P.M.

MARITA WAS PROPPED UP ON MY CHEST studying my eyes. She'd gripped my trapezius muscle so tight when we were making love, I thought I was going to scream. Instead, it weirdly worked. Her exotic eyes were almost luminous against her bronze skin, by the light of the muted television. I asked, "Do you do that a lot?"

"You were so tense I could feel the knot in your shoulder. I rubbed it out."

Something was bothering Marita. After all her passion subsided, a dejected stillness seemed to settle over her. This was a problem, as I went there too easily myself.

I asked, "What's your story, Marita?"

With a flicker of a smile, she said, "I was born in Thief River Falls."

"So, what's it like for black Latina woman in the great white north?"

"I felt like the spokeswoman for nonnative minorities much of the time, but it was alright." She smiled, "Here's some history. Thief River took its name from the Anishinaabe phrase, Gimood-akiwi ziibi. It literally means stolen-land river. The Anishinaabe tribe lived in the area. When they realized a band of Dakota Indians occupied a secret encampment along the river, they called it the thieving-land river. Plus, we're the home of Arctic Cat."

"Snowmobiles?"

"Yes—more ATVs, today. But our five hundred miles of snowmobile trails are a big tourist attraction."

I smiled, "You don't strike me as a snowmobiler."

"There's a lot you don't know about me. Hearing that engine purr as I race across the frozen tundra is a rush—reina del rodeo!"

"And that means?"

Marita laughed, "Rodeo queen."

"Where does the dancing come from?"

"Dad is Venezuelan, my mom is African. I'm Creole. And in my house—we danced. We spoke with my global extended family regularly. You have heard of the internet, haven't you?"

I had wondered about her personal history, and it warmed my heart that it was pleasant.

She said, "It's bothering me that I haven't been fully honest with you. I don't want to lose you."

I stopped myself before saying I wasn't actually hers to lose. It was easy to say, "I can be very forgiving," not because I was a great guy, simply because I wasn't invested. I had no reason to be jealous.

"I need to tell you something about Danny."

She had my attention now.

Marita closed her eyes as if sharing would be painful. "Danny helped everybody—no questions asked—because he believed in the goodness in people. But he was clearly bothered whenever Bobby's name came up."

"What did he say?"

"Nothing. He would just become silent."

This had me thinking. Was it grief for Bobby's loss or guilt?

Marita inched closer. "Danny and I had sex once. He talked me into a threesome."

"Not with Lachelle?"

She smiled, "No, it wasn't Lachelle. And I won't tell her you said it. She's already mad enough at you."

I closed my eyes for a second. "I don't know what to say to Lachelle. I'm sorry. I was a jerk. I don't deny it. I just can't change it—and I was only fifteen at the time."

Marita said kindly, "Lachelle is a great person. She becomes someone else when she's around you—someone she doesn't even feel good about. It was just a hard time in her life. Sometimes it's easier to blame it all on one person."

I liked that she stood up for her friend.

She purred as she said, "Before you judge me as a slut, imagine you're drinking at a lake one hot summer night with two women. You're single and one of them suggests you all skinny dip. And not too long after, you're all standing kind of close to each other in the water talking and you're all a little buzzed. The women suggest you all fool around." She carefully studied my reaction and added, "Danny and his partner invited me to join them. Danny and I were friends. We all were drinking. That's all it was."

"Who was his partner?"

"He was a married man." She leaned up on her elbows. "I didn't know that at the time. That would have been a dealbreaker." She rested her chin on my chest and continued, "Danny wanted to experiment and told me they'd both be gentle with me. I said, 'What the hell.'" She paused, "I'd never do it again. It was weird. They were both more into each other than me, which did nothing for my self-esteem. I felt left out for a bit. Danny made me promise I wouldn't tell anyone he was gay—but he's dead, now. I don't think promises are a thing after you die."

Dead men keep secrets forever. I told Marita, "I don't imagine his lover's wife was wild about this."

"The guy he was having the affair with was married to another man. Danny was ashamed of it, but he liked the guy."

I wished I wasn't lying in bed with Marita, and I wasn't blaming her. As they say, I'd made my bed. I'd sleep in it— tonight. Maybe you couldn't always just be in the moment. Sometimes you needed to have a foot into your future. I only agreed to this hookup after it was clear she had nothing related to the investigation. That may have just changed.

It would've been nice to have gone out for a beer with Lauren. The rumor was she was involved with an older professional, so I always assumed she wasn't available.

Marita prodded, "What are you thinking?"

"I need the name of Danny's lover."

23

"Not only would we uncover the truth and the historical record, and not only would we allow these bodies to talk in the courtroom, we would get these bodies back to their families."
—CLEO KOFF

2021

JON FREDERICK

10:00 A.M., FRIDAY, APRIL 15
HENNEPIN COUNTY MEDICAL EXAMINER'S OFFICE
530 CHICAGO AVENUE, ELLIOT PARK, MINNEAPOLIS

The week had started out productive but had quickly fizzled into distractions. A new police shooting of a young black man, on top of the Chauvin trial, had pulled Zave and me away from the investigation to help keep people and businesses safe. Jada was spending every extra minute helping Sean recover, but she was also being lured into the Minneapolis story. On the plus side, I thought we were a good team, when we were together. We willingly shared information and we were all open to suggestions.

Zave and I were meeting with Dr. Amaya Ho today, to discuss the evidence on Ray Fury. Amaya could potentially secure the conviction, since she completed an analysis on the evidence before it was all thrown together. She and I had worked a number of cases together in my previous gig with the BCA and we were comfortable being open with each other.

While we waited for her, Zave smiled slightly and asked, "Am-I-a-ho? Really?"

"It's hard to unhear it once you've made the connection, I know. Actually, Amaya has two definitions in Japan. It can mean *night rain*, and it can mean, *you can depend on me*."

Zave laughed, "It's not the *Am-I-a* part I'm concerned about."

"The name Ho comes from one of her Korean ancestors. It's one of the most common surnames in Korea, where it means *tiger*."

Dr. Ho entered the room with a packet full of reports and pictures. Her straight ebony hair was woven into a sensible braid and hung down the back of her white lab coat. She set the packets on the conference room table for each of us to peruse.

Zave and I sat across from her with our legal pads, eager for information.

Amaya told Zave, "Jon has already shared that the evidence box is in disarray. I'm not sure how useful my reports will be. This was a case where I didn't discover a lot of evidence that will lead you in a direction. Instead, I can tell you what it wasn't. For example, Sadie didn't die by Plymouth Creek."

It was something I suspected when I first noticed only half of the murder weapon, the belt, was by the body. I picked up the picture of Sadie's body lying in the high grass.

Zave asked, "How do you know?"

Amaya matter-of-factly said, "Her blood had pooled to the front of her body, indicating she died lying face down. As you can see, she's lying on her back when the body's discovered."

He suggested, "The killer could've just turned her over."

Using her pen as a pointer, Amaya directed our gaze to Sadie's face, then her torso, and then her knees, as she said,

"Where are the dirt and grass stains? Sadie wasn't face down in that field. Her body was transported there."

I thought out loud, "She could've been killed in the truck." That was where the remainder of the belt was found.

Amaya countered, "Not likely. She wasn't on the ground and there was no evidence of a struggle in the truck."

AMAYA POINTED TO THE PICTURE I WAS HOLDING of Sadie's body at the murder scene. "What are your thoughts?"

"The body seemed staged. Her bra and underwear weren't tampered with, yet her shirt's off and her jeans are open. It's odd that someone would have started a sexual assault, but not touched her underwear."

Zave asked, "Do you mind?" as he reached to look at the picture.

Amaya gestured to the folder in front of us. "It's in your packet."

He pulled it out and studied it.

Amaya respectfully waited for Zave to say something. When he didn't, she continued. "The rape conviction wasn't based on my report." She handed me her report. "I couldn't determine with certainty that Sadie had been raped. There was no facial bruising, but if I had to pick yes or no, I'd guess she was raped vaginally and anally. The minor tearing was consistent with a victim who complied but didn't necessarily consent. If she was into rougher sex, then maybe she wasn't raped at all. But the County Attorney had a second autopsy done and this examiner reported Sadie had been raped. My report was never introduced in court." She raised her eyebrows and refocused on her file. "I can't say with certainty that the second report is wrong. Sometimes it's not clear." Amaya added, "Sadie did have intercourse with Ray Fury in the previous twenty-four hours."

Zave said, "Fury is claiming he had sex with Sadie *three days* prior."

"Impossible," she said. "His sperm were still alive in her. He had sex with her fewer than twenty-four hours before her death."

"So, he's lying," he said. "And this supports Bobby's claim that Fury had sex with her after she left for work at three in the morning." Zave looked from me to Amaya, a question on his face.

Amaya clarified, "Yes, but all I can say is they had intercourse within a day of Sadie's death."

Zave asked, "Why didn't you ever DNA test the belt?"

"It was never given to me to test."

I considered, "Did you ever test the beer cans for DNA?"

She nodded. "Yes. One was wiped clean. The other had a police officer's DNA on it."

Zave questioned, "Bobby Long's?"

"No. Daniel Baker."

He was startled by the revelation. "Danny never told me he was at the scene."

Amaya told us, "Dan Baker discovered the body. When I shared my evidence that his prints were on a beer can at the site with Sergeant Collier, he told me Bobby and Danny shared a beer after the body was discovered, while they were waiting for the crime scene techs. Collier said he jacked them both up about it."

Zave suggested, "Doesn't that seem weird?"

"Dan was camping with a friend when Bobby called him," she continued, "and told him Sadie failed to show up for work. Dan agreed to help look for her. He came straight from the campsite, so had a cooler of beer in his trunk." Amaya hypothesized, "Maybe he thought it would calm Bobby."

I considered, "Could Dan have killed Sadie?"

Zave quickly responded, "No. Dan was kind." He appeared to be working through some grief over the loss of his friend as he softly added, "And he wasn't attracted to women—so there's no motive."

Deciding to give Zave space to process his thoughts, I paged through Dr. Ho's report and turned to her. "You wrote that the time of death was within the last twenty-four hours. I saw a video of the body being loaded at eight in the morning." I could still picture Sadie's body remaining stiff on the gurney when the paramedic slipped. "Sadie's body was rock solid. Rigor mortis was in full force. She had to have died before midnight."

Amaya gave a half-smile. "You've learned well. But it is possible that, under the right conditions, a body could solidify only a few hours postmortem."

I asked, "Did those conditions exist that night?"

"I can't give you a clear yes or no answer. Probably not, but maybe."

Zave was studying the second examiner's report. "This document suggests Sadie died somewhere between three and seven in the morning. That's very specific."

Amaya muttered with contempt, "He based this assumption partially on Bobby's claim that they showered together before Sadie left for work. If this is true, Fury's DNA had to be introduced after."

He pressed, "And if it's *not* true?"

"It had to be introduced in the previous twenty-four hours." Amaya gestured to the report he was holding. "I can't testify that this report is wrong. My report is based on physical evidence, rather than anybody's word. With that in mind, I can't be that precise on the timeframe."

Zave asked, "Any thoughts about the fire?"

Amaya shared, "The fire was fresh. The killer started it, perhaps thinking it would destroy evidence, but the flames were out before they reached the body."

I was still sifting the new information through my head. I said, "I think the killer was in a fantasy fugue-like state when he posed the body. And when he was done, the reality of the situation set in. But I still don't understand why, after taking his time, he fled before the fire reached the body."

Amaya commented, "It's your job to answer that question."

Zave proposed, "His ride showed up."

ZAVE AND I LEFT AS CONFUSED ABOUT THE CASE as when we started.

I said, "The ride idea has the wheels turning in my head. One of the pieces I've struggled with, looking at this case, is if Bobby killed Sadie, how did he plan on returning home? Sadie supposedly left in Bobby's truck, and it was left at the site where her body was found. Now with his prints on the beer can, we know Dan was there before the crime scene techs arrived. He could've been Bobby's ride home."

Zave shook his head in disbelief.

We had a lot to process. I said, "I've already got forty hours in this week. I'm going home to spend some time with Serena and the kids. I'll meet you back at the office on Monday morning at eight. If you decide to put in any extra hours, you won't get overtime, but you will be comped for it, so you'll get that time off before you have to return to your regular work."

He muttered, "I've got nothing going right now. If you're okay with it, I'd like to hear what Sadie's family has to say about the investigation."

24

"Anyone who has ever struggled with poverty
knows how extremely expensive it is to be poor."
—JAMES BALDWIN

2021

XAVIER "ZAVE" WILLIAMS

10:30 A.M., SATURDAY, APRIL 16
5TH STREET NORTHEAST, FRIDLEY

Seeing the small, one-story house where Sadie Sullivan was raised intensified my appetite for a healthy serving of justice. Growing up, Sadie and her brother shared a bedroom with a sheet hung from the ceiling between the two beds for privacy. Her three sisters shared the other bedroom. Sadie's mom kept her own clothes in the unfinished basement and slept on the couch. Despite their poverty, Sadie had described her family as decent, law-abiding Christians, who treated others with respect. Looking through the small house, I understood how a proposal to live with just one other person would be incredibly appealing.

Sadie's sisters, Brittany and Katie, indicated their mom and youngest sister, Nina, had no interest in talking to me about Sadie's death. Her murder, followed by their brother's suicide, was too painful for them to revisit. The murder had been unsolved for two years before Fury's long trial. They just wanted it to be over.

Brittany and Katie huddled close together on the couch in the small living room, while I sat in a patched-up recliner as we talked. Brown duct tape was holding the torn pleather together.

Brittany had dark hair like her sister, while Katie's was an unnatural platinum, with incoming roots matching her dark eyebrows. Both were in their late twenties and like Sadie, had pretty, Italian features. Even though Brittany and Katie were only one and two years older than Sadie, respectively, they had both married right out of high school, creating a template for their sister to follow.

Katie swiped at a stray tear. "Mixed emotions pour from my heart when I come back to this house. Being poor sucks. You can only afford cheap things, so they break, and you have to buy them again or accept living in a place where nothing works. But when we were all home, it didn't matter. We were happy." She sniffled, "I *hated* living in this cramped house, but man, do I miss it. I miss Sadie and Liam." She had to stop to dry tears, pulling the sleeve of her white hoodie over her hand and dabbing away, black smears of mascara soaking into the fabric.

Brittany gently rubbed her sister's back and took over. "The house emptied out quickly. After Katie and I married, Sadie was murdered, and Liam died by suicide. Liam lived at home until—" she didn't finish.

Katie said sadly, "Mom and Nina each have their own bedrooms, now."

I asked, "Do you mind if I check out Sadie's old bedroom?"

Brittany led the way, and then both sisters peered in the doorway when I went inside. It was a small room. Clothesline hooks were screwed into the ceiling on each side of the room, where a wire once held a curtain to split the space in half.

Brittany saw me looking up and explained, "Mom opened up the hem of a sheet and ran a wire through it so Liam and Sadie each had their own space."

"It must have been a big sheet if it divided the room."

She smiled sadly. "It didn't divide the entire room, but it did provide privacy for them to dress."

I couldn't help thinking how awkward it must have been for Sadie, as an adolescent, to have a brother, five years older, sleeping on the other side of a sheet from her. "And you always lived here?"

Katie answered, "Mmm-hmm. We didn't have room for another girl in our room so, from birth on, Sadie was with Liam."

Sadie shared a bedroom with Liam all the way through puberty. I didn't want to say what I was thinking, but I needed to. "Do you think it's possible Liam could have abused Sadie?" He did kill himself after her death.

Katie and Brittany responded in unison, "No!"

"They were close," Katie said quickly, "but Liam always saw himself as her protector. He wanted Sadie to keep the baby and said they could all share this room. But Mom said we just couldn't."

That wasn't reassuring. What if Liam abused Sadie and she threatened to tell Bobby about what had happened? The family had already been through enough. I would only have to test the DNA of Sadie's daughter and the father to address my lingering thoughts.

I was thankful I kept my thoughts to myself when Brittany added, "Liam would ditch his friends to comfort Sadie after she gave up her baby. He was a great man. His suicide doesn't change that."

I said, "I knew Sadie from Cub. She was a wonderful person and always spoke well of her family. She was proud of both of you and excited to have you in her wedding."

Katie's eyes brimmed with fresh tears. "Sadie was always so kind—to everybody."

I decided to start with a nice, safe question. "I noticed her nails were cut very short. Isn't that unusual for a woman who is about to get married? I'm no expert, but don't women usually try to grow their nails out?"

Brittany smiled, "Sadie and I had a conversation about this the Sunday before she died. She chewed her fingernails and didn't want people seeing her stubby, ragged nails on her wedding day. I told her if she wanted to end that disgusting habit, cut 'em down, and she did."

That took care of the theory that they were trimmed down to hide DNA.

I asked, "What did you think about Bobby?"

Brittany gushed, "He was her knight in shining armor. He would've done anything for Sadie."

"Did they ever fight?"

"No. Never."

I slid my eyes over to Katie. She was a year closer and maybe Sadie shared more with her. She added carefully, "Not really. They never *physically* fought."

Pressing her further, I told her, "Sadie shared with me that she was having second thoughts about the marriage."

Brittany looked surprised, but Katie understood. She said, "There were times Bobby could be a little controlling, but he only wanted what was best for her. Before him, Sadie didn't always have the best taste in guys. She was beautiful and guys always hit on her." This seemed to trigger a memory and Katie smiled, "Sadie would say, 'He's not interested. He was just being polite—' even when it was so obvious to everyone else. Bobby was afraid she might give some guy the wrong impression."

"Do you think Ray Fury could be one of those unhealthy guys she dated?"

Brittany hardened. "No way." She was bristling; I'd have to be more careful.

I looked to Katie, who agreed, "No way in hell! She'd help someone like Ray, but he was too scary and intimidating for Sadie. We sat through the murder trial. Have you seen the darkness in his eyes? At heart, Sadie was a chicken."

Brittany chastised her, "Don't speak ill of the dead."

Katie laughed, "Oh, come *on*, Britt! She's up in heaven smiling at me right now because she knows I'm right. That's why she only dated guys who put a lot of energy into being with her. And those guys weren't always the best because she didn't choose them—they chose *her*."

I interjected, "Sadie made a comment to me I'll never forget. 'Vulnerability is our best expression of courage.'"

Warm smiles covered both faces.

Katie said, "She was nice to everyone. Vulnerable to everyone. Maybe that's why she was such a chicken when it came to dating. She was afraid she had nothing left to give."

After a pause, I said, "Your cousin has made a statement that she saw Sadie and Fury out to eat together at Pizza Lucé."

Katie mused, "Lucé's does have good pizza. Their Margarita pizza is *the bomb*. But no—Sadie never went out to eat with Ray. No way."

There was a passing glance between the two sisters that suggested to me there was a story of hurt involving their cousin. I asked, "What aren't you telling me?"

With smallest shake of her head, Brittany seemed to signal to Katie that this topic was closed. It was as if the vault had opened for a fraction of a second and then slammed shut.

Katie continued like the stinging pang had been nothing more than a mosquito bite. "As time passes, more and more people come out of the woodwork claiming to be Sadie's confidantes. Our cousin, Frannie, was always jealous of Sadie. Frannie likes to poke her nose where it doesn't belong."

Brittany agreed. "She always has something to say, when nothing should be said. If people were complimenting Sadie about her kindness and beauty, Frannie would throw in, 'Too bad she's damaged goods. Having a kid at fifteen and all . . . '"

RATHER THAN THE JIGSAW COMING TOGETHER, I left with more puzzle pieces turned upside down. Instead of clarifying my suspicions, I added more suspects. Ray probably killed Sadie. Bobby could've done it. Liam may have done it. Hell, even Frannie could have killed her.

2:30 P.M., SATURDAY, APRIL 16
XERXES APARTMENTS, 5211 XERXES AVENUE NORTH,
BROOKLYN CENTER

CHEYENNE SCHMIDT LIVED IN AN apartment complex fewer than two miles from the recent shooting in Brooklyn Center. Washington County was taking over the prosecution of Officer Kimberly Potter, so the Hennepin County Attorney could avoid criticism of bias. (The prosecutors and the police worked closely together in a county.) I put in some hours last night helping quell looting in Minneapolis, in response to this tragedy.

The county would pay a huge sum to the victim's family, and nothing would change. The state left people in poverty, swore at the high crime rates, accidently shot people, and then paid their families millions of dollars. It was a sadistic lottery that cost the poor families in my community a loved one. Black Lives Matter grew out of the frustration that this happens every damn year. We should've made changes the very first time someone was accidently shot. Brooklyn Center is 38% white and none of the 71 Brooklyn Center police officers lived within city limits.

Cheyenne reluctantly let me stop over before she went to work. She met me at the door, barefoot, in a tight pink tank top and real short, black shorts, barely covering what God gave her. Now at twenty-seven, she was as cute as I remembered. Her dark hair was split into two youthful ponytails that somehow worked. She waved me in, all pouty, then perched at on one end of her ratty couch. Cheyenne crossed her legs and the top one started bouncing in irritation when I joined her at the other end. I didn't have a lot of confidence the springs weren't going to give way once I sat down.

Cheyenne picked up a Diet Mountain Dew from the scuffed coffee table in front of her, gripping it so hard the aluminum crinkled in protest. "I know why you're here. I'm sorry, but I'm not going to testify." She took a gulp of pop and burped quietly into the back of her hand. Quickly changing the subject, she asked, "Did you hear J-Lo and A-Rod broke up?"

It was an insane time in Minnesota. The Derek Chauvin trial was going full force. Daunte Wright was just killed by a white cop, and former Yankee star, Alex Rodriguez, was trying to buy the Minnesota Timberwolves basketball franchise.

I shared my rant, "The Wolves have been the worst team in professional sports for thirty-two years. Despite this, they only hire from within the organization." I held up my hand as if I was signaling someone to halt. "It defies logic."

Cheyenne seemed to enjoy the dramatics, so I continued, "Get this—the T-Wolves' management offered to advise A-Rod. Two days later, he breaks up with Jennifer 'J-Lo' Lopez. I'm not saying they wanted them to break up, but all it took was for A-Rod to agree to listen to them, and just like that his relationship tanked. A-Rod and J-Lo were together for four years and engaged for two. Two days of advice from the Timberwolves and they fall apart. Whatever they've got working in that office, they should see if it will break down plastic. They probably traded J-Lo for three, six-and-a-half-foot forwards who can't post-up, shoot threes, or dribble."

Cheyenne teased, "I see I struck a nerve."

"No need to get the violins out. I'm a basketball fan, but the T-Wolves continue to destroy my love of the game. Nobody plays defense." I grinned, "I'll probably be okay—with years of intensive therapy. How about you?"

Cheyenne lost her smile. "I can't say I worry about the Timberwolves—like, maybe I should." She played with the hem on her shorts, lifting it slightly.

I wasn't sure if she was intending to be seductive, but she caught my eye. Back in the day, Lachelle used to warn me, *There's nothin' more trouble than a white girl on the prowl.*

She looked back up, admitting, "I struggle every night at work with my anxiety—since the assault. I see every man in the club differently and I cringe when they touch me." She shuddered, and then turned away and wiped a tear away with the heel of her hand.

"It's time to find new work."

"Easy for you to say," she sighed. "I'm not qualified to do anything."

"Have you thought about college or vocational school?"

"I can't do school." She took her soda into the kitchen and attempted to block my view, but I strained my neck enough to watch her pour a shot of Fireball into the can. She continued over her shoulder, "And I can't go through what Elizabeth went through on the stand. I swear I'd scratch that defense attorney's eyes out."

I asked, "Do you always drink before work?"

Cheyenne eyed me. "Wouldn't you?" When I didn't respond, she slouched. "Just since the assault. I didn't think you saw that." She looked me over and asked, "Are you single?"

Oh, boy. I needed to keep her talking if I was going to have any success getting her to testify. I smiled, "That's a good question. I'm not sure."

She snickered. "How can you not be sure?"

"I recently went out with someone, but I'm not sure if we're going out again."

"Would you ever consider going out with someone like me?" She was flirting now, and not doing too bad a job of it. She corkscrewed a lock of hair around her finger, her hot pink nails so long they were curling. I wondered how in the hell she could do normal things with those, like putting on a fitted sheet or hell, wiping her ass, without causing injury.

Avoiding the question, I said, "I can't believe you're not in a relationship—an attractive woman who's surrounded by men all the time."

Cheyenne blew out a long breath. "I'm not—but there's a guy who thinks he's with me. Jimmy was the one who got me work at the Gentlemen's Club, but I've been second-guessing our whole relationship. My best friend asked me what kind of boyfriend gets me a job at a strip club. The more I think about it, the more I realize the answer is *the kind I don't need*. I'm just doin' this till something better comes up." She stared into my eyes. "You never did answer my question."

I wasn't better than anybody. "Yes—I would go out with someone like you. But someone who works as a stripper? No."

She rubbed her thumb and index finger together. "It's just about the *money*. Everybody could use a little more money."

"Not at that cost. I'd be much happier living with less."

Cheyenne simpered and, kittenish, curled her legs up under her. "I guess I'll have to find a new job."

Getting to task, I told her, "We really need you to testify against Ray Fury. I wish I had time to give you to think about this, but we don't have time. We need to prosecute before we run into issues with the statute of limitations."

She chewed at the claw that was her thumbnail. "That attorney is going to tear me apart."

"We'll help you prepare for the questions." I leaned into her. "Cheyenne, I promise, I'll help you through this."

She shook her head, "I don't know."

"You could save someone else from being raped."

"I thought he was in prison."

"He is, but there's a good possibility he'll be released."

She closed the distance between us and was now sitting uncomfortably close. "Will you *honestly* be there for me?"

"Of course."

She purred, "To support me—answer my calls anytime of the day—*or night?*" She emphasized "night" with a hand on my thigh, causing more concern for the damage those nails could do.

The prosecutor told me to do whatever I needed to do to get her to testify. I could answer phone calls. I reluctantly agreed. "Yes. I am going to find a way to help you see him prosecuted."

And once again, I was making a promise I wasn't sure I could keep. I eased my leg out from under her daggers and made my excuses to leave. As I headed toward my car, Cheyenne propped herself in a pose against the doorframe that just left me feeling sad.

25

*"Love makes your soul crawl
out from its hiding place."*
—Zora Neale Hurston

2021

XAVIER "ZAVE" WILLIAMS

7:30 P.M., TUESDAY, APRIL 20
WEST RIVER ROAD, HAWTHORNE, MINNEAPOLIS

I went to St. Peter Claver Church on Sunday, praying for some peace in Minneapolis. It was the oldest African American Catholic church in the state. It was where I was baptized, received first communion, was confirmed, and where I completed my Eagle Scout project.

My prayers were answered. Derek Chauvin was found guilty on all counts, including Second Degree Murder, Third Degree Murder, and Second Degree Manslaughter for ending the life of George Floyd. Today, Americans across the nation were celebrating this verdict and it felt like our entire country breathed a collective sigh of relief. One of the best things we did was to secure the help of community groups such as the Minnesota Freedom Fighters, We Push for Peace, New Salem Missionary Baptist Church, A Mothers Love, WW Protection, and Second Chance. They walked the streets during the Chauvin trial providing a buffer between the protestors and the police. There were a lot of hugging and smiles on the streets of Minneapolis tonight. All was peaceful.

Not only did I want the world to change, I wanted to change, too—starting tonight. While I was by-the-book and disciplined at work, I allowed my personal life to wander like a piece of driftwood on the sea. I'd been a terrible person in relationships. Indecisive. I didn't let people know what I wanted and, when it didn't play out exactly as I hoped, I allowed myself to get busy at work and didn't call back. Being more assertive would be kinder. I should've called Lachelle and shared my worries about my future and listened to her stressors. I should have told Sadie I would've dated her if she was available. And then, there was a series of one-time dates with women I should've called back. They weren't necessarily one-night stands, as that implied more than how most of my dates went. I just safely held my distance and vanished at the first sign of stress.

I sat on my front steps looking down the embankment in front of my house, at the powerful Mississippi. The *Great River*, as the Anishinaabe called it, was almost two football fields wide on the other side of the road from my house. The forces of nature had a way of making me feel so small.

After some deep soul searching, I decided to call Lauren Herald. We both shared some sense of relief over the Chauvin verdict. Fishing for date ideas, I asked, "Tell me about a guilty pleasure."

After a pause, she shared, "Mint chocolate ice cream—but not from a franchise. I like the small shops."

"We've got to hit Milkjam Creamery sometime."

Lauren asked, "And your guilty pleasure is?"

I smiled, "Dark chocolate-covered almonds. No matter the size of the container, it's always one serving."

She laughed, "Well, you wear it well."

Silence ensued.

"Can I ask you something?" As the words left my mouth, I thought—stupid question! I was asking her something.

"Sure. What's on your mind, Zave?"

"I'm embarrassed over the way I was, the other night, when you stopped over."

She casually responded, "You had no idea I was stopping over—and that's not a question."

"When you showed up, a light went on in my heart that's been dark for a long time." I hoped this wasn't sounding like one of Danny's pick-up lines. "Maybe it's not what you intended, but the thought of enjoying some time together gave me hope again. Sometimes, you don't realize something is missing until you get a glimpse of it."

Lauren said with kindness, "I've only known you to be considerate and helpful. It seems like we're taking the long route to your question."

I couldn't tell what she was thinking. I opted to dig myself in deeper. In for a dime, in for a dollar. I told her, "I try to be kind, but I've felt sort of disconnected lately—like I'm just going through the motions. When I think about the possibility of spending time with you, I feel nervous and excited, and most of all optimistic."

She remained silent and the demons in my head started screaming, *Cut ties and run! Pretend it was a wrong number.*

I filled in the space, "Would you consider going on a date with me? Look, if you want nothing to do with me, I will respect that. I'm not a creeper. I just couldn't let it go unsaid."

Finally, she said, "I wasn't expecting this."

For a hot minute, I regretted making the call. I just made everything between us at work weird.

She asked, "Why now? I mean—I've always been here."

"I thought you were with someone."

"I was. Do you know who?"

I had no idea. "No. Does it make a difference?"

"Not to me. I'm interested, Zave, but I'm going through my own metamorphosis. I need to warn you that I'm looking for a serial monogamist, not the bachelor-bachelorette experience. I date one guy at a time and I'm going to expect that my man dates only me—to give us a chance. I'm not a hookup gal."

8:30 P.M., WEDNESDAY, APRIL 21
ANGRY INCH BREWING 20841 HOLYOKE AVENUE,
LAKEVILLE

I AGREED TO MEET LAUREN AT THE TAPROOM at Angry Inch Brewing. On the third Wednesday of each month, Dan Baker and I would meet at a taproom for a cold glass of Pilsner. Although last time, I believe Dan had the Lies & Lederhosen, while I went with the Lonely Monk. I arrived early, to be respectful of Lauren, and sat at a small table with my glass of beer.

Of all people, Marita came in and sat down at my table. She said, "I figured you'd be here."

Dan had obviously shared our routine with her. We toasted to Dan.

Marita said, "Describe yourself in three words."

"Horrified, nervous, frustrated."

She gave me a disheartened glance. "Not the words I picked." She explained, "My words are sad—for Danny, comfortable—with you, and hopeful—for us."

Just then, Lauren entered the taproom.

I explained to Marita, "I am meeting someone tonight. I can't do this."

She coyly smiled, "We'll get together another time."

"I don't think so."

"I know you, Zave—better than you know yourself. She followed my gaze. When blondie tries to get too close, you'll call me."

Lauren wore a loosely crocheted, wheat colored sweater and distressed jeans. Short brown boots showed a glimpse of tanned ankle at the end of her jeans.

Marita asked, "Is that her?"

"Yes."

She was hurt, but teased, "Ooh—sexy without being obvious. You can see her lace cami through her sweater. Nice touch!" She winked, "If I wasn't so damn hetro, I'd do her."

Lauren approached our table.

I told Lauren, "Marita and I were both friends of Dan's."

She kindly offered to Marita, "You should join us."

I quickly intervened, "She was just leaving."

Marita hesitated, waiting for another offer to stay, as I stared hard eyes into hers.

I interjected, "Lauren, let's go to the bar and order. You can taste the options and get some advice from Sne."

"Sne?"

"Snezana, if you want to be formal."

Lauren was quick to pick up on the friction between Marita and me and wisely responded, "I have to meet her." She turned to Marita, "It was nice meeting you."

Marita politely departed. I'd have to thank her.

Lauren studied me, "Her eyes are captivating. You can't deny that."

There was no safe way for me to respond to that. I said, "Lauren, you look amazing!"

"Thank you." She asked, "Was she the woman at your place when I stopped over?"

Please Lord, end this conversation! "Yes." I couldn't even look at her.

With no more said, she took my hand and led me to the bar.

After we made our selections and were seated, I asked, "Where did you graduate from high school?"

She beamed, "Pierz. Football state champions every other year since 2015. Or perhaps you know us better for Bologna Days and Thielen's meats."

I teased, "Didn't Springsteen write a song about that?" I sang, "*Bologna Days. They'll pass you by. Bologna Days. By the wink of a young girl's eye.*"

Lauren spit out her beer in laughter.

Embarrassed, she grabbed a napkin and wiped her lips. "Sorry. I believe Springsteen's song was *Glory Days.* But if The Boss would have been to Bologna Days, I'm sure he would've changed it." Her blue eyes lit up as she requested, "Sing more."

"Nah, I'm not much for singing, but you'll have to hear me play guitar. That I can do."

"What style?"

"I started out country, because that's what the uncle who taught me was into, but I've gravitated to rock and blues."

Lauren was so attentive. She made me feel important, which said something remarkable about her.

"I would love to hear you sometime. Zave—you're not what I expected. I need to know more. Where did *you* go to high school?"

"Robbinsdale Armstrong. I'm a Falcon." I jibed, "We're named after a Star Wars spaceship. Our claim to fame is that Bee Vang is an Armstrong graduate."

She laughed, "Pardon my ignorance, but who is Bee Vang?"

"The guy who played Thao in Eastwood's Grand Torino."

With genuine admiration, she shared, "I bet you were a star in high school."

I didn't remember the last time someone looked at me like I was really something special.

I smiled as I drank in those heavenly blue eyes. "I had my moments. It seemed like such a big deal at the time, and now it seems so small." I felt good about my performance as an athlete but embarrassed over my inability to see beyond my own needs. "I can't imagine the line of guys who were waiting to date you."

A little embarrassed, she said, "I didn't date in high school. And in college, they called me the *ice queen* because I didn't respond to guys' rude propositions. They weren't real creative—" She flipped a strand of her blonde hair. "Elsa-like hair."

I cut in and crooned, "My advice is, *Let it go.*"

She leaned into me and gently squeezed my arm. "That's terrible."

I felt a warmth in our conversation I hadn't felt in a long time—maybe ever. And then my phone rang. I looked down and it was Cheyenne. I didn't answer and it rang again. This time, I answered and abruptly explained, "Hi, Cheyenne. I'll call you back later. I'm kind of busy right now." I hung up.

Lauren had such a pleasant smile and she so easy to talk to. I felt drawn to her and for once, I was exactly where I was supposed to be.

My phone buzzed again. *Come on, Cheyenne—give me a break!*

I reluctantly picked it up and she immediately begged, "Don't hang up on me again. I need to talk, *now*. I'm having a hard night. My boss is pissed—says I don't smile like I used to . . ."

Lauren watched as I cradled the phone like a stone I wanted to cast to the bottom of a lake.

I suggested to Cheyenne, "I can call you later."

She whined, "You said I could call anytime. I really need to talk—*now*."

Dammit. I turned to Lauren. "I'm sorry, but I have to take this call for work. Can I step out for a few minutes?"

Disappointed, Lauren asked, "Do you want me to leave?"

I told Cheyenne, "Let me call you right back." She protested, but I hung up.

Lauren asked, "Is that Cheyenne the stripper?"

"Yes. It's my job to make sure she's okay to testify. I told her she can call anytime she needs."

"Look Zave, I like you, but you've got to learn to establish some boundaries."

My phone buzzed again. It was Cheyenne.

Lauren offered a weak smile and a wave goodbye.

I took the call and sadly watched her walk away, but then immediately hung up. I sprinted as fast as I could after Lauren.

She had already started her car and was pulling away.

I yelled, "Lauren!" and ran next to her car.

She stopped and buzzed her window down. "What, Zave?"

"I'm so sorry. It's just until this trial's over. And it's phone support. That's all I'm doing."

She smiled as I struggled to catch my breath. "Well, you running after me is a better end to this date, than *he took a call from a stripper.*"

"I took a call from a *rape victim,*" I emphasized. "It's the sole reason I'm talking to her. She needs help."

Lauren held my stare and her face softened in empathy. She nodded, "Fair enough. I won't refer to her as a stripper again. How about if I refer to her as a kinesiologist?"

"A kinesiologist."

Her eyes shimmered, "Someone who specializes in body movement. Take the call." She drove away.

I think I love that woman. My phone buzzed again, and I took the damn call.

26

*"As I walked out the door toward the gate
that would lead to my freedom, I knew
if I didn't leave my bitterness and hatred
behind, I'd still be in prison."*
—NELSON MANDELA

2021

JADA ANDERSON

1:30 P.M., THURSDAY, APRIL 22
SHOPPES OF LITTLE FALLS,
102 1ST ST SE, LITTLE FALLS

I drove and hour and half north on Highway 10, to meet with Sadie Sullivan's cousin, Francesca. The Shoppes of Little Falls was like walking through an arts and crafts fair. Sean would've loved the wall light made from a saxophone with blue light shining out of its bell. Decadent chocolates, jewelry made from real spider webs, mystery novels, and the handcrafted wood were all appealing, but I had my eye on a fused glass necklace.

Francesca Sullivan was more enamored with the clothing items. She was a little heavyset, with natural dark hair, heavy brows, and sharp, attractive Italian features, like all the Sullivan women. We both wore masks—hers white, mine black.

As she wrapped scarves around her shoulders and surveyed herself in the mirror, she said, "As I told you on the phone, I don't really have a lot to say. And, by the way, you can call me Frannie."

I made this trip because I had to see Francesca in person, to decipher whether she was lying.

Frannie stopped at a wooden placard that read: *To be a Christian means to forgive the inexcusable, because God has forgiven the inexcusable in you. C. S. Lewis.* A sadness unexpectedly descended over Frannie, pulling her features into a mask of regret. "Katie and Brittany haven't spoken to me since I made my statement to Ray Fury's attorney."

I asked pointedly, "Did you honestly see Sadie and Ray Fury dining together in a restaurant?"

She paused and looked directly at me. Her response was matter of fact, "Yes, I did."

"Where?"

"Pizza Lucé. And I watched them because I was in *shock*. My engaged cousin was holding hands with a *black man*." She grimaced as she fiddled with one of the scarves and said, "I'm sorry—I didn't mean anything by that. Sadie and I both went to Fridley High School and the students are mostly black. Luke wrote in the Acts of the Apostles, *God shows no partiality, but in every nation anyone who fears him and does what is right is acceptable to him.*" She nervously added, "I've dated black men."

I smiled, "You don't need to convince me God doesn't give a damn about race—beyond having a special love for those who are persecuted."

Frannie nodded in agreement. "Sadie wasn't just having food with this guy—she was leaning into him, hanging onto his every word."

"Could you hear what they were saying?"

Frannie clarified, "I wasn't close enough to *hear* them, but there was no mistaking their affection for each other. And they kissed before they went their separate ways."

I pressed, "Why didn't you testify at Fury's trial?"

She shrugged, "I didn't think it was relevant. It was three days before Sadie was murdered."

I explained, "Sadie's case was prosecuted as a stranger rape and murder. The family insisted Sadie and Ray never had a relationship. You could've helped him. Are you sure it was Ray Fury?" I skewered my gaze into hers.

"Yeah—pretty sure, anyway. It was years ago, now, but I've seen pictures of him. Seeing engaged Sadie, all cozy with a ripped black man, was such a shocker."

I didn't want to create problems, but I had to test the doubts expressed by Sadie's family. I said carefully, "Her sisters suggested you made the statement out of jealousy and a need for attention."

Frannie clutched the frothy scarf close to her throat in defense. She was hurt. "I *was* jealous of Sadie," she admitted. "We were in the same grade. I tried to be the perfect Italian Christian girl, while Sadie was spending her sophomore year in the backseat banging some dirtball. And even after she's pregnant and gives away her baby, everything was still about Sadie. *She's so beautiful. She's so nice.*" The tone of her voice became brassy with indignation. "Well, you know what? You're *supposed* to be nice. The reward isn't bigger in heaven because you're pretty!"

She searched my face for agreement, but I wasn't giving it to her. I waited quietly and watched as Frannie gathered her composure, and then asked, "Are you okay?"

"Yeah," she said, looking away. "I'm sorry about that diatribe. The truth is, I saw Sadie in that restaurant with Ray Fury and I feel guilty I didn't tell someone. I think I didn't because I knew how her family felt about me. I was afraid they'd say exactly what they're saying now—that I just said it for the *attention.* I don't want to see an innocent man in jail. I want to see the man who murdered Sadie punished."

Frannie busied herself returning the scarves to their hooks and smoothed them into place. She said, "I'm over my jealousy and I'm grieving her loss. Sadie was always kind to me, even when I was a brat to her. I'll never forget saying something so mean about her in seventh grade. She looked at me with incredible hurt in her eyes but didn't say anything in response."

"What did you say?"

"It was intended to be a joke, but it was mean. It wasn't true, so what difference does it make?"

I calmly repeated, "What did you say?" Comments were particularly hurtful if they were partially true.

Frannie dropped heavy arms to her sides and slumped. "We were with a group of girls teasing each other about our stupid idiosyncrasies when someone made fun of the three-D Prince poster in my bedroom. And I threw out, 'Well, Sadie sleeps with her brother!' I didn't realize until I said it that I was the only one in our group who knew she and her brother shared a bedroom. When I saw the shocked expressions on the girls' faces, it occurred to me Sadie never had anyone over to her house. I only knew the sleeping arrangement because I was her cousin."

I studied her expression closely as I asked, "Do you think it's possible Liam sexually abused Sadie?"

Frannie looked me earnestly in the eye and said, "Absolutely not. They were careful to always dress and undress behind the curtain. The door was on Liam's side of the bedroom, so he had no reason to go on her side, and he didn't. He wouldn't even *look* for something on her side of the room—even when she wasn't home. Somebody else always had to go look if Sadie had borrowed something of his. It was actually annoying." Frannie walked to a display and began perusing the chocolates.

I stayed close and she turned to me, "I am ashamed of how petty and jealous I was back then. My insecurities didn't make enough room for love in my heart. When I received the invitation for Sadie's wedding, I went to her and apologized for my jealousy and pettiness. She was her usual gracious self and forgave me. She apologized to *me* for being pregnant at fifteen and the embarrassment that must have brought me." Frannie shook her head. "We hugged and laughed. Today, I try to act with Christ in my heart. I'm trying to do the right thing, here. And I'm so glad I went to her when I did . . . "

If Ray Fury was having an affair with Sadie, he had no reason to kill her. He had never killed anyone. I didn't know why he lied about the day he had sex with Sadie. He admitted to having sex with her—what difference did it make? Maybe Ray simply got the date wrong.

27

"If you are neutral in situations of injustice, you have chosen the side of the oppressor."
—DESMOND TUTU

2021

JON FREDERICK

4:35 P.M., THURSDAY, APRIL 22
ROUNDHOUSE BREWERY,
23836 SMILEY ROAD, NISSWA

The faulty logic of some criminals was disturbing. Last weekend, a man protesting the Daunte Wright shooting fired shots at National Guard members who were trying to keep Minneapolis businesses open. The bullets penetrated a military Humvee and two guards were injured. I tried to understand the shooter's logic: *Because I'm upset that an innocent person was shot, I'm going to shoot innocent people.* Fortunately, the shooter was caught and arrested. How did he see himself as better than a cop who accidently fired a gun? The National Guard was made up of our friends and neighbors who were trying to keep peace. Imagine if one would have been killed.

I was pleased with the Chauvin verdict and another night of peace in Minnesota.

Jada called me on her way back from visiting Frannie in Little Falls and shared the details of their conversation.

She sounded sad, so I asked, "Are you okay?"

Jada grumbled, "Sean's been a little weird. But his heart attack and the wedding have got to be a lot. The man was still declaring himself a lifetime bachelor into his thirties. And all this COVID crap makes being a reporter complicated."

"Does he still struggle with jealousy?"

"He says he doesn't. Lately, I feel like he's pushing me away."

"You're one of my favorite people, Jada. I hope the two of you find a way to work through this."

"Jon, you and I used to talk for hours," she said wistfully. "Now it's just a few minutes about a case and done."

She was right. "This is just the way it needs to be."

"Is Serena jealous of our friendship?"

"It's me. Do unto others as you'd have them do unto you. It would bother me if, every day, Serena was talking to a guy she once had a four-year relationship with. So, I reduce our contact to what's necessary."

To be honest, I liked Jada a lot, but didn't plan on working with her again. Serena has struggled with being insecure about my love for her recently and it pains my heart. Serena was so amazing! A simple wink from her could make my day. I wanted Serena to feel safe and secure in our marriage; I was beginning to realize a clean separation from my past was necessary. Abraham Maslow proposed that you needed to feel safe before you could think at a higher level. I believed security was also essential to love at a higher level.

I told Jada, "I want to thank you."

"For what?"

"Now that I've returned to the BCA, I've thought about what a blessing it was for me to have you to talk to when I first started out. I was a lost soul at the time, and you kept me going in the right direction. It's funny, when you reach success, you think it was inevitable. But honestly, there were a hundred times I wanted to just head back home get drunk with my old friends. You would ask me, 'What are you going to do if they call you in for a special assignment?' Or, 'I was hoping you could help me with . . . ' And it took a bit, but I was there when the windows of opportunity finally opened. So, thank you."

"That's kind of you, Jon. It worked both ways . . . "

I respected Jada, but unfortunately, she wasn't firing on all cylinders. The information I gleaned from her interview with Frannie left me with a lingering suspicion. Jada would've picked up on it if she didn't have a smorgasbord of stressors on her plate right now.

I called Frannie. She told me if I wanted to speak to her, I'd need to meet her at Roundhouse Brewery, as she was on her way to Grandview Lodge for the weekend.

Frannie was waiting for me on the patio, where we could sit at a picnic table unmasked as we spoke. There was a bit of a spring chill in the air, although the sun was feeling warmer every day. Frannie was hunched into an oversized, buffalo plaid flannel shirt that looked two sizes too big. I was glad I hadn't shed my jacket.

I asked Molly what they had on tap and ultimately selected an Angel Seat Amber.

Frannie and I sat at a remote table. She said, "I've already talked to Jada. I agreed to testify. What else do you want from me?"

"Something's been eating at you for a long time that you haven't been able to talk to anyone about. You told Jada that Ray didn't kill Sadie—which basically means you believe Bobby did. Why are you convinced Bobby killed Sadie?"

Frannie wanted to run. She skittishly revealed, "Ray and Sadie were friends. I saw them together."

"What was said?"

She avoided eye contact. "I didn't hear the conversation and I couldn't see much of his face. But I could see Sadie's and she was ogling him."

I took a sip and set my glass down. "When you went to Sadie to apologize before her wedding, it was for something bigger than what you shared with Jada."

Frannie remained silent, rubbing the beads of sweat off her glass of Sinful Tropical stout.

I thought out loud, "I've heard about how kind Sadie's sisters are; it doesn't quite compute that they'd maintain resentment toward you for insulting Sadie in junior high." I decided to just put it out there. "You slept with Bobby. And somehow her sisters found out."

Frannie's busy fingers stilled but she did not look at me. She asked softly, "Why does it matter?"

"I need to understand Bobby's mindset at the time of Sadie's death."

Splotches of embarrassment blossomed on her cheeks. She bowed her head and made the sign of the cross before speaking, "God forgive me. It was a chance event. We both happened to be at an after-bar party and Bobby drove me home. Sadie had already left for work."

"How did her sisters find out?"

"When we were leaving the next morning, we ran into Liam. He and Bobby were buds and he stopped over to see if Bobby wanted to go fishing. Liam looked at us and said, 'You've *got* to be kidding.' I told him we were both drunk. It was a mistake. I promised it would never happen again. Bobby begged him not to tell Sadie. Liam didn't tell Sadie, but he obviously told Brittany and Katie."

"Did *you* tell Sadie?"

"No. When I recieved the wedding invitation, it was clear she didn't know. I drove over to tell her, but I just couldn't bring myself to do it. So, I apologized for the way I treated her in junior high."

"What did Bobby think about your affair? Did he want you over Sadie?"

"No—God no. And it wasn't an *affair*. It was one sinful night." She took a large swallow of beer. "I saw a side of Bobby I hadn't seen before. The next morning, he told me, "You don't have anyone to blame but yourself. He said, 'You wanted it and you got it. I hope you're happy.' He told me if Sadie ever found out it would break her heart."

Frannie finally met my eyes. "I just want to go to the lake."

7:00 P.M.

COLD STREAM LANE, EDEN PRAIRIE

I TOOK FLYING CLOUD DRIVE TO PIONEER TRAIL, to Sunny Brook Road, to Cold Stream Lane, to find the home Bobby Long had been staying at since his release from prison. His probation officer told me Bobby's dad helped find him a house in a nice suburb to help him avoid the blowback he'd receive in the inner city for his behavior as a police officer.

When he answered the door, Bobby was immediately defensive. "What's this all about?" Prison had bulked him up and thinned him out. His skin was pale as alabaster, but overall, Bobby looked strong, healthy, and perhaps more dangerous than ever. His snug, plain white t-shirt showcased his new physique, and his navy workpants hung a bit loose on him.

I said, "The BCA has asked me to look into Sadie's murder."

Bobby turned and stalked to the kitchen table.

I followed him and we sat across from each other as adversaries. Like most narcissists, he wasn't about to lawyer up. Talking gave him the opportunity to show off. He also knew his cooperation would look better for his probation.

I asked, "How was your prison time?"

He looked past me as he spoke. "Hard. How do you *think* it is for a cop in prison?"

"I heard you joined the Aryan Cowboys."

He slid flat eyes toward me. "It was the only way for me to live through it. I haven't had any contact with the Brotherhood since my release. I told them my PO won't allow it, but I'm done with them."

I observed, "You were six years older than Sadie."

"Still am."

"Did you ever pull Ray Fury over?"

"Not that I remember. I could've. A cop pulls a lot of people over."

I said, "He has a friend claiming he was with Fury when you pulled them over and told Ray to stay away from Sadie."

Bobby growled, "That never happened. If I thought for a second Sadie was with Fury, I would've ended it with her. But if I knew he was going to rape Sadie, she'd still be alive." He added, "I'm not sure he would be."

That line of questioning wasn't productive, so I switched tactics. "Who'd you date before Sadie?"

Bobby replied, "Not relevant."

"It's a chance to prove you're a decent man in a relationship."

"I'm sure she'd have nothing but good things to say, but I'm not dragging any of my old friends into the mess I made of my life. It just isn't right."

Chivalrous or hiding something? I asked, "So, how'd Sadie respond when you told her you slept with her cousin?"

He seemed to debate denying it, but finally said, "Frannie was always itching to one-up Sadie. I didn't expect that Bible-thumpin' babe to come after me all horned up. She caught me when I was drunk and took her opportunity. Then the next morning she's all repentant. If I'd have handed her a whip, she would have flagellated herself. Changed my attitude about super saintly women. They need to tell everyone how they should behave to fight their own temptations."

I decided to let him keep rambling.

Bobby stretched his arms and, after a bored yawn, said casually, "Sadie never knew, so no damage done. Can't you see—I had no reason to kill Sadie and she had no reason to think I would. If I was unhappy, I could've just left."

"Did you ever argue about infidelity?"

"No. Sadie trusted me."

That's unfortunate. I revealed, "There's a report from prison that you made the statement, 'I killed my nigger loving fiancée.'" Just saying the word left the taste of ashes in my mouth.

Bobby frowned. "Yeah."

"Did you say that?"

"What difference does it make?"

"You admitted to killing Sadie."

He stared at me. "If I said it, I said it to get protection from the Brotherhood." He raised the sleeve of his t-shirt to reveal a shoulder tattoo of a skull wearing a Nazi helmet. The Iron Cross protruded from the helmet. Wings were attached to the side of the skull and the helmet had ACB written across it. Bobby said, "I did what I had to, to survive. I didn't kill Sadie, but if I had to say something disgusting for protection, I did. It's all about survival in there."

"So, you acknowledge that you stated you killed Sadie."

Bobby's smarmy smile set my teeth on edge. He said, "I'm not going to deny it. I'm not going to admit it, either. I know the law. The threat could be perceived as a hate crime since it includes racial disparagement. I don't need any additional charges. If I said it, I didn't mean it. I will say this, if Ray Fury gets out of prison after what he did to Sadie, I may be talking to my Aryan Cowboy friends."

"Is that a threat?"

He maintained his grin. "Just saying I might need some emotional support."

We both knew he meant it as a threat.

Bobby continued, "I hear Fury has a court date coming up for one of his rape charges. I plan on attending."

He didn't pose a particular threat to Fury in that setting, since he would have to go through a metal detector to get into the courtroom.

"How did Dan Baker manage to find Sadie's body so quickly?"

He corrected, "It wasn't *quickly*. Her work called at three forty-five and said Sadie still hadn't arrived. She was always on time. So, I began searching immediately and called some friends to help. It was hours before Dan spotted my truck. When he searched the area, he found her body."

"And then the two of you had a beer by her corpse."

Bobby snarled, "Bite me! I wanted to go to Sadie and hold her. Dan stood in my way and said I couldn't—the CSI team was coming, and he didn't want me to contaminate the scene. Dan wasn't working when I called him. He had a cooler of beer in the trunk and offered me one to chill out."

I asked, "Why did you wipe your prints off the can?"

Bobby shook his head. "I don't remember doing that. You know as well as I do people often don't leave prints when they hold things."

"Do you still have the phone you were using back then?" I wanted to verify that he was at home when he called Dan.

"Nobody has the same phone eight years later. I called the phone company to try to prove my innocence, but they don't have records from 2013 anymore."

"How'd you get home?"

The question seemed to surprise him. "After I made sure her body was loaded respectfully, Dan gave me a ride. I couldn't leave with her still lying there."

This still didn't make sense when I considered the chronology of events. "If Dan had to give you a ride home, how did you get to the scene? You just told me you began searching immediately." The possibility existed that Bobby drove that truck with Sadie's body to the scene.

His eyebrows lowered and furrowed close together. "I knew a tactical approach would be the most productive. So I started calling friends and coordinated the search with a map at home. As soon as Dan spotted the truck, I had him come and get me."

I told him, "This confuses me. If the body of a woman I loved was discovered, I'd get in my car and head there immediately."

"I just explained my strategic course of action. Nothing I did could have saved Sadie at that point." He huffed, "Beyond that, Sadie took my truck—and I hated driving her little car. I barely fit in it."

His double excuse raised a red flag. People who were honest sometimes had more than one explanation for their behavior. Liars always had two. I considered, "So, did Dan call the CSI team before he picked you up, or after?"

Bobby hesitated, "I don't know. You'd have to ask Dan."

"Dan's dead."

He sadly acknowledged, "Yeah, I heard that."

28

"To be free is not merely to cast off one's chains, but to live in a way that respects and enhances the freedom of others."
—NELSON MANDELA

2021

JON FREDERICK

10:00 A.M., FRIDAY, APRIL 23
HERON DRIVE, CHANHASSEN

The Department of Justice—the Feds—announced they were starting an investigation into the Minneapolis Police Department. U.S. Attorney Merrick Garland stated, "The investigation I am announcing today will assess whether the Minneapolis Police Department engages in a pattern or practice of using excessive force, including during protests. The investigation will also focus on if the department engages in discriminatory practices. Yesterday's verdict in the state criminal trial does not address potentially systemic policing issues in Minneapolis."

It seemed appropriate, with all that had taken place. There had been no violent protests in Minnesota since Derek Chauvin was found guilty of murdering George Floyd, so Zave and I were back to the investigation fulltime.

IT TOOK ME A COUPLE DAYS TO TRACK DOWN Bobby Long's old lover. I spoke to some of his former coworkers before they finally got the name straight. After finding her current address, I had to work out a time when she was available to talk. Isabella Carlson was a registered nurse. She now lived in a neighborhood off Audubon Road, just down from Prince's Paisley Park.

Isabella answered the door in a charcoal turtleneck and jeans, appropriate for today's cool weather. Her thick mahogany hair, dark eyebrows, and pretty face immediately registered that *Bobby has an attraction template.* People often had a specific look to which they were attracted, and Isabella had features similar to Sadie Sullivan's. The difference was Isabella had green eyes and fuller lips, like my wife, Serena.

She lived in a nice, middle-class home, in a gentrified neighborhood. As she welcomed me in, she requested, "Please, call me Bella."

She led me into her living room, and we sat in elegant but comfortable chairs with a coffee table between us.

I began, "I need to ask you about your relationship with Bobby Long. I assume you've heard about his criminal charges and his recent release from prison."

Bella's lips transformed from an inviting smile to a grim line. She glanced away and answered, "Yes." The melancholy that overtook her features immediately indicated her memories weren't all pleasant.

She said, "My first impression of Bobby blew me off my feet. He washed and vacuumed my car on his days off. Fixed things in my house. My friends all said, 'You need to hang on to that one.'"

"What changed?"

Bella's hand quickly came up in a gesture to stop my train of thought. "I want to clarify he was never abusive to me. He never forced anything on me. He never struck me."

"So, his charges had to be a bit of a shock."

She carefully considered her response. "The level of brutality—yes."

I patiently waited for her to continue.

She threaded graceful fingers into her hair, holding it off her face. "Bobby loved me. But I began to take notice that his efforts weren't guileless. He was writing down the mileage and checking if the numbers squared with where I said I'd been. He was rummaging through my mail and personal items to see if I had other love interests."

"That had to be unnerving."

"I am not a perfidious lover. I was just busy with work and didn't always check in with him. But he didn't believe me. When I'd forget to tell him I'd stopped somewhere, we had arguments. One night, when my car wouldn't start, I got a ride home from work. I'd had my fill of it all, so I didn't return his calls. After I went to bed, I received a call from my neighbor that a man was by the sliding doors trying to get into my house. I called the police and they caught him." She sighed, "It was Bobby."

"He wasn't charged."

With a little regret she said, "No. Bobby said he intended to surprise me with a gift. I admitted to the officer at the scene that Bobby was my boyfriend and that was that."

"What was the gift?"

Bella snorted, "Good question. I never did find out. I ended it. I threatened to talk to his supervisor at work if he called me again, but that didn't stop him. When I finally made good on my promise and called his supervisor, and gave him the whole story, Bobby quit with the calls. But even after that, I'd see him driving by my house at night."

"I give you credit for being so assertive. It's the only way to end stalking."

She smiled, "Thank you. It was a relief to see he was engaged to Sadie. I hoped the best for them. He could be accommodating, but it proved to be only a means to an end, rather than from the goodness of his heart. I expected he'd eventually get into trouble, but I didn't expect it to be that serious."

I showed her a picture of Sadie. Bella smiled, "Wow. She could be my sister. Skinnier, but the hair is mine. I even used to have a shirt like that. Do you think he's infatuated with me?"

"It might be a type. You could all look like one of his junior high teachers. Has Bobby contacted you since his release?" If he was obsessed with her, she'd see him somewhere.

"No. I was granted a no-contact order. His supervisor helped me get it and it's still active. If Bobby violates it, he goes back to prison and he knows I'll report him. His old boss said since his charges, there have been other complaints about his past behavior."

"Do you think he could've killed Sadie?"

Bella took her time contemplating the question. "Wasn't someone already convicted for that?"

"Yes, but I'm reopening the murder book. I know you can't say with certainty, but do you truly believe Bobby could have killed Sadie?"

"No. He was never violent to me. Isn't past violence the best predictor of future violence?"

1:15 P.M.
ST. PAUL WESTERN DISTRICT PRECINCT
389 HAMLINE AVENUE NORTH, UNION PARK, ST. PAUL

THE MEETING WITH BELLA LED ME BACK TO Bobby Long's former supervisor at the Western Precinct in St. Paul. Police Chief Wade Watson was in his late fifties—a stocky white man with stubble for hair. He was clean shaven, which was wise, as his jaw appeared considerably larger than the top of his head, creating a pear effect.

I sat on the other side of his desk, telling him, "I've heard there were complaints about Long's behavior as an officer. I need the names."

Wade cracked, "Yeah and I need more demands like I need a hole in my head."

"I'm not going to put a hole in your head, but your list of demands won't diminish if you don't cooperate." I didn't like threatening, but some people needed an impetus to cooperate. I reminded him, "I'm a BCA agent and we have the authority to investigate police departments."

Wade stubbornly complied by getting up and digging through a file cabinet. He pulled a file and, after glancing through it, informed me, "A woman named Merri Rae Collins suggested I talk to some of the women Long's pulled over. I called a few, but none of them had anything disparaging to say. You know how it is, everyone who gets a ticket complains. It doesn't mean the officer did anything wrong."

"But we know Bobby was a bad cop."

Chief Watson agreed, "Yeah, yeah, I know. I'm not going to defend the bastard. If it was up to me, he'd still be in prison."

"Can you give me an address for Merri Collins?"

He checked the file. "She lives in Harding."

I asked, "Do you mean on Harding Street, or the St. Paul Harding school district?"

"Neither. Some town way up north, in the middle of nowhere."

I smiled, "I know where Harding is. You should visit. It's the home of the famous weather rock and Urban Legends. One-time home of the Harding Honeys, Harding Supersonics, the Derelict Convention . . . "

Wade had already turned his back to me and was busy with the next complaint, uninterested in my trivia.

8:00 P.M.
QUEST ROAD, PLATTE LAKE TOWNSHIP, HARDING

MERRI RAE COLLINS WAS LIVING WITH HER lover on Platte Lake, fifteen miles from Harding. Depending on when they bought their home, they might have received a great deal. Platte Lake was only twenty-three feet deep; during one exceptionally cold winter, it froze through completely, leaving dead fish all along the shore. Although it was a disgusting cleanup, lakes could recover from this, and Platte was one that did.

When Merri didn't answer her phone, I gave Serena a call. Her grandparents lived in Harding. She agreed to see what she could find out from them.

Serena called me back, "Merri Collins is living with her lover, Zoey Taylor. Grandma Mae said Merri and Zoey have helped her with the large garden she insists on planting every year. She described them as a kind, loving couple."

I had to smile when I thought of Mae. "You know how unassuming and gracious your grandmother is? Zave tells me Sadie Sullivan was like that."

Serena commented, "Gentle, but so vulnerable." She added, "Grandpa offered to give us a ride out to their place."

I laughed. Her grandfather drove so slow, we used to joke that you could read his tires when he drove by. "If your parents can stay with the kids, I'll pick you up and have you come along for this interview."

"Thank you. If you can get me Zoey's number, I'll call and tell her we're coming . . . "

SERENA'S NUMBER BUZZED AGAIN ON MY PHONE. She said, "Merri's not home. Zoey said she went shopping in St. Cloud and hasn't returned. She suggested we check out the St. Cloud bars. Merri has been struggling since Bobby Long's release from prison. Do you have any idea what happened?"

"No, I don't. Zoey wouldn't give you a clue?"

"She said it wasn't her story to tell."

"Okay. It will take all night to get through the St. Cloud bars. I'll call the St. Cloud police and see if anyone's picked Merri's car up on an LPR." Some of the squad cars had license plate readers mounted on the front, so if you were looking for a car, you could put the plate number in the system, and it would tell you the exact site where the squad car drove by that plate.

Within ten minutes, I received a call back from the St. Cloud P.D. I was informed Merri's car was in the parking lot behind Beaver Island Brewing Company.

10:00 P.M.
BEAVER ISLAND BREWING COMPANY,
216 6TH AVE S, ST CLOUD

THE BEAVER ISLAND BREWERY WAS NAMED after the numerous islands on the Mississippi River—typically fifteen to thirty, depending on water levels. The islands were named the Beaver Islands by Zebulon Pike, in 1805, as the islands were heavily inhabited with beavers when his expedition floated by them down the river. St. Cloud State University owns the majority of the islands.

The taproom's walls and ceiling were overlaid with rustic wood, with aged sliding railroad doors in front of the outdoor patio. I asked the bartender, Holly, if she'd seen Merri, and shared her license photo.

Holly told me, "She had a couple glasses of blueberry ripple and left with some guy just a few minutes ago."

We made our way to the full parking lot behind the taproom.

Serena spotted Merri first and held my arm before we proceeded further.

We could only see her from the shoulders up, over the roof of a car. Merri was leaned back against the car; her eyes were closed, and she had a concentrated, almost pained grimace on her face.

I asked, "Is she having a seizure?"

A sly grin crept across Serena's face. "That's not how I'd describe it."

When we walked around the side of the car, I saw a man on his knees in front of her, with his head completely covered by the front of her dress.

Serena commented, "Well Investigator, how do you want to proceed?"

I yelled, "Bureau of Criminal Apprehension!"

The man hustled to his feet, swiping the back of his hand across his mouth, as Merri smoothed her dress back down.

Merri suggested, "He was just looking for something."

I remarked, "Aren't we all."

Serena gave me a friendly nudge on the shoulder.

I stepped toward them. "I'm not interested in ticketing anyone. We just need to talk to Merri."

Ashamed, Merri rubbed her face with her hands and told the man, "Just go."

He said, "Take out your phone and I'll give you my number."

She responded, "Not interested," and turned her back to him.

I left Serena with Merri and stepped away briefly with the man. He said he'd just met Merri that night. I suggested next time he find a private place and sent him on his way.

When I returned, Merri was asking Serena, "What the hell am I doing?" She paced back and forth. "When I get drunk, I make a man do exactly what I was forced to do. And here's the kicker. I'm not even *attracted* to men."

I remained at a distance and listened.

Serena replied, "It's called a trauma bond. Victims often repeat their victimization until they work through it."

"All these barflies claim to be so good at it, so I challenge them. *Put your money where your mouth is.* Truth be told, nobody can pleasure me like Zoey." Bewildered, she said, "And after, I feel incredible shame and hope like hell I never run into the guy again."

Serena said, "It must be hard on your relationship."

Merri stopped in her tracks. "Zoey pretends like she doesn't know, but she knows. We just don't talk about it."

Serena was gentle with her guidance. "You're pushing her away. Punishing her because she loves you. Eventually, she's going to walk away."

"I expect she'll leave tonight, after she hears this."

Serena studied her for a moment, "Is that what you want?"

"It's exactly what I don't want."

I interrupted, "Is Bobby Long the one who abused you?"

She looked over at me. "What's this about?"

I approached them and told Merri, "I'm investigating the murder of Bobby Long's fiancée. I need to know as much about him as I can." I gestured to her short, chocolate brown hair, "Was your hair longer at the time you were assaulted?"

She thought back. "Yes. Quite a bit longer."

I continued, "Bobby seems to have a fascination with controlling Caucasian women with long brunette hair. Would you be willing to press charges?"

Merri studied her cuticles for a moment before looking back up. "No. He pulled me over for a DWI and I told him I'd do anything to avoid being charged. And I did. My life would be a hundred times better if I would have just taken that damn ticket."

Serena glanced my way. It was her nature to comfort, but I'd told her sometimes it was best to say nothing. Let them keep talking.

Merri started talking again, "I hate myself. I deserve to be alone. Despised."

I interjected, "So, you're abusing Zoey for loving you and living a tribute to Bobby Long."

Her eyes darted toward me. "Screw you."

I didn't let up. "You've made Bobby Long the star of your life, by letting him ruin it for you."

Serena turned toward me, "Jon, that's enough." She went to Merri and put a careful, but comforting arm around her shoulders. Merri's expression was conflicted; she looked like she was leaning into Serena and pushing her away all at once, as if compassion was just too much for her to bear. Serena said, "Let me drive you home. We can talk on the way." She turned to me. "Follow us."

I followed her instruction. I felt badly for Merri, but someone needed to stop sugar-coating her slide to the bottom. I'd been in Zoey's position before and it sucked. Before we were married, Serena took our daughter and moved away, telling me she needed to work through her past trauma. During that time, she became involved with someone else. Okay, my own trauma bond was getting in the way of being a decent person. *Time for me to shut up and refocus.*

Serena called me. "We're going to stop at Gilberto's Taco Shop and eat in the car."

"Am I on speaker?"

"No."

I felt foolish. "Good. Sorry for being an ass."

"We can talk about it later. Are we good, Jon?"

"Yeah. I love you. But I have a big favor to ask of you. Even if Merri doesn't want to prosecute, we need to find out exactly what happened and what was said. You know how profiling is—it's paying attention to repeated patterns. I need to know what Long said and did during the offense. I have this information from all of Fury's reported victims. I need them from Long's."

"Okay. Hang tight. I'll call."

This should've been the simplest case I'd ever worked. Sadie was murdered by one of two people. But based on the evidence I'd seen, so far, I didn't have enough to convict either of them. This was a problem, since Ray had already been convicted for her murder.

11:25 P.M.

GILBERTO'S MEXICAN TACO SHOP
2301 WEST DIVISION ST #100, ST CLOUD

WHEN THEY WERE FINALLY READY FOR ME, I joined Serena and Merri in Merri's car, in the parking lot.

Serena told me, "Long pulled her over for a DWI and offered to let her out of the ticket if she performed oral sex on him. He drove her to some gardens in St. Paul, which were abandoned for the night, and pushed her to her knees."

Merri said, "I was trying to tell him I didn't want to, but then he took me by the back of the head and just started it." She stared vacantly at the traffic driving down Division. "I don't remember exactly what he said, but I do remember hearing the word, *whore*, a lot. Oh yeah, he recited the poem, *Mary, Mary, quite contrary.* Only that pig could make a children's poem gross. I'm sorry, but I can't recall more."

I questioned, "Do you know what that poem's about?"

Merri softly said, "No."

"Abuse of power," I said simply. But the history quickly played in my brain. When King Henry VIII died in England, he left the throne to his fifteen-year-old Protestant niece, Jane. His daughter, Mary, should've been the successor, but Henry had declared that his marriage to her mother was illegitimate. Mary the First had Catholic supporters who reinstated the legitimacy of the marriage, making Mary queen, and she emerged with a vengeance. Mary had Jane and 250 Protestants executed. The *silver bells and cockle shells* refer to torture devices, such as corkscrews and clamps that were applied to genitals. The *pretty maids all in a row* referred to Jane and other Protestant women Mary Tudor put to death. Protestants called Mary the First *Bloody Mary.* She executed her fifteen-year-old cousin, who never wanted to be queen in the first place, even though Jane was only queen for nine days. A priest was sent to convert Jane to Catholicism before her execution. She never converted; instead, she became good friends with the priest. Lady Jane Grey was considered a Protestant martyr. Jane recited Psalm 51 before she was executed, which was a heartfelt request for God's forgiveness. I shook my head—a mental exercise similar to clearing an Etch A Sketch—and dismissed the thoughts.

Oblivious to my mental calisthenics, Serena told Merri, "You're doing great."

I asked, "What was Bobby like, after the assault? What did he say?"

She gave me an agitated glance, and then drifted back to the assault. "It was weird. He almost became human again. He told me he'd drive me home and I'd have to get my car the next day."

I considered, "What did he tell you when he dropped you off?"

"He held my arm and wouldn't let me go until I heard him out. He said my silence wasn't just for my sake—anyone who loved me would hate me if I told them what I did. They'd be nice to my face, but underneath would see me as a sellout whore—*his* words. He reminded me I just blew a stranger when I had someone who loved me at home. And then he finally let go and I ran. And I've been running since. I moved north, started a new relationship, and everything was good until I heard he'd been released."

I said, "I'm sorry you had to go through that. It was his job to help you—to protect and to serve." When she didn't respond, I added, "I'm sorry for my comments in the parking lot."

Teary-eyed, she turned to me with a sad smile, but maintained her silence.

12:45 A.M.
SATURDAY, APRIL 24
PIERZ

SERENA AND I WERE FINALLY HOME FOR the night. She curled up next to me in bed, asking, "What was that all about?"

The time in my car following Serena and Merri had given me a chance to reflect. "I guess I'm still bothered by the fact that you were never sorry for leaving me after Nora was born. I'm grateful we worked it out, but I never felt like you considered what it was like for me."

She raised her head. "Why didn't you say something?"

"Because I don't want to stop enjoying every moment I have with you, to dump my trash."

She laid her cheek against my chest. "But the moments can be even better once you lose the baggage." A brief shiver shook her. Serena kissed me and said, "I am so sorry for leaving with Nora. It scares me now when I realize I could've lost you. But like you, I haven't brought it up because I didn't want to poke at an old wound. Why rehash my shame when you seem to be dealing with it so well?" She studied my eyes. "Why now? What triggered this?"

I sat up. "When you had COVID and were staying with your parents, I had an IT guy clean up our computer. He asked me if I wanted to keep some old personal emails that had been deleted—he thought you sent them to me. I realized that they were your messages to your lover during our separation."

Serena was bothered. "And you read them." After a reluctant nod from me, she said, "I'm so sorry. What stuck?"

She knew me better than I knew myself. "In one letter, you commented about how you wondered if you accepted my marriage proposal because you were pregnant with my child. But *you* proposed to *me*. There are enough legitimate reasons to hate me; you don't have to make crap up."

Serena wrapped an arm across my chest and a leg across my legs and hugged me hard with her body. "What did you do with the emails?"

"I deleted them—as you intended."

She pled, "Can we just start over? It's been all you since we got engaged."

"I've said what I needed to say. I'm done."

"I don't want to turn you into a pistanthrophobic."

"Pistanthrophobia?"

"It's the fear of trusting others. We need to get back to talking like we did before I got COVID."

"I agree."

She added, "It was hard when I had to go stay at my parents'. I have routines with the kids and was worried you were messing them all up. You were letting them sleep in our bed."

"Just on Friday and Saturday nights. We'd watch a Disney movie all snuggled together and I'd carry them to their beds when they finally bit the dust. I'd think of innocent people like Sadie dying so young, and then I couldn't get myself to let the kids fall asleep lonely and scared—knowing Mom's not home. In the U.S., we push to get the kids to sleep in their own beds, but in Europe, their parents let them crawl in with them at night. Studies show there's absolutely no difference between the mental health of both groups when they become adults."

Serena said, "I'm not being mean—just needing balance. I need my time alone with you." She kissed me tenderly and continued, "But I'm learning Nora and Jackson are much more resilient than I give them credit for."

I teased, "I didn't ruin them?"

Serena shifted to her back and said to the ceiling, "No. I hate to admit it, but in some ways, they're a little more responsible."

I leaned over her soft, warm body. "Can we stop talking? It's been a long week."

She said, "Honey, sometimes we need to talk, even when we're tired." She teased, "It's not all fun and games."

I was afraid she'd say that. "I was just looking for fun. I'm fine with skipping the games . . . "

29

"Every day that we wake up is a good day. Every breath that we take is filled with hope for a better day. Every word that we speak is a chance to change what is bad into something good."
—WALTER MOSELY

2021

XAVIER "ZAVE' WILLIAMS

10:00 A.M., SATURDAY, APRIL 24
SAMMY'S AVENUE EATERY,
1101 WEST BROADWAY AVENUE, #1
COLUMBIA PARK NEIGHBORHOOD, MINNEAPOLIS

I called Marita again, just as she prophesized, but it was simply to identify Danny's married lover. Evan White agreed to meet me at Sammy's where we could both enjoy some java.

Evan was a white-collar guy who tried to carry off a blue-collar look. He wore a commercially faded chambray shirt and jeans, but the Escalade he parked outside gave him away. I needed to get an idea if Evan's husband could have killed Danny in a jealous rage.

My first question was, "Do you deer hunt?"

A little taken aback, he responded, "I do."

"What kind of a rifle do you use?"

"A Remington eight-seventy. It's better for small game, but I've had good success hunting deer with it. I need to be a little closer, but that's part of the challenge. If I wanted to blow up deer from five hundred yards away, I'd get a rocket launcher."

"What does your husband use?"

Evan chuckled, "Mac isn't an outdoorsman. He's mixed race and says, 'There's no way in hell I'm heading to the woods with a bunch of white guys with rifles.' I don't believe he's ever even fired a gun."

"Was Mac aware you and Danny were having an affair?"

"Danny and I weren't having an affair."

I let my head tilt to the side and gave him my *don't bullshit me* stare. "Come on, I have witnesses."

He quickly explained, "Look, it's not like that. Mac and I were married, but we'd been separated for a year when I met Danny. Mac and I hadn't spoken for over a year when Danny died."

This made sense to me. I didn't see Danny as a man who'd try to break up a marriage. "Do you have any idea who would've killed him?"

Evan shook his head. "No. I thought it was a gang shooting."

"I don't know what it was. We've worked every angle with the Disciples for three years and we have nothing. I'm starting to wonder if it was something else. What did Danny say about Bobby Long?"

Evan sat back. "He didn't like talking about Bobby. The most I could get out of him was that Long was going to cost him his job, someday." He swirled the stirring stick in his coffee. "Honestly, I didn't mind that he was working with Bobby—no reason to be jealous. I was a *little* envious when he began working with you, though."

That was absurd, but love was indeed ridiculous. I had to ask once more, "Can you think of *anyone* he worked with, or arrested, or had a relationship with, who went off the rails on him?"

"No. Can you?"

"No. Everybody at work loved him."

Evan added, "Only because he hadn't come out."

"I'll admit, I work with some rednecks, but none who would hunt him down over it. Whoever killed Danny called him to that house and shot him once he arrived. The shooter wanted Danny dead." If it hadn't been a premeditated murder, someone would have admitted calling him to that house.

After a thoughtful silence, Evan said, "Sorry, but I can't think of anyone. Unless you'd consider—" he stopped himself. "No—no one."

I had to know. "Who are you thinking about?"

"There was this girl named Marita who was always calling Danny. We were out at the lake one night and Danny was hinting for her to leave, but she wasn't getting it. She suggested we all skinny dip and then wanted to join us. It was just weird. But you know how Danny was. He didn't want her to feel bad, so he suggested we go along with it . . . "

1:30 P.M.
ALLOY BREWING COMPANY, 2700 COON RAPIDS
BOULEVARD NORTHWEST COON RAPIDS

I HAD TO SPEAK TO MARITA. WHEN I CALLED, she insisted I have a drink with her. I agreed to meet her at Alloy Brewing, which was one of my favorite taprooms near Minneapolis. Coon Rapids was a suburb just north of the city. I ordered Erik's Red Runner Irish ale, while Marita insisted on the Sexy Green Tractor IPA.

We found a table away from customers so we could talk.

Marita wore a fitted, colorful slim tee with a slight sheen and midnight blue jeans. There was something dangerous about her opposing eye colors. The green seemed to suggest *go for it,* while the blue one was harder to read. I never understood exactly what lay beneath her exotic beauty. Was it the sad blues, or the blue biblical reference to peace?

Marita asked me, "What is your urgent need, Zave?"

"I spoke to Evan. He thought that you had stronger feelings for Danny than you let on, and maybe were a little hurt when he didn't return your affection."

She started laughing in her deep, throaty way. "There's nothing more threatening to a gay relationship than the possibility of a straight lover."

I quietly reminded her, "You did have sex with him."

With a flash of her eyes, she dismissed this. "Danny was my best friend. And he was my connection to you." She reached across the table and took my hand. "I'm not looking to rein you in. You and I are the same. What Lachelle detests about you, I like. You're wise enough to enjoy the moment, knowing none of us are guaranteed tomorrow."

"But what Lachelle detests about me, I don't like either. My relationships don't make me happy. I wouldn't want to be with someone like me."

"Must be hard—hating yourself."

I didn't know how to respond. It wasn't that I hated myself. I just wasn't happy.

She asked, "Are you ever afraid of dying?"

"Yeah." I was afraid I was going to die just as I had lived. All alone—with a million acquaintances and no friends. "Sometimes I feel like I'm one wrong turn away from getting shot to death by someone I don't even know—like so many of us have died this year in Minneapolis. Some jackass will be out there spraying bullets because of his fragile ego and I'll get caught in the crossfire."

She rubbed my hand and smiled. "Zave, we have this wink in time—we're both single—both lonely—both yearning for affection."

I pulled my hand back and thought out loud. "You had no reason to kill Danny."

Marita's piercing eyes threw an electrical storm my way—I had to fight the urge to duck. She spat, "*That's* why you asked to meet me?" She pushed her beer away, sloshing golden liquid onto the tabletop, stood up, and blew out of there so fast, napkins from nearby tables fluttered to the floor in her wake.

9:30 P.M.

WEST RIVER ROAD, HAWTHORNE NEIGHBORHOOD,
MINNEAPOLIS

LAUREN AND I WERE SITTING ON THE COUCH and had just finished the first episode of *Queen Sugar* on Hulu. She was casually dressed, in a teal t-shirt and beat-up jeans. The tee was snug against her body and was stenciled with the words, "Be Kind." I couldn't stop myself from reading it. I wouldn't have had to look to know it, but it was an added benefit. We matched perfectly as I was a t-shirt and jeans man at home. Lauren had piled her hair into a glorious mess on top of her head that I thought was sexy as hell. Her peacock feather earrings suited her—the Christian symbol of purity.

I said, "Tell me a little more about your hometown of Hillman."

She had a knockout smile. "It's a booming metropolis. The population increased by one- third from 2000 to 2010."

I teased, "From two to three."

"Tenfold. From twenty-nine to thirty-eight."

"I can't say I've been through Hillman."

Lauren grinned, "Of course you've never been *through* Hillman. It's not on the way to anywhere. Hillman is a desti-nation. You have to drive into Hillman, and then back out. Did you know the Hillman Bar was once a three-room school? It now has outdoor seating."

"Does it have indoor seating?"

"Don't imply we're hicks. That's what we do. We used to have a pickle factory. We still have a bartender named Bart."

Lauren's smile suggested something great was always just a second away. Her natural beauty and easy manner felt so refreshingly honest.

I told her, "Speaking of northern Minnesota, the St. Cloud police bought a house right in the middle of a Somali neighborhood."

She kiddingly interrupted. "Umm—St. Cloud is only northern Minnesota for people from the Twin Cities. It's in the southern half of the state."

"I stand corrected," I made a mock bow of apology. "Anyway, the police have book and pizza nights with the kids in the area. The Somali neighborhood knows all the officers by their first names. This is what we need in Minneapolis."

"You're getting a little excited," she observed with hint of a grin.

"I *am*. There are solutions to the unrest. We just need to be creative. Maybe you could do a drawing night."

Her smile widened. "Now *I'm* getting a little excited."

I put my arm around her, and she turned her face to mine.

Our lips were so close it was all I could do to hesitate. I asked, "Is it okay if I kiss you?"

The words barely left my lips when she kissed me. She pulled me close and our bodies gravitated together.

And then my phone rang.

She pulled away and I looked at the time on the phone. I blew out a long breath. "Cheyenne's on break. Worst possible outcome is the call lasts fifteen minutes."

Lauren sighed, "Okay."

I picked up the phone and began pacing.

CHEYENNE SPOKE FOR THE ENTIRE FIFTEEN minutes of her break before I was able to escape. I returned to Lauren on the couch. "Where were we?"

We kissed again, although she seemed a little more hesitant.

And then there was a knock on my door.

Lauren stopped kissing me and I stood up to answer it. I was hoping it wasn't Jon with more work for me tonight. Instead, it was worse.

When I opened the door Marita marched in. "Who the hell are you, to accuse me of killing Danny? You never appreciated what a good friend he was. I *loved* Danny! He was my best friend."

I pointed to Lauren, "Marita. I have company."

She spat, "I don't give a damn if sister golden hair has to hear this."

Lauren stood up and said, "I was just leaving."

I turned to her, "Please, just wait." I needed to get Marita to leave. I was on the verge of losing someone I longed for. I turned back to Marita, "Look, I'm sorry. I shouldn't have accused you. I'm just trying to sort this all out."

Marita said, "I never would have harmed a hair on Danny's head. He was the only one who truly understood me—appreciated me."

"Okay—okay. I'm convinced. I'm sorry." *Now please, leave.*

Tearful, she leaned into me for a hug, and I awkwardly patted her on the back.

I quickly released her and said, "I'm sorry. Are we good?"

She nodded and glanced over at Lauren, who was ready to slip out the door.

I guided Marita to the door. "Lauren and I need to be alone."

Mercifully, Marita left with no more drama; Lauren was about to follow suit.

I pleaded, "Please, Lauren. Stay."

She sighed sadly, searching my eyes. "Boundaries, Zave. I can't do this. I won't *date* this way anymore."

"I'm sorry about Marita. Everything should calm down when Cheyenne's trial is over."

Disheartened, she said, "Don't call me until then." On that note, she took off.

I don't know how long I stood there staring after her.

30

"She tried."
—Sister Thea Bowman

2021

CHEYENNE SCHMIDT

3:30 P.M., THURSDAY, MAY 6
HENNEPIN COUNTY GOVERNMENT CENTER, 300 SOUTH
6TH STREET DOWNTOWN WEST, MINNEAPOLIS

On the advice of the prosecutor, Paul Tierney, I wore a conservative, medium length black skirt, black suit jacket, and ivory blouse. My hair was straightened and secured in a sleek knot at the back of my head, to make me look as classy and un-stripper-like as possible. On Zave's advice, I didn't wear makeup.

My testimony with the prosecutor went smooth. As instructed, my answers were short and to the point in my explanation of Fury's attack on me. But now, I had to face the very part I'd been dreading. There was a good-looking man I'd met at the club sitting behind the defense table. I wasn't sure why he was here. I hadn't told Zave about him, because I didn't want him to see me as that kind of person.

The Honorable Dora Morales was presiding over my case. She was in her sixties and Zave said she was good. *I guess we'll see.*

Margaret Brown took her time as she sauntered toward me, prolonging my misery as much as she possibly could. She was a scrawny thing somewhere north of 50. Margaret held her knobby, creased hands in front of her chest with her fingers entwined and her elbows jutting out to the sides like wings. Her nose was narrow and beak-like, completing the resemblance to a chicken. She finally asked, "Cheyenne, what do you do for a living?"

I cleared my throat and said, "I work at a gentleman's club."

Margaret sneered, "*Gentlemen*, indeed. So, what exactly do you do there? Are you an accountant, or a custodian?"

"I dance."

"By yourself?"

I reminded myself of Zave's advice. Be as short as possible with your answers. Everything I needed to say was said with the prosecutor. I nodded, "Yes. Sometimes with other women."

"They call you Candy at the strip club, right?"

"Yes."

"Why is that? Wouldn't *Shy Ann* be the obvious moniker? But you're not shy, are you?"

The prosecutor stood. "Objection. Irrelevant."

Margaret smiled over her shoulder at Tierney. "I'll withdraw the question." Turning back to me, she asked, "Candy, what do you wear when you dance?"

I didn't answer.

Margaret repeated, "What do you wear when you dance?"

"Different outfits."

"Are you topless at times, when you dance, Candy?"

I didn't answer. Zave advised me not to answer to *Candy*. He said she was going to try to implant in the minds of the jury I was *just a stripper*, not a person worthy of respect.

I took some pride in the fact that Margaret's feathers were a little ruffled by my silence. After trying to stare me down and intimidate me, she turned to the judge, "Do I have permission to treat this woman as a hostile witness since she's refusing to answer my questions?"

I interjected, "My name is Cheyenne. You addressed the question to *Candy*. Candy is a name I go by during a performance, like a character in a movie."

The judge smiled. "She has a point. Call her by her name and I have a feeling she'll answer."

Margaret turned to me, emphasizing my name in two separate words. "Okay *Shy Ann*. Is it true that sometimes, when you dance, you are wearing little more than a two-inch swatch of fabric covering your vulva?"

I wanted to crawl into a hole, but told myself, *I can do this.* "It's a little more than that, but it isn't much."

In the galley, Zave gave me a nod of approval. He had advised me to be honest. Trying to make it sound better than it was got witnesses into trouble.

Margaret turned her head, jerking it around like she was pecking for feed. "Do you sometimes do private dances with men in a back room?"

I squirmed in my seat. "Yes."

"And what happens during those dances?"

Tierney stood up. "Objection. Irrelevant."

Margaret turned to the judge. "My client is accused of making sexual advances on this woman. I think it's relevant to establish where she draws the line."

The judge pondered for a minute. Judge Dora's silence was unnerving. Deep in thought, she tapped her lips with her forefinger, and then finally ruled, "Sustained. I don't feel it's been established that the attack had anything to do with her work."

I took a deep breath and, with a sigh of relief thought, *Thank you Dora!*

Margaret said, "Okay. Can I ask questions about her attitude toward men?"

The judge nodded.

And just like that, Margaret went back to my work.

She asked, "Do you love the men you strip for?"

"No."

"Are there some you don't even like?"

I didn't want to answer, but finally said, "Yes."

"Have you ever given a lap dance to someone you couldn't stand?"

"Yes—I needed the money."

Margaret clucked, "Like you needed money and help when you met Ray Fury."

Tierney shouted, "Objection! The defense attorney is testifying."

The judge agreed. "Sustained."

Margaret glared at me with angry, beady eyes. "I'm not going to ask you to go through your entire sexual history—I'm not sure we'd have time for that."

Tierney stood again. "Objection. She's still testifying."

The judge stated a little more firmly, "Sus*tained.*"

Unfettered, Margaret continued pecking, "How many men have you had sex with, in the last year?"

"Five." I realized I had answered before Paul had time to object.

Margaret looked confused, "Didn't you just say you did lap dances in the back room?"

"Yes."

She smiled. "And is it safe to say that men achieve an orgasm, at times, when you're grinding your derriere into their crotches?"

The Honorable Judge Morales warned Margaret, "Careful with the language."

I answered, "Yes."

"And you have only had five of those?"

"No."

Margaret challenged, "You just committed perjury."

I swallowed hard and tried to explain, "No—I don't count those as sex."

She laughed out loud. "How convenient. You see, *Shy Ann*, I think *most* of the world would consider rubbing your naked body against a man until he achieves orgasm, sex. By this definition, how many men have you had sex within the last year?"

I thought, *at least a couple a week.* I answered, "About a hundred."

She prompted, "But it could be more."

"It could be."

"So, Candy, you initially said five sexual partners and now you're saying the truth is you've had sex with more than one hundred men." She grimaced theatrically. "When you have sex with so many men, so often, how do you even know if someone is forcing sex?"

It suddenly occurred to me it wasn't that many. I'd forgot about getting shut down for COVID, but I didn't get a chance to explain.

Margaret continued to hammer away at me. "Are you a prostitute?"

I had to clear my throat before I bitterly reminded her, "My name is Cheyenne. And I'm not a prostitute."

"So, what do you consider yourself?"

"A professional dancer."

Margaret crowed, "That's aggressive dancing when it leads to hundreds of orgasms."

The prosecutor stood. "Objection."

Judge Morales slammed the gavel. "Sustained." There was an angry assertiveness in her tone when she quietly said, "You're trying my patience, Margaret."

Margaret apologized to the judge. "I'm sorry. I have evidence the witness is lying, which draws all of her testimony into doubt." She turned back to me and repeated, "Are you a prostitute?"

"No, I'm not. *How many times do I have to say it?* I added, "I don't have sex with the men I dance for at the club."

Margaret stated, "But if you did have intercourse with them, you would count them among the men with whom you'd had intercourse, in the past year—by your definition of sex, correct?"

"Of course."

"Could you name the men with whom you've had intercourse, by your definition, in the last year?"

Tierney stood up. "Objection."

The judge immediately responded, "Sustained."

Margaret said, "I'll ask this another way. Was Randy Smith one of the five men with whom you had sex, by your definition of sex, last year?"

"I don't even know a Randy Smith."

She walked over to the handsome man behind the defense table. "Let me refresh your memory. *This* is Randy Smith. Did you meet him at the club two weeks ago?"

Shit! I was in trouble. He had set me up. I'm so stupid! I forced out, "Yes."

"Did he pay you five hundred dollars for sexual intercourse?"

I could see Paul Tierney was upset with me even before I answered. I admitted, "He gave me five hundred dollars to cover my rent. Since the rape, I haven't been doing well."

Margaret demanded, "Did you have sex with him?"

"Yes."

She leaned into me. "Candy, you just lied to us."

I put my head down and didn't respond.

Margaret turned and shook her head in front of the jury, as if to say, *poor, poor pitiful Cheyenne.* "Candy, what do you think the five hundred dollars was for?"

"Rent."

The bantam hen had the nerve to start laughing.

I remained silent. I wasn't answering to Candy. I was pissed at myself that I'd just done it, but I was so flustered. Her antics were so preplanned it was sickening. I wanted to scream at the jury, *Don't you see what she's doing? She's blaming me for being raped!*

Margaret grinned. "And after he gave you the money, you had sex with him."

All smart-alecky, I remarked, "I was very appreciative."

When I looked into the galley, I saw Zave disagreeably shaking his head. His silent message was *tone it down.*

Margaret laughed in my face. "I bet you were, Candy. That's a lot of dollars down the G-string."

Judge Morales stared daggers at Margaret, as she directed, "Ask a question or be done."

Margaret was careful not to irritate the judge further. She politely asked, "How long have you been employed as a stripper?"

"Eight years."

"And there are nights you lose money as a stripper, since you need to pay for the staff, correct?"

"Yeah."

"It's estimated that, when it comes down to the hours invested, the average stripper makes about twenty dollars an hour and it appears your situation isn't any better than that. According to your tax records you've never made forty thousand a year. Is that accurate?"

"Yeah."

As if a sudden insight occurred, Margaret glanced back at me, "Shy Ann, were you struggling financially and emotionally at the time you parked with Mr. Fury?"

"I was just out of high school. I was still learning to manage my money."

"And *Shy Ann*," the pause after *Shy* was extra-long this time, "did people offer to help you after you reported Mr. Fury may have kissed your breast?"

Zave told me to be honest, so I said, "My name is Cheyenne—one word—and the answer is yes." I should've added that I still struggled financially and emotionally, even more now.

I was about to say this when the hen powered on. "And you would do just about anything for some attention. Take your clothes off. Grind a man to orgasm. Maybe accuse someone of trying to force sex on you."

I looked to the prosecutor to object. Even Judge Morales appeared to be anticipating an objection, but it never came. It felt like Paul was punishing me for not being completely honest with him. I was on my own, now. I quietly said, "I don't lie."

Margaret emphatically pointed out, "You said you were not a prostitute, yet you took money for sex. Isn't that the basic definition of a prostitute?"

I tried to stop my shaking hands by clasping them. I cleared my throat again and answered. "I didn't know his name was Randy Smith. He called himself Bo." I wasn't going to fold and give in to Margaret and Ray. I decided to tell it exactly how I rationalized it. "Mr. Smith gave me five hundred dollars to help me with my rent and I had intercourse with him that night. Two separate things. Sometimes when people are nice to me, I feel affectionate toward them." Honestly, I knew sex was implied, but it wasn't explicitly stated. If Margaret wanted to play games with words, I could do that, too.

She cackled at me again and I was fighting the urge to get up and push her down. "Isn't that basically what all prostitution is—quid pro quo—one thing in exchange for another."

She was getting to me. I remarked, "There was no guarantee. If your husband gives you money and says, 'Get yourself something nice,' and you later have sex with him—are *you* a prostitute?"

Margaret's smile darkened. "I get to ask the questions, Candy."

I quickly added, "I'm not a prostitute and I'm not familiar

with what prostitutes do, so I can't answer your question." Even I realized my tone had reached full-on smartass. In the galley, I saw Zave patting his hand down, signaling me again to get it together. I took a deep breath and blew it out slowly.

Margaret spoke at the jury when she stated, "You initially said you didn't have intercourse with men you danced for at the club. Now you're admitting you had sex with Randy, for whom you danced at the club."

"I didn't dance for Randy." I remembered how persistent he was in wanting to help me. I was so stupid.

Margaret clarified, "You were dancing, Randy gave you five hundred dollars, and then you had sex with him in the club—correct?"

"No. Randy approached me during break and asked what was bothering me. I shared that I was worried I couldn't cover my rent. He offered to help. We got together later. We didn't have sex in the club." We had sex in the back of his Tahoe in the parking lot.

Margaret shook her head in disbelief.

Her assistant turned and handed Randy a notepad and a pen. Randy scribbled something on it and handed it back. The assistant then shook her head, *no*, to Margaret.

Margaret decided to move on. "And you drove Ray Fury behind the back of closed store and parked in the dark. What did you think was going to happen?"

I tried to get a grip. "He asked me to drop him off there."

"But there was no one there who can verify your story, is there?"

I reluctantly agreed, "There was no one there when we pulled in."

"This wasn't really a rape, was it? There was no penetration. You're basically accusing him of kissing your breast."

"There was no penetration because I *escaped*. He slammed my head against the steering wheel."

In her most innocent tone, Margaret chided, "Where are the bruises?" She held up a picture of my face taken at the hospital.

I explained, "The steering wheel is padded. It stunned me and the bruising didn't show until a couple days after."

Not one to give up, she asked, "Did you need help at that time in your life, when you and Ray," she cleared her throat, "parked behind a dark, closed store?"

"Yes."

"Have you received help?"

"Yes."

Margaret held up a picture of my legs taken at the hospital on the night of the assault. They were smooth and unscathed. She said, "Nice legs. You claimed that Ray dragged you on the tar. Where are the scrape marks?"

"I was wearing thick sweats."

"I thought you said he pulled your pants down."

I tried to explain, "Not past my knees." My sweatpants were bunched up, so my knees were cushioned.

Margaret smiled, "We don't really have any evidence that you were assaulted, do we?"

I softly muttered, "My word."

"What?"

"I said—my *word*."

Margaret ended with, "Well I'm afraid *your* word isn't good enough." Disgusted, she dismissed me with a wave of her hand, as she announced, "I'm done with you."

Paul Tierney was offered a chance for rebuttal, but he declined. He obviously felt I'd done enough damage.

Completely humiliated, I stepped down and sat back at the table with the prosecutor. I felt so pathetic. Paul wrote, *Perfect*, on the notepad in front of me. I knew he was pissed with the way I messed up; I didn't need his sarcasm. Paul set a folded note on the table in front of me. He then stood up as Margaret objected to his final witness.

Margaret was telling the judge, "This last witness is ridiculous. The prosecutor subpoenaed someone who used to work in the public defender's office with me. This has no purpose other than to be gamey."

Paul said, "She is a witness, as listed."

Margaret argued, "A witness of what?"

Paul smiled, "You will soon find out."

Judge Morales patiently told Margaret, "You were granted some leeway in your cross-examination. I think it's only fair I grant the prosecution the same."

Paul told the judge, "Thank you your honor, but it won't be necessary."

I carefully unfolded the note in front of me. It read, *Happy Cinco de Mayo! This witness is my gift to you! Zave*

A petite, white-haired African American woman in her seventies was sworn in. I had no idea what she was going to mean to my case.

After she stated her name was Bonnie Carter, for the record, Paul Tierney asked, "Could you please explain what you witnessed on August 28, 2013, at 9:15p.m.?"

Bonnie calmly replied, "I was driving west on Broadway in the Hawthorne part of Minneapolis."

Now brooding, Margaret's jaw dropped.

Bonnie continued, "I turned north on Fourth Street when I heard a woman scream. I pulled behind the empty business and turned toward a car in the parking lot with the door open. A woman was crawling away—trying to escape—from a large man who was after her."

Holy crap! This was the woman who interrupted Fury's assault on me.

"Were you able to identify them?"

"The woman was white, and the man was black. It was dark, but my headlights were on them."

Paul suggested, "Please continue."

"The woman was trying to get away from him, but he grabbed her by the collar and began dragging her on the tar—like he was dragging out the garbage. They both turned toward my headlights, and he took off. That's her," she pointed to me, "right there. The white girl started running toward my car and then I left."

Tierney questioned, "Why?"

Bonnie waved a hand as if it should be obvious. "I was afraid he was going to keep coming after her. What's a seventy-eight-year-old woman with a bad hip and a heart condition going to do? *Look* at him." She pointed to Fury. "One punch from him and I'm dust. I called nine-one-one. The dispatcher said they had a squad on Broadway and, before I was out of the area, I saw flashing lights headed toward the scene . . . "

I BREATHED A SIGH OF RELIEF. PAUL HAD told me that one collaborating witness would make all the difference. Zave had found one. I looked back at my handsome superhero. The name Xavier means a *bright and splendid friend*. While the hearing wasn't technically over, for all practical purposes, it was. The damage done by Bonnie's collaborating testimony against Ray Fury couldn't be undone—not even by the marvelous Margaret Brown. Everyone knew the prosecution had won.

When the judge dismissed us for the day, Zave came right to me and gave me a brief, but tight hug. I could have just kept hanging on.

Prosecutor Tierney smiled, and said, "Your testimony was the perfect setup." He explained, "We had to send a disclosure of our witnesses to the defense. I decided to take advantage of the fact that Bonnie once worked with Margaret and they didn't get along. I included a large amount of information that referenced a feud the two of them once had in the office. Beneath that information was our primary reason for subpoenaing Bonnie."

Zave added, "Paul said once Margaret saw how trivial her arguments were with Bonnie, she would never read through it all. It was clear she hadn't."

Paul smiled and turned to shake hands.

I hugged Zave once again and, this time, clung to him. "I am so glad that's over. Let's get out of here. Take me somewhere to celebrate."

He backed away, "I can't."

Confused, I asked, "What do you mean? It's over, now. You're no longer working with me, so that's okay. I quit my job. It's wide open for us." I tugged his arm, "Come *on.*"

Zave wasn't budging. "Cheyenne—you're great. I just can't."

I pleaded, "Please. Are you trying to tell me, in all those late-night calls, you were just *pretending* to care?"

He seemed so cold. "No. I care about you, Cheyenne. You're wonderful and kind. It's just not right for me."

"You're no different than Margaret."

Zave said, "I wanted you to have the justice you deserved. And now you're going to finally get it. I served my purpose and now I'm off to the next case."

He was just one more man using me. Embarrassed, I ran out of the courtroom and kept running until I was on the steps in front of the courthouse crying.

After a few minutes, I heard a man saying, "You did a terrific job in there. Fury deserves to be punished for what he did to you and to so many other women. What you just did took guts and I respect that. I know all of this had to mess with your head, but is there anything I can do? How about if we just go across the street and I'll buy you a sandwich. Nothing worse than being miserable on an empty stomach."

I looked up at the generous man. His pale skin nearly glowed—talk about a *white knight.* "Thank you." I reached my hand out and he helped me up.

"My name is Bobby . . ."

31

*"You'll find in life when you are free, your
true creativity, your true self, comes out."*
—TINA TURNER

2021

LAUREN HERALD

8:30 A.M., WEDNESDAY, MAY 12
HENNEPIN COUNTY GOVERNMENT CENTER
300 SOUTH SIXTH STREET,
DOWNTOWN WEST, MINNEAPOLIS

I sat in the Hennepin County Courthouse listening to the
testimony in Ray Fury's appeal. Sean Reynolds asked me
to attend and report my findings to Jon and Zave. He said
they'd pass the information on to Jada Anderson. It was my
preference not to deal with Jada face-to-face. I'd heard she
could be difficult.

Fury was escorted into the courtroom in a shiny gray,
sharkskin suit. As he entered, his eyes searched the galley and
immediately fixed on mine. By his knowing look, it was clear
he knew that I was the person who identified him. Even after
he sat at the defense table, he turned and looked straight at me
with an expression that gave me the shivers.

I wasn't about to give him the satisfaction of knowing he intimidated me, so I stared right back just long enough to say *I'm no coward*, and then casually dug in my purse like I had more important things to do. In truth, he scared the hell out of me.

Finally, the judge entered and Fury's attorney, Margaret Brown, nudged him and directed his gaze to the front.

9:00 A.M.

DR. AMAYA HO WAS ON THE STAND LOOKING as professional as usual, in navy suit jacket and slacks, with a white shirt buttoned to the very top. The very best experts, like Amaya, made their testimony the focus of the court rather than their clothing.

Margaret asked, as she handed Dr. Ho a document, "Is this your report?"

Amaya paged through it and replied, "Yes."

Margaret stated to the judge, "Let the Court note that this was accepted as evidence document number twelve." She turned to Amaya. "You're very familiar with testifying in court. According to our records, you are used by the Hennepin County prosecutor more than any other medical examiner in the state. Does that sound accurate?"

"I testify for the prosecution frequently. I am not familiar with your data."

Margaret continued, "Do you think it's odd that they didn't use your report when they prosecuted Ray Fury?"

"I examine the evidence and turn in a report. Attorneys decide what is used for court. I have confidence in my reports; I am not insulted if they don't use my work."

I liked Amaya, but I wasn't sure I believed her.

Margaret pried, "Your report suggests Sadie Sullivan was never raped."

Amaya responded coolly, "I specifically stated that I could not prove with certainty that Ms. Sullivan had been raped."

"But there are many cases where you've testified *with certainty*," Margaret emphasized, "that someone had been raped, correct?"

"Yes."

"Do you understand the implications of your report? If Mr. Fury didn't rape Sadie, he had no reason to kill her."

Amaya pointed out, "My task is to report on the physical evidence in a case. I spend no time examining motivation. It is not my role."

"Did the police look into any other suspects than Mr. Fury?"

"I cannot answer that question. You need to ask the police. The DNA profile was placed into CODIS, but there was no match at the time."

Margaret directed the Court, "But CODIS only looks for criminals and you're saying Sadie may have been involved in a consenting sexual relationship, correct?"

Amaya responded, "Yes."

"Did an investigator recently ask you to test DNA to see if Sadie's brother, Liam, was the biological father of Sadie's daughter?"

Amaya's composure slipped briefly in surprise, which on her looked like a quick widening of the eyes and a flutter of her lashes, but I wasn't sure anyone else would have noticed. She replied, "Yes. Investigator Xavier Williams asked me to run the test, which demonstrated—"

Margaret cut her off. "You've already answered the question."

Prosecutor Tierney immediately rose to his feet. "Objection. Let the witness answer the question."

Judge intervened and directed Dr. Ho, "You are allowed to finish answering the question."

Amaya said, "The DNA test indicated that Liam Sullivan was not the father of Sadie's child. The father is the man Sadie Sullivan identified eight years ago."

In relentless pursuit of something that would help her case, Margaret asked, "Were you asked to perform a DNA test on the belt used to murder Sadie Sullivan, back when Mr. Fury was convicted for this offense?"

"No."

"Don't you think it's odd that you weren't asked to test the murder weapon?"

Amaya had regained her stoic composure. "I test what is sent to me. It would be a waste of time for me to consider the purpose of the testing. So no, I did not consider it odd. I didn't even consider it."

"Did an investigator recently ask you to test for DNA on the belt that was used to strangle Ms. Sullivan?"

"Yes. BCA Investigator Jon Frederick made this request."

"Did you find any DNA on the belt?"

"No."

Margaret scratched her head, feigning confusion. "The prosecutor's theory is that Mr. Fury raped Sadie, leaving DNA on her. Doesn't it seem bizarre that an out-of-control rapist wouldn't leave DNA on the very belt with which he strangled her?"

"No, I would not say bizarre. He could have worn gloves to strangle her." Dr. Ho hesitated a beat and then dropped a bombshell. "There were traces of soap on the belt."

Margaret raised her hands as if in shock. "Are you kidding me? Isn't it even more preposterous that Mr. Fury would rape Ms. Sullivan and leave DNA, and then go wash the belt?"

In her typical, unemotional manner, Amaya said, "No. I am not kidding you. As for the rest, I can only tell you what the forensic evidence indicates. As I stated earlier, exploring why people do what they do is not my role."

10:30 A.M.

FRANNIE SULLIVAN WAS UP NEXT. SHE NERVOUSLY asked the Bailiff, "Should I sit there?" pointing to the only empty seat in the front of the courtroom, before taking the stand. Margaret tried to calm her. "I'm going to make this quick and painless for you. Did you see Ray Fury dining with your cousin, Sadie Sullivan, just three days before she was murdered?"

Frannie stated, "Yes, I believe so."

Margaret clarified, "You couldn't recognize your cousin?"

"It was Sadie—talking to a black man—I'm pretty sure was Ray."

Margaret reminded her, "I believe the exact word you used, when we spoke, was *flirting*, correct?" She picked up her notebook and read, 'Sadie was flirting with Ray. They held hands and even kissed.'"

Frannie nervously glanced over at Sadie's sisters, and then quickly looked back at Margaret. "Yes, that's all true."

Margaret commented, "And this was at Pizza Lucé."

Frannie corrected, "I had the restaurant wrong. It was Lu's Sandwiches."

Margaret told her, "The restaurant isn't really significant, as long as you're clear it was Sadie and Ray."

"It was Sadie and a black man I thought was Ray . . ."

5:30 P.M.

AFTER I WAS DONE REPORTING TO SEAN, I called Zave and told him, "Ray Fury is now a free man." I explained, "They introduced in court a statement from Piper Perry saying she believed Bobby Long would have killed her if she hadn't complied. That opened the door to reasonable doubt on Fury's conviction. Dr. Ho's report, combined with Frannie's subsequent testimony, freed him. Frannie swore she saw Sadie eating and flirting with a black man. If Fury didn't rape Sadie, he had no reason to kill her."

Zave asked, "'A *black man* or Ray Fury?'"

"She said a black man she *thought* was Ray. It was just three days before Sadie was murdered. Frannie amended her original statement, clarifying that the restaurant wasn't Pizza Lucé—it was Lu's Sandwiches."

Zave quickly growled, "That son of a *bitch.*" He quickly apologized, "I'm sorry for swearing, Lauren. *I* was the man who ate with Sadie at Lu's Sandwiches. Fury just got away with murder!"

I immediately had more questions, but this wasn't the time. I asked, "Did you know the belt that was used to strangle Sadie had been washed?"

"We received that report this morning. I don't know what to think about that."

"And there's your reasonable doubt. Ray might've gotten a *get out of jail free* card, today."

Zave said, "He still has sentencing for the rape conviction."

"It was all settled in court today. He won't serve any more prison time unless a new charge comes up. Fury's attorney threatened that he would sue the city for false imprisonment, if he wasn't given credit for time served for his conviction for the attempted rape of Cheyenne Schmidt. The court accepted the agreement and Ray walked free."

"Fury wouldn't have received more than the five years he'd already served," he explained. "Sentencing for sex crimes is all about the level of penetration, rather than the implied threat. No sexual penetration occurred with Cheyenne." He sighed, "Even if we find evidence now that he did indeed rape and murder Sadie Sullivan, he can't be tried again."

"I don't feel good about his release. Ray stared me down when he first came into the courtroom."

"If you want to meet and talk about this, I'm open. I owe you. I greatly appreciate you being there for me when Danny died."

He was kind. "Thanks, Zave, but I'm meeting with someone tonight."

7:00 P.M.
BOROUGH, 730 NORTH WASHINGTON AVENUE,
NEAR NORTH, MINNEAPOLIS

MY MAN REQUESTED WE MEET AT A RESTAURANT at Else Warehouse, on the second floor above the Borough Bar. I walked from my place in Hawthorne, believing I'd receive a ride home, but my date hadn't shown up. I knew his work was intense and demanding, but I didn't like being set aside. He'd never been as committed to making this work as I'd been, and it was wearing on me. I ordered a dessert, a strawberry Danish koldskål, so I didn't appear to be loitering.

I lived in Hawthorne, as it gave me ample opportunities to create drawings of strife in the inner city. I heard a ruckus in the bar downstairs and my heart raced for a moment, before I realized it was just a boisterous group of friends.

I called him, but the call immediately went to voicemail. I used to worry that he had an accident when he didn't show. Now I worried that he had a purpose—other than me.

My dessert arrived. I slowly stirred my spoon in it as I thought about the sorry state of my relationship. *How do you keep it from crashing? I don't want it to crash, but I don't know how to pull the throttle and raise the ailerons on the wings.* I had wasted time on a man who really didn't care. I was just an appetizer. Hell, not even that—I was a free sample. I hated being so sad. My family told me to move back home, but for me, *Home is where the art is*—not to mention my work. I dipped my spoon in the koldskål. The danish was good. I just didn't feel like eating.

I tried calling one more time—no answer. I dug out some cash and decided to just leave.

When I walked downstairs to exit through the bar, a man with his back to me stepped away from his huddle of friends at the end of the bar and blocked my exit. Flamin' Ray *effin'* Fury stepped directly in front of me.

"It's Lauren, right? That's the name I got from my attorney."

I looked down and tried stepping around him. "Excuse me, I have a ride waiting for me."

He maneuvered his bulk to block my retreat. Bar patrons jostled into us, pressing me closer to Ray to the point I had to look up to see his face, looming nearly a foot over me. The proximity shot a dose of cortisol through me—*flight, flight, flight!*

Ray spoke to me with affected casualness, but the menace in his tone tightened the muscles in my neck. "You sent me to prison. Don't you think you at least owe me an apology?"

He caught me at a bad time, and I was flustered. I swallowed hard and mustered up my angriest tone, "Let me leave!" I said it loud enough so everyone in the bar could hear and pushed myself a step backwards into a couple gals behind me, unconcerned about their exclamations of "Hey!" and "What the hell?"

As people began paying attention, Fury threatened me in his quietest tone, "I'm not done with you, Blondie." He then moved aside.

Once outside, I ran north on Washington Avenue toward my apartment in Hawthorne. After about a block, I ducked into Spyhouse Coffee and stayed to the side as I watched out the window. It wasn't long before a black convertible Camaro came cruising by with Ray Fury in the passenger seat. He was looking for me. He must've seen that I left on foot. I called my friend again—no answer.

The vehicle headed north on Washington. My closest friend is in Austin for the week. I hadn't told anyone else about my relationship and I had no desire to, now. This might've been one of the most careless decisions I'd ever made, but I slipped out and continued on my way. *It was under two miles. I could do this.*

I needed to get around Target Field. I crossed 394 and was feeling better about ditching Fury. I tried calling my date to complain about the predicament he left me in, but once again, it just went to voicemail. If I had a friend who'd been stood up as often as I had, I'd question her sanity. I walked casually, like I didn't have a care in the world, as my insides were frayed cords of live wires. I went past the Cancer Survivors Park and reminded myself I was lucky that all my troubles were changeable. I was still frustrated about my relationship but feeling more confident about surviving my walk home.

My heartrate blew up when I heard thumping bass coming from a car behind me. I looked back, and there was the black Camaro pacing along side of me. Ray was pointing to the side of the road, apparently instructing the driver to pull over. I decided to call Zave, but even he didn't answer. I began to wonder if my cellphone was working.

I knew it looked crazy, but I broke into a full sprint, grateful I'd decided against the heels I'd planned on wearing tonight. I'd heard of the damage Ray inflicted on women and I wasn't going to wait for someone to rescue me. I thought about running to a house and pretending like I lived there, but how would I feel if Fury broke into that house later?

I looked back and saw he and his friend were still creeping along in the Camaro behind me. When I turned to look ahead, I crashed into a Native woman who was just exiting the Smack Shack. I quickly apologized, "I'm sorry." And then said, "Pretend like you know me."

The woman was initially surprised, but quickly registered the fear on my face. Her features melded from a bright greeting to a combination of empathy and ferocity I couldn't describe. I wanted to draw her.

She said, "Well, I'm Crystal. And you are . . . ?"

"Lauren."

"There. Now we don't have to pretend anything. What's going on?"

I pointed back to the Camaro, "There's a very dangerous man following me. I'm not sure I can keep outrunning him."

She pulled me into a tight hug that spoke of protection and loyalty. "You're shaking." She released me, but still kept firm hands on my upper arms. "Do you want to call the police?"

Her embrace was momentarily comforting but, still frustrated, I said, "With all the craziness in Minneapolis right now, do you honestly think law enforcement is going to respond to this?"

Crystal glanced back at the car and said, "Probably not. Okay, friend, you're going to walk with me to my car and we're going to come up with a solution. Lucky for you, problem solving is my jam. We can't problem solve with the same level of thinking that created them. Do you know who said that?

I guessed, "Albert Einstein?"

"You're off to a good start. Need a ride?"

I felt like crying. There were amazing, kind people in the world. Grateful to have someone on my side, I simply breathed, "Thank you." *Wow!*

As we walked together, Crystal confidently eyeballed the driver. The Camaro sped up and disappeared around a corner, red brake lights glowering back at me in warning.

Crystal will always be my friend.

32

"People think about the word 'fearless' to mean without fear. I see it to actually mean 'with fear, but you do it anyway.'"
—LUVVIE AJAYI JONES

2021

JADA ANDERSON

8:30 A.M., FRIDAY, MAY 14
BUREAU OF CRIMINAL APPREHENSION OFFICE
1430 MARYLAND AVENUE EAST, ROOSEVELT, ST. PAUL

Ray Fury was a free man. I wasn't sure if it was right or wrong and that was the crux of the problem. You shouldn't keep a man incarcerated if you weren't sure if he was guilty. Our system was set up where the proof required was *beyond a reasonable doubt,* yet it was so often ignored when a black man's life was at stake. My stories gave the case attention and ultimately had a big part in Ray's release. *Why didn't I feel better about it?*

I looked over the duo Sean had put together for me, with a sense of appreciation. We all shared an insatiable desire for truth and justice. Jon was a reticent country boy whose factual nature could come across as uncaring. Nothing was further from the truth. Zave had the reserved cockiness you get from growing up in the inner city and knowing there were times when you were your only resource. I wondered if their personalities led them to the field, or if the field quieted people down over time.

Jon sat back in a forest green, untucked button-down shirt, with the words *Truth, Wisdom, Faith* embroidered in copper thread along the bottom. The cursive copper writing stood out above his black jeans.

Zave enjoyed being out of uniform and wore a comfortable, navy blue MPD hoodie and faded blue jeans. He wasn't happy with me, as he was never convinced of Fury's innocence. His sullen, concerned demeanor was kind of endearing.

He commented to me, "Fury followed Lauren his first night out of prison. She ended up being saved by a Good Samaritan."

I asked, "Who's Lauren?" That name had popped up a lot recently.

Jon responded, "Lauren Herald. She's the sketch artist who IDd Fury prior to his arrest."

Zave added, "If Fury's innocent, why wouldn't he admit that he had sex with Sadie within twenty-four hours of her body being discovered—a fact that Dr. Ho stated is undisputable?"

Jon interjected, "Let's look at the day before Sadie's body was found. Bobby Long had the day off and was home most of the day. According to Bobby, he left for a couple hours when Sadie was napping in the afternoon. He said Sadie wasn't even aware he'd left."

Zave said, "So, Fury either raped her then, or raped her as reported, after she left for work. Either way, there wasn't time for her to set up a consenting encounter with him. Sadie never would have invited Fury to Bobby's home, and she was never late for work." He stood up and directed his frustration toward me. "*I* was the man who ate with Sadie at Lu's Sandwiches. Sadie's sisters were right about Frannie—she always has something to say when nothing should be said."

I apologized to Zave. "I'm so sorry. I'm the one who interviewed Frannie. I thought she was telling the truth." I'd messed up. My work was falling apart, along with my fiancé and engagement.

Jon immediately supported me. "*Frannie* thought she was telling the truth. She could've passed a polygraph because she *believed* it to be true. There's no way you could have detected this." Perplexed, Jon added, "But why would Fury kill Sadie? He raped Elizabeth the next day and didn't kill her. It doesn't make sense. If Elizabeth could survive Ray, couldn't Sadie?"

Zave agreed, "For damn sure." Sadie would have found a way—for her daughter's sake.

Jon commented, "But I don't imagine there was a lot of negotiating prior to Sadie's murder. The guy who killed her caught her by surprise. She was lying face down, according to Dr. Ho. He wrapped a belt around her neck and tightened it until the life was out of her. Fury did it as an afterthought, when he was done raping her, or Bobby did it in anger. Either way, Sadie didn't see it coming."

I added, "Someone either hated her or needed her silent."

Jon told us, "Amaya Ho believes Sadie reacted by trying to grab at the belt and loosen it."

I could tell Jon wished she would've done something else. "What should she have done?"

"She wasn't going to pull that belt loose. Her best hope was to try to rock him off her body and loosen his grip."

I didn't know that I could forgive myself if Ray Fury hurt someone again. I didn't bother to tell them, but I was going to have one more conversation with Ray. He promised me an exit interview.

8:30 P.M.
FARVIEW PARK, 621 NORTH 29TH AVENUE,
HAWTHORNE, MINNEAPOLIS

RAY FURY AGREED TO GRANT ME MY interview if I'd go to him immediately. He wanted to meet close to home, since he hadn't renewed his driver's license. Fury told me to meet him by the purple raindrop at Farview Park, in the Hawthorne neighborhood. If I wasn't there by 8:30, he'd be gone.

When I pulled to the side of the road by the park, I could see Ray's oversized form sitting on a bench behind the fifteen-foot raindrop. Hawthorne was dangerous on a Friday night and the sun would be setting in ten minutes. Ray was the only sign of life in the park tonight. Ominous shadows cast by the trees hovered over him like a posse of demons. There were houses across the street, one hundred fifty feet away. I considered the damage he could do to me before someone noticed or called the police.

With Sean's precarious heart, I couldn't tell him I was meeting Ray. I told myself this was what reporters did. *We go to dangerous places to gather information in the interest of truth.*

When I approached, Ray removed a folded piece of paper from his back pocket. He sat back in a black muscle shirt and jeans, unfolded the page, and then handed it to me.

It was a nondisclosure agreement—a simple contract between the two of us, to keep today's interview confidential. I raised an eyebrow and looked down at him.

He explained, "I learned about the law in prison. I told you if you helped me get out, I'd tell you what I couldn't say during our last visit in lockup. But here's the catch—it's not for print. It's just between you and me."

I'd grabbed my mail on the way out and stuffed it into my purse. I rummaged around for a pen and pulled one from the recesses of my bag, spilling letters on the ground. I sat by Ray and signed it. I then bent down and retrieved my mail.

Ray ordered, "Bring your purse back to the car. I'm not takin' no chances with this bein' recorded. I'm searchin' you when you return. No phone—no nothin'."

As directed, I went back to my car and tossed my phone in my purse. I locked the doors and pocketed my key fob, my house and office keys the only defense I'd have if things got hairy. All the times Sean advised me to keep Mace on my keychain—now I saw it. *Too little, too late.* I was tempted to take off, but the reporter in me wouldn't allow it. My news reports were the impetus that freed this man from prison. I had to have some credibility with him. When I returned, he passed on searching me and patted the bench next to him.

I sat, though not as close as he suggested.

"I'm tryin' to make a go of it on the outside. One of those prison ministers lined me up a job. He didn't want me to go back to a moving gig."

"You were working for a moving company?"

"Cash work. Off and on." He looked regretful as he added, "I coulda been a heavyweight boxer." He studied me. "You know what they call those guys? The Undisputed Champions of the World. That should've been me. Instead, it's all I can do to avoid life in prison—for something I didn't do."

I maintained eye contact. It was obviously a dream that was important to him, and I had no reason to doubt it.

In his baritone voice, he continued, "I know I sound like every has-been. But at fourteen, I had the size and ability of a champion."

"You needed guidance."

"No shit. And I needed the facilities. If I was in Eden Prairie, they woulda had me training for the NFL, or for a heavyweight title fight. Instead, I was hangin' out."

"So, when did the assaults start?"

Ray scrutinized a house across the street, his sharp eyes in contrast to his seemingly relaxed posture—a token of a viperous lifestyle. "I was fourteen the first time I went lookin' for sex. The guys were runnin' a train on a girl, and I was invited to join." His eyes slithered back to me, waiting for a reaction.

I gave him a blank look and said nothing, so he continued, "After that, I was muscle for the gang and they'd tell their girls, 'Take care of Ray.' When that wasn't available, I found the snatch and took care of it myself."

"It?"

"You know—that itch you get that sometimes can't be ignored or shut off—it's gotta be scratched."

I needed him to give me something specific. "What's the worst thing you've done?"

Ray sighed. "The kid was a mistake. I watched the house and after the girls went to sleep, I jimmied a door open. Looked like their parents were gone for the night. I was after the older sister, but I went in the wrong room. It was dark and I wasn't thinkin' clear. I never got charged with that one, but I could've, just as well. All the cops see me as the guy who raped a twelve-year-old girl. She bit me. Any man would bite a chick if she bit him on the dick. She asked for that. And they shoulda had better locks."

Listening to offenders rationalize behavior was a pet peeve of mine, but I needed to keep him talking. "How many rapes have there been?"

"No matter. It's not why you're here. I'll tell you about Sadie and then we goin' our own ways. We're even. My debt to you is paid." He brushed his big paws together in finality, but doing so wouldn't get the dirt off his soul.

I told him, "I can't tell anyone, so give me the truth. I know you lied to me about having sex with Sadie a couple days earlier. And you lied to me about eating in the restaurant with her. You never dated her."

He nodded. "I never dated her. I was movin' boxes into a house across the street—fillin' in for my cousin 'cause he was hungover. My name wasn't on any of the paperwork. We just traded days. I watched this hot babe walkin' in and out of the house all morning—waterin' the flowers. Lookin' like one of those Karens who think they're too good for a brother. I couldn't stop thinkin' about her."

"So, you raped her?"

He looked away and nodded. "Yeah. I did." He looked back, "Would you have helped me if you knew I raped her?"

I didn't say it, but the answer was a hard no. Instead, I asked, "When?"

He couldn't look at me, which I found curious. At once, all bravado, then shamed nudged through his hard demeanor. Maybe there was hope for him, yet. He continued, "At about two in the afternoon, I saw her close the curtains in an upstairs bedroom. And then I saw her boyfriend get in the car and drive away. I didn't know he was a cop at the time."

"Would it have made a difference?"

He sneered, "Maybe—but I'm not sure for the better or the worse. I walked across the street and the door wasn't even locked." He shrugged as if that explained everything. "There it is. If Bobby woulda just locked the door, I mighta walked away."

"Did you *ever* walk away?"

"Minneapolis is a big town. There's always another house. Sadie was sleepin' when I went in the bedroom. I got on top of her and covered her mouth and punched her in the stomach with my free hand." He shook his head in disbelief. "And here's the funny part. She begged me not to punch her in the face—said she was gettin' married the next week. She said, 'I don't want everyone to see me as a rape victim at my wedding. I'll go along. Just leave my face alone.'"

There was no funny part.

Ray added, "I wish they could all be that easy. Took her from the front then flipped her over and took her from the back. When I left, she was shakin' and cryin'—tryin' to get dressed. I remember thinkin', *Who's too good for who, now?* I just left. And that's it. Her fiancé was a cop. Lock the damn door."

The little I knew of Sadie I liked. Zave loved her. "Why kill her?"

"I never said I *killed* her. You still don't believe me, do you? Here's the problem. If killers always lie, you never really know if someone is innocent when they say they didn't do it, do you?" Ray smirked. "They lied to put me in prison, and I lied to get out."

I questioned, "So an unlocked door is justification for rape?"

He minimized his behavior. "Worse shit happens to people than what I did."

"But you're a gifted athlete. And your victims were all so vulnerable." I ran through the four I knew of, "Developmentally disabled, twelve-years old and sleeping, stumbling intoxicated, a stripper—and you left them so damaged." It made me sick.

It was all it took to flare Ray's anger. He glared at me, and his voice dropped an octave. "You shamin' me, bitch?"

Trying to tone it down, I softly expressed, "No. I want to believe that beneath that hard surface is some compassion. A minister was taking time out of his life to talk to you in prison. Didn't you learn anything?"

Ray started laughing, "I learned somethin'. I'm outta prison."

There was a black emptiness in his eyes that horrified me. My last words to him were, "But for how long?"

I felt the hair stand up on the back of my neck. My instincts screamed run. I suddenly realized it was completely dark around us. There was no time to think about it. I bolted toward my car, fumbling the fob out of my pocket, ready to press the unlock button so I could jump in. I couldn't get out of there fast enough. When I looked back, Ray was gone. *Crap—I didn't have my phone. Where did he go?*

With my heart pounding, I heard the satisfying clunk of doors unlocking and yanked the door open. Once inside, I locked the doors again and tore down the street. I glanced in the rearview mirror to see Flamin' Ray standing in the middle of the street. Ray had pursued me. I reminded myself, *one more reason I work out!*

10:30 P.M.

KING'S POINT ROAD ON HALSTED BAY, MINNETRISTA

AFTER SEAN AND I PUT ISAIAH TO BED, I TOLD him what I'd done. As I anticipated, he was furious.

Sean stood in front of my large window overlooking the lake, lecturing me. "You can't go into that situation without backup . . . " After his rant finally died down, he faced me and asked, "So, did he kill Sadie?"

"I don't think so. He made some weird comment like, *Am I lying?* It felt dangerous, so I just left. I do believe he raped Sadie. He had no problems sharing the details about that. He admitted raping her at two in the afternoon, in her house. Fury was working for a moving company across the street and saw that she was home alone."

Deep in thought, Sean rubbed his chest as he watched a lit-up boat crossing the dark lake. He turned to me. "It's time to call Serena."

"What are you talking about? Jon's Serena?"

He nodded. "When Jon asked for work, he said they need the money. Serena and Jon were private investigators together. I'm sure she'd appreciate the work. Serena sure looks a lot like Sadie. Imagine if we planted her where Bobby Long's working now. Who knows what he'd share with her?"

I was still a little frustrated with Sean's condescending tone toward me. When we argued, it was easy to think the worst. I wondered if he invited Jon into the investigation because he was over his jealousy, or if he knew from the onset that Serena could be used as bait to get Bobby talking. Serena would never work this investigation without Jon. I opted not to say what I was thinking. I had my bachelorette party tomorrow night, and I badly needed a night out with my girls.

I sighed in resolution and asked, "Did you get a letter regarding the final menu from our wedding venue? They said they mailed it, but I haven't seen it . . . "

33

"Nazi anti-Semitism and the Holocaust was a calamity almost beyond comprehension. It will be years before we understand the damage."
—W.E.B. Du Bois

2021

XAVIER "ZAVE" WILLIAMS

8:30 P.M., SATURDAY, MAY 14
XERXES APARTMENTS, 5211 XERXES AVENUE NORTH,
BROOKLYN CENTER

I made it my mission to find Cheyenne Schmidt tonight. She wasn't working at the club anymore. While I didn't want to get back to talking to her regularly, I did want to make sure she was okay. Rape cases take a toll on victims; I liked to leave people with resources.

I knocked on her apartment door.

Cheyenne answered in high-waisted black leggings and a cropped t-shirt, showcasing the smooth skin of her flat stomach. She held the door partially open, looking a little worse for wear as she softly spoke, "What are you doing here?"

"I wanted to make sure you're okay."

She glanced back into the apartment, then turned back to me, "You shouldn't have dumped me." I could smell booze on her breath.

"Cheyenne, you're a good person, but I can't be in a relationship with you—you were someone I needed to protect. You're honest and open, and that was so refreshing. But when the case was over, I had to move on. I have the name of a great counselor who helps people work through trauma, if you want to give her a call." I handed her a card.

Cheyenne softly said, "You're too late, Zave."

Just then the door swung open and there stood Bobby damn Long. He took the card from her hand and turned to me. "What are you doing here?"

I flashed my badge. "I was offering her a resource to help her deal with her trauma."

He smiled, "She has one right here."

Cheyenne disappeared back into the apartment.

Bobby pulled up the sleeve of his t-shirt, revealing an Aryan Cowboy Brotherhood tattoo on his shoulder. "Know what this means? *Not welcome.*"

I was juiced with anger at the thought of this QAnon asshole, but there was nothing I could do. I told him, "I'm glad you and your friends had the time to do some coloring in prison. The Nazi helmet is a nice touch—having matching hats and all—kind of like that cone clowns wear."

He was at a loss for words, but his middle finger was still functioning as, like a little kid, he stuck it up in my face, then slammed the door.

34

*"A man must be at home somewhere,
before he can feel at home everywhere."*
—HOWARD THURMAN

2021

JON FREDERICK

8:30 P.M., SUNDAY, MAY 15
PIERZ

Nora and Jackson were in the backyard with me, planting an herb garden with cilantro, chives, dill, rosemary, sage, and lemon thyme. We had a large country yard that ended at a forest.

With a little direction, Nora dug, planted, and watered, while I helped Jackson follow in her footsteps. We'd finished watering my hops, which I planned on using for a beverage experiment. In theory, if you poured beer over recently harvested hops, it was supposed to give the beverage an incredibly fresh and clean taste. The process was called *wet hopping*. It was a peaceful, but hot spring day, which made watering our future harvest enjoyable for my dynamic duo.

Jackson hunched over and focused on a honeybee hovering over a dandelion. He asked, "What it doing?"

"Bees get their food from flowers. It's gathering nectar."

The bee suddenly flew away, and Jackson's eyes curiously followed its direction. "Where it go?"

I asked, "Where do you think it went?"

He responded, "Prob'ly Target."

I smiled. It *is* where people go. Serena or I mentioned every week, *We need to stop at Target.*

Serena stepped outside looking pensive as she studied us. Nora and Jackson abandoned me for the playset. It was unlike Serena not to join us.

She wore a faded apple green cotton top with her cropped jeans, which accented her emerald eyes. Serena looked down at my soaked tennis shoes and commented, "I swear, if you'd just find the right sandals, you'd never want to wear tennis shoes again. Your toes could finally breathe."

I teased, "That is quite a feat. Pun intended."

She hit me in the shoulder. "Okay, so, we need to talk. Sean Reynolds just called me. What would you think about me joining your investigation next Wednesday?" She explained Sean's suggestion. "Bobby Long is working for a cleaning company. He goes into an accounting firm two consecutive nights during the week to clean. Sean wants me to sit at the desk as a receptionist when Bobby's there, to see if he'll open up to me."

I'd thought about how both Bobby Long and Ray Fury have attractions to brunette, white women, with similar features. Sadie Sullivan was a taller version of Serena. "Do you understand they'd being using you to draw out information from a rapist?"

"Yes. I don't love the plan, but it could work."

I considered, "What do they have for security? We're talking about a man who put a gun to a woman's head and raped her—*twice.*"

"They have hidden cameras throughout the office and will have an officer watching and listening to every interaction in a van outside. Then I could stay with you on Wednesday nights, so the only nights we'd be apart are Monday and Tuesday."

It worried me, but I had to keep in mind my work constantly worried her. "If this is what you want, I have no issue."

She smiled, "I already checked with my parents. They'll watch Nora and Jackson. I wanted to check with you before I called Sean back."

"Okay." I had to fight off my urge to scream, *Please don't do this! It's too dangerous.* That would've been quite hypocritical. It was what she wanted to do and, therefore, what she should do.

11:00 P.M.

PIERZ

THE LIGHTS WERE OUT, AND THE FIREPLACE was on, to provide a soft orange glow. I had finished rubbing Serena's feet and had drifted off to sleep on the couch next to her. She was watching the end of the Mare of Easttown. This was our typical end to the evening. She'd fill me in on what I missed tomorrow.

I woke to Serena's hand gently rubbing my cheek. The TV was off. She said, "Someone's texting you."

I grabbed my cell phone off the coffee table.

The text from Jada read, "Wearing THE dress for my wedding to Sean. It finally makes it to a church."

I texted back, "You're kidding, right?"

"No. It has a great history . . . "

I responded, "Terrible idea."

"Sean has no idea. Money saved. Nothing hurt."

It was crazy and so unlike Jada. I texted, "If you need to borrow money for a new dress, I'll find a way to help."

"OK—accepting the money. The other dress I considered is $11,000."

The preposterousness of it all finally hit me. I texted back, "Whoever has Jada's phone, wish her a happy bachelorette party for me."

Serena rubbed her eyes. "Who's texting you at this time of night?"

I handed her my phone. I had told Serena about the rooftop meal with Jada. I hadn't told her that Jada was wearing a wedding dress. *The stupid lies we keep, even when we're trying to be open and honest.*

Serena glanced at the texts and handed the phone back. Without a word said, she headed upstairs.

When I plugged my phone in for the night, I noticed there was one last text from Jada. "Sorry! They were teasing me about my first time in a wedding dress and I told them the story. Maybe shouldn't have."

35

"Any time things appear to be going better, you've overlooked something."
—Shirley Chisolm

2021

SERENA FREDERICK

8:30 A.M., WEDNESDAY, MAY 18
BUREAU OF CRIMINAL APPREHENSION
1430 MARYLAND AVENUE EAST, ROOSEVELT, ST. PAUL

I joined Jon's investigative crew for their morning meeting. Xavier, Jada, and Jon had already compiled so much information. I wasn't officially a BCA agent. I was a part-time Community Liaison to the BCA.

Zave was telling Jon, "Bobby's relationship with Cheyenne isn't illegal, but *man*, is he an opportunist. Sadie was innocent and needy. Cheyenne wasn't innocent, but she was craving someone who would tell her what to do. He's gonna destroy her. In a year, she'll be an eating-disordered, anxiety-ridden mess."

Jon agreed. "Here's what we have going for us. Bobby seems to have a honeymoon period with lovers where they think he's wonderful. So, we have a little time to work with."

Jada was particularly quiet, today. She offered, "I'm sorry. Sean meets with the cardiologist tomorrow and I want to be there. I know I haven't been much help. I'm here to tell Serena what I know about Sadie, and then I need to step away for a while."

Everyone shared that they understood.

Jon explained to me, "Your role is to sit behind the counter and let Bobby come to you. When the opportunity arises, engage him in personal conversation."

"What if he doesn't initiate a conversation?"

Jon smiled, "He will."

Zave commented, "If he doesn't, just look sad or distressed and he'll be on you like white on snow."

Jon asked me, "What are you going to do if someone recognizes you?"

I nervously squirmed. It was certainly possible. I used to work in billing in the metro area before I was married. Jon had been running through possibilities all weekend in his effort to talk me out of this. I didn't want to lose this opportunity. I offered, "I'll use my maiden name."

Silence weighed upon the room. Jada finally lifted it by telling me, "Zave got us a number of pictures of Sadie from her sisters." She handed them to me. "Buy the same style of blouses and fix your hair and makeup to look as similar as possible. It's kind of a pain, but you'll need to use a purchase order, since it's being paid for by the BCA."

Jon warned me, "Don't introduce any topics involving Sadie."

I assumed that, but I realized he likely felt the need to say it. I flipped through the pictures. Sadie liked airy blouses that didn't cling to her body.

"They'll show you around the office today," he continued, "but after today, you'll only need to be at the accounting office at five-thirty. Bobby comes in at six, when everyone's supposed to be gone, and he leaves at eight." He paused, "I won't be there."

Jada explained, "You and Jon are too close for him to be working your surveillance. Sean's afraid Jon will interfere."

I was comfortable working with Jon, but I assumed they knew what they were doing. I could see he wasn't happy about it.

He turned to Zave, "I'm going to continue to trace the path from Sadie's home to her body, to see if I can find anyone or any video that will help clarify who drove the pickup. It would be a lot easier if the murder hadn't occurred eight years ago."

Zave nodded. "That's good. Bobby's continually denied driving the truck that night, so if he's driving, he's our killer. If Sadie, or Fury, is driving, the killer is Flamin' Ray."

8:30 A.M., THURSDAY, MAY 19, 2021
51ST STREET & WASHBURN AVENUE SOUTH,
FULTON AREA OF MINNEAPOLIS

MY FIRST NIGHT AT THE OFFICE WITH BOBBY was a success. When he finished cleaning, he leaned against the counter and spoke to me for an extra half hour, after he was supposed to be done. I suggested to him that I was single and was working extra hours, because I needed the money. I was both nervous and excited about gathering more information tonight.

Agnes and I sat at her kitchen table, enjoying warm tea. She told me, "I enjoy the company, but I'm curious—are you here so much because you don't trust Jon?"

No topic was ever off limits for Agnes. "No." Since having COVID, my thyroid levels were all over the charts, varying from hypo- to hyperthyroidism. When my Thyroid Stimulating Hormone (TSH) levels were low, I was depressed. When they were high, I was anxious and jealous. It was insane how a physical issue could have such an impact on one's personality.

I told Agnes, "I'm helping with the investigation. But truth be told, Jon and I are not in a great spot, and I want to get back to what we once had."

She grumbled, "You're very physical. I'm not sure what to think about that."

Without giving the question much thought, I said, "It's quicker." I didn't share that, along with being more anxious, I was also aroused more. There was a weird upside. It was how the nervous system worked.

Agnes cackled, "I imagine it is. Not exactly how I was raised, though."

I smiled, "Not how I was raised, either. Even though Jon isn't a touchy-feely guy, my contact is very significant to him. At home, he rubs my feet every night. I've come to realize it's as much for his sake as mine. It's his way of connecting with me in a manner no other person can."

"I need to find a guy who connects by rubbing my feet," she said wistfully.

We were interrupted by a knock at the door.

I peeked out the side window and saw Bobby Long. *This is a problem. He must have followed me here from work last night.* I stepped back from the window and continued to observe, just out of his view.

I told Agnes, "Don't let him in and don't tell him I'm here."

Agnes held the door open a crack and rudely spat, "Whatever it is, make it quick. I'm an old woman with not a lot of time left."

Taken aback, Bobby stated, "There's a woman named Serena who stayed here last night. Is there a man in her life?"

"There's a man in my life—standing at my door."

Frustrated, he asked, "Is Serena in a relationship?"

"What's it worth?"

Bobby said, "It depends how much you're willing to tell me. Is she sleeping with him?"

Agnes remarked, "I imagine she felt obligated to—after she had sex with him."

I touched Agnes' arm and shook my head *no*.

Agnes glanced my way and changed tone. "But he hasn't been around for a while."

Bobby wondered, "Is someone else inside with you?"

"No. It's just that stupid cat I'm watching for my sister. They say curiosity killed the cat. Well, I was a suspect."

"The guy with Serena—what's his name?"

"Jon."

I tugged at her arm again and mouthed, "*No.*"

She continued, "Jon Kennedy."

He laughed, "You're kidding, right?"

"No. If your last name was Kennedy, wouldn't you name your kid Jon?"

"What does he look like?"

"A lot like you. Sickly pale—insecure—annoyingly curious. Do you have a brother?"

I'd forgotten how insulting Agnes could be. The fact that she hadn't skewered me, recently, reminded me that I'd made significant progress with her

Bobby told her, "I don't have a brother." He hesitated, "You said she's not seeing him anymore."

Agnes quipped, "You're a sharp one. I only have to repeat myself a couple times."

He said, "Please don't tell her I stopped."

"My silence has to be worth at least a Jackson."

"What?"

"Twenty dollars for those who can't read their money."

He argued, "It doesn't have his name on it."

She flatly responded, "You're an idiot."

He took out his billfold, removed a twenty, and glanced at it. "By God, you're right."

Agnes held her hand behind her ear and pretended she didn't hear him. "What was that?"

He said louder, "You were right!"

Agnes tormented him, "I still didn't quite hear you."

Tired of the game, he handed her the twenty.

I stepped away from the window as Bobby turned to leave.

Agnes gloated, "It's a pleasure doing business with you."

She shut the door and said, "You don't see Jon anymore. I would argue that you see him a little less these days."

36

"Success is to be measured not so much by the position one has reached in life as by the obstacles which he has overcome while trying to succeed."
—Booker T. Washington

2021

BOBBY LONG

8:30 A.M., THURSDAY, MAY 26
COLD STREAM LANE, EDEN PRAIRIE

Life throws you curveballs. It hasn't played out exactly as I hoped, but after prison, I'm living with a beautiful woman and have another at work flirting with me. They say a bird in the hand is worth two in the bush, but can I trust Cheyenne? I thought Sadie was cheating on me. This time I need to know for sure.

I have a number of items I've taken from past home breakins. I don't feel bad about it. I'm sure the homeowners' insurance covered them and a couple more items doesn't change the robber's sentence. I pull a laptop out of my secret storage unit. With it, I create an email account in the name of *Zave Williams* and decide to send my beloved Cheyenne a note. First of all, I don't believe their relationship was platonic, as Cheyenne insists.

Strippers basically lie to men for a living. But I've got a good thing, here, and I don't want to cut her loose without knowing. Prison has taught me the importance of certainty.

Cheyenne,
I'm writing to let you know I still care about you, and I'd like to meet up with you. Seeing you again reminded me of my love for you. We need to pick someplace secluded and dark, so we don't get caught. We'll resume the passion we had before you left. Thinking of you . . .
Love,
Zave

This email is a win-win for me. If Cheyenne tells me about it, I'll know she's committed to me. If she doesn't mention it, then I know she's still thinking about the possibilities with Williams.

8:00 P.M.
EQUITABLE ASSOCIATES, TECHNOLOGY DRIVE,
EDEN PRAIRIE

I'M SWEATING FROM WORKING SO FAST. I have to get the cleaning done so I have more time with Serena. When I'm finished, I wash my hands and face clean in the bathroom and go to the counter to get another look at her. She has so many features and mannerisms of Sadie, it's freaky. But they aren't exactly the same. Serena has fuller lips and vibrant green eyes. She has a nicer ass, but Sadie had bigger breasts. Sadie was taller and a little thinner. But wow! They both could be models.

Serena leans over the counter in her baby blue blouse and smiles as we share stressors of the day.

When the conversation tires, I ask, "Would you ever be interested in grabbing lunch with me, sometime?"

All flirty, she says, "Maybe."

My palms are slick. How can I be so nervous? I faced threats every day in prison and here I am sweating like a pig from talking to a girl. I force out, "I know this is a little bold, but are you seeing anyone?"

Troubled, she says, "No. I was dumped a couple months ago."

"He had to be out of his mind."

Serena asks, "How about you?"

"Would I be asking you out if I was in a relationship?"

"Some guys do," she says with a perky shrug.

"I've always considered faithfulness to be the greatest quality of a lover. Everything else you can learn to live with . . . "

10:00 P.M.
COLD STREAM LANE, EDEN PRAIRIE

CHEYENNE IS WAITING FOR ME AT THE DOOR when I arrive home. She's a cutie in her little black t-shirt dress—but she's no Serena.

She teases, "It's taking you longer and longer to end your shifts. You're not working with some hot little number, are you?"

How do women always seem to know when you've stepped out of line for a second? I tell her, "I go into these businesses by myself to clean. I'm not on a crew."

She purrs, "I just miss you." Cheyenne wraps her soft arms around me. "Hit the shower. I'll join you."

With Serena having some interest in me, I can amp up the competition. "Cheyenne, I'd like you to dance for me tonight. Like I was one of your guys at the club."

She studies me. "I don't do that anymore."

"You can for me." When she hesitates, I add, "I think you should get a job."

"I thought you wanted me at home waiting for you."

"I did, but now I'm thinking I was being selfish. Wouldn't it be nice not to ask me for money?"

"I suppose," she agrees.

I pull her close. "But not stripping or anything like that." The odds of her getting a shift that matches mine are almost nil. This would allow me time at home alone with Serena.

Cheyenne softly asks, "Anything else?"

"This is just an observation, but you seem to be putting on a little weight. It will be good for you to get out of the house." I could add something about her drinking, but that's enough for one night. No need to be cruel.

She sadly turns away.

I ask, "Have you heard from anybody interesting today?"

With guilt oozing out of every pore, she responds, "No."

Leaving Cheyenne in the living room, I head to the bedroom and dig out my laptop. I have to see if Cheyenne responded. Sure enough, she did.

Zave,
Pick up where we left off? There was nothing between us.
I have no interest in meeting you. I'm with a great man
now. A man who knows how to take care of a woman.
Don't contact me again.
Cheyenne

Her words put a grin on my face. Tonight, will be a good night!

37

*"One man cannot hold another man
down in the ditch without remaining
down in the ditch with him."*
—Booker T. Washington

2021

SERENA FREDERICK

8:30 P.M., THURSDAY, JUNE 3
EQUITABLE ASSOCIATES, TECHNOLOGY DRIVE,
COLD STREAM LANE, EDEN PRAIRIE

I initially felt relieved that Jon wouldn't be directly overlooking my undercover work with Bobby. But as the conversations with Bobby got more intense, I began wishing Jon was involved. I knew he wouldn't let anything happen to me.

Minneapolis had lit up with gunfire. Three children, in three separate incidents, ages six, nine, and ten, were shot in the head by stray bullets. Sean believed gangs were spraying areas of enemies with automatic rifles. Jon had been temporarily pulled from heading this investigation to help make some arrests. Shootings were up 150% in Minneapolis, while the community was trying to restrict the use of armed officers.

Zave had also been pulled to help the Minneapolis Homicide Unit and was working our investigation primarily after his shift. Jada came and went as she was able. I didn't blame her; she was trying to attend all of Sean's medical appointments. This left me basically working this alone, with a man in a surveillance van listening in and occasional phone calls from Sean. I was still spending Wednesday nights with Jon at Agnes' house, which brought me comfort.

Bobby was progressively spending more and more time with me. I'd allowed him to walk me out when he left, recently, *for my safety*, according to Bobby. He asked me tonight if I wanted to sit in his truck and talk a little before we went our separate ways.

He walked me to a jacked up white Ford F150 Raptor with oversized, off-road tires.

I commented, "That's a lot of truck."

"It's a 2017, but it's in great shape because it sat in a shed when I was—" he caught himself, "for a couple years when I wasn't driving it."

I walked around the back to see metal bull testicles hanging from the trailer hitch.

Bobby laughed.

I commented, "So you like people looking at your balls when you're driving around?"

"It's just a joke."

I teased, "I get it. I have a metal vulva on the back of my car."

He squinted. "What?"

Bobby walked over and looked at the back of my rusting gray Ford Fusion.

Attempting to appear surprised, I said, "Oh, I guess that's just the muffler."

He walked back to his truck. "You've got a sense of humor, girl."

I stepped up on the running board and, with the help of what Jon's brother Victor referred to as the "holy shit" handle, pulled my short self in and settled in on the passenger side.

Bobby's eyes gave my body a quick once-over, as he commented, "How does an amazing woman like you end up single in her thirties?"

"The average age for a woman to first marry in the U.S. is twenty-seven." *Okay—that was a Jon statement.* Needing to pry deeper, I said, "My boss told me you were in prison. I looked up the case."

Frustrated, Bobby ran stubby fingers through the smattering of hairs left on top of his head and turned away.

I said, "It doesn't seem like the man you are now. But I would like to know, where did all that anger come from?"

He slowly turned back. "Everyone's quick to judge, but no one's ever asked me that."

"I'm not running away, Bobby," I assured him. "I wouldn't be much of a Christian if I didn't believe people could change. The articles suggested you grew up in the suburbs, in a happy home."

He smiled, "I grew up in the suburbs. They got that much right. I hated my dad, growing up. He treated me like an annoyance, until he finally left. When I tried to visit him, he told me I wasn't his kid. When I asked my mom about it, she said she'd tell me when the time was right. Then she'd make comments about random guys, like, *maybe he's your father.* When I was fourteen, she was mad at me and told me that a black serial rapist was actually my father and that, after he raped her, my father couldn't love her again."

"What a terrible thing to learn at fourteen."

"And then to later find out it wasn't true. As a young adult, I sent my DNA into ancestry-dotcom to learn a little about my history. I started getting names of people in my dad's family sent back to me as relatives. So, I went back and confronted my mom. She said she had to say what she did to make sure my father never got custody of me. It was all a lie, created out of spite. She hated my dad more than she loved me."

I took his hand. "I'm so sorry you had to go through that."

He shrugged. "Well, it's done now. I told my dad what she said. He never apologized. Said it wasn't his fault, but he has helped me out since I got out of prison. He got all *godly* and found religion, so I suppose he felt some obligation. I don't speak to my mother anymore." He squeezed my hand. "That's enough about me."

I wanted to see how he'd respond to this. "My man left me for an African American woman."

Bitter distaste filled his eyes. "Are you kidding me?"

"I am not. She's a beautiful, successful, professional woman."

"He's trying to prove to everyone how open-minded he is. But it's just shallow, right-wing, jungle fever bullshit."

I conjured up the hurt I felt when Jon and I had separated. On cue, tears began pooling in my eyes.

Bobby said, "Hey, it's okay. He's a dumbass. Look, it happened to me, too. My fiancée was seeing a n—a black guy. She never admitted it, but I have friends. People told me they saw her talking to him again and again—in the store—out to eat. I didn't know what to do."

I looked at him. "What *did* you do?"

He put his arm around me. "Let me kiss you, first."

And I let him. It was disgusting, but I let him.

He placed his hand on my breast.

I gently pulled away. *How far do I let this undercover crap go? It's already gone too far.* I asked, "I have to know. You must have been so hurt, Bobby. What did you do?"

He pulled his arm away and looked out his window. "I had her swear to me she'd never see him again."

"Did she?"

He silently nodded. And with that, Bobby started the truck and revved the engine to punctuate the end of conversation with an obnoxious roar. "I think I'd better call it a night."

I gave him a peck on the cheek and left.

I felt so dirty—I just wanted to get home and shower. He was so close to telling me something significant, but if I had pushed it, I'd have blown my cover. I wanted to be done with him.

After Bobby's truck rumbled away, a van pulled up and Sean Reynolds stepped out. "What did he tell you in the truck?"

"Bobby thought Sadie was having an affair with a black man. He made her swear she'd never see him again."

He directed, "Keep him talking. Now we need a mic on you. Once you leave the office, you're not mic'd. Do you want it in your purse or bra?"

"I'll have Jon drop a bra off." I looked sideways at him. "I thought you were out of this."

Sean grimaced. "Jon's going to be busy helping out with the Minneapolis shootings the next couple weeks, but I'm still working this case. The BCA oversees cop investigations and as the boss, I need answers about Bobby Long, here." He started to walk back to the van, and then turned back. "Don't tell Jon what happened tonight. You can tell him when this is all done. You know as well as I do, if you tell him, he'll intervene. It'll mess up all the work you've done."

I asked, "How could you see what happened?"

Sean pointed to the roof of the office building. "Bobby always parks in the same spot, so we mounted a night vision camera that's aimed directly into his windshield."

I wasn't sure if that made me feel better or worse. *At what price to my own dignity do I continue to do this work?*

I decided to drive back to Pierz, so I could be home when Nora and Jackson woke up. When in doubt, spend time with the kids.

38

*"Misery won't touch you gentle. It always
leaves its thumbprints on you; sometimes
it leaves them for others to see, sometimes
for nobody but you to know of."*
—EDWIDGE DANTICAT

2021

JADA ANDERSON

9:30 P.M., FRIDAY, JUNE 4
KING'S POINT ROAD ON HALSTED BAY,
MINNETRISTA, MINNESOTA

I'd made salmon sandwiches on wheat bread, with capers and an egg with a melting yolk for our evening meal. Sean worked late, so his yolk now coagulated in the fridge, while mine filled my belly.

This problem began long before Sean's heart attack. *If you're not going to show up, just call and let me know.* I opened a bottle of Napa Valley Dominus—purported to be nuanced and complex, filled with the opulence of wildflowers and deep valley fruits. I settled into my favorite, buttery-soft, cream leather chair, and propped tired, bare feet on the matching ottoman while I savored the wine. It was actually a pretty good cabernet, and I didn't imagine cheap. Sean had bought it for me for some special occasion. I'd planned on sharing this with him, tonight. If he wasn't going to come home, I was going to drink it.

Where the hell are you, Sean? You just had a heart attack!

Before I finished my mind rant, he rushed in the door. "Sorry! It took a little longer than I anticipated."

"You missed Isaiah. I just put him down." I studied his glossy eyes. Either he was drinking, or he just got out of bed. The first option seemed most likely. "You stopped at a bar."

"I did. I thanked some of the staff for following through with my responsibilities in my absence."

"So, how does that work with your cardio rehab?"

With a dismissive wave, Sean dropped heavily onto the couch. "I need to talk to you about something."

My first thought was he had more bad news about his health. "What now?"

"I don't think we should get married."

"*What?*" My feet were instantly on the floor, as I braced to spring from my place of comfort. A small droplet of deep burgundy cab sloshed from my glass and splattered onto the off-white leather of the ottoman I'd worked so hard to keep Isaiah's busy fingers from staining. I fought the urge to run for a rag and the 409.

My parents and family had flown in from Chicago to help me get everything in place for our upcoming fall wedding. "Are you *kidding me?* What's this about, Sean?"

He was having a hard time looking me in the eyes. "I'm ten years older than you and now, I have a bad heart. Think about the decades you'll be spending alone."

I stared hard at him until he finally looked at me. "I know what I want, Sean. Don't put this on me, like somehow you walking away is *good* for me. What else? Is there someone else?"

He laughed without humor. "Don't be ridiculous. You hover over me like my mother. You're driving me nuts." His mahogany eyes softened. "I feel terrible for what I've put you through, Jada. You're working the Fury case only minimally, because you're taking care of me—going with me to the doctor; making sure I'm not alone. I don't need a babysitter. If I die, I die. But I need to *live*," he implored. "I need to work."

Fuming through clenched teeth, I said, "Last thing I want is to have another child to *mother*. Grow up." His comment stung and I couldn't let it go. Hell with him. "You know what? If you want to leave, *leave*. Walk away from us."

I stomped to the kitchen for the 409 and grabbed the roll of paper towels. I doused the stain on the ottoman and started scrubbing furiously—that spot didn't stand a chance. The leather didn't either, really. This couldn't be happening.

Sean sat rigid, saying nothing—*doing* nothing.

I pointed to the door and repeated, louder, "Leave!"

Without another word, he stood up and walked out.

11:30 P.M.

THE WINE WAS GONE. I WAS CURLED UP IN BED, alone and miserable. Of course, it had started to rain, to match my bleak mood. The wind was blowing hard enough to cause the vines on the side of my house to scrape and creak in protest against the steel siding.

Sean and I had spent so much time together, I imagine he felt smothered. I had to admit, I started to resent that I'd abandoned my work for the most part. There were interviews I should've gotten to—ones that didn't work with his appointments. We were adjusting to a new reality. The biggest problem was Sean needed to accept that we couldn't go back to the way things were. His lifestyle led to his heart attack. It had to change—if not for Sean's sake, for Isaiah's.

Lost in ruminations, I was shaken to the present by what sounded like the downstairs doorknob rattling.

I sat up and strained my ears to make sense of what I was hearing. I slid quietly out of bed and slipped my phone into the pocket of my pajama pants. I crept out of my bedroom without a sound. I first checked on Isaiah. He was still sleeping like an angel. After tucking his chubby arms under his blanket, leaving all the lights off, I made my way down the steps to the back door. I held my breath and listened intently. I heard the light, steady rain; I registered the vines scratching against the siding, but now there was nothing else. The wine was getting to me. I chastised myself, breathed a sigh of relief, and started back to my bedroom.

It was then that I saw the shadowy figure outside, crossing by my living room window. I fumbled my phone out and quickly called Sean to see if, by some chance, he had returned.

He answered, "I'm sorry. I know you're just—"

I cut him off. "Are you outside?"

"No—I'm in Hawthorne."

"There's someone outside my house." My heart started galloping maniacally in my chest.

"I'll call the police. I'm a half hour away, but I'm on my way!"

I heard breaking glass from the other side of the house. "Sean, he's coming in!"

"Stay on the phone, babe. Where's Isaiah?" I could hear panic escalating in his voice.

I told him, "Call me right back," and hung up. I slid my phone down the carpeted steps into the basement. His call could create a distraction and buy me some time.

Soon as I let go of the phone, I bolted upstairs and snatched a groggy and confused Isaiah out of his peaceful slumber. I tried to have a plan for every possible emergency I could be in, with my three-year-old boy, even as I prayed I'd never have any such crises come to fruition.

I whispered, "Shhhh. Hold your blanky around you."

I could hear movement downstairs. I held Isaiah tightly and headed to the extra bedroom. My little bruiser was already over half the size of my body. I stood him by the window and carefully slid it open. He was so beautiful, with his loose black curls and weary caramel eyes, staring at me in bewilderment. My little superhero in his black and blue, Black Panther pajamas, needed rescuing tonight. He seemed to sense there was trouble and silently trusted that I knew what I was doing.

The intruder was now coming up the next flight of stairs and would soon be on the same level. He was trying to be quiet, but he had some weight to him, as the wood under the carpet complained beneath his steps.

I crept out the window onto the roof of my garage. Isaiah wasn't about to stay inside by himself and had already started crawling out when I turned to pull him through. I gently closed the window behind me. The stone granules on the shingles felt like coarse sandpaper on the tender soles of my feet and the cold rain quickly soaked my thin pajamas. It was too dangerous to jump off the roof with Isaiah in my arms, so I sat on the scabrous shingles and inched up against the cold steel siding, just out of sight from the bedroom window. The icy shock to my system unleashed a shudder from deep inside me. I locked my fingers together behind Isaiah's back and pressed him to my chest.

He softly said, "It's raining."

"I know, honey." I snuggled my baby boy close and sheltered him as my stomach knotted with fear. Tears and rain drizzled down the both of us. I could no longer hear the intruder and the house remained dark. I rocked back and forth with Isaiah as I silently wept, praying for rescue.

As we waited for the cavalry, an insight occurred. When I met with Ray Fury, my mail fell out of my purse. I'd been missing a letter from our wedding venue ever since. If he picked up any of my pieces of mail, Ray had my address. I'd freed him—I brought this on my family. *I am so sorry, Isaiah.*

After a few cold and quiet minutes, Isaiah tried to comfort me. He put a dimply hand on my cheek, smiled slightly, and said, "Is okay, Mama."

My boy could make me smile under the direst of circumstances. While I once proclaimed I'd never be a mom, Isaiah was a golden ray of light from heaven.

I whispered, "I love you, Isaiah."

Finally, the glorious sound of sirens cut through the night. I nuzzled my face against Isaiah's and said quietly, "It's okay. We're gonna be okay, now, baby."

As soon as I heard officers inside, I eased carefully back to the window with Isaiah locked in one arm and pounded on it with my free hand. I needed both hands to slide the window open, but the roof was getting slippery, and my hands were wet. I didn't want to risk dropping Isaiah to open the window.

Soon, a knight in navy blue was framed in the window and, after carefully scanning the roof, the officer slid the window open. I nearly went limp with relief. I gingerly handed Isaiah to him, and the officer gave me his other hand to help me back inside.

I quickly toweled off and changed Isaiah out of his rain-drenched PJs. Shivering with both adrenaline and my own soaked clothes, I wrapped a beach towel around me and went to speak with the officers downstairs. Sean had arrived and confirmed the window had been broken for entry, but the intruder was gone by the time the law arrived.

39

*"Time, as far as my father was concerned,
was a gift you gave to other people."*
—Michelle Obama

2021

XAVIER "ZAVE" WILLIAMS

1:30 P.M., SATURDAY, JUNE 5
NORTH LYNDALE AVENUE,
HAWTHORNE, MINNEAPOLIS

This would have to go down as the most insane year in the history of policing Minneapolis. The U.S. Marshalls Fugitive Task Force came riding into town, today, and cornered a fugitive on the top of a parking ramp in Minneapolis. The cavalry shot and killed the man in a vehicle, while a female passenger sat next to him; fortunately, she wasn't hurt. While the Marshalls announced that metro police departments participated in the arrest, they didn't share that they wouldn't allow the Minneapolis police officers to wear body cameras. Not wearing cameras was standard procedure for the U.S. Marshalls. I just didn't know how long they were going to get by with that and I didn't want any more rioting. I personally felt the Marshalls should've been held accountable, just like all the rest of us.

I was running through the number of reasons why working with Jada, today, was a terrible idea. I was currently up to twelve, and still counting. Jada insisted on confronting Ray Fury, *today*, and she was going whether I went with her or not. I couldn't let her go alone and, with Sean's heart condition, I didn't blame her for not telling him.

As Jada and I approached Flamin' Ray's front door, I asked her one last time, "Are you sure you want to do this?"

With the unwavering confidence of the righteous, she said, "I'm doing this."

Fury answered the door in a maroon Minnesota Gopher's t-shirt and gym shorts. He didn't seem too surprised to see us and flipped a nonchalant hand toward the living room, suggesting we have ourselves a seat. He and I sat at each end of a shabby couch, while Jada planted sassy hands on her hips and stood directly in front of him.

She was livid and not hiding it. "I want the letter you picked up when we met the other day."

Feigning ignorance but missing the mark, Fury asked, "What letter?"

Jada recklessly invaded his space, eyes on fire. I was glad not to be on the receiving end of her gaze—I didn't know that I wouldn't give under the rage in this sister's interrogation. Her full lips thinned as she pulled them over bared teeth. She told Ray, "I need it for my wedding."

It was interesting to watch Fury's instincts kick in; he slanted himself away from Jada, like this wasn't the first time he'd been under the scrutiny of an angry, authoritative woman. He almost sounded like a kid as he claimed, "I don't know what you're talking about."

Jada wasn't letting up. "You were in my house last night.

I just want you to know, the next time that happens, I'll be waiting for you and I'm gonna put a bullet in your head."

Fury got ahold of himself as he saw where this was going. He smiled in defiance, a little more swag in his tone. "I was home all night. Check my phone."

Jada railed on, "Yeah, I'm sure you learned *a lot* in prison," she said nastily. "Like don't bring the phone because they can track it. I want you to know you haven't fooled anyone. I now have undercover police protection, around the clock."

That wasn't true, but I understood her reasons for saying it.

Fury quipped, "You're welcome."

Jada wasn't having it. She leaned right into his face and, if possible, her wrath intensified. She poked him in the chest. "*Next time*," she sneered, "they're carrying you out in a body bag."

Fury shook off his short-lived intimidation and stood up, now towering over Jada. "You *threatening* me?"

As he advanced on her, her bravado crumbled and she backstepped toward me. The reality of her predicament registered and the barely contained fear in her eyes gave her away. Fury sensed it like a mamba, and he seemed to uncoil himself into something even larger before our eyes.

He unleashed venom in Jada's face, eyes slitted and dangerous and head tilting as he screwed his menacing glare into her eyes. I'd seen that look just before he knocked an opponent into next week. "Did you come over here to threaten my life?"

That was my cue. I stood up and put my body between them. Ray was bigger, but I was just angry enough. While he advanced with the powerful intimidation of a monstrous serpentine, my honor and adrenaline wouldn't allow me to stand by and let this rapist intimidate another woman. I stood tall and used my chest to direct Fury back toward the couch. I put some extra bass in my voice when I told him, "Sit down."

From a safe distance, Jada shouted over my shoulder at him, "Consider my threat to be the premonition of a psychic that I'm sharing for your benefit! Take *heed*, asshole." She marched toward the door and turned to me, "I'm done."

Without taking my eyes off Ray, I said, "I'll join you in a minute."

After Jada slammed out, I said to Fury in a voice I hardly recognized, "Side note—stay away from Lauren Herald." I had to meet him at his own state of cool. I internally ordered my body to chill out before this turned into something I couldn't come back from.

Obviously lying, he remarked, "Don't even know who you talkin' about."

"She does a lot of work for law enforcement—all agencies. If something happens to her, you're going to be in a world of hurt."

"Threaten, threaten, threaten. Y'all are boring me."

His nonchalance was heating up my attempts at being frosty. "Just giving you fair warning, Ray."

He picked up his game controller and resumed playing a video game—*Duke Nukem Forever*. He settled back on his raggedy couch, all pulled together now. I almost envied his ability to deescalate, as the best I could do was reduce my tension from full boil to an unstable simmer. He commented with a jut of his chin toward the TV, "Got some of my old video games out of storage."

I was familiar with the game. I made the parents of juveniles I dealt with destroy it. *Duke Nukem Forever* is a first-person shooter game that came out in 2011. The game featured breasts on walls that players can slap, aliens who forcibly impregnated women, frequent references to fellatio, and the players could spank women, if the women objected to being dragged off.

I squinted, "Should you really be playing this?"

Eyes now focused on the TV, he lackadaisically replied, "I have no restrictions on video games."

While he played, I helped myself to a search through his home.

Fury called after me, "You ain't gonna find nothin."

"Good," I echoed back. After a bit of looking around, I opened the top drawer of his dresser and found an envelope addressed to Jada Anderson. I walked out holding it.

He registered the envelope and gave me flat eyes. "Illegal search and seizure. There ain't a damn thing you can do with that."

That was true. I was pretty sure he was going to burn it as soon as I left, anyway.

"Shut the damn game off."

He humored me and complied, a smartass challenge on his mug.

"I watched you box years ago," I said. "You were something. I thought you were a brother who was going to get outta this 'hood."

Ray stared hard ass at me, then I watched the attitude on his face transform to resignation. He muttered, "I did, too."

"I've heard all of your justifications. So, you're okay if someone rapes your mother—if she forgets to lock the door?"

He barked out a laugh. "Good luck raping my mother. Ma is the only one who's ever knocked me out." Not wanting to appear weak, he quickly added, "I was only twelve at the time. After that, she just Maced me."

Trying to go easier, I reminded him, "You've got a second chance, *because* of people like Jada. What're you gonna to do with it, man? You get arrested again, they're going to civilly commit you. You're in lockup forever."

"Believe me, I've learned," he said. "Next time, they ain't findin' a body." He stood up and laughed at my bugging eyes. "It was a joke." Ray's posture deflated. "You have any idea what it's like for a sex offender straight outta prison? And a brother, at that? Try findin' a job."

"I understand it isn't easy, but employers are looking for labor all over, especially now with what's left of COVID and people getting paid for not working." I tried another approach. "You could still be a man you could be proud of. This time, instead of knocking people down, you could help 'em up. You could be an example of a man turning his life around."

I was frustrated when he didn't respond. I walked over to the gaming system and ejected *Duke Nukem.*

Fury watched through narrowed eyes as I walked into the kitchen with it. He remarked, "I know what you dicks do. You confiscate these games, then go home and play them."

I held his eyes hard as dropped the video game on the floor and crushed it under a twist of my heel. "Woops! Dropped it," I shrugged. "Play a game other than rape one-oh-one."

Jada was still at the door, taking it all in. I handed her the envelope as I breezed past her, and we left.

8:30 P.M.

WEST RIVER ROAD NORTH,

HAWTHORNE, MINNEAPOLIS

WHAT THE HELL WAS HAPPENING TO ME? I didn't go into people's houses and destroy property—at least until now. My morality was circling the drain and I needed to get myself back out of the sink.

I called Lauren. My morality, like my relationships, was meandering afloat and I was afraid of getting caught in the sucking whirlpool. I needed someone with her rudder set to true north to change course.

I pointed out, "The case is over with Cheyenne and I'm no longer speaking to her. No women have stopped over to chew me out for weeks, and I haven't dated since our last date. No hookups. Just being my miserable self, alone."

"I like you, Zave. I just came out of a relationship where I felt I was played. I'm not doing it again. I know you're a good man. It's your boundaries that make me nervous."

I suggested, "Help me out, then. I was directed to get Cheyenne to testify. She agreed to, but only if I would be at her beck and call. If you have a suggestion for how I should've handled it different, please tell me."

And she did. "Come on, Zave; you're better than that. You should've told her you would be available to talk from four to five p.m., each day. That way, you could have blocked out the time and it wouldn't have interfered with your personal life."

"But it isn't what she demanded."

Lauren's laugh tinkled like fine crystal. "Few people get what they demand. If you would've set a boundary, she would have complied. Maybe I'm wrong, but I think most strippers are an empty vat for attention and affection. She would've taken anything you offered. So, when an attractive young man offers her everything, she's hittin' it—hook, line, and sinker. I don't even blame her."

"Good point. This is exactly why I need to talk to you." I could imagine her smirking on the other end. "By the way, weren't you going to refer to Cheyenne as a kinesiologist?"

"Yes. Sorry. I meant—like most kinesiologists." She offered, "Do you want some more advice?"

"Is it going to cost me?"

"Dearly."

"Wow," I laughed hopefully. "Okay—your wisdom might still be worth it."

"This would be a good time to ask me out . . . "

40

"Women don't need to find a voice, they have a voice, and they need to feel empowered to use it, and people need to be encouraged to listen."
—MEGHAN MARKLE

2021

JADA ANDERSON

9:30 A.M., MONDAY, JUNE 7
LUTHERN SOCIAL SERVICE OF MINNESOTA
COMO AVENUE, FALCON HEIGHTS, ST. PAUL

It was time for me to have a conversation I should've had long before now. With some assistance from Zave, I was able to locate the intellectually disabled woman Ray Fury was acquitted of raping, years ago. Her name was Marian Mays.

Marian was husky woman of European descent, who was physically in her early thirties. She was dressed comfortably in a striped, button-down cotton shirt and high-waisted, out-dated jeans. What some jokingly referred to as "Mom jeans" seemed to fit Marian perfectly. We sat together at a picnic table in the backyard, while a group home staff person leaned against the back door, smoking and observing.

Marian's hair was thick and straight—lighter, with almost a reddish tone—unlike Fury's other reported victims.

His type clearly wasn't hair color. He was an opportunist. When he got the itch, he simply looked for the first vulnerable victim available. I wondered how many African American victims Fury had raped, who never reported him, out of fear of retaliation from him or the Disciples.

Marian brought out her book of sea creatures, so I took my time paging through it with her, looking at pictures.

I asked, "Did you know that your name, Marian, means graceful star of the sea?"

She beamed, apple-red cheeks pushing her eyes into a delighted squint. "No! Why didn't they tell me that?"

I smiled, "I don't know."

She pointed to a dolphin and said, "I bet you think that's a fish. It's not a fish. It's an animal."

"It is. And it's a mammal."

"Yeah—a mammal." She repeated to herself, "mammal," in an effort to remember this.

There was picture of a submarine, so I pretended to be confused. "Hmmm. Now, what do you think a submarine and a fish have in common?" I wanted to get a rough idea of her intellectual functioning.

Marian looked expectantly at me waiting for me to say it.

I patiently waited for her to say *they're both in water*. I offered a clue, "Think about it. Where do you see them?"

With a proud grin, she said, "In restaurants! They're both sandwiches."

It took me a second, but I laughed as I hugged her. "You're right!"

Excited, she lifted her foot and twisted it to and fro, showing me her bright pink Crocs.

"They are beautiful!"

She exclaimed, "Hot pink!"

I hated to switch to a painful subject, but there was no avoiding it. I took her hand in mine and said, "Marian, I need to talk to you about Ray Fury. He was the man you said raped you, ten years ago."

Marian looked at the staff as she responded, eyes wide, exuberant cheeks now slacking, "He is a bad man. They wouldn't let me ride the bus by myself—for five years!"

"Did you meet him on the bus?"

She emphatically replied, "No! It didn't even happen on the bus." After a pause she added, "It was at the bus *stop*."

"What happened?"

"He told me to walk with him." Her sweet face crumpled in distress. "I told him I'm not supposed to go with strangers. He said staff said it's okay. That was a lie!" She hung her head. "And then he took me behind a building."

"And he had sex on you."

"Yep."

"Did you call him a name when he was done?"

"Nope."

"Why did he hit you?"

"I asked him if he was going to be my boyfriend. He punched me hard and told me I couldn't tell anybody about him. I held my head and cried all the way home. And staff got it out of me." She smiled slightly, "But I didn't have to go to court. They took care of it for me."

It was obvious she wasn't told he was acquitted. "Did you want to have sex with him?"

"No!" she defensively responded. Marian looked shyly at me. "But I *did* want a boyfriend. They moved me to St. Paul, so I'd never have to see him again." She brightened, "And now I got a boyfriend! He doesn't drive, though."

"As long as you don't have to drive him around, it's a nonissue."

She made an exaggerated show of rolling her eyes and chuckled, "I don't *drive*."

Her openness warmed my heart. "Is he nice to you?"

"Yeah." She leaned closer and whispered in a tone anyone could have heard, "He told me he loves me."

"How did that make you feel?"

Marian glanced back at staff, and then quietly shared, "I love him, too." She giggled joyfully.

I put my arm around her. "I could talk to you all day."

She responded seriously, "No, you can't. Because I eat lunch at eleven-thirty . . . "

41

*"Luck is when an opportunity comes
along and you're prepared for it."*
—DENZEL WASHINGTON

2021

JON FREDERICK

1:00 P.M., WEDNESDAY, JUNE 9
BUREAU OF CRIMINAL APPREHENSION
1430 MARYLAND AVENUE EAST, ROOSEVELT, ST. PAUL

From the onset of this investigation, I'd tried not to poison the well, even though I had strong beliefs about who killed Sadie Sullivan. Sean reassigned me to help investigate some of the shootings in Minneapolis. I understood it, but it had taken me longer than I'd hoped to talk to people along the stretch from Bobby Long's home to Plymouth Creek, where Sadie's body was found. There were no surviving videos and no witnesses who could identify the driver of Bobby's truck. So then, I looked for accidents or events—anything that could've happened between 3:00 and 4:00 on the morning of August 31, 2013, which could be used to trip Bobby or Ray Fury up in a conversation.

I finally found something. Plymouth Creek was close to the Twin City Tennis Camps. While there were no events going on early in the morning, there were two tennis players who had returned at 3:30 that morning, from a tournament in Colorado.

The University of Minnesota had recruited a couple high school tennis stars—Rachel Hart from Minneapolis North and Megan Zang from Los Gatos Christian High School in San Jose, California. That summer, they'd been working at the Twin City Tennis Camp and playing in tournaments nation-wide. Both were still in Minnesota, so I called them into the BCA office to meet.

Megan was a lean and wiry Asian woman, vibrating with intensity. When I laid out my timeframe of interest, she said, "We drove straight through after finishing the tournament in Denver. It took thirteen hours."

Rachel added, "We were both anxious to get home. My car was still in the lot by the tennis camp." In contrast to her friend, Rachel's Nordic background was evident in her height and broad shoulders, with waxy blonde hair raked into a no-nonsense ponytail. Neither looked near their reported ages of thirty-something.

I asked, "So, what did you see when you arrived?"

"We saw a truck in the lot," Rachel said. "It stood out, because it was the only vehicle there, but no one was in it."

"Did you hear anything?"

"Just occasional cars cruising four-ninety-four. The lot is close to the freeway."

"You didn't see or hear anything?"

"No. I would've come forward if I had."

Megan added, "I saw a belt—or part of it—lying on the ground. It looked like it might've fallen out of the truck. It was like seeing a lone shoe on the side of the road—how does a person lose a shoe? Or a belt? I didn't think much about it."

I imagined Sadie's body being dragged out and part of the torn belt falling to the ground.

Her angular features intersected with tension as she remarked, "It was creepy to hear that woman had just been raped and murdered, right before we arrived. I'm sorry we can't be of more help."

"I appreciate you both coming in and talking to me. This still could be helpful."

Rachel asked, "How so?"

"Even though you didn't see him, he might have seen you. Were there any other times, that summer, when you came home so late?"

Rachel responded, "No. It was the first time and, after learning of the murder, we vowed we'd never be there that late again." Her forehead crinkled in worry. "Do you really think he saw *us*? Should we be worried?"

I didn't know. I said as much and advised both pay a bit more attention to their surroundings until we solved this case.

Megan added, "It's lucky neither of us pulls out and drives away until the other is doing the same."

I pointed out, "Lucky or wise?"

4:30 P.M.

51ST STREET & WASHBURN AVENUE SOUTH,
FULTON AREA OF MINNEAPOLIS

I JOINED SERENA IN THE BEDROOM AT AGNES' home, so we could talk while she got ready for another evening at work with Bobby Long. I sat on the bed and watched her dress.

After I filled her in on my interview with the tennis duo, I told her, "We need to get Bobby to say something about seeing tennis players late at night by the courts. They claim it was the only night, all summer, someone returned that late at the Twin City Tennis Camp. This would place Bobby at the site where Sadie's body was left, at the time it was dropped off. He claimed he didn't arrive until much later."

Serena hugged me, running her hands through my hair as she stood over me. "I know you worry, Luv. Sean is just outside the building. I'll be fine." She tilted my face up to hers and held it as she kissed me in reassurance.

"You were bothered, last time—enough that you didn't even spend the night with me."

"I wanted to be with the kids when they woke up."

Scenarios of Bobby kidnapping Serena and killing her tripped through my brain. I will never forget working my first murder book. Serena had been trapped in an armoire by another demented man, thrown into a cesspool, and nearly died. It was the first time I took a man's life and I'd do it again for her.

But today, Serena was a good investigator, and I didn't have the right to deny her the opportunity to work. She'd kicked some serious ass to save a child; still, I warned, "Don't let your guard down. Bobby has raped and killed. He's dangerous."

Appreciating the seriousness of my concern, she said, "I won't. I promise." She drawled, "Not my first rodeo, darlin'."

"I know. And I hate it—I never wanted you to be in danger again, but here we are. I know you can handle yourself, but it's not gonna stop me from worrying. Violence is a natural response for Bobby—it isn't for you. Tell Sean I want immediate intervention if Bobby does anything aggressive. *Anything.* You can't let him escalate."

Serena stepped back and tried to lighten the mood. "I have my mic'd bra on, now. Is this how I do it?" She aimed her breasts at my face and laughed.

"Only when you're around me."

42

"I want to be remembered as someone who used herself and anything she could touch to work for justice and freedom . . . I want to be remembered as one who tried."
—DOROTHY HEIGHT

2021

SERENA FREDERICK

8:30 P.M., WEDNESDAY, JUNE 9
EQUITABLE ASSOCIATES, TECHNOLOGY DRIVE,
EDEN PRAIRIE

I was so nervous; I could've thrown up. Bobby had worked like a madman to preserve time for us together at the end of his shift. I had to give him a little credit—he was a worker. The CAO (Chief Accounting Officer) told me Bobby checked in with her regularly, to make certain everyone was satisfied with his work. He was very skilled at ingratiating himself with others.

Bobby put away his cleaning items and had obviously washed his hands and face thoroughly, before coming to the counter to greet me. He nonchalantly leaned elbows on the faux granite countertop and asked, "Are we at the point where we can just sit in my car and talk, rather than making me stand at the counter?"

I sauntered around the counter over to him and smiled. "I don't know. Do you have something to say to me you can't say here?"

"Yeah. I wanted to explain myself. I felt bad about just leaving last time."

I looked back at my computer, pretending to have a significant amount of work to do, then said, "You know what? I'm just going to shut it all down and finish this later."

Pleased with my response, he said, "I'll wait for you outside."

After we climbed into Bobby's beastly truck, he said, "I'm sorry for leaving. I was sitting here with a beautiful woman, and I just let my emotions get the best of me. I didn't want you to see me like that. I like you—a lot."

"Thank you, Bobby," I dredged up gushing against all my instincts. "That's very kind. I've come to appreciate our conversations. I talk to people all day, but I don't really share myself with them, like I feel I can with you." I wanted to rush into the reasons for practically prostituting myself and say, *Tell me about Sadie's death*, but I'd learned from watching Jon interview that they tell you more if you let them introduce the topic.

When I didn't fill the dead air with chatter, Bobby hung his balding head a bit, and said, "Sadie's death has been hard on me. I said things I never should've said."

I offered a "hmmm," to keep him talking. "Something about it still lingers."

He looked at me with what I knew was affected remorse, but he was going for a heartfelt confession, so I played along with empathy in my eyes. "We argued before she died because of the rumors she was having an affair with a black man."

I searched for the right question, but I couldn't think of one that wouldn't give up my cover. I finally asked, *"Was* she?"

"Now that I look back, I don't think so. She was just being Sadie. Talked to everybody—she was kind and open but without fail was on the verge of being used by some degenerate."

He then quickly gathered himself and sat up straighter. "That's what I like about you. Sadie was everybody's muse. You're just for me."

It was unnerving to see his grandiosity restored with barely a beat, as he went from lamenting over his deceased, soon-to-be bride, to suddenly referring to me as his muse. I took a chance with my next question. "So, what did you say to Sadie that you still regret?"

Bobby took a breath and surveyed the parking lot in front of us intently. "I accused her of the affair. She cried and told me she'd been raped. I didn't believe her. Nobody in their right mind would've believed it—it was too *convenient*," he groused. "I accuse her of an affair and, all of a sudden, she comes up with, *I've been raped.*" The disgust on his face was almost equal to the disgust I felt for him churning around in my stomach. He turned to me, so incredulous, and asked, "Would *you* have believed her?"

Yes!!! But I didn't say it. "What did you do?"

"I walked out the door. Left her lying on the bed, crying. And that was the last conversation we had."

What a guy. My teeth ground at his story. It was all I could do to not verbally tear this nasty man into strips. Instead, in character, I asked, "What happened?"

"She just stayed like that until she had to go to work. She worked at three a.m., so that was her sleep time. I ignored her. Sadie's dead because of Ray Fury. Fury killed her. And now he's a free man. Where's the justice?"

Where's the justice, indeed.

"How do you come to terms with this?"

"I've been waiting for another chance to be with a beautiful, sweet woman—and here you are—my shot at redemption." He leaned in and kissed me.

I tamped down the bile in my stomach and allowed it, but then pulled away, soon as I could. The bench seat in his truck made me nervous. A console would have provided some forced space.

Once I secured a bit of distance between us, which took some doing, I said, "My sister wanted me to ask you a question and I'm afraid if we keep doing this, I'm going to forget."

He puffed up, the big man ready to be a hero. "What is it?"

I made a show of sighing with gratitude. "We're not from the metro. I've only lived here a couple months. She has a daughter who's into tennis and wanted to know about training camps in the area."

Bobby's head jerked back a bit, not ready for this question. He pursed his foul lips and thought for a bit, then said, "There's actually one near where they found Sadie's body. I only know about it because I spent time in the area investigating on the days after her death."

"She wants one that only has players involved during the day," I encouraged his need to be something important. "You know how some of those youth sports are, they have kids competing day and night, every day of the week."

Bobby liked giving advice. "I'm sure she could find a program that would just be daytime matches during the summer."

Taking advantage of his need to be the expert, I tried to appear engrossed in every word he shared. "Great. So, they don't do any of that weekend and late evening stuff?"

"Well—they do, but I think that only involves adults."

"Oh, wow—how late do *they* go?"

"I've seen them pulling in at three in the morning."

Bingo! That was what I needed to hear. Having achieved my mission, I relaxed—let my guard down. *Okay, Sean, you can rush in with the troops any minute.*

Bobby seemed to stop and think about the night he saw the tennis players, and then looked like he was bothered by what he had revealed. He shook himself and said, "Enough about that." He came across that bench seat and tried to kiss me harder.

I again I allowed a chaste kiss, but when he attempted to lunge his dirty tongue down my throat, I backed away and asked, "What are we doing here, Bobby?" I'd heard Jon's rough friends comment that there is no better cock-blocker than a woman wanting to talk about the relationship.

He was annoyed. "I can show you better than I can tell you."

And then he said something that brought a chill of terror to my very soul.

With a lascivious grin, he recited, "Peter, Peter pumpkin eater, had a wife and couldn't keep her. He put her in a pumpkin shell and there he kept her very well."

He'd recited a nursery rhyme just prior to raping Piper and Merri. This rhyme originated from a man whose wife was a prostitute. When he couldn't *keep her* at home, he murdered her.

Bobby forced me onto my back and began grinding his body into mine. He was strong and difficult to fight off. He forced a kiss and began running his hands over my body. *Sean, where the hell are you?* I had lost control of the situation. I needed to find a way to stop this, soon, as rapists reach a point of no return.

After being thoroughly groped, I panted, "I can't. My boss is coming back. I can't lose this job."

He hesitated just enough for me to wrestle out from underneath him. He still maintained his grip on my left bicep. *Had he felt the mic?* I had to say something to convince him I wasn't betraying him, or he'd kill me.

He gazed over to the dark shadows.

I offered, "Let's go to your place." It was a concession I knew he couldn't comply with.

It didn't take him long to come up with an excuse. "My dad's visiting. How 'bout yours?"

"I live with a crazy lady. Last time a guy visited me, she called the police."

He looked around, "It's dark enough on the east side of the building."

I shook my head. "No. I swear, my boss will be back in a matter of minutes. There was a report I finished she wants to send out tonight."

When he let go for a second, I opened my door and said, "Another time," and backed away—careful to be aware of his movement.

He seemed to consider coming after me, but he didn't. Finally, he grumbled, "Are we okay?"

"Sure we are." *As good as a woman is after being groped by a rapist.*

He tore out of the parking lot. I could hear his gears shifting as he gunned it down Flying Cloud Drive.

He might've been angry, but I doubted his rage was anywhere close to mine. I could've been raped. I wasn't just mad at him—I was furious. *Where the hell was my backup?* They could see everything. They could *hear* everything.

I drove around to the back of the building where the surveillance van was parked. I yanked open the door, ready to scream at the crew.

There Sean was, by himself, hunched over the steering wheel, clutching his chest. *Dear God!* I dialed 911.

43

*"I've learned that people will forget what
you said, people will forget what you did, but people
will never forget how you made them feel."*
—MAYA ANGELOU

2021

JON FREDERICK

10:30 A.M., THURSDAY, JUNE 10
BUREAU OF CRIMINAL APPREHENSION
1430 MARYLAND AVENUE EAST, ROOSEVELT, ST. PAUL

Zave, Serena, and I met at the BCA office to determine where to go from here. Serena managed to get Bobby to reveal enough to arrest him, but we lost the evidence. In the moments Sean thought he was dying, he frantically hit buttons, trying to signal for help, effectively shutting off the recording of Serena's work. We could see the video from the roof, but there was no volume. So, Bobby was still a free man.

Sean was hospitalized and Jada remained at his side. He didn't technically have another heart attack. He had severe angina as a result of pushing himself too hard since his heart surgery. He thought he could cover the surveillance by himself, last night, so he could have more agents out investigating the shootings in Minneapolis. I was enraged over it but refrained from running to the hospital and cursing Sean out. He wasn't a terrible man. We were all over-worked and dealing with a flood of guns being sold illegally in Minneapolis. A woman bought 47 guns in May and sold them all out of her trunk to anyone who could pay in Minneapolis. A man did the same with 33 more, beginning in June. The police confiscated twice as many illegal guns in 2020 in Minnesota than they did just ten years earlier.

Serena had put her body—if not her life on the line, and we had nothing to show for it. While she was fighting Bobby off last night, Zave and I were responding to another shooting in Minneapolis that left one man in the hospital. We determined the shooter had escaped in an oxblood red Dodge Charger with tinted windows and we had a partial plate number.

As we were about to start the meeting, Jada walked in and told us, "I'm sorry, but I have to be done with this investigation."

I said, "I understand."

Frustrated, she shared, "Sean needs to get it through his head that his options aren't changing or going back to his old life. His options are changing or *dying*. This is going to take all of my energy." Jada turned to me, "I'm sorry for getting you involved in this and then stepping away."

"It's all good, Jada. I understand. Family is first."

Before leaving, she asked, "Is Lauren Herald married?"

Zave told her, "No."

Jada's eyes narrowed as she asked, "Is she working this investigation?"

He said, "We've brought her into it, here and there."

Perplexed, she simply muttered, "Hmm," and left.

Serena had been quiet in Jada's presence. Once Jada was gone, she shared her new information with Zave.

He said, "So, it sounds like Ray raped Sadie that afternoon, as Jada suggested, and Bobby came home and accused her of having an affair."

Serena nodded. "Yeah. He didn't say a word about showering with her before she went to work, as he originally claimed. Bobby said they argued, and Sadie remained lying in bed. He told me that, after he accused her of cheating, he never spoke to her again. But none of his incriminating comments were recorded. Instead, we just have a silent movie of Bobby groping me." She shuddered and my fists tightened in renewed anger for my wife.

I told her, "You could file an attempted sexual assault charge on him."

She scoffed, "All he'd get is a misdemeanor for forced over-the-clothing contact. He's not getting by that easy. I want a *murder* conviction." Clearly agitated, she breathed deeply. "I'll go back and talk to him, if you and Zave do the surveillance this time."

Zave was quick to state, "I'm in."

"Alright." I respected Serena's resilience. We needed to finish this. It was all I could do, though, to tamp down my primal urge to throw her over my shoulder like a caveman and haul her home where she'd be safe.

Zave switched gears and asked, "What do we do about the break-in at Jada's?"

I said, simply, "It's not our case. It belongs to the Hennepin County Sheriff's Department."

He reacted, "You know they're not going to do anything about a home break-in where no one was assaulted and nothing was taken, when they have all these shootings going down."

"I know," I agreed. "But it's not our case. Jada has had a security system installed." Both Ray Fury and Bobby Long were escalating, but we didn't have enough evidence to arrest either.

Serena said reluctantly, "So, I'll go back and see Bobby again tonight."

And then my phone buzzed and Zave's buzzed right behind it. They'd located the Dodge Charger driven by the Minneapolis shooter. We were both requested to help search the area. A man who had opened fire in public last night was walking around Big Lake. It was an emergency we had to address. Knowing this could tie us up all day, Serena agreed to call in sick at the accounting office. We'd have to get back to Bobby next week.

I felt better that Serena was going home for the weekend. After last night, it would be good for her to step away from the investigation for a spell.

11:15 A.M.
HIGHWAY 10, NEAR KELLY FARM ROAD, ELK RIVER

ZAVE AND I WERE HEADED TO BIG LAKE IN separate vehicles when I received a call that the shooter was on the move, heading south on Highway 10. A police helicopter informed us the minute there were no cars between the Charger and us, so we used our vehicles to block the south lanes on Highway 10, and then waited. We were instructed to not engage with the driver, but we didn't have time to go anywhere for cover.

I grabbed the mirror I had strapped to Jackson's car seat for him to use during long drives. Zave and I each retreated to the backsides of our cars. We sat behind the wheels, as bullets would go through the body of a car.

I used the mirror to look under the car and watch for our shooter.

Zave commented from the other lane, "I need to have a kid."

"It might be easier to just buy a mirror."

I texted Serena: *Avoid Highway 10.*

I held the mirror below the frame of my car and watched as the Charger slowed upon approaching the blockade. It stopped about fifty feet away. The driver's door opened, and a Chicano man stepped out with a handgun. Not missing a beat, he opened fire at our vehicles. I wasn't sure if he thought we were slouched in the cars, or if he wanted us to show our faces.

Through the clatter of bullets ripping through metal, I maintained phone contact with the Hennepin County deputy directing this arrest. We were advised not to return fire, so we didn't move. This was insane. Zave and I looked at each other incredulously at the ridiculousness of it.

When he stopped shooting, squads skidded in and blocked the Charger in on all sides. Over the phone, I could hear the sergeant directing officers to go to nearby houses and instruct people to hunker down in their basements.

1:45 P.M.

WE SAT ON THE ROAD LISTENING TO A negotiator trying to talk a 26-year-old man named Izon DeLeon down. After two hours, Izon shot himself. The police fired no shots. No riots, tonight. I would never know what led to the exchange of gunfire in which Izon was involved, or the tragedy of this young man's life. Zave and I would spend the rest of the afternoon assisting the investigation by picking up shells, gathering evidence, and completing paperwork related to the incident. Even though it wasn't our case, we couldn't simply pass it off to another team; everybody was dealing with shootings.

44

"I had reasoned this out in my mind; there was one of two things I had a right to, liberty or death; if I could not have one, I would have the other."
—HARRIET TUBMAN

2021

CHEYENNE SCHMIDT

9:30 P.M., THURSDAY, JUNE 10
WEST RIVER ROAD NORTH,
HAWTHORNE, MINNEAPOLIS

The chilly night air raised a minature tent village of goose-bumps across my arms. West River road overlooked the dark waters of the ominous Mississippi. I searched up and down the street. Desolate silence, quite unusual for Hawthorne, surrounded me. I finished carefully putting my makeup on in the rearview mirror. I didn't dare do it until now, out of fear I'd run into Bobby before I got here. If he knew what I was doing, I'd be dead. I looked in the mirror. *This is as good as I'm going to look. You'd better appreciate it, Zave.*

The last few days, I'd received email after email from Zave, begging me to give him another chance. At the same time, he didn't answer my calls. He must've had a girlfriend checking his phone, and he wasn't going to dump her until he knew I was a sure thing. I was tired of being used by men. Whatever feelings Bobby had for me were gone and, in his own words, I'd become his *own private whore.*

I slipped on my navy hooded windbreaker and carefully covered my face with a matching mask. Even though the mask mandates had been lifted for outdoors, lots of people were still wearing them and I didn't want to be recognized. It was drizzling, so I could pull off wearing a windbreaker.

Zave had invited me to his place, tonight, through emails. I could read men; I felt his longing for me when his eyes slid across my thighs at my apartment. There was no comparison between Zave and Bobby. Zave had a perfect, ripped body; he was nicer and more respectful. He told me to call him when I arrived, if he wasn't home. *Finally, the right man reached out!* I was so excited I made the call as I headed up the embankment to Zave's house. *He could've turned the outside light on for me.*

"Zave, I'm almost at your door."

He hesitated, then asked, "Cheyenne?"

"Not funny, Zave."

A gunshot rang through the night. Startled, my phone went flying out of my hands and slid down the slope. That shot was close. I didn't waste a second looking for my damn phone. I ran. I thought I heard a body drop at Zave's door.

I stumbled as I slid off the hill onto the level tar, and my hands scraped raw on the road when I dropped to my knees. I scrambled to my feet and raced to my car. I put it in gear and tore out along the river road, ripping my mask off so I could breathe.

9:50 P.M.
COLD STREAM LANE, EDEN PRAIRIE

WHAT THE HELL JUST HAPPENED? Had somebody killed Zave? I didn't have time to grieve. I needed to get somewhere safe.

As I drove to Bobby's, my adrenaline cooled, and I could think again. I couldn't go into his house wearing this new blouse and with my face all made up—not to mention the grass stains on the knees and probably on the ass of my light-washed jeans. I slowly cruised by. The house was dark; Bobby's truck wasn't home. I should be okay. I still had my apartment in Brooklyn Center. I could just go back there if I had to. But then Bobby would be convinced I cheated on him. I needed to be here when he got home.

Once inside, I slapped at the light switches to see what I was dealing with. I couldn't chance him waiting for me in the dark. No sign of Bobby—so far, so good. I raced to the bedroom, grabbed some clothes and, in a drawer, beneath my underwear, felt for my gun. Bobby helped me buy a nine-millimeter when I first moved in. He told me he wasn't losing another girlfriend. Honestly, I feel he wanted me to get it so he'd have quick access to a gun. I rushed to the bathroom and tucked the gun under my towel, so it would be there when I got out of the shower.

I let the warm water stream down my body as I tried to relax. It was an incredible relief to scrub my makeup off.

I took some deep breaths and, my guilt and evidence finally washed away, turned off the water and stepped onto the bathmat. *Where was my gun?* I shook my clothes in a panic and moved junk around on the vanity; the gun fell to the floor. *Oh yeah. Under the towel.* I was officially a hot mess.

With a sigh of relief, I shimmied into my yoga pants and went to the living room.

When I went to pull the curtains, I noticed a burgundy Taurus parked in front of the house. There was a thin, athletic man a little over six feet tall, at my door. His untucked shirt matched the color of his car. I watched him click off the safety on his gun as he approached.

I followed suit. I held my gun straight out, in firing position. *Bring it, asshole. I'm not going to lie in wait for you to find me. If you're comin' in, I'm ready. I'm tired of being scared. You wanna have it out, let's have it out—right now!*

I let the door slowly swing open.

The man vaulted to the side of the door and shouted, "This is Jon Frederick from the BCA! I need you to drop your gun and slide it out the door."

Good God, I was seconds away from a shootout with the flippin' police. *What the hell was I doing?* I tossed the gun out the door. *Sweet niblets—I should have put the safety back on.* It clacked down the steps. I held my breath, hoping it wouldn't fire; my air whooshed out when the gun landed without going off. I put my hands on the back of my head, walked out, and dropped to my knees.

10:20 P.M.
BUREAU OF CRIMINAL APPREHENSION, 1430 MARYLAND
AVENUE EAST, ROOSEVELT, ST. PAUL

I FOUND MYSELF SITTING IN AN INTERROGATION room across from a polite investigator in his thirties, who had again introduced himself as Jon Frederick. He asked me to explain how I came to know Xavier Williams. After I finished telling him how Zave came to my rescue and helped me through court, I began to consider where this was going.

Jon set my phone on the table.

He knew I was at Zave's house. I asked, "Is Zave dead?"

He didn't answer. I told him, "I swear to God, I had nothing to do with it. He and I were emailing. He asked me over and I went. I was going up the steps when I heard a shot. That's why I was holding the gun when you arrived. I was afraid the shooter was coming after me, too."

Jon slid a picture of a Latino-looking woman toward me. "How do you know her?"

I'd never seen her before. "I don't."

"Her name is Marita Perez . . . "

45

"I'm sick and tired of being sick and tired . . .
We have to build our own power."
—Fannie Lou Hamer

2021

CHEYENNE SCHMIDT

6:30 P.M., SATURDAY, JUNE 12
COLD STREAM LANE, EDEN PRAIRIE

Bobby finally came home. I'd spent most of the day applying for jobs at convenience stores and restaurants and had a couple promising leads. My stomach churned with jitters; I walked on eggshells around him, worried about how much he knew.

Bobby directed me to sit by him on the couch. "Whatcha been up to?"

My skin was tingling with nervous warm sweat. Knowing he still might have some cop friends, I told him, "I was brought in for questioning about a murder."

"Who was killed?"

"Some woman named Marita Perez."

"Where did it happen?'

There was no way I could explain what I was doing at Zave's, so I said, "I don't know. I had nothing to do with it."

"Who's Marita Perez?"

I swallowed hard. "I honestly have no idea."

Bobby was irritated. "That doesn't make any sense. You were questioned about shooting someone you didn't know, and you have no idea where it happened?"

He seemed to know I was lying. "Honestly, I don't know how I got dragged into this."

Bobby stood up. "You're lying to me. You need to leave."

I remained seated. "Please—not now. I'm afraid. I can't be alone right now."

He paced until he finally left the room and returned with a notepad and a pen. He ordered, "I want you to write on this paper, 'This is my address,' and then write your address."

"Where I'm living, now, you mean? Here?"

"No. Your apartment in Brooklyn Center."

I did as I was told and handed him back the notepad. "Why do you need my address? You know my address."

Bobby barked, "If you want to have any chance with me, you're going to need to do something *for* me."

I timidly consented, "Okay."

"I want you to put on a miniskirt, heels, and the skankiest top and makeup you have, and we're going for a walk."

"Why?"

He impatiently ordered, "Just do it or get the hell out."

7:20 P.M.
NORTH LYNDALE AVENUE,
HAWTHORNE, MINNEAPOLIS

BOBBY DROVE TO FARVIEW PARK IN THE Hawthorne neighborhood and parked his car at the end of the block.

He told me, "Take your time and promenade up this block and back. I'll be around the corner, just out of sight when you return."

Was he trying to get me raped? "Bobby, don't do this. You can't leave me here."

"I'm not leaving you. I just want to see you make the walk. Then we'll get in my car, drive home, and make love. I promise, I'm not leaving you here."

"Do I have to?"

"If you want to stay with me tonight—yes."

"*Why?*"

"Consequences for choices. It's an easy punishment. All you have to do is walk. C'mon--scoot."

No matter how much I argued, I was going to end up doing this. I got out of the car and started the slutty stroll. I'd pulled on my high-heeled black boots that went up to my thighs—I used to joke that they were my "gravity boots," as my knees always seemed to end up in the air when I wore them.

The walk up the block went better than anticipated. People gawked out of windows, but no one said a word to me. When I finally reached the end of the block, I saw him. There was Ray Fury, sitting in a lawn chair, leering at me from a porch as I strutted by. My anxiety skyrocketed. I could feel my head pounding, like I was being struck again and again. I quickly turned and hurried back.

Ray was about to say something to me, when a woman rushed out of a neighboring home and yelled, "Skanky bitch! If I see you on this block again, I'm tearing you apart with my bare hands."

I wasn't sure what I was going to do if Bobby bailed. *If I just wouldn't have gone to Zave's. Then after the shooting, Zave acted like he never invited me. He set me up. I'm so stupid.*

To my relief, Bobby was around the corner, as promised. *Thank you, Bobby!* I quickly got in and we drove back to Eden Prairie.

ONCE IN THE HOUSE, HE DIRECTED ME, "Go stand by the couch. Drop your underwear and bend over."

Oh, come on. Couldn't this be enough? "I've told you, it's painful for me to do it like that." I had a tipped uterus, so intercourse that wasn't face-to-face was not enjoyable.

He couldn't have cared less. "I'm not going to ask again. If you don't, I'm throwin' your ass out of here. Your call."

If this was what needed to happen for him to get over my betrayal, I'd suffer through it. "Okay."

I did as I was told. I squeezed the upholstered arm as needed to get me through the pain. It's been said Jack the Ripper killed his victims in this position, cutting their throats when he was taking them from behind. I found some comfort in the curtains being open. He wouldn't kill me where everyone could see. This was all about humiliation. Bobby got this way when he was angry. The episode would run its course and we'd be good again.

When he was done, he told me, "Take a nice warm bath and I'll make us something to eat."

The moment of relief had finally arrived. It was over. I felt so degraded but was relieved to finally move on.

AFTER A LONG, SOOTHING SOAK IN THE TUB, I stepped out in my most comfy lightweight pajama pants.

Bobby was waiting for me. "Kneel on the floor and kiss my feet."

"I'm not doing that, Bobby."

He handed me my car keys and said, "Then goodbye. I don't want you here. I can't even stand to look at your lying face when we screw. Get the hell out."

I pleaded, "I didn't do anything!"

He smacked me with a hard backhand. "Go run back to your buddy, Zave."

The anger behind that slap was a clear message that I wasn't safe, here. I opened and shut my jaw trying to work the soreness out. Bobby knew this whole time. For him, it was simply a matter of seeing how much humiliation I'd tolerate before I'd find the self-respect to leave. Every concession strengthened Bobby's sense of superiority over me.

46

*"Friends take up time,
and I didn't have time."*
—Richard Pryor

2021

BOBBY LONG

9:45 P.M., SATURDAY, JUNE 12
51ST STREET & WASHBURN AVENUE SOUTH,
FULTON AREA OF MINNEAPOLIS

I'm feeling an incredible rush from watching Cheyenne grovel for affection. Did she really think I could feel anything for her after she went to Zave? Stupid bitch. And it was all willing. No probation violation for me. My hands are clean. But to keep them clean, I need to disappear for a bit after tonight.

I know it's late, but I'm feeling good, and I have to see if Serena will go with me. Even though I wanted her the other night, I respect that she wouldn't have sex in public. I pull in front of where she's staying and hope Cruella, or whatever that crazy woman's name is, doesn't answer the door again.

No such luck. If forty-year-olds are Generation X, this battle-ax must have come from Generation A.

I barely hold up my hand to knock and the old biddy swings the door open. I ask, "Is Serena home?"

She answers with a question. "Do you know what time it is?"

"Yes. It's nine forty-five." I push my way past her through the door, damn near knocking her over. I don't care. Let her break a hip. "Is Serena home?" I repeat and call out, "Serena!"

There's no answer, but I can hear the shower running, so I make up my mind to stay a bit.

The sea hag follows me. "Get out of my home! Do I need to call the police?"

I turn to stare her down, which is easy as I stand a good foot over her. "I *am* the police." Well, I *was* the police, anyway.

Guarded, she obediently steps back.

"If you can be honest with me, you have nothing to fear," I tell her. "What's your name?"

"Agnes. Like the bull."

It's angus, but I don't bother to correct her. "Tell me about that Jon Kennedy guy. What does he do for living?"

I swear I catch a glimpse of a smile when she answers, "Reduction mammaplasty. If that's too complicated for you— tit shrinking. How do you think Serena met him? She took her shirt off and it was love at first sight. But I guess it was a little too much."

Is she serious? They felt natural. Maybe the Doc went a little too far. "Why would Serena have breast reduction surgery?"

Agnes continues, "She was running a fever."

"What?"

She taunts, "You're such an idiot. Why would anybody have breast reduction surgery?"

"I mean—" I stop myself. "Forget it."

Agnes laughs and, trying to be hip, cackles, "I'm just pulling your chain—dawg! That feather-brain isn't smart enough to be a doctor."

I could snap her in half like a Triscuit. Can't say I'm not tempted; she tries my patience. "Okay, what's this Kennedy guy look like?"

Agnes says, "He had a patch over one eye. Wore one of those Steve Van Zandt headscarves. Had a prosthesis on one leg."

"What the hell? Is he a pirate?"

Agnes scolds, "I don't appreciate you making fun of the disabled."

I raise my hand in retreat. "Sorry. I thought you said he was like me."

She goes on, "I said there are *similarities*. He was chubby, insecure—not very smart."

The shower is now off, and I wait for Serena to come out of the bathroom.

Instead, a petite Asian woman in a robe and a scarf over her head steps out. She immediately stops and asks, "Who are *you?*"

"I'm looking for Serena."

Agnes immediately interjects, "Serena drove up north to visit her family for the weekend. You should've just asked."

The Asian woman asks Agnes, "Do you want this man here?"

Agnes responds, "No. Absolutely not. This guy's like the south end of a Clydesdale, headed north."

Her roommate tries to hold back her laughter as she tells me, "I think you'd better leave."

"If you talk to Serena, tell her Bobby's looking for her."

47

"I can accept failure.
Everyone fails at something.
But I can't accept not trying."
—MICHAEL JORDAN

2021

FLAMIN' RAY FURY

11:00 P.M., SATURDAY, JUNE 12
NORTH LYNDALE AVENUE,
HAWTHORNE, MINNEAPOLIS

I'd been thinking about Zave's words to me. *I could be a man I'd be proud of again.* I got it. No more drunks, retards—I could do that.

I shouldn't have gone after Jada. But she pissed me off—rubbin' it in my face like she did. If Ma saw me with a woman like Jada or Sadie, she'd laugh and say, *She's out of your league, son. Don't go foolin' yourself. Know your place.* Well Ma, my place was anywhere I wanted to be.

Still, Zave's words kept ringin' in my head. Could I be a decent man yet? What would that even look like? I'd just get up and go to work. Keep my nose clean. Maybe someday I'd get an award for bein' an example.

I smiled at the invitation I'd received.

Cheyenne's strut was hot tonight. Those boots popped a chubbie in my jeans. There was no mistakin' her intentions . . .

48

"Don't ever let anyone make you feel like you
don't matter, or like you don't have a place in
the American story—because you do. And you
have the right to be exactly who you are."
—MICHELLE OBAMA

2021

CHEYENNE SCHMIDT

11:30 P.M., SATURDAY, JUNE 12
XERXES APARTMENTS, 5211 XERXES AVENUE NORTH,
BROOKLYN CENTER

I'd never been more alone. I now had nothing. No money. No friends. No resources. Bobby didn't like my friends and, to keep the peace, I had distanced myself from them. I had become financially dependent on him and had barely any food left in my apartment. I did manage to find an old bottle of cooking wine in the cupboard, which I polished off. I finally felt my nerves had calmed enough to sleep. I double-checked that the door was locked and stripped down to my panties. It was hot in here tonight and I couldn't afford to run the air conditioning. Instead, I'd sleep with as little on as possible. I opened the windows and blinds, hoping for an evening breeze. The glow from the streetlights gave my apartment the dusky, shadowy twilight vibe you'd find in a closed bar. *Tomorrow's another day.*

I thought about trickin' myself out for cash and drawing unemployment. But there were a couple problems with that. The first was that strippers were self-employed. The clubs do this so they can avoid paying unemployment and medical expenses. The second was that I wasn't a welfare whore. The only time I didn't have a paycheck, since I was sixteen, was when I lived with Bobby and believe me, that *was* work. I didn't care what Margaret said, I wasn't a hooker. Having a guy working for her to set me up was entrapment.

I had an offer to begin working at a convenience store Monday. I was going to take it and work as many hours as possible to survive. The manager said I wouldn't have any trouble getting additional shifts. Everyone was struggling to find help.

My last thoughts before I drifted off to sleep were, *Bobby still has a key to my apartment. What am I going to do if he returns in the middle the night to humiliate me one last time? It was so weak and pathetic of me to allow myself to be demeaned by him. I'd kill him before I'd allow him to do that again . . .*

1:25 A.M., SUNDAY, JUNE 13

IT WAS SO HOT, I SLEPT FITFULLY, ROTATING from my side, to my back, to my other side, to my stomach, like a broiler chicken on a rotisserie. When I flopped to my back for the hundredth time, the air in the room felt different. I slowly opened my eyes and there was Flaming Ray Fury standing over me, removing his jeans.

He laughed at me, "Curiosity got the better of you, girl. You needed a taste of the flame. Well, here I am, home delivery, burnin' hot."

This had to be a bad dream. I squeezed my eyes shut and opened them again, hoping I could blink him away.

Ray was still there. Now completely naked.

I gathered my sheets around me, scooted up to a sitting position, and demanded, "Leave."

He was damn cocky when he said, "Not happenin' girl. Not yet. We got some business to attend to."

He crawled onto the bed like a panther, sleek with sweat and tensed to attack. He roughly yanked my sheet away. "Get that last piece of clothing off."

"No. Please, leave. I swear, I'll scream."

Ray smirked with confidence, "The hell you will." He ripped my panties off and squeezed the corners of my jaw until my mouth was forced open. He shoved my sweaty underwear into my mouth and pushed my mouth shut.

I gagged and coughed as he hovered over me and managed to push the fabric back out of my throat.

When he pawed my legs apart, I slid my hand under my pillow.

I swung my nine-millimeter out and dug the barrel into his ribs. I pushed the underwear out of my mouth with my tongue and spat, "Get. Off!"

He smiled, "That's the plan, bitch."

And then I fired. Again, and again, and again—four shots in two seconds. The blasts echoed through the apartment and my ears began ringing like a bell choir had taken up practice inside my head. I was covered with bright red blood. I remember thinking *I have to get that bleeding creature out of my bed. I have to sleep here.* When I pushed the beast off me, I felt the vibration of his body thud onto the floor, and then the reality of what just happened sank in. I swiped my hands on my sheets, leaving smears no amount of bleach would ever remove. I grabbed my phone and thumbed in 911.

I walked with wobbly legs around Ray's lifeless body, keeping my distance, like his hand might shoot out and grab me. I made my way to the bathroom and stood naked in front of the mirror, numb to the sight of my body painted with blood. I didn't recognize myself—my eyes were empty like someone else was staring back at me. I tried to use my makeup wipes to clean myself up, I suppose to not ruin any other linens, but kept dropping them. I finally gave up and threw on a t-shirt and shorts.

My legs carried me into the kitchen and my hand grabbed my bottle of Fireball off the counter. I took a big pull straight out of the bottle, my throat and lips instantly on fire. Dispatch said police were on their way.

As I waited, I found myself thinking, *What the hell happened to me?* When I fell asleep, I thought I was at my lowest point. Now I might be on my way to prison. If I'd grown up in Stillwater, it would be a clear case of self-defense. But in Brooklyn Center, it was a crapshoot. I thought about the statue of Lady Justice in the courthouse. The weights are unbalanced, and she's blindfolded. That was a clear message to me—don't expect it to be fair. *Regardless, I'm glad I tucked my gun under my pillow before I went to sleep.*

2:25 A.M.

I FOUND MYSELF SITTING AT MY SMALL kitchen table talking to Zave, who was now a homicide investigator. In the heat of the night, he was sweating through his blue MPD t-shirt.

I asked, "Where's the white guy?"

"Investigator Frederick is on his way."

I reached for my Fireball, but Zave slid it out of my reach. I think I was still in shock but, with emotions darting all over the place, I asked, "Did I break up a date?"

Zave was angry, and not about to waste a second on casual conversation. "Why were you at my house the night Marita was shot?"

I glanced over at the crime scene techs who were within hearing distance. "Are you sure want to discuss this here?"

Zave sternly enunciated each word, fully and distinctly, as he spoke. "Yes. Imagine what it was like for Marita's parents to hear from me that their beautiful daughter was murdered on my doorstep, and I have no idea why. Marita was creative and loved—she never hurt anybody."

"You emailed me," I reminded him. "Told me to meet you at your house. I didn't know where you lived until you sent me your address."

He struggled with this. "I didn't email you, Cheyenne. If what you say is true, someone was catfishing you." He scratched his head. "Why would someone set you up for Marita's murder?"

"I swear, I don't know."

Zave pursed his lips but didn't say anything, initially. He pointed toward my bedroom. "You have some explaining to do. There's a dead man on your bedroom floor, with a note from you—with your address—and a key to your apartment in his pocket."

"What? No. That's not right," I was so confused. "That's impossible." And then it finally sank in. The walk. Writing my address. Bobby had my extra key. I mumbled, "Bobby sent him here."

Doubtful, he questioned, "And how would that happen? Ray and Bobby aren't exactly friends."

I asked, "The night Marita was murdered—what was she wearing?"

"A black windbreaker and jeans."

I couldn't wrap my stupid brain around how he played me. "Bobby did it. He intended to shoot *me*. I was supposed to be at your door." I felt my body curling inward and started rocking to shake the shock and shame loose; I was suffocating from it.

He argued, "It's not like you could be mistaken for Marita. You told Jon you were wearing a white blouse."

"I was—underneath the windbreaker." I used my bought-and-paid-for nails to scratch down my bare arm. The pain cut through enough to bring me back to reality. "Okay—I wasn't completely honest with Jon. I was wearing a navy-blue windbreaker over the blouse, with the hood up and a black facemask. I was afraid if I told him I dressed as a cat burglar, I would never convince him I wasn't guilty."

"So why *were* you dressed that way?"

"I lived with *Bobby*," I said. "Duh. You know what he's like. If somebody would've recognized me and told Bobby I was going to see you, I was dead . . . "

3:40 A.M.

THE ADRENALINE WAS FINALLY WEARING OFF and my eyelids were heavy. A perky little brunette had come with Jon Frederick. While he and Zave were in my bedroom with the body, she sat down at the kitchen table next to me. Her face was too open—too *nice*. I didn't trust her. Women didn't treat me like this.

"I'm Serena," she said. "Are you okay?"

I laughed at her. "I'm a lot of things, but one thing I'm not is *okay*. Am I going to jail?"

"No," she gently took my hand. "It was clearly self-defense." When I said nothing, she asked, "Can I try to be your friend?"

"Why?" This Laura Ingalls Wilder chick—what could she possibly know about what my life is about? She looked to me like she hadn't lived a hard day in her life. Still, something deep in me was cracking under her kindness. *Dammit.*

With an understanding smile, she said, "Looks like you really need one, here."

"You got that right," I said. I was surprised to feel the beginnings of tears prickling behind my eyes but wasn't ready to let them go—I wasn't sure I'd ever stop. I changed the subject. "So, you're with Jon?"

Serena nodded.

"I saw the two of you come in together and I could tell. Look, if it's a work thing, I won't tell a soul."

She smiled, "I'll help you, but you can't give up my name to anyone."

"Far as I'm concerned, I've never met you." I couldn't keep the snotty out of my voice and didn't care. She'd go away soon enough; might as well help her along.

Serena softly said, "Jon and I are married."

Huh. I didn't even consider a legit relationship. "So what are you, the good cop?"

"No, but I have been a rape victim."

I decided to hear her out, but first had to ask, "Why would you help *me?* I'm a drunk stripper who lied to your husband and was screwing a crooked cop."

She teased, "I like to keep a good mix of friends. Do you know how hard it is to find someone who meets all of those criteria?"

I accidentally laughed and a member of the crime scene unit, who had wandered into the kitchen, glanced over at us.

Getting back to the seriousness of my situation, I told her, "I don't think anybody realizes how good Bobby is at this. Under his direction, *I* set this up—and I didn't even know it. He wanted me to either be raped or to kill Fury and it happened. And Bobby's hands are clean."

"Believe me," Serena said, "Bobby isn't fooling me. I personally have no tolerance for men who assault women and Bobby's a bully. I'm your ally through this." She briefly squeezed my hand and added, "You've been given the opportunity to call a friend and you haven't called anyone."

"I don't have anyone." That was hard to say out loud.

"Okay." I hated seeing myself through her eyes. The kindness and pity were almost too much to take.

And then she stepped up like no one had ever stepped up for me in my life.

"Your place is a crime scene, so you can't stay here. And I assume you can't afford a hotel."

I was too tired to be proud and bitchy anymore. "How do you know that?"

"Because guys like Bobby drain all the love, cash, and friends from women before they kick them to the curb. But never forget, you're the hero here, Cheyenne. You're the only one who legitimately got Ray Fury convicted of a crime. And when he came back after you, you survived. You're made of some pretty resilient stuff and I'd like to learn more about that."

Talking to her felt good. "So, what do you suggest?"

"I'll take you to a thirty-day inpatient chemical dependency treatment program."

I needed to be honest with her. "I don't think drinking is my main issue."

With a gentle smile she agreed, "I don't think it is, either. But, if you'll voluntarily put yourself into treatment, it will buy us thirty days to secure work and another place."

"I'm supposed to start a new job—as a *cashier*," I emphasized, "on Monday."

"I'll talk to your employer and the treatment program and see what we can do."

"But—why? Why are you helping me?"

"Maybe a couple of years from now, you'll pay it forward. But you don't have to—it's your call."

"I will." The tears threatened again and finally, I let them go. As I sobbed a lifetime of helplessness, fear, and anger into my hands, Serena sat quietly and rubbed my back. *Thank you, God, for sending me this angel!*

49

*"I prefer to be true to myself, even at
the hazard of incurring the ridicule
of others, rather than to be false,
and to incur my own abhorrence."*
—FREDERICK DOUGLASS

2021

XAVIER "ZAVE" WILLIAMS

12:30 P.M., FRIDAY, JUNE 18
WEST RIVER ROAD NORTH,
HAWTHORNE, MINNEAPOLIS

As Charles Dickens once said, "It was the best of times, it was the worst of times, it was the age of wisdom, it was the age of foolishness, it was the epoch of belief, it was the epoch of incredulity, it was the season of light, it was the season of darkness, it was the spring of hope, it was the winter of despair."

The worst—my painful conversation with Lachelle Lewis when I stopped home for lunch on Friday. She was waiting for me when I arrived. Lachelle had a lot to be angry with me about, but I let her in my house, anyway.

A tumultuous storm of hatred and grief flashed in her eyes like lightning.

I was ashamed for abandoning Lachelle when her dad died and ashamed again for not calling her back after Danny's death. And now her best friend was murdered just outside my door.

The muscles in her face tensed as she demanded, "Why is Marita dead?"

"I wish I knew. She randomly decided to stop over to talk, and someone shot her. I wasn't home—I didn't invite her over."

"But you'd invited her over before, right?"

"Yes."

"And now she's dead. Killed at your doorstep. Does it even bother you?"

I softly told her, "It torments me, Lachelle. I liked Marita."

She studied me, "I want to scream at you, but you've got the saddest look on your face." I watched her sharp, angry features transform into soft disappointment, if not pity. I wasn't sure which was worse. I had to look away and took an instinctive step back, as if her opinion of me would simmer over and stain my shirt. She sighed, "I got the best of you. Back when you were fifteen, for a little while, you cared. You listened and you wanted to know everything about me. Now you're just empty."

I didn't want it to be true but had nothing to say.

This seemed to incite a fresh wave of rage, as Lachelle snarled, "Look, I don't believe you killed Marita, but you're *poison*," she hissed like a street cat. "Stay away from me and stay away from my friends . . ."

She slammed the door on her way out and left me standing there, staring at the floor.

THE BEST—OCCURRED ONLY MOMENTS LATER. Lauren called and asked, "What do you have going this weekend?"

"Work, I imagine, unless you have a better offer."

She hesitated, "I know this is gutsy, but I have to ask. I just received a call from a couple I did a drawing for. They offered me use of the cabin they rented for $4000 a week on

Fawn Lake, all weekend, in appreciation of my work. They were called back to the metro and said it's all mine, if I want it. The cabin sits on a peninsula, so it's surrounded by water on three sides. There's no Wi-Fi, but there is a warm fireplace. I thought it would be perfect—if I could go with you."

I needed this. Grinning, I told her, "I'm already packing in my mind. I will pick you up the second you are ready . . ."

50

"It just looks like we're not hurting."
—TERRIE WILLIAMS

2021

CHEYENNE SCHMIDT

10:30 P.M., SATURDAY, JUNE 19
PARK AVENUE WOMEN'S CENTER FOR ADDICTION
2318 PARK AVE, PHILLIPS, MINNEAPOLIS

A guest speaker, Alice, had shared her history of alcohol addiction. Alice was a dirty blonde with a Texas twang, weathered features, and thin muscular arms. She was once pretty, but her hard life left her with wrinkled eyes squinted into the slits of a chronic skeptic. When she was done speaking, Alice hung around and I bent her ear with my story of sexual victimization as an adolescent, rape from Ray Fury, followed by an abusive relationship with a cop. I felt so important—she was listening to me and believing me.

Alice asked if I wanted to step outside for a smoke. I told her, "I better not. I'm not supposed to leave the building." Serena made me promise I wouldn't leave the facility. I was protected, as long as I stayed inside.

Alice teased, "Far be it from an addict to break a rule." When I didn't respond, she added, "Tell you what, give me your phone and I'll put my number in it. You can call me anytime you need to talk." I handed her my phone; she entered her number and handed it back. "There. Well, I'm stepping out for a minute."

I looked back. Nobody was paying attention to us. I said, "Hell with it. I quit smoking, but I'll come out with you to keep you company."

Alice dug in her pocket as we exited and, coming up empty, she asked, "Would you mind walking with me to my car, so I can grab my lighter? I'm parked in the Abbott North-western ramp."

The ramp was clearly in sight, and it was a nice warm night.

She added, "There's safety in numbers." As I processed my second thoughts about this, she said, "Don't worry about it. I'll just run."

I assured her, "It's fine. I could use the exercise."

It was quiet for a few minutes as we hurried along. Finally, Alice told me, "You're such a brave soul. It was gutsy of you to share that you were involved with a dirty cop. What was his name?"

The balls it took to ask that question almost sent me into a panic attack. We had entered the ramp and she was parked in the back row. *Why had she singled me out?*

I told her, "I don't think I'm ready to give that up."

Suddenly, out of the darkness, emerged Bobby Long.

I am so stupid! I turned to run, but Alice immediately wrapped her skinny arms around me from behind, the things binding like bale wire. She held me still until Bobby sauntered over. Alice handed me off.

Bobby crowed, "Dallas Alice comes through for me. She said she'd find you, but I didn't believe her. Thanks, Alice!" He removed a handgun from the back of his jeans and told her, "You can go now."

Alice responded, "She didn't give you up, but I could've got her to."

"Okay, you're dismissed." He waved her away, "Scoot."

Proud of herself, Alice said, "I'm boot scootin'," as she disappeared into the inky recesses of the ramp.

With his gun grinding into my side, Bobby dragged me to a car in the darkest corner of the ramp. There would be no happy ending for me. I felt like my parents put a bright orange tag on me that read, *Abuse Me*, and it would remain until my miserable life ended. I felt lightheaded and sick.

Bobby said, "You've been talkin' to investigators."

"Only because they keep grilling me. I haven't said anything about you, Bobby."

With a maniacal grin, he said, "I don't believe you. I still have friends, Cheyenne. Talk to me."

"I mean it, Bobby. I didn't give 'em anything."

"Alright, we'll do this your way." He recited, "Cheyenne and Zave went to their grave, with a lesson that I taught her. Cheyenne fell down and broke her crown and Zave came tumbling after." He sneered as he unbuckled his belt. "That nursery tale never did rhyme, did it?"

"What do you want?" A familiar feeling of dread began to take over my body. *Not again.*

He grabbed my shoulders and turned me away from him. "Bend over the hood of the car."

I stood strong and told him, "Bobby, I'm not having sex with you."

And then I felt his belt around my neck. I reached to grab it as it cut into my skin.

He rubbed his groin against my buttocks. "How about one more time, just for old time's sake?"

I realized this was the first time I didn't have the numbing buffer of booze when he forced himself on me. The belt tightened and I couldn't breathe. My survival instincts kicked in and I bucked against him, but he was too strong.

Bobby pressed me harder against the car and grunted, "I know when you're lying Cheyenne. There's something you aren't telling me."

I was starting to slip away. I finally croaked, "Okay—stop."

He loosened the belt. "What?"

"They've got someone close to you who's giving them information."

"Give me a name."

It would've been so easy to give up Serena, but she was my one friend. Trying to buy time, I said, "Alice."

Bobby tightened the noose.

I closed my eyes and saw stars.

He spat at me, "Lying whore, how stupid do you think I am?"

When my eyes opened, I could see tears of pain splattering on the hood of the car.

He loosened his grip for a moment, and I told him, "Just kill me, Bobby. Just fucking get it over with."

Bobby bent me back over the hood and slammed all of his weight on me. I felt the hood dent in. Then he removed the belt and backed away.

I remained sprawled across the hood until he slapped my ass hard and said, "I have no desire to kill you, Cheyenne. You serve a purpose. Get the name and call Alice with it. You've got her number. I tell you what, you get me that name and I'll leave you alone . . . "

51

"No one is born hating another person because of the color of his skin, or his background, or his religion. People must learn to hate and if they can learn to hate, they can be taught to love, for love comes more naturally to the human heart than its opposite."
—Nelson Mandela

2021

JON FREDERICK

10:30 A.M., SUNDAY, JUNE 20
BERKSHIRE LANE, EDEN PRAIRIE, MINNESOTA

Serena and I drove along Purgatory Creek in Eden Prairie, toward the home of Bobby's father, Truman Long. Since Serena was now a BCA Community Liaison, *whatever that means*, she could help with the interview.

I told her, "The same rifle was used to kill Dan Baker, Wesley 'Dreads' Washington, and Marita Perez. Do you know that Bobby Long was free when all of those shootings occurred?"

Perplexed, she said, "I thought he was arrested for rape before Dan was shot."

"He was, but he was released on bail, pending trial."

"And you think he shot all three of them."

"Yes. There's no doubt in my mind he disappeared after Marita was shot to avoid gun residue testing. If I would've found Bobby that night, I would have tested him."

Serena commented, "When they asked Dan to help reinvestigate Sadie Sullivan's murder, they really put a rope around his neck."

"I think it's possible he volunteered because of his doubts about Fury's guilt. And somehow, Bobby got Dan to respond to a call for an officer in distress in Hawthorne. When a cop gets shot at a gangster's doorstep, they don't spend a lot of time looking at other suspects."

"But why shoot Dreads?"

"Bobby's a racist pig and he wanted to kick off a race war. A cop is killed, then a gang member. Fortunately, neither the police nor the Disciples took the bait. A race war would've taken the suspicion completely off Bobby."

She added, "Witnessing the carnage would be immense pleasure for a narcissist like Bobby. People dying and getting shot—all orchestrated by him. But why would he kill Marita?"

"He thought he was shooting Cheyenne and he was setting Zave up to be the fall guy."

"Poor Marita." She paused, "Okay, but then why kill Cheyenne?"

"It addressed two desires. One, it got her out of his life and made room for you. And second, it was a chance to implicate a black man for one of his crimes. Think about it. How does Zave explain that a stripper, who was calling him all hours of the night, was found dead outside his house?"

"I feel terrible."

I took her hand. "You didn't do anything wrong, Serena. Bobby was going to be Bobby. He was going to try to kill Cheyenne once he had proof that she set her sights on Zave. It's a narcissistic injury that his redneck ass couldn't forgive. Think about it. He killed Sadie right after she'd been raped, because he couldn't get over that she'd been with a black man. He couldn't even hear what she was trying to tell him over his own hatred and bigotry. You're not the reason Bobby killed anyone. You're the reason he's finally going to be held account- able." I paused. "*I* made the biggest mistake."

"How so?"

"I thought we'd have a honeymoon period where Bobby would be good to Cheyenne. I didn't consider that, when you entered the picture, he'd trash her out so quickly."

We reached Truman Long's home.

Before we got out of the car, Serena asked, "How did you know Bobby killed Sadie? I've never seen you so fixated on one suspect."

"The evidence we've had from the very beginning. The first stuck with me after watching the video of Sadie's body being loaded to be taken to the medical examiner, eight years ago. Her body was solid. Rigor mortis was in full force. This timeline put her with Bobby at the time of her death, because he claimed she left for work at three a.m."

"Why didn't that free Fury?"

"Because circumstances can exist where a body stiffens relatively quickly—so it's not one hundred percent."

She considered this. "And the second piece?"

"This is the clue I can't let go of. The killer positioned Sadie's body. That was a mistake. It's hard dressing a dead body. It was clear Sadie had dressed herself. Think about this from the perspective of both suspects. If you're Fury, you rape Sadie. Let her dress. Drive her out to a rural area. Kill her, and then expose her underwear to make it look like she had been raped." I paused to let this sink in. "It doesn't make sense. Fury raped her. He didn't need to make it look like she'd been raped. Flamin' Ray would've left her naked. His MO is to leave them broken, but alive, at the exact location where he raped them."

"Isn't that what the Boston Strangler did?"

I had to give her credit for her research. "That's good. He posed them at the site of the assault—but he left them naked. Okay, now think about it from Bobby's perspective. He doesn't believe Sadie was raped. He kills her in a jealous rage, but he wants to make it look like she'd been raped, and he wants to pin it on the black man she had sex with. Still, he loved Sadie, so he didn't want to totally humiliate her. He settled on exposing her underwear and posing her."

Deep in thought, Serena agreed, "Yeah."

Not certain she was convinced, I added, "And here's one more piece, if you need it. Only Bobby could've removed the plastic bags from the evidence box. If Fury was guilty, Bobby would have wanted that box of evidence to remain as intact as possible. The prosecutor was angry that the contaminated evidence couldn't be used against Fury if he got a retrial. It also couldn't be used to convict Bobby Long."

Truman Long strolled up the sidewalk, ambling home from church. Truman was a big man with a scraggly white moustache.

As we watched him mosey toward his front door, Serena said, "Don't mention that we're law enforcement unless you have to. It's possible Bobby's told his dad about me."

We got out of the car simultaneously, catching Truman's attention. He paused with a gnarly hand on the door handle and cocked a bushy white eyebrow at us as we approached him.

Serena started the conversation. "Hello, Mr. Long. I'm Serena and I'm looking for Bobby. He came by looking for me, but he didn't leave an address."

Truman's wrinkles smoothed as his face relaxed and he smiled, taking my wife in, in a way I didn't necessarily appreciate. "Well, he could do worse—in fact, he *has*. I'm glad he finally got rid of that tart, *Cheyenne*." He said her name with derision. "I had to look at the floor every time I stopped over. I tell you what, that harlot must not own a brassiere, and all she's always wearing are short shorts and skimpy tank tops. It's ungodly." He stopped himself. "You don't need to hear that—I apologize, ma'am."

Serena smiled warmly. "It's okay."

With that, Truman brightened and offered, "Can I offer y'all a cuppa joe? I was just gonna brew a pot."

"We'd love that," said Serena. "Thank you."

Truman ushered us into his home. As he puttered in the kitchen, I absorbed his meticulously kept space. His furnishings boasted of the 70s era, but all had been well cared for. There wasn't so much as a wisp of dust on his Lemon-Pledged wood surfaces or a crumb on the oyster-colored linoleum floor. I was particularly pleased with his spotless kitchen, as the opposite would have made it difficult to graciously accept a cup of coffee. Even as I wasn't a coffee drinker, much preferring a cold Dr. Pepper, I'd occasionally had to suffer through coffee to be polite or to gain confidences.

As Truman waited for the coffee to brew, Serena asked him, "Did you see on the news that Ray Fury was murdered last night?"

Truman looked pleased. "You should only speak good of the dead, so let me say this. Fury is dead—good. He murdered Sadie and ruined my son's life. And now, I s'pose they're lookin' to blame Bobby."

Serena assured him, "No, they know who killed Ray. He attempted to rape Cheyenne last night and she shot him to death."

"Well, maybe I've been a little too hard on the girl. I ought to send her a thank you," he chuckled. As he poured steaming coffee into plain white mugs, Truman said, "Look, missy, I'd love to help you, but I don't know where Bobby is." He pulled out a quart of cream and held it up in a question to us both. I nodded, hoping the French vanilla would help, as Serena shook her head. Truman plopped some cream into his and my mugs and passed the drinks all around.

As Serena cradled her mug, she casually asked, "If he stops by, will you tell him I was looking for him?"

I finally engaged in conversation, which also saved me from the java. "Do you think Bobby might've gone to the same place he was a couple days ago?"

As if he only now registered my presence, Truman gave me a scrutinizing stare. "Who are *you*?"

Serena rescued me. "He's my brother. My roommate said Bobby sounded a little frantic, so I asked him to help me find him."

He gave me a once-over and, seeming to accept the ruse, Truman grumbled, "Bobby got mud all over my Enclave."

I asked, "Do you mind if we take a look at your Buick?"

Truman shrugged, "I guess it can't hurt anything." He pulled a set of keys off a small brass hook by the garage entry door and tossed them my way. He opened the garage entry door and reached in. I soon heard the hum of his garage door opening, as he said, "Here you go."

"Mind if I back it out?"

"Help yourself. Don't know what good it's gonna do ya."

Truman stayed inside while Serena and I stepped out to look at the SUV. I backed it into the daylight and shut it off. The inside was as meticulously cleaned as Truman's home. As we looked it over, we noted mud sprayed on the fender behind the wheels, in contrast to the immaculate interior.

I rubbed my finger along the dirt and observed, "Loamy soil."

Serena teased, "Now you're just showing off. What does *loamy* mean?"

"It's a mixture of sand, silt, and clay found in the soil of central Minnesota."

"Okay, Sherlock, lemme guess. You're going to send it to the lab and find that it only exists in small area of the state?"

"I could. Although half the state's population lives in the stretch we refer to as *central* Minnesota." The 2020 census indicated that this area was the fastest growing population in Minnesota, increasing in size about 12% in the last decade.

I smirked and told Serena, "I was thinking I would just use the OnStar system. The Enclave has a find-my-vehicle app, so its location is constantly projected to a satellite and stored in a data system."

She teased, "Well, aren't you a smarty? So, that means we probably aren't going to get the data on a Sunday."

"True." I got back into the Enclave and started it up.

Serena leaned into the driver's side window I'd opened.

I continued, "Unless it's stored in the vehicle's previous destination data." I scrolled down the list and asked, "Would you mind making a note of these three addresses on your phone?" She was simply much faster at it than I.

With a half-smile, she leaned in and used her cell to take a picture of the addresses on the screen. I could've done that. When she was done, I pulled the SUV back into the garage. We returned the keys to Truman and left him with two mugs full of coffee and a bewildered expression on his face.

As we drove away, Serena and I agreed to check out the last address and we'd ask Zave to go to the second last. If we didn't have any luck, we'd all travel to the third address.

52

*"Love is an endless act of forgiveness.
Forgiveness is me giving up the right
to hurt you for hurting me."*
—BEYONCE'

2021

XAVIER "ZAVE" WILLIAMS

12:30 P.M., SUNDAY, JUNE 20
HIGHWAY 94, MONTICELLO

Lauren and I had a downright magical weekend on Fawn Lake. It was north of Brainerd, next to Lake Ossawinnamakee. *Cabin schmabin.* This place was twice the size of the homes in my neighborhood. It was a log, A-frame deal, with a second story balcony that overlooked the lake. There was a wood fireplace in front of a comfortable couch. I had to admit, those might have been the best two days of my life. I felt something with her I'd never felt. I didn't want to leave.

When I reflected on the poor choices I was about to make, I could only say, *I am so sorry, Lauren!*

As we were driving back to Minneapolis on I-94, I received a text from Sean Reynolds:

"I need you to check out an address on Pickerel Lake— 405 Old Viking Boulevard, Nowthen, MN. Bobby might be hiding out there. Scouting mission. I want you to get the credit for finding him."

I showed the message to Lauren. She concentrated for a moment, and then said, "Sean must have gotten a new phone."

That was an odd comment, but I was immediately distracted by a call from Jon Frederick. I decided not to take it. Instead, I smiled at Lauren, "I'm not back at work yet. *Boundaries*."

Lauren relaxed a little. She was leaned back with sketchpad in hand, making some minor adjustments to a drawing she started of me over the weekend.

After thinking about it, I said, "I'd like to check on the address Sean sent me. It's on the way back." When she didn't immediately respond, I told her, "I'll drive you home first— just to be safe."

She shrugged, "We could swing over. It would be quicker than driving me all the way back to Minneapolis. If it's nothing, maybe we could have a little more time together tonight." Lauren took my hand and kissed it. "Let's hope it doesn't come to that. What are you thinking, Zave?"

"When you finally get the right perspective on a case, everything makes sense. I could never understand why Dan made the call—*officer in distress*—before he walked up to that gang house. I believe, at the very end, he considered that Bobby Long might be setting him up. But he was a trusting enough guy; he followed through as directed anyway."

Lauren rubbed my hand. "That's sad."

"It pisses me off." I pulled my hand away. "Jon seemed to know from the onset it was Bobby. I think I had too much exposure to Ray to have the right perspective."

"Do you like working with Jon and Jada?"

"I don't mind, but it's been frustrating. Jada's been in and out of the investigation—now officially out. Jon and I are constantly being pulled out to deal with Minneapolis shootings and I don't know what the hell Sean is doing. It would be easier if he'd just get healthy and let us handle it. And then, all of a sudden, Jon's wife, Serena, is working with us? It's too weird."

"I wonder how Jon managed that."

"Honestly, I don't know. I do appreciate that Jon has either met with me or called me, daily, and shared new information. I guess I'm just skeptical of how this ends. I've too often seen the white guy march in and take all the credit at the end."

"Like Chief Collier did when you arrested Ray Fury."

I remarked, "You know damn well, if there would've been any shooting, it all would have landed on me."

Lauren recited the poem:

"It's not my job to run the train
The whistle I don't blow.
It's not my job to say how far
The train's supposed to go.
I'm not allowed to pull the brake,
Or even ring the bell.
But let the damn thing jump the track
And see who catches hell!"
(anonymous)

I laughed, "The brothers' creed. I want to follow up on Sean's lead because I feel like he's giving me a solid."

She commented, "Jada is such a prima donna. I can't imagine working with her."

"Have you worked with Jada?" It wasn't like Lauren to sound so snarky.

"No." She quickly backtracked, "I'm sorry—I shouldn't have criticized her. I was just going on what a friend had said and that's not fair."

After an awkward silence, I decided to pull a page from dating Marita. "Tell me about your worst date."

Lauren laughed. "There was this guy who took six calls from a kinesiologist," she paused for effect, "who takes her clothes off for a living—on our first two dates."

I was a little embarrassed over that.

She saddened and said, "To be honest? My worst was when the man I'd been dating exclusively admitted he had an ongoing sexual relationship with someone else, throughout the entire time we'd been dating. When I pried further, he admitted he was engaged to her."

Her manner was unnerving. I flashed to Jada asking, *who is Lauren Herald?* A terrible insight washed over me. "The older man you were involved with was Jada's fiancé—Sean Reynolds."

I threw a sideways glance at her, and she nodded, looking humiliated. "I wanted to tell you, but you said it didn't matter. This weekend, we were amazing together."

"You're the reason Sean and Jada aren't getting married." My perfect Lauren, creeping in on someone's engagement. What a hypocrite! *Boundaries*—right? As my frustration escalated, my foot responded, and I realized I was a good fifteen over the speed limit. I leveled out the speed, but my adrenaline still raced.

She focused her gaze out the passenger window, chewing nervously on a thumbnail. She finally looked back to me and pled, "Please don't take me home. I love you, Zave."

Thinking back, the pieces kept falling into place. "Sean was with you when he had his heart attack."

"I was trying to end it."

"So, while I was explaining every reason for every conversation I had with women, you were sleeping with an engaged father. You lied to me . . . lies by omission are still lies."

1:10 P.M.
405 OLD VIKING BOULEVARD,
LAKE PICKEREL, NOWTHEN

LAUREN'S PLEAS WERE EXHAUSTING. I WAS SO overwhelmed, I had nothing to say when we reached the final turnoff. We faced a winding gravel driveway that cut through the woods.

I turned to Lauren, "This is where we part ways. You'll need to wait in the truck for me."

"I love you, Zave," she repeated.

Once again, I didn't respond. I should have, but I didn't. I was hurt.

Lauren frowned.

I told her, "If I'm not back in a half hour, take my truck and go call Jon Frederick. I'll give you his number." I couldn't resist getting one more jab in. "I guess you could call Sean if that's easier . . ."

53

"Be thankful for what you have; you'll end up having more. If you concentrate on what you don't have, you will never, ever have enough."
—OPRAH WINFREY

2021

LAUREN HERALD

1:30 P.M., SUNDAY, JUNE 20
405 OLD VIKING BOULEVARD,
LAKE PICKEREL, NOWTHEN

It was hot and I didn't feel like sitting in a truck when I was this close to a lake. Sketchpad in hand, I strolled to the trees and grass that butted up to the edge of the abandoned shore. For a moment, as brief as it was, Zave and I had the intimate magic that lovers dreamed of, and it had already slipped through our fingers.

I first met Sean when I was twenty. He was an investigator for the BCA, at the time. I interviewed him in college and told him I was an artist who was interested in forensic work. He took me out to eat and was polite and respectful. I had captured the interest of a powerful black man, who was both respected and impeccably dressed. At the end of the night, he dropped me off at my dorm. I wrote my number down but he wouldn't take it. Sean smiled and said, "Too young."

Five years later, our paths crossed again, and this time he took my number. I honestly didn't know he was a decade older—I knew he was a *little* older, but he was in better shape than most of my classmates.

Sean told me he was a father. When I confronted him with the rumors that he was engaged, his response was, "Not really." He explained that his baby mama was trying to pressure him into it. When I discovered the wedding plans, I was out. I made a commitment that, from then on, my man just dated me. No more players.

I held the sketchpad at the ready, but I couldn't free my mind enough to draw.

Suddenly, I heard a voice behind me. "Woman, what in God's name are you doin' here?"

I turned to see a grubby-haired, white man about my dad's age, with a Fu Manchu moustache. He wore a red baseball hat, a dirty, sleeveless white tee, with jeans and hiking boots; he was carrying a rifle. The ink of a majestic buck with antlers was tattooed on his right shoulder.

I fumbled for words. "Drawing nature."

He asked, "You here by yerself?"

I thought for a second. It was careless to admit I was alone, but I didn't want to give Zave up. "Yeah."

"I like your black truck. What year is it?"

"I actually don't know too much about it. It's my boyfriend's. He lets me borrow it when I set out to capture nature in its undisturbed state in my drawings. He doesn't want me to get stuck."

"Can I see your sketchpad? I just wanna make sure there ain't some other ulterior motive."

Skittish, I handed it to him.

He flipped through pages of drawings of Zave and, with a good ol' boy grin, said, "I'm no expert, but this is what you see when you look out at this here lake?"

I nervously quipped, "It's an anamorphic illusion."

He seemed to know I was pulling his leg, as he sniggered, "A what?"

"An anamorphic illusion can only be seen when it's viewed from the right spot. Okay, truth is, I just got here. I have to gaze at my subject for some time before I'm inspired to start drawing."

His face broke into a wide grin, making his need for dental work glaringly apparent. "The hood of that fancy truck was still warm; that checks out. So, where's your boyfriend?"

"At home."

He spat a gob of chew on the ground and asked, "Tell me, how does this brother treat you?"

"With kindness and respect."

With hardened skepticism, he studied me. "That so?"

"Yes—always."

I noticed a small tattoo of a cross under his stag tattoo. I had a low tolerance for racist rednecks who claimed to be Christian.

I pried, "Do you remember the shooting at the African American Evangelist church in South Carolina, back in 2015? A white supremacist walked into the church and parishioners sat with him and prayed with him. The shooter killed nine people because they were *black*. Reloaded his gun five times, as he fired seventy-seven shots into the congregation. He later said that he almost didn't shoot them because they were so nice to him." The vibe I got from this guy was that he wasn't going to hurt me, so I challenged, pointing toward his tattoo, "How does that fit with your Christianity?"

Somewhat troubled, he gave it some thought and recited, "God will not hold any blameless for the killing of innocents— Deuteronomy. That killing spree was an unforgivable atrocity. That was a cardinal sin, sweetheart." He added, "I'm not a racist. You found a kind one, good for you. Just lookin' out for you."

I countered, "There are good ones and bad ones in every race."

"Not arguin' with you, sister."

He was beginning to doubt my motives and I was beginning to question the wisdom of my need to challenge his thinking. The man directed, "Alright, then, draw something for me. It can't include my face."

I sketched an acropolis with the words, Tykes Carpet Castle written over it, similar to the symbol on his hat.

He grinned again, "Damn, you're good." The man gazed pensively out at the lake. "Nothin' good is gonna come out of you bein' here, darlin'—and there's potential for a lot of hurt. Do yerself a favor and just git—alright? I can't explain why. Just heed my warnin'."

I quickly stood up, "Okay. Thank you!" Didn't need to tell me twice. I'd been feeling dread creeping up the back of my neck the more we talked.

He watched me as I hurried to the truck.

I started it and pulled away. I needed to drive out of sight and then carefully return. I wouldn't want Zave to think I'd abandoned him.

54

*"Never be afraid to make some
noise and get in good trouble.
Necessary trouble."*
—JOHN WILLIAMS

2021

XAVIER "ZAVE" WILLIAMS

1:45 P.M., SUNDAY, JUNE 20
405 OLD VIKING BOULEVARD,
LAKE PICKEREL, NOWTHEN

When I considered I might be approaching a racist killer who'd love to see me dead, the woods felt menacing. I used binoculars to scan for movement. Birds hidden like snipers above me announced my arrival with loud chirping and then taking flight. I wanted to yell, *Shut up!* A rafter of turkeys trouped in single file ahead of me while a scurry of squirrels rummaged about. Ninety percent of the time I'd ever walked through the woods, I saw nothing. Today, I felt like I was in the middle of a clanging parade. All that was missing was a neon arrow hovering along above me, flashing to point out my location.

I somehow managed to survive the cacophony and made it to the large, two-story dwelling along the lake. Parked in the driveway sat Bobby's tricked-out white truck, sticking out like a sore thumb in the rustic surroundings. I took out my phone to call for backup, but of course, had no reception. *What is this, Petticoat Junction?* Gimme city life all day long.

Wanting visual verification of Bobby's actual mug, I crept along the woods by the edge of the lake. I spotted a man with his back to me, standing in the shallows, fishing. When he turned to the side to survey the lake, I realized I had ol' Bobby Long, in the flesh, in my sights.

I drew my gun and carefully approached. When I was close enough, I called out, "Bobby Long, you're under arrest for aiding and abetting the assault of Cheyenne Schmidt."

He turned and cocked off to me, "Yeah, I don't think so, bud."

I directed, "Put your hands behind your head and drop to your knees."

Bobby defiantly remained standing. "My friends tell me you're all jazzed up about convicting me for killing Sadie."

When I didn't respond, he kept on, "Don't you wanna know why she died? All I have is a fishing rod. I'm no threat to you."

Surprised by his willingness to talk, I played along. "Why?"

"You. *You're* the reason Sadie's dead. Hitting on her at the store. Taking her out to eat. I was tracking Sadie's movements. I saw you kiss her. She was engaged to be married. To *me*."

My stomach flipped at even the idea I'd somehow contributed to Sadie's demise. At the time, I didn't even consider the hypocrisy of being so pissed at Lauren. I focused on keeping a bored expression. "Engagement didn't render her mute. She could still talk and be a friend. Sadie was a great listener."

"But she was *mine*," Bobby fumed. "So, when my neighbor called and said he just saw a black man leaving our house, I rushed home. I confronted her about the black man, and she said she'd been raped. I didn't believe her—why would I? She'd been out whoring around with you. So, that's all on *you*. You're the reason I didn't believe her. Sadie laid down in her bed and I lost it. I was tired of being disrespected."

He was such a narcissistic dick. I felt my breaths coming faster at his sick disregard for such a beautiful human. "You had Dan pick you up after you dumped the body." I couldn't believe Dan went along with this. "Why kill him?"

Bobby dismissed this. "I told him Sadie'd been raped and murdered by a black guy, and I didn't want her body found in my bed, so I drove her to Plymouth Creek. Dan wasn't happy about it, but he agreed to help me—until he figured it out. When I saw he volunteered to help reopen the investigation, that was the end of Danny Boy."

"And Dreads?"

Bobby shook his head, "I expected the police to react stronger to Dan's death. When they didn't, I stirred the pot a little by killing a gang banger. You keep tossing matches at a powder keg, it eventually blows. And I've gotta admit, it's all working out nicely. The Murderapolis riots showed the true colors of the city. Last year was the first time the Minnesota murder rate was higher than back in 1995. Cops were assaulted in record numbers—two a day throughout 2020. For three years in a row, blacks have committed more murders than any other race."

The arrogance of this prick, to assume this has all been about him. My finger involuntarily twitched on the trigger, but I needed to continue gathering information, so I asked, "Why kill Marita?"

"Collateral damage," he shrugged. "Cheyenne would pay a price for going back to you."

I argued, "But I never contacted Cheyenne."

"I did, on your behalf. And it ended up working out even better. What do Sadie, Dreads, Dan, and Marita all have in common? You were the one who arrested Dreads, right?"

I reluctantly nodded. "And why are you telling me all this?"

"This is all falling down on you. The more you try to implicate me, the less believable you'll be." He smirked, "I'm not killing you—not saying you won't die—but it won't be by my hand. You might even do it yourself when all's said and done."

I wasn't exactly sure how he thought he was going to manage this, but I imagined he'd been working on this scheme ever since he discovered I was spending time with Sadie.

Bobby changed the topic by sneering, *"Black Lives Matter*—but not to blacks. Killing your own children with stray bullets. Torching businesses and making people afraid to drive downtown. And then you come back and say it's bad policing. I call bullshit! You created the bad cops. Minneapolis is a pressure cooker; the pressure has to come out somehow. If your people wouldn't have attacked Sadie, I wouldn't be in this mess." He pointed his finger at me. *"You* made me the man I am today. Don't ever forget that."

I laughed at him and sarcastically said, "Yeah, *I* did. I am personally responsible for all of your shitty choices." Talk about projection. I told him, "I take accountability for my behavior. I'll expect that you take accountability for yours."

And then I heard the cock of a rifle behind me. An angry voice ordered, "Drop your gun."

When I turned, there were four white, hillbilly-looking characters with rifles aimed at me. I dropped the gun. I'd been so wrapped up in my frustration with Lauren, it never occurred to me that the text I received from *Sean* actually came from Bobby. I'd been lured here. I hoped to hell Lauren got away.

Bobby pulled a pair of handcuffs out of his tackle box and approached me. "We saw you coming in our motion sensor cameras in the woods. Lots of action out here, today."

Two of the hillbillies stepped aside and spoke, and then ran to Billy's truck.

I was pushed along to the house and into the basement. A chain was wrapped around my cuffs and then Master-locked around a six-inch square, wooden support beam. I needed to drag out my survival as long as possible and prayed Lauren called for help. I shouldn't have dismissed her when she said she loved me.

55

"I believe that there will ultimately be a clash between the oppressed and those that do the oppressing. I believe that there will be a clash between those who want freedom, justice, and equality for everyone and those who want to continue the systems of exploitation."
—Malcolm X

2021

XAVIER "ZAVE" WILLIAMS

2:30 P.M., SUNDAY, JUNE 20
405 OLD VIKING BOULEVARD,
LAKE PICKEREL, NOWTHEN

My heart sank when a cuffed Lauren was escorted to the basement by Bobby and two of his Aryan soldiers.

Bobby barked a laugh at me. "Another lamb to the slaughter on you—*negro.*"

I waited for them to unhook my chain, assuming they'd use it to also secure Lauren's cuffs to the pole. These huckleberries were about to have the fight of their lives.

But they didn't loosen my chain. Instead, a second chain was used to fasten Lauren to the same post. I thought about still trying an attack, but knew I had no chance of resolving anything until I was free.

Lauren was trying to put on a brave face, but the wild fear in her eyes gave her away. I prayed I would find a way to get her out of here, unharmed.

Bobby looked at the two of us and said, "We're going to have a little fun with your dolly before the night's over, so live it up with her while you can. I don't have a lot of love for girls who go to the dark side." He chuckled pompously.

I knew better than to respond. They weren't going to kill me, here—this place was too secure to give up. They wouldn't want to leave blood evidence. And, most likely, they wouldn't want to carry me. Corpses were heavy and awkward to maneuver. I needed to remain as healthy as possible so I could fight when the opportunity arose.

Bobby and his henchman headed back upstairs. I asked Lauren, "Did you call Jon?"

Her resolve broke and her brittle posture threatened to crumple like an aluminum can. She shook her head as she inspected the cuffs and chains with trembling fingers. "No. I'm sorry. When I tried to drive to where I could get reception, they ran me off the road." Exhausted, she asked, "Mind if I sit down?"

Lauren's chain was above mine on the post. The only way she could sit was if I did, too. "Yeah, that's fine."

As we eased onto the floor, she said, "I didn't want to leave you, so I waited. When they ran me off the road, I jumped out and took off, but they hunted me down. It's a game to these guys." Her eyes were bright with tears. "They're going to kill us." An angry red welt was slapped across her cheek; I was sick at the image of her running, terrified, through the woods with these maniacs on her tail.

I looked up at the two-by-six. It was secured with sturdy metal T-straps to the above support beam. The chain couldn't be removed at the top of this beam.

Lauren softly asked, "Do you know why I went to your house that first night?"

I shook my head.

"I was lonely. Sean stood me up and I was tormented by thoughts of him with Jada."

I considered this. "And you thought I'd be a good one-night stand."

Resigned to our fate, she sadly leaned into me. "I don't know about good, but I thought that's the guy you were. Easy peasy. No regrets. But Marita beat me to the prize."

"So that's what this weekend was—one prolonged one-night stand."

"No. But that was the vibe I first got from you. I don't think I've ever seen you with the same woman twice."

It was the same image Marita had of me. In my defense, I pointed out, "Our paths never crossed much."

"Fair enough." She leveled her blue eyes on mine and I tried to look anywhere else, but she put a soft palm on my cheek and turned my face back to hers. "But getting to know the real you blew me away. The gentleness of your voice comes from a caring, tender soul. You let down the mask and allowed me in. I feel like I'd been one turn of a page away from a classic novel, but all I'd ever seen was the paper dust jacket."

Feeling insulted, I said, "I've always cared."

She smiled, "Zave—you *do* care. But it's, 'Are you okay? Here, talk to this person. Alright—good luck—bye.' You've helped hundreds of people and that's kind, but you always hand them off. Then you never have to share too much of yourself. I get it—it's safe. But I got to know the real you and I'm grateful."

Lauren was dead on. I'd never really thought about it. Instead, I selfishly responded, "I can't wrap my mind around you and Sean. It makes me feel like I don't know *you.*"

"That's not surprising," she said sadly. "Hell, *I* didn't know me." She studied the floor as she added, "I was frantic—crazy with the idea that I needed Sean. I was afraid if I let go for one second, I'd lose him. You know how intimidating Jada can be."

"She never struck me as intimidating."

"That's because you're a man. Imagine being a woman competing against her. Jada could be walking a runway. She's stunning, eloquent, and was at every social event Sean had to attend."

I couldn't help thinking Lauren had it backwards. Jada was a news reporter and Sean didn't really need to be at most of those events. "Have you slept with him since we've dated?"

"Once. I'm sorry. I didn't know you like I do now."

That burned, so I refocused on our situation. I flatly said, "I'm sorry I brought you here. I should've taken you home. I didn't think—"

She cut me off. "Zave, you still don't get it. We could die, here—*today*. Maybe in minutes. You gave me the best weekend of my life; you opened my soul to a man of great spirit and noble ways. I don't regret if my last minutes will be with you. So, if you have something to say to me, you'd better say it. If not, I want you to know that this weekend was gold, in a lifetime of never coming closer than mustard."

Instead of screaming, *I LOVE YOU*, I found myself rambling on, "I think I was so hurt, because I've always thought you were what I should aspire to be."

With a sad acceptance that I would simply never say the right thing, Lauren dropped her head on my shoulder and said, "I'm sorry."

My engine didn't turn over as fast as it should, but I wasn't giving up. I sighed and tried again, "Let me explain. It would be easier if you were perfect, and it was just me who had to iron down the rough edges. I'd have complete control of that. But maybe we could be even better if you weren't perfect. If you struggled—like me—and we worked through this together. Then I'd know your love for me occurred in the face of all your temptations—not just because altruistic love is what perfect people give. I'd know that, somehow, despite my imperfections, I'd have earned your love. That I was worthy of being loved by someone as amazing as you."

Lauren elicited a heartfelt, "Ahhh. Now that's the Zave my heart sees."

I told her, "I love you, Lauren."

"I love you too, Zave."

And then the basement door opened.

We quickly scrambled back onto our feet.

With my wrists chained to the support beam in front of me, I was in a terrible position to fight.

Bobby elicited the ugliest laugh when he told me, "The boys are going to have some fun with Blondie. Don't worry, she'll be waiting for you with open legs when we're done."

Screw this noise. I'll take my chances. When Bobby and his sasquatch of a friend got close enough, I hauled off and kicked his sidekick in the balls like I was going for a fifty-yard field goal. The squeal of pain from his pig-mouth was beyond satisfying. He crashed to the floor and writhed around, cupping his boys with both hands.

Bobby stepped back and Tased me. Hot agony instantly boiled through my body, and everything stopped working. As I spasmed to the ground, Lauren let out a yelp. My limbs were jerking and useless; I watched helplessly while Bobby quickly unchained her.

Lauren turned feral. She lunged forward and bit into Bobby's bicep, locking down tightly until the now recovered, large white supremacist drilled his knuckles into her jawbone to loosen her grip.

Bobby was apoplectic, watching blood dripped down his bicep. He growled, "You're gonna pay for that one, mud shark."

I tried getting to my feet, but a hard kick from the giant's steel-toed boot to my ribs buckled me to my knees.

Lauren was dragged away, kicking and screaming, "No! No!" By the time I could think clearly and get my feet under me, I heard a soft plea, "Zave?" just before the basement door closed.

Her faint cries continued, *"Please, no."*

Shortly after the door slammed, I heard men arguing.

My arms weren't wrapped around the post. My handcuffs were connected to a chain around it, secured by three Master locks. I yanked at it and was reminded my cuffs were painfully tight. The locks weren't going to break. The clock was ticking for Lauren—75% of women abducted by strangers were dead in an hour.

While the beam was attached to support framing at the top, it wasn't fastened to the concrete floor. I sat down and started slamming both feet into the bottom of the post. I realized this beam wasn't supporting the weight of the house. It moved ever so slightly with each kick. My only hope was to kick this post out of place and slide the chain underneath it. I had to make this work, and fast.

As I stomped my feet against the post, I realized I could've made every second with Lauren loving—but I hadn't. I couldn't get over my own ego soon enough. I'd brought her into my mess; I needed to get her out of it.

I froze when I heard a gunshot upstairs. I held my breath and strained my ears, but no longer heard Lauren. Instead, I heard more male voices barking back and forth and, after a couple minutes, there were two more gunshots.

Now rabid, I kicked at the post like my life depended on it—Lauren's life did—but it wasn't giving enough.

The basement door opened; I stopped, turned around, and leaned my back against the post.

Bobby came marching down the steps, as arrogant as ever, wearing gloves and holding a Browning hunting rifle. He was all too happy to report, "Lauren gave one of the good old boys a nice ride. She took a bullet, but I'll still get my turn while she's warm."

He was holding the rifle out in front of him and, when he came close enough, I charged him and kicked it out of his hands.

Startled, he crab-walked out of my reach.

I scrambled on the floor, grabbed the rifle with my cuffed hands and aimed it at Bobby. I fired.

He made no effort to run.

A loud bang rang out—but no bullet fired. The rifle had been reloaded with a blank.

Bobby smirked, "I was going to leave the rifle for you, anyway. The prints on it are all yours. Gun powder residue on you." He whistled as he walked away. "Lauren's spread eagle and waiting for me. I promise, I'll use a condom."

I realized I was now holding the rifle used to murder Danny, Dreads, and Marita. Only my prints would be on it. But I wasn't particularly concerned about the long game, at the moment. I dropped to the floor and got back to kicking at the bottom of that damn post with everything I had.

56

"If you talk to a man in a language he understands, that goes to his head. If you talk to him in his own language, that goes to his heart."
—NELSON MANDELLA

2021

JON FREDERICK

2:30 P.M., SUNDAY, JUNE 20
405 OLD VIKING BOULEVARD,
LAKE PICKEREL, NOWTHEN

The address Serena and I visited yielded nothing. It concerned me that I hadn't heard back from Zave, but he had earned time off and I was hoping he was enjoying it. We needed to get some confirmation that Bobby was in the area before we called for back-up. Serena and I were now headed to the second address, which was on Lake Pickerel.

I told her, "Nowthen's named after the town's first postmaster who used to say, *Now, then,* frequently in conversations."

Accustomed to my random trivia, Serena silently grinned. Based on her advice, we were driving an unmarked Ford Fusion—the same vehicle she drove to work when she met with Bobby. Since we had no indication that her cover had been blown, she thought it was wise to maintain the option of talking to Bobby as a friend. I made it clear, if we found him, I didn't want her entering the home alone. Bobby was dangerous and likely had connections who had informed him we had a warrant for his arrest.

Serena asked, "Did you bring your new toy along?"

"I did." I had bought a parabolic microphone. You'd see them on the sidelines at NFL games. They looked like a big circular snow sled. Event staff aimed them at the quarterback, so they could pick up his voice over the crowd noise. When I was in college, some nerdy physics students I knew would sit by an open window on the third floor of the science lab, aiming it at students walking about campus. You could listen in on conversations hundreds of feet away. A company called Sound Shark had now made a nine-inch parabolic mic that was supposed to pick up a conversation two hundred feet away, and I bought it for our investigative work.

She asked, "Is it legal?"

"The Minnesota Statute states that interception and dis-closure of oral communication through an electronic device is illegal, without consent of one of the parties."

Surprised, she asked, "Both parties don't need to be consenting?"

"No. Minnesota is a one-party consent state."

"That's unnerving." She paused and added, "Well, then you can't use it. You won't have consent from either party you're listening to."

I smiled, "There's an exemption. It's legal for officers to use in the normal course of their employment while engaged in an activity that is necessary to the rendition of their service, provided they don't intentionally divulge the contents of the communication to anyone other than another officer."

"Just by the way you said that I have a feeling you're taking liberties with your interpretation." She quickly looked up the statute on her phone and said, "That exemption appears to be intended for employees of a wiretap company who are engaging in the task as part of their work."

I asked, "Would you rather I marched inside that house uninformed, or first listened to what they're saying?"

Glancing out the passenger window, she unemotionally responded, "Use the parabolic mic. But put it away when you're done. And promise me you'll wait for backup if it's warranted, alright?"

I nodded.

As we rumbled down the gravel road, Serena spotted Zave's truck angled toward the ditch. We quickly hopped out. My biggest fear was finding a body inside.

The side of the vehicle was scraped, indicating it had been run off the road. We ran to it, but it had been abandoned. *Thank God*. But that also begged the question, *Where is Zave?*

I turned to Serena, "Call nine-one-one and then call Sean. This is no longer a scouting mission."

She looked at her phone. "There's no reception, here. I just had bars a few minutes ago."

I tossed her the keys. "Drive until you have some coverage and then call."

"What are you going to do?"

I opened the trunk and pulled out my backpack. "I'm going to find Zave."

From the GPS system I'd been following, I knew we were within a mile of the address, and it was north of where I now stood. I turned to Serena, "I love you. I couldn't have done better."

She ran to me and we kissed. "Don't say it like that. I love you, too. Help will soon be on the way."

"If this is what I think it is—a militia hideaway—these groups will be well armed and they're not giving up without using their toys. I need to see what we're in for. In all likeli-hood, it all ends here, tonight." I envisioned people dying here.

Serena offered with diluted optimism, "Maybe they've left."

"No such luck. They would've hidden Zave's pickup before they departed and the hood's still warm. We're going to have a showdown right here, right now. Mark my word—bullets will fly. Call for help and stay away."

"I pray Zave's still alive." She knew the clock was ticking. Lives were lost in seconds. Serena sprinted back to the car and the tires spit gravel when she tore away.

Zave was in serious trouble. The advantages he had over me during our investigation of Minneapolis crimes were lost in rural Minnesota. I dug through my backpack. Before I'd have use for my parabolic mic, I'd need my RF Spectrum Analyzer. It looked like a walkie-talkie but picked up on hidden cameras in any given area. From conversations with my hunting friends, I anticipated that, if an Aryan group was hiding Bobby Long, they had motion-sensitive cameras camouflaged in the woods. My friends used them all the time to scout for deer, moose, bear, and wolves.

I took a calming breath and started traipsing north through the woods. *Showtime!*

Within a half mile, the RF alerted me to the presence of hidden cameras, so I carefully avoided them. My concern for Zave intensified. His walk through the woods would be analogous to me walking to the Disciple's gang home in Hawthorne, without backup.

I reached the edge of the woods and took in the two-story lake home. Two armed men stood by the side of the house arguing. Behind them sat a metal, life sized statue of an eagle, the American symbol of freedom and strength, perched on a four-foot marble pedestal.

I slid my mic on and aimed it. Through my binoculars, I saw a large, muscle-bound skinhead exchanging words with a man with long, dirty hair and a Fu Manchu. Skinhead had a bull's head and the Latin words *Lorem Ipsum* tattooed on his bicep. This was a common symbol of Mixed Martial Arts fighters, even though the statement was meaningless. Lorem Ipsum was a nonsensical phrase used to indicate where text will be placed in a design. The Fu Man Chu man captured my curiosity. He had tattoos of a stag and a cross on his shoulder. *Where had I seen him before?*

The familiar man was arguing, "Are you all out of your frickin' mind? We never should've brought that gal back here. Is this what you signed up for? It sure the hell wasn't what I signed up for. She had nothin' to do with what Bobby's got goin' on."

The skinhead responded, "We couldn't let her go. She'd talk."

Shaggy asked, "So, what are we going to do with her—*kill* her? Spread the word—if anyone harms that woman, I'm coming after him."

When skinhead didn't respond, the scraggily man continued, "I'm supportin' anything that makes America better. But this—this ain't it. What's the plan, here?"

"If we don't put some faith in Bobby, we're gonna have a thousand different ideas and sound like all the left-wing extremist liberals."

Instead of agreeing, Fu Manchu said, "I'll run reconnaissance. I'm warnin' you—you better not've got me into some crazy shit." He turned on his heel and began stalking angrily toward the perimeter of the woods.

The skinhead headed in the other direction.

I stepped behind a large tree and waited for Fu Manchu to come to me. As I heard him approaching, I leaned my back against the tree and tossed rocks deeper into the woods, hoping to lead him past me, so we wouldn't meet face to face. I was trying to avoid one of us dying.

Stealthy, thoughtful steps headed my direction. They were soft and surreptitious. This man was ex-military. When he finally walked by, I put my gun to his back and ordered, "Drop your rifle."

He complied and raised his hands, "What do you want?" I estimated him to be in his fifties. He slowly turned to me, keeping his hands raised.

I'd seen this guy before. Even though my father and I hadn't always seen eye to eye, Dad had lots of friends. I said, "I think you know my dad—Bill Frederick. And you're protecting Bobby Long?"

Taken by surprise he said, "Yeah, I know Bill. We were on the USS Stark when an Iraqi jet fired two missiles into the side of the frigate. The jet was in a blind spot in our radar system. Thirty-seven sailors lost their lives. One of the rockets failed to detonate—leaving flamin' rocket fuel in its path. There would've been more dead, if it wasn't for heroes like your dad, who were immediately out there dousin' the fire. Bill's a good man." His expression hardened as he refocused on the moment at hand. "Somebody's gotta step up, here. This country's goin' to hell."

I pointed out, "Zave Williams is a cop. A *good cop*. And you know as well as I do, Bobby wasn't. He murdered his fiancée, a police officer, and an innocent woman who was just trying to make a life for herself."

Frustrated, he looked back at the house. "I didn't know about all that. I was told a black guy was after him and he needed protection."

I asked, "Who's the woman?"

Surprised by my comment, he said, "You've got better surveillance than we do."

Not necessarily better. Rather, the right tools for this situation. Instead of showing my cards, I told him, "You might want to keep that in mind."

"Lauren something-or-other. She came with him."

"And you're going to let Bobby rape and kill her? This is what you mean by stepping up?"

"Hell, no. I don't like Bobby. Never have."

"In an hour, this place is going to be surrounded with law enforcement, and if this ends in a shootout, you lose, because our reinforcements are going to keep coming until we win. We'll bring the National Guard in if we have to. Is this how you want to be remembered—dying for a cop-killing rapist?"

He dropped his hands and stared past me. "No. Hell, no." He put a calloused hand out and said, "Call me Buck."

I stared at his hand for a beat, then took a risk I wouldn't likely tell Serena about and shook it. "Jon." Knowing the prototype of a militia member, I decided to use a Christian reference. "Let's reason together. We were both washed in the same blood. Though your sins may be scarlet, they shall be as white as snow."

The man smiled, "That's from Isaiah. You're a Christian?"

"Yes."

He squinted toward the house, and then turned back to me. "Okay. I ain't interested in fightin' cops. Part of the reason I'm in this is to give law enforcement back some power. But if I help, you've gotta have my back when this is over. What can I do to get out of this?"

Sean would go ballistic if he knew what I was about to do. I told the man, "I'll make a deal with you. If you want to walk out of here without hard prison time, get one of those hostages out of there."

Buck nodded, "They're armed to the gills, son. You can't match their firepower without backup. I'd do this for Bill's family. He'd do the same for mine." He calculated, "There's five of us, including me. The cop and Lauren are chained up in the basement."

"I don't see the hostages surviving without some inside help."

Clearly bothered, he recited, "Shedding innocent blood is an abomination—Proverbs." He spit on the ground. "All right. Let's do it. I'm not fightin' against Bill Frederick's son. Bobby really killed his fiancée?"

"Yes. Because she was raped—he didn't want anything to do with her."

Buck was a lot of things, but insincere didn't seem to be one of them. He looked truly dyspeptic. "Thank you for lettin' me make this right."

"Don't thank me, yet. I simply don't have a better plan. I know if I go in alone, my wife and kids are burying me before the week's out. I don't know how far away my backup is from here." I added, "If we survive this, I will do everything in my power to see you don't do time."

I picked up his rifle and, after giving it some thought, cautiously handed it back to him.

Buck grinned as he took possession of his weapon. "You're taking a hell of a chance. When I get thirty yards away, your chances of hitting me with that pistol aren't good. My chances of hittin' you with this rifle are still damn near a hundred percent." He turned and started walking to the house. After a few steps, he looked back and said, "I like your style, son. We need guys like you alive. Don't ever give a man you don't know a weapon superior to your own, again," and continued on his way.

My intent wasn't completely altruistic. If he came back without his rifle, the rest of the crew would know there was trouble in the woods, and they'd be out here hunting me down.

57

*"I'd rather regret the risks that didn't work
out than the chances I didn't take at all."*
—Simone Biles

2021

SERENA FREDERICK

2:45 P.M., SUNDAY, JUNE 20
405 OLD VIKING BOULEVARD,
LAKE PICKEREL, NOWTHEN

With no reception, I had no way of communicating with Jon. We were left to make our best individual decisions in a fluid situation. As I drove my rusting Ford Fusion right up to the lake house, I imagined Jon's worry was going through the roof.

I was afraid for Zave's life. I agreed to be part of this team and I was the one person whose presence might keep Bobby from killing someone—if my cover hadn't been blown. Considering that possibility had me squinting one eye shut, bracing myself to get shot at, as I rolled onto the property. Gunfire never came.

A musclebound skinhead met me in the driveway, and I immediately told him, "I'm with Bobby."

He brought me to the door and yelled, "Bobby, keep your pants on. You've got company."

I hoped that comment wasn't literal.

Bobby came out of a bedroom and, surprised, said, "Serena! How'd you find me?"

"I went to your dad's—this address was still in the Buick. Agnes said you sounded pretty desperate when you stopped over. I wanted to make sure you were okay."

He studied me skeptically. "Dad doesn't know where this place is."

I attempted to curb his fears. "Bobby, I was worried." I put my hand on his shoulder. "I was afraid you were going to do something drastic. Your dad said you used his Buick. I found this address in the navigation's previous destinations."

Assured, Bobby smiled, "You should be a detective." He took my hand and escorted me into the home. "Okay—some crazy shit went down here but we're leaving. There's a place up north we can stay at for a bit. But we need to leave soon. You okay with that?"

I said, "I don't know—how long are we talking about?"

He stared into my eyes. "Not sure. It's a quaint country place where we can start over—together. I know it's a lot to ask. It's gotta be better than living with that crazy old biddy you're staying with."

Trying to appear excited, I asked, "Can I run home and pack?"

"I'm sorry, but no—we have to go. I'll buy what you need." When I hesitated, he said, "Make a list of what you need, and I'll have one of the boys get it for you. I need to go from here and I want you with me."

"This is crazy—but okay."

He hugged me, then stepped back. "I need to talk to the boys, quick, before we head out. Wait here."

Wanting an idea of the home's layout, I asked, "Where's the bathroom?"

He pointed down the hall.

Once I was out of eyeshot, I opened the bedroom door closest to the bathroom.

The sight was sickening. Lauren was lying, lifeless, on the bed. Her hands were raised above her head and handcuffed. A bright red splotch on her forehead dripped blood and there was a bullet hole in the wall behind her head. She was dressed on top; her bottom half was covered with a blanket. A scruffy haired man with a Fu Manchu was dead on the floor, two bullet holes in his chest.

Swallowing back bile and panic, I quietly closed the door. When I turned to head back, I met Bobby in the hallway.

He confronted me, "Did you go in the bedroom?"

I could feel a lump in my throat. *Had he seen me?* This was a life-or-death situation. I gestured to the door and forced out, "Yes—I peeked in. I wish I wouldn't have."

"I can see it on your face. There's a black guy downstairs who caught Buck raping his girlfriend and shot them both to death. One of my men will take care of him."

I argued, "But if you kill him, won't it look like you did this? Wouldn't it make more sense to leave him alive?"

He first argued, "Since the Minneapolis riots, almost half the homicides have gone unsolved. It might be the only way we get justice."

I pled, "Please don't, Bobby."

Mercifully, he didn't take much convincing. "You're right. Okay, would you mind hauling the box on the kitchen counter out to the back of my truck?"

"Sure." I walked to the kitchen, passing a burly, lumberjack-like man in the hallway. Before leaving with the box, I stopped out of sight and listened.

Bobby quietly told the man, "Kill him."

I wrestled the heavy box outside. *Where are you, Jon?* I had a chance to get in my car and drive away, but I didn't. Instead, I glanced back at the house and, with no one obviously watching me, I quickly opened my car door and retrieved my Sig P365, tucked it into the back of my jeans, and covered it with my blouse. It was an easy to grip handgun I could conceal. I'd never used it for anything but target practice and had honestly hoped this day would never come. I quietly closed the door and re-entered the house. Once inside, I heard a ruckus in the basement.

Bobby hollered, "Let's get out of here," and ran to me.

58

"Our history did not begin in chains."
—MALCOLM X

2021

XAVIER "ZAVE" WILLIAMS

2:55 P.M., SUNDAY, JUNE 20
405 OLD VIKING BOULEVARD,
LAKE PICKEREL, NOWTHEN

I was sure it was going to break my back, but I finally slammed the kick home that separated the bottom of the post from the floor. I leaned forward and slid the chain underneath it. I was still handcuffed and now dragging with me a length of chain, weighted with Master locks.

The basement door opened, so I made a large circle around the perimeter of the room, to avoid being seen by whoever was coming down the steps. I went to one side of the enclosed staircase and swung the chain and locks head-high into my visitor like a knight's flail.

Taken completely by surprise, my large guest bent over and covered his battered face.

I dropped down on him like an avalanche, wrapped the chain around his neck and tightened it.

At that point, I realized he had a gun in his hand; he pointed it over his shoulder to fire at me.

I managed to duck my head away from the barrel as my ears echoed with the *BANG! BANG! BANG!*

I held the chain tight as if I'd lassoed a bull and with the weight shift, he fell off balance, face first to the floor, effectively shaking the gun free from his grip.

Still on my feet, I bent over him and walked in a circle, periodically stepping over his body. This process tightened the chain around his neck, link by link, in an unforgiving stranglehold. It was minutes before his struggle for life ended, reminding me Sadie's death was no short endeavor. My anger toward Bobby energized me. Finally, it was over for this man.

One down, four to go. I dug through the dead man's pocket and found the handcuff keys, and quickly freed my wrists. I picked up his gun and crept upstairs.

Even though my ears were ringing, I could hear Bobby talking to a woman down the hall. It wasn't Lauren, so I headed to the first closed door down the hall, looking for her.

When I opened the door, my heart plummeted into my gut. Blood dripped down Lauren's forehead and there was a bullet hole in the wall behind her head. I would later discover that there was also a deceased white man on the floor. I was so overwhelmed with my view of dead, still Lauren, I didn't even notice him.

I blew out of the room in a rage. Down the hall, I caught a side view of Bobby growling at a woman I couldn't yet see.

59

"Champions aren't made in the ring.
They are merely recognized there."
—JOE FRAZIER

2021

JON FREDERICK

2:55 P.M., SUNDAY, JUNE 20
405 OLD VIKING BOULEVARD,
PICKEREL LAKE, NOWTHEN

I wished Serena never would have entered the house. Waiting for an opening was no longer an option. She wasn't going to survive without help. My work had taught me people had anger problems because they needed to be angry, at one time, to survive. Bobby and the boys were angry. That anger was in me, but I didn't know that it was in Serena.

I watched the large skinhead circle the house like a hayseed nightwatchman. His water bottle rested by the eagle statue. After he walked by it this round, I quickly went to it and dumped it out. I bumped the base of the statue, and the bronzed bird wobbled precariously. It wasn't attached, and I caught it just before it tipped onto the ground. I steadied the bird and then set the water bottle on the ground, trying to make it look like the cap hadn't been tightly secured and it'd simply leaked out. I retreated to the edge of the woods and waited for him to return.

This round, he stopped at the water bottle and curiously studied it. After looking around briefly, he swore under his breath, set his rifle down, and retreated to the house.

I raced over to his rifle and emptied it. I ducked back out of sight and waited, with the intention of Tasing my martial arts opponent as soon as he returned. The Taser had to work. I didn't dare shoot an unarmed man. If it didn't do its job, I'd be left to battle a superior opponent. I hadn't been in many brawls. I tried to use my wits and reasoning to get out of altercations. It was rarely in someone's best interest to fight, but it was still occasionally a necessity.

I found myself thinking about the Muhammad Ali and Joe Frazier fights. They called Frazier *the tank* because he just kept coming. Ali was clearly the superior fighter and he pounded Frazier, but Smokin' Joe beat him once by surviving until he had an opening. It didn't come until the final round. Ali was confident and got a little too aggressive. Joe caught him with a left jab that dropped Ali to the canvas—and subsequently gave the fight to Frazier.

I could hear skinhead coming and, when he stepped around the corner, I fired the Taser, striking him right in the chest where his leather vest was open. The metal hooks bounced off his dog tags and fell impotently to the ground. Before I could draw my gun, he was on me, trying to gut me out with his hunting knife.

With fury backed by raw strength, he drove the blade toward me.

I pushed it down, realizing I was running the risk of taking it in the groin.

It was all I could do to force the thrust lower, but I didn't have enough power to get it clear of my leg. The knife sank into in my upper thigh; I saw it before I felt it. *Shit.* Adrenaline-infused, I twisted his wrist with both hands, digging my fingers into his tendons until he let go, leaving only the hilt of the knife sticking out of my leg.

Skinhead stepped back and said, "Okay, Longmire, you wanna punch it out with me, let's go."

Cocksure, he danced on his toes, as I limped heavily toward the eagle, hoping to perhaps use it as a shield. That blade could've been embedded in my femoral artery; if he pulled it out, I'd bleed to death.

Before I could take cover behind the statue, Skinhead unloaded a volley of punches to my torso and head. I held up my forearms and deflected them the best I could, trying to anticipate where the next strike would land. My leg burned and his blows painfully thumped like they were backed by hydraulics.

I had a fraction of an opening, so I advanced toward him and tried to blast him with a jab to the solar plexus, but he quickly twisted away from my effort, and I only caught air.

I had extended myself too far and left myself vulnerable. He took advantage with a rocket punch to my ribs.

I retreated, again using my forearms for self-defense, as he kept coming with more rapid-fire punches. Each blow painfully bruised, and I was starting to feel dizzy. While I was deflecting the brunt of the blows, I was swinging too wildly and wasn't landing any punches. He was beating me down and I was weakening from my injuries. It was just a matter of time before I was defeated.

He finally stepped back and laughed. "I could do this all day. You amuse me."

I was in trouble. *What would happen to Serena if I didn't win this?* I reached back for my gun, but before I could grip it skinhead thundered a punch toward my head.

The combination of my ducking back to avoid it and the blow sent me falling backwards. I broke right into a backward summersault and came back to my feet again. I had returned to standing next to the eagle.

Skinhead came at me again. Contrary to his words, he wanted to end this quickly. He darted at me, this time lunging for the knife.

I grabbed the eagle's feet and swung the thing like a club, cracking him upside his skull. He dropped to the ground like a sack of flour.

The eagle stands for justice, and justice was served.

Careful not to disturb the knife in my body, I knelt on him, pulled his wrists back, and cuffed him.

I moved out of his reach and tipped over, staring up at a brilliant blue sky scattered with unperturbed clouds ignoring the violence below. The shape of a bird came gliding into my blurring view. A proud white head and tail feathers came into focus, and I was sure the majestic eagle gave me a nod of approval. I wanted to keep moving but I was so dizzy, I needed to rest for a second.

60

"Sometimes, there are days like this when slow, steady effort is rewarded with justice that arrives like a thunderbolt."
—President Barack Obama

2021

SERENA FREDERICK

3:05 P.M., SUNDAY, JUNE 20
405 OLD VIKING BOULEVARD,
LAKE PICKEREL, NOWTHEN

When the shooting started downstairs, I froze.

Bobby grabbed me hard by the arm and yelled, "Get moving!"

When I turned to leave, he let go of me and went back to the kitchen to retrieve a rifle. *What had he seen?*

I followed behind him and could see out the window, over his shoulder, that Jon was involved in an all-out brawl with a skinhead. I flinched with every strike that landed on my husband. To my relief, Jon knocked him out—with a metal bird, of all things. He was laying on the ground now, not moving. My instincts screamed to run to him.

Bobby turned around and almost ran me over. He ordered, "Meet me at the truck. This will only take a minute." He raised the rifle to his eye and aimed it at Jon.

I intentionally bumped the rifle. "No—Bobby. Let's just leave."

Fuming, he jabbed the butt of the rifle hard into the side of my face, knocking me off balance and to the floor. "Stupid bitch, I told you to leave."

I reached behind my back and drew the gun from my waistband.

Bobby's eyes widened in shock.

Angry at the abusive prick, I did something I may never feel good about. I fired, *BANG!* The gun recoiled, jerking my hands back, but I didn't let up. *BANG! BANG! BANG! BANG!* Honestly—at that moment, Bobby wasn't aiming his rifle at me or Jon. I was tired of him feeling me up and knocking me around—and I had a loaded gun on me. I didn't think I could ever shoot someone, but I did.

Bobby fell to the ground in a gruesome heap of torn flesh and blood.

I finally peeled my finger from the trigger and set the gun down. Bobby Long was dead.

I leaned back and closed my eyes. Still in shock, I hadn't anticipated one more player.

When I opened my eyes, a fit blonde woman stood right over me with her gun fixed on my head. Her sweat-stained muscle shirt revealed the defined veins in her arms. She wore an American flag bandanna around her neck and tattered jeans. The sinewy muscles in her forearms flexed as she gripped her firearm.

Blondie jeered, "I told Bobby not to trust you. He told me to just keep an eye on the surveillance cameras and stay out of his personal life."

I raised my hands in retreat and pled, "I have no grievance with you."

She growled, "This is a war, and the yellow rose of Texas beats the belles from Tennessee, sweetheart."

I had to assume the belle reference, like Disney's Belle, was about my brunette hair.

Out of nowhere, Zave flew into her, and her single shot was lethal only to a lamp. With a fury I'd never seen in him, Zave pinned her face down and roughly tore the gun from her hand. He wrenched her arms behind her back, ignoring her howls of protest.

Zave ordered, "Bring me that lamp."

When I handed it to him, he yanked the cord free and used it to hogtie the woman's wrists and feet in a tight knot behind her back. She fought him every step of the way, unleashing a combination of expletives punctuated by flying saliva.

Sirens closed in and squad cars soon could be heard skidding to a halt in the driveway.

I ran to the window and saw an exhausted Jon, now struggling to his feet. The man he'd been fighting lay handcuffed on the ground. The inside of Jon's leg was soaked with blood.

Heart in my throat, I ran outside and yelled, "Jon! Are you okay?" I closed the distance between us faster than I thought I could move.

"Yeah—I'll need some stitches."

Zave opened the door to check on us.

Jon yelled to him, "How many of the militia are accounted for in there?"

Zave called back, "Three."

Jon responded, "I only got one. There's one more."

I shouted, "There's one dead in the bedroom."

Jon sighed with relief, "Okay—we're good. There were five." He dropped to his butt and lay back down on the grass.

I crouched beside him. "What do you need?"

He spread his legs. "I need to be careful with my movement until this blade's out of my body."

A hunting knife was buried to the hilt in his thigh. I told him, "Don't remove it. It's better if we leave it in until you're at the hospital."

Jon nodded as he massaged his forehead. I could tell he was in pain but he wasn't one to say anything about it. Instead, he asked, "How about Lauren?"

It was agonizing to have a colleague killed. "She's in a bedroom. It looks like she took a bullet in the forehead."

He paled and muttered, "Damn it!" With a grim expression, he said, "Help me up. I need to see the scene."

Zave was hovering over Lauren when we entered, tears in his eyes, but with hope, he said, "She has a pulse." He rubbed his thumb across her bloody forehead and said with curious surprise, "I don't think she was shot."

Jon limped over to the dead man on the floor and said, "Sorry Buck." After a quick prayer over the man, he turned and studied Lauren's body on the bed.

She slowly started coming to. Lauren's cuffs were removed, and she sat up. Oddly, she didn't appear to have injuries beyond a cut on her hand.

It took her a few minutes to collect herself, before she told us, "This guy named Buck insisted he get first shot at me when they dragged me into the bedroom. Once he locked the door and it was just the two of us, I was ready to fight him like a wildcat—even with cuffs on. But he quietly told me he was going to save my life. He made a cut on my hand with his knife and told me to hold the wound against my forehead, so it would look like blood was dripping down my forehead. Buck told me to lie still until the cops came for me—so I did. He fired a shot behind my head into the wall and the last thing he said was, 'One more thing. I'm going to knock you out.' Before I could register what he meant, with a blast, I was out. When I started coming around, I was covered with a blanket from the waist down, but my jeans were still on, thank God."

Jon asked, "Who shot Buck?"

"I'm not sure. I played dead and my mind was still hazy. I caught a glimpse of a big, burly guy and I could hear Bobby. I remember Bobby was angry Buck killed me before he got his chance. I heard a shot, and then heard Bobby say, 'We're okay. They'll think Zave did it.' The shooter was standing next to me, but I was too terrified to open my eyes."

Zave assured her, "I'm staying at your side tonight. I'm so sorry."

Lauren continued, "Do you want to hear something really sick?"

No one responded.

She continued, "After a few minutes, Bobby returned alone and said, 'I'm going to have you anyway.' I could hear him unbuckling his belt, but then it was announced Serena arrived and he left."

Two Anoka County investigators entered the room.

Jon insisted, "Don't move her yet." He pointed to three perfectly circular dots of blood on her torso. Jon directed one of the investigators, "Photograph those. We need those drops of blood sampled for DNA." He explained, "This is blood from the man standing over Lauren. Perfect circles mean Lauren was no longer moving when they dropped on her. This is how we identify the man who shot Buck."

After the photos were taken, I announced, "There's an ambulance outside. Both you and Jon should get checked out."

Zave pointed toward my cheek. "You've got a pretty nasty bruise forming, yourself." I felt where I'd been struck with the butt of the rifle.

Jon studied me. "Are you okay?"

I nodded. I didn't want to talk about it right now. Jon picked up on this and said no more.

Zave groaned, "I wouldn't mind seeing an x-ray of my ribs. But I need to have a conversation with the *yellow rose of Texas* first." He turned and kissed Lauren. "If that's okay with you."

She smiled. "I'll be waiting."

Zave commented, "I want to take down Bobby's entire network." He told Lauren, "I won't be long. I just want to let the investigators know what we're dealing with. I'll catch up to you at the hospital."

As I helped Jon to the ambulance, he told me, "I was trying to take him alive. I tried Tasing him, but the hooks bounced off his dog tags, rendering it useless. And then he came at me full bore with his knife." Trying to make light of the knife sticking out of his inner thigh, he said, "Damn near ruined my whole weekend."

I smiled, "I should write a Kama Sutra book and how to make love to an injured lover."

"I might not read it, but I promise to look at the pictures."

"You know what your mom's going to say, don't you?"

"I imagine something like, *the Lord works in mysterious ways.*"

I teased, "She'll say God meant for you to have another child."

Jon remarked, "Well for damn sure, She meant for me to at least try . . . "

6:10 P.M.

ANOKA COUNTY SHERIFF'S OFFICE

13301 HANSON BOULEVARD NORTHWEST, ANDOVER

I WASN'T ALLOWED TO RIDE IN THE AMBULANCE with Jon because of lingering COVID restrictions. Instead, Zave and I were brought to the Anoka County Sheriff's Department, where we were interviewed by a husky white investigator in an interrogation room. Our statements were being recorded and I imagined Sean Reynolds and the sheriff watched on the other side of the one-way glass.

A Chicano investigator, Mateo Morales, joined the team and had me walk through everything that had transpired after I arrived at the lake house. As I sat, I occasionally applied an icepack to my swollen cheek.

Once I had covered the basics, Mateo came back to the shooting. "Could you explain why you shot Bobby Long?"

I wasn't even a hundred percent sure, myself. It all happened so fast. I hoped to hell it wasn't just because he hit me in the face.

I knew better than to process my thoughts aloud, so I repeated, "He aimed his rifle at Jon. I bumped it to keep him from sighting Jon in his crosshairs and he struck me in the face with the butt of the gun. I had my handgun in the back of my pants so I grabbed it and fired at him."

Mateo tapped the table. "You fired five shots."

I tiredly remarked, "I'm not a great shot."

"Do you have a permit to carry?"

"Yes."

"How long have you had it?"

"A couple months."

Investigator Morales was thinking the situation over. "You said Bobby was holding a rifle. Was it aimed at either you or Jon when you fired at him?"

"No."

"We have a witness who claims Bobby was just standing there, presenting no threat to you, when you unloaded your gun on him."

I touched my swollen cheek. "Bobby had just belted me with the butt of a rifle. He didn't have time to re-aim." Frustrated with the interrogation, I asked, "What do you *think* was about to happen? Do you think after Bobby knocked me to the floor, he was just going to give up and turn himself in? People were dying in that house."

Mateo commented, "My concern is that they were all killed by the investigators."

"That's not true."

He dismissed my comment and pointed out, "The only one you saw killed was Bobby, right?"

In resignation, I admitted, "Yes."

"And we have no evidence that Bobby killed anyone."

I sat back, "That's ridiculous."

He leaned into me, "Is it? Zave admits to killing a pretty damn big man in the basement. Only Zave's prints are on the rifle that killed Buck. And it appears to be the same rifle that killed Dan Baker, Wesley Williams, and Marita Perez. All people Zave interacted with."

I thought back about his witness. "Did your witness tell you that she tried to blow my brains out? Zave saved my life."

"She's in custody as we're sorting it all out . . . "

LAUREN WAS IN THE WAITING ROOM WHEN I was done. We mutually grimaced as we caught each other's injuries. I had a nasty bruise on my cheek. She had a swollen bump on her forehead and her hand was wrapped in bright white gauze. Her interview had also ended.

We hugged tightly and she said, "Thank you, Serena."

They had performed the concussion protocol on the scene and determined Lauren didn't need to be hospitalized.

When Zave's interview finished, he offered to give me a ride to North Memorial, where a trauma team was performing surgery on Jon to repair the partially severed muscle in his leg.

We piled into his truck, with Zave driving, Lauren in the passenger seat and I sat in the extended cab. I wish I would have gone to the hospital with Jon. If my worries for my husband and intensifying guilt weren't enough, something was bothering Zave, and it soon would be directed at me.

Zave remarked, "Serena, Jon should never have asked you to go in there. Do you realize that, as someone working for the BCA, you could get prison time for that shooting?"

"Jon didn't tell me to enter that house. I chose to because he and I feared you'd soon be dead if we didn't intervene."

He took a frustrated breath and continued, "I appreciate that, but stop and think. Kim Potter is going to prison for shooting a man with a weapon charge. Kim's a commended officer. Saved a kid during an amber alert, talked a suicidal person down, negotiated the safe release of a kidnapped child—it goes on and on. I'm not defending her shooting—I'm just saying she has a better defense than you do. While no one hates Bobby more than I, but Bobby was just a suspect. And the witness claims he was no threat to you when you shot him."

I clarified, "Bobby aimed his rifle at Jon and was going to shoot him."

Zave looked perplexed.

I was feeling nauseated. "Zave, I went back in the house with the gun after I heard Bobby tell the giant to kill you. When I heard the shots downstairs, I was afraid it was too late. Tell me—what *should* I have done?"

Lauren interjected, "If Serena wouldn't have come in when she did, Bobby would've raped me. Honestly, she saved my life."

Zave clarified, "Serena, I think you're a hero. I just feel it was unfair for Jon to put you in that situation."

Am I a terrible person? Did I kill Bobby out of my own reactive anger? I wanted to clarify, "Jon didn't put me in this investigation."

Surprised, Zave asked, "Who did?"

"Sean Reynolds. Jon didn't want me to work it. Sean asked me to. And if I'm going to do this job, I'm going to do everything I can to save my colleagues, regardless of my lack of experience and wisdom."

Lauren reached back, squeezed my hand and repeated, "Thank you!"

Zave hung his head. "I'm sorry. I didn't know all of that . . . "

10:10 P.M.

PIERZ

IT'S INSANE THAT PEOPLE ARE RELEASED the same day they have surgery. Fortunately, Jon's procedure went fine. Sean made sure a vehicle was delivered to the hospital so I could drive Jon home. Ever the father, he insisted we return to Pierz for the night so we could have some time with Nora and Jackson. Mom let them stay up and watch a Disney movie until we arrived. I got the kids ready for bed, and then I watched Nora read My First Bible Stories to Jackson. Nora sensed my sadness and acted so grown up.

Jackson, with his father's big blue eyes, eagerly hung on to every word his sister shared.

When the story was finished, Nora told him, "God helps us when we need it. He's all around us, but he doesn't come in the house or anything like that. He's kind of like Silencia, the girl who mows our lawn."

How could you not love that! Their hugs and laughter pulled me out of my daze of self-induced guilt. Still a little groggy, Jon showed the kids his wound and told Nora how the warrior training had saved him.

AFTER THE KIDS WERE ASLEEP, WE RETREATED to bed. I lay in the crook of Jon's arm, telling him, "I killed a man today. I never wanted to ever kill anyone. I wonder, if I wouldn't have been a past rape victim, would I have killed Bobby?"

Jon ran his hand soothingly through my hair. "Being a victim doesn't mean you'll never have to kill someone. You saved my life. I will be forever indebted to you."

I revealed, "I saved your life when I bumped his rifle. He wasn't aiming at you when I shot him."

"If you gave him another second, he would've killed both of us. Nora and Jackson would be crying themselves to sleep."

"I keep thinking, what if I would have just yelled, *Drop the rifle?*"

"Do you think this man—a man who murdered his fiancée, his partner, and his ally—was going to drop his rifle? He would have killed you and then me."

With a dolorous attempt at a smile, I said, "I'm a terrible shot. I wish I would never have learned to fire a gun."

"Then it would've just been me going into that house and that wouldn't have played out well. I had one guy to take down and he almost killed me. What kept me fighting, when he was getting the best of me, was knowing you were in there." He kissed me and added, "I needed someone to have my back and you did. There's no one I trust more than you."

"This is so stressful." I finally agreed, "Sometimes there are no good choices."

"Anytime you have anxiety about what happened, remember I wouldn't be here, and your kids wouldn't have a mother. Bobby created a situation that forced you to end his life. You're not to blame for that."

I snuggled him even tighter, "Thank you." And then I said something I once jacked Jon up for saying to me, when he came home from work all stressed out. "I don't want to talk anymore tonight. I just want to make love and fall asleep."

I think God made making love simple, to force us to hold someone close and get out of our heads.

61

2021

SERENA FREDERICK

10:00 A.M., TUESDAY, JUNE 22
PARK AVENUE WOMEN'S CENTER FOR ADDICTION
2318 PARK AVE, PHILLIPS, MINNEAPOLIS

I wasn't really in the mood to attend Cheyenne Schmidt's reunification session with her father this morning, but I would follow through as promised. Cheyenne had asked, "What do you wear to meet a father who sexually abused you?" I suggested she wear a modest shirt and jeans. She decided on an off the shoulder, flowery romper that highlighted her long legs. It was an outfit she felt comfortable in.

Cheyenne and I sat in a conference room waiting for her father. Teary-eyed, she told me, "Thank you for killing Bobby. I'd lost hope."

I wasn't sure how to respond to that.

She took my hand and revealed, "He cornered me in the parking ramp last Saturday. He was never going to let me go, Serena."

How the hell did Bobby get in here? I slid my chair closer and hugged her, "I'm so sorry, Cheyenne. What happened?"

She squeezed me tight. "Bobby choked me with his belt. He wanted me to give up the name of the insider. But I wouldn't give your name, Serena. You give me hope."

I just held her, until her breathing finally calmed down. I suggested, "Maybe this isn't a good day to meet with your father."

Cheyenne quickly brushed away tears. "I'm okay. I need to bring resolution to something. I need this."

I studied her and shared, "Okay."

Her father was escorted by staff to our room. The staff person closed the door when she exited and left the three of us. Sig Schmidt had thick black hair, starting to gray on the sides and combed straight back.

Cheyenne was given complete control of the session and I was present as her support person. She shared that she was working at a convenience store, about to graduate from chemical dependency treatment, and greatly enjoying her new hobby of riding bicycle with the Twin Cities Bicycling Club. Cheyenne was also struggling to find a place she could afford.

I told her, "Cheyenne, you've done great, here. And there's nothing better for a person than getting outside and getting some exercise."

Sig said carefully, "I'm proud of you."

After an awkward silence, he added, "I completed sex offender treatment in 2017. The CORE program involves some intense soul searching. I'm starting over. I'm married now and have a five-year-old daughter."

Cheyenne was taken aback. "That's bullshit! Why do you get to have another family? You abandoned me. Mom hated me. And you get to just go on? Bullshit!"

Sig patiently gave her time to collect her tears, and then told her, "I'm sorry. I wanted to tell you how sorry I was—but I couldn't. I was court-ordered to stay away. And I didn't *just go on*. I made a huge mistake. An unforgivable mistake. And after going to jail, and then treatment, I slowly put things back together. I'm sober. I work a fulltime job. I have regular visitation with your brothers."

Cheyenne cut him off, "And you replaced me. Like I was nothing."

"There's no replacing you," he said softly. "It was only with your permission that I was finally able to lift my no contact order. I wanted to apologize to you a million times. This is the first day I've been allowed to speak to you."

I felt badly for Cheyenne. She hadn't done anything wrong, yet she lost so much.

Again, a pregnant silence settled around us.

Sig finally asked, "Can I read you a letter? I feel I don't deserve to enjoy a conversation with you until I apologize."

Cheyenne let out a pained, labored breath. "If it makes you feel better."

Sig pulled a worn, folded letter from his back pocket. It looked like it had been there for ages. He cleared his throat and somberly read:

"I'm sorry for sexually abusing you. As time passes and I no longer get to enjoy our conversations, the damage I caused weighs heavy on me. I feel incredible guilt for hurting you—an amazing, fun-loving young girl. I've tried to come up with a way to make this right but have accepted that there is nothing I could do in a thousand years that could ever make it right. All I can do is tell you how sorry I am and hope that, over time, you can move forward from it and have a good life. It was my job to care for you—to protect you. But I failed. A father's trust and protection should be a given. You should have been able to confide in me without worry that a sacred boundary would be broken. I'm sorry for violating your trust. Someday, you'll need to be able to trust decent people. I was stupid. I should've got help before I hurt you. I regret that it took you turning me in, for me to face my sins. Group therapy helped me understand the full ramifications for my behavior."

Cheyenne listened intently, tears spilling freely. I felt like an intruder.

Sig's voice thickened as he continued, quiet sniffling giving away his deep regret.

"I understand if you hate me for what I did. That's a normal healthy feeling toward a man who was neither normal nor healthy at the time. I give you credit for turning me in. That was courageous, and so much to put on a young girl. I want you to know I'm sorry and completely responsible for everything that happened. As a child, you did your best by telling when I, as an adult, did my worst by violating your trust. I wish the best for you and have nothing but respect for you. From now on, you get to pick how much I'm in your life. If you say go to hell, I accept it. If you say I'll see you sometimes, I'll accept it. If you say holidays, I'll work around your schedule. I thank God I had the chance to give you this apology. Don't ever think you need to consider forgiving me. There is no forgiveness for what I did. For me, there is only trying to be a decent man every day and hope that people see my commitment to this. It is on me to try to make up for my sins, for the rest of my life, and to hope for salvation."

Cheyenne stood up and reached to her dad for a hug. They embraced and tears flowed from both.

She finally pulled away and said, "Dad, I killed a man."

Sig nodded. "I know. It wasn't your fault. He's lucky you didn't kill him the first time. I blame myself. If I would've been there for you, that situation never would have happened."

The forgiveness shared between the two was important for me to hear. If they could be forgiven, why couldn't I?

Cheyenne said, "I want my dad back."

Sig suggested, "This is a lot to ask, but would you consider moving in with Dawn and me? We've already discussed it and my wife has agreed. It's the least we can do. You could get to know your sister. We don't have a lot, but we can offer you a place to stay, rent free, until you find something better—and free meals. But we can't have any alcohol or drugs in our home."

Cheyenne smiled through renewed tears. "Sounds perfect. I miss you, Dad."

Sig's response was genuine. "Not any more than I miss you. It's time for us to start over. I've prayed for you every night, and twice on Sundays."

62

*"Caring for myself is not self-indulgence,
it is self-preservation, and that
is an act of political warfare."*
—AUDRE LORDE

2021

JADA ANDERSON

6:00 A.M., WEDNESDAY, JUNE 23
KING'S POINT ROAD ON HALSTED BAY,
MINNETRISTA, MINNESOTA

The gorgeous man lying in my bed had now fallen pleasantly asleep. I slid out of bed and peeked out the blinds at the bright lemon sun emerging with a beacon of optimistic light over the lake.

We were both under a lot of stress and we debriefed with a little too much alcohol last night. Bobby Long was dead. Less deserving—but still deserving—Ray Fury, was dead. I was celebrating the end of my involvement in this case last night and we became affectionate. Maybe I was mad about losing another partner to a white girl. I didn't see myself as racist, but the idea of it seemed to induce an extra burn. Surprisingly,

I didn't feel guilty. Instead, I felt a sense of redemption. After last night, I'd be single for a while.

Sean attempted to apologize but I didn't want to hear it. He told me it was a mistake. When you bumped into a valued piece of art and broke it, *that* was a mistake. Sleeping with someone else during the entire course of an engagement was malicious. Sean said he was afraid of getting old and dying; he wanted one last fling before our marriage. Maybe I needed a fling, too. I got it, but marrying Sean was now off the table.

I shook my lover. "It's time to get up. You have a deposition this morning. And I don't want you here when Isaiah wakes."

He silently complied, but then grumbled as he gathered his bearings. "It's better if we don't say anything to anyone about this."

I smiled, "Is it?"

He slid his shirt on that chiseled body and said, "Yes, it is."

I placed my hand flat on his bare chest, stopping him from continuing to button. There was something about the gesture that made him uncomfortable—as if it brought back a disturbing memory. I asked, "What?"

"Sadie did that same thing, years ago, the last time we spoke."

I taunted, "I'm a reporter. It's in my nature to tell—but okay, Zave." I slowly pulled my hand away. "I have no desire for drama, but I'm not going to lie for you. Are you a little worried about Lauren?"

"She's afraid of you."

"She should be—but it isn't warranted. I don't have time to waste on your lily filly." Playing with his nervousness, I added, "Say hi to her from me."

After he finished dressing, he faced me awkwardly and said, "I don't know what to say."

"*Thank you* would suffice." I smiled. "You do have me rethinking the wisdom of my dating older men."

Zave seemed to be struggling to pull it all together.

I asked, "Do you remember getting pulled over last night?"

He rubbed his eyes, "Shit. I do, now."

I flashed back to the night before.

12:30 A.M.

HIGHWAY 394 BRYN MAWR, MINNEAPOLIS

I HAD INTENDED TO CALL FOR AN UBER; but Zave offered me a ride home. There was a tender place in my heart for a kind gentleman with tortured morality. As the night passed, I found myself drawn to him, to the point of leaning against him during our conversation before we left.

His truck was parked on the street and when we approached it, I asked, "Are you sure you're okay to drive?" I had stopped drinking two hours ago; he hadn't.

He grinned a little sloppily. "I'm fine."

Zave didn't seem that bad at the time. I watched him remove his shoulder holster from beneath his shirt, set it behind the seat, and cover it with a jacket. A move I'd later appreciate.

I stepped up on the running board and into the passenger seat. I teased, "I can do that, too." I removed my bra by pulling it through my sleeve, placed it in my purse, and drank up the desire in his amorous glance.

We were soon cruising east on I-394. Zave had a Clickbait tune he insisted I listen to, and he was bobbing his head to the thumping beat when a squad car pulled alongside his truck and paced us for about half a mile.

The squad finally pulled back and flashing blue lit up behind us.

Zave slowly pulled his truck onto the shoulder of the interstate. Now irritated, he turned to me, "I wasn't doing anything wrong."

He was right. Zave was simply a black man driving a new truck. Now that I studied him, I realized he was more intoxicated than I had first thought.

He lowered his window and waited.

A white officer blinded us with the mag light he beamed through the window. Seeing we were unarmed, he hopped up on the running board and shouted, "I need to see your driver's license and insurance."

Zave commented, "We're not hard of hearing. Can you tell me what I did wrong?"

The light searched through the truck. When it landed on me, I realized my blouse was clinging more than I wished. But I sat frozen, hands on my lap, fearful any movement could bring gunfire.

The officer finally turned to Zave. "You look like you've been drinking. You're going to need to step out of the truck."

Zave hadn't missed the extended time the officer kept the light on my body, and he was angry. He remained seated. Instead of getting out, he responded, "I'm unarmed. You can keep the light on me. I'm going to grab my wallet."

The officer drew his gun and pulled open the door as he stepped down onto the road.

Zave held his wallet up in the air, opened it and showed him his badge.

The officer lowered his gun and grabbed the billfold. He read out loud, "Xavier Williams—Investigator." He handed it back and then glanced down the freeway. The officer said to me, "Can you drive this truck?"

I gave him my most pleasant smile, "Yes."

He slapped the door and said, "Have a safe drive home," and walked away.

6:15 A.M., WEDNESDAY, JUNE 23, 2021
KING'S POINT ROAD ON HALSTED BAY
MINNETRISTA, MINNESOTA

ZAVE WAS NOW DRESSED.

I commented, "The blue code."

He argued, "He never should've pulled me over in the first place."

I pointed out, "If you wouldn't have been a cop, the best possible outcome would have been spending the night in the Hennepin County Jail."

He responded, "So a black man should never get a break."

"This is how it all starts. Now you owe him one."

He said firmly, "No one will ever be abused on my watch. I don't care if I owe the officer my life."

I smiled, "Right answer. I'm just warning you."

With remorse, he softly shared, "Message delivered. I shouldn't have driven home." He stuttered, "I—I need to go."

"You do. I hear that's what you're good at. *X and his one-night sex*. No hard feelings. I knew the game going into this."

I watched him back his truck out of my driveway and head on down the road.

To quote Shakespeare, "Parting is such sweet sorrow." Lauren stepped in on my relationship with Sean. I stepped in on Lauren's relationship with Zave. I might have gotten the better of that exchange . . .

63

"Every man must decide whether he will walk in the light of creative altruism or in the darkness of destructive selfishness."
—Martin Luther King Jr.

2021

XAVIER "ZAVE" WILLIAMS

8:00 A.M., WEDNESDAY, JUNE 23
4TH PRECINCT, 1925 PLYMOUTH AVENUE NORTH
WILLARD HAY NEIGHBORHOOD, MINNEAPOLIS

Last night, Jon, Serena, Jada and I went out to Wabasha Brewery to let off some steam over this case. Jon and Serena left early. Jada and I didn't. *What the hell is wrong with me?* It was so stupid! The demons in my head were telling me, *It's okay. Nobody needs to know.*

When I walked into the precinct, my colleagues rose to their feet and clapped. I was at the pinnacle of respect from my colleagues and at the moment, I felt like the worst man I'd ever been. I shook some hands and took what I needed from my desk. An internal investigation was taking place regarding the deaths at Nowthen and I was suspended until it was completed. The good news was it was a paid suspension. I headed across town for my interview with Jon Frederick.

9:00 A.M.
BUREAU OF CRIMINAL APPREHENSION,
1430 MARYLAND AVENUE EAST ROOSEVELT, ST. PAUL

JON WAS THE BCA AGENT SUPERVISING THIS case, so was asked to take a deposition from me about the Nowthen skirmish. Since he was also involved in the event, he wouldn't have the final say, but his recommendations would guide how my involvement was handled. This was no small ruling, as I killed two people at the scene. There was a process in law enforcement called the *continuum of force*. A police officer should only use deadly force if it is a necessary response to escalating aggression by the perpetrator. I was nervous. My first killing met the criteria, but the second did not.

Jon met me in the parking lot and said, "Before we go in and take your recorded statement, I think we should go for a walk and talk a little off the record."

"Okay."

We strolled down Prosperity Avenue, past the L'Etoile du Nord French Immersion School.

Jon asked, "Is there anything you would change in your statement from the time you arrived until you killed the brute in the basement?"

"No."

"Okay. I have no questions up to that point. After reviewing the statements, it's clear the man was sent to kill you. The fact that you escaped from being chained to a post and killed him in handcuffs is impressive."

I didn't respond. This wasn't the part I was worried about.

Jon continued, "But once you got upstairs, your statement gets confusing. I listened to the tape three times, and I still don't understand it."

Palms up, I asked, "What do you want me to say?"

"The truth. I have the ballistic reports back. Serena didn't kill Bobby Long."

I rubbed my forehead. I'd reached a point in my life where the truth would bury me—in every aspect of my life. "I respect the fact that you and Serena entered the lion's den for me, but you're a BCA investigator and your recommendations could send me to prison. I'm going to need an attorney."

"This walk is entirely off the record."

"How do I know that?"

"Apparently, you don't. I am a man of my word. It might be helpful for you to know that I'm not out to make a name for myself at the BCA. I'm considering heading back into private practice when this is all said and done." Jon gave me a deadpan look and said, "I told you I'd keep you updated on all of the information I had throughout this investigation. Did I?"

"You did," I admitted. "I appreciate that." I paused, "What if I was out of my head for a minute? Just spun out."

"I'm not sure you were. Let me be the judge of that. You were chained up and had to fight for your life. I don't feel like you made any illogical decisions. I battled one man and damn near lost. Those boys were tough."

I said, "I stepped into the bedroom and saw Lauren. I thought she was dead. I was so overwhelmed I didn't even take in the dead guy on the floor."

"What happened when you left that room?"

The voice in my head was saying *ask for an attorney*, but instead I was going to put some trust in this farm boy.

I revealed, "I moved toward Bobby's voice. I could see his side perfectly, but I couldn't see who he was talking to. I raised the Glock, aimed it where I could hit his heart, and fired. I didn't give a damn if he was a threat at that moment. I wanted to watch him die, and that's my truth. Enough is enough. Sadie, Danny, Marita, and at the time, I believed Lauren."

"And you hit your target."

I admitted, "I didn't realize Serena had fired at the same time. I just knew she continued to fire four more times. I didn't need to."

Jon pointed out, "Serena put a bullet in his right shoulder, a bullet in his left shoulder, two bullets in the wall around him, and then hit him in the balls. Her shots certainly would have incapacitated Bobby but wouldn't have killed him."

I explained, "I waited until I knew she was done shooting to approach. And then the blonde stepped in. I'd forgotten about her. She was with the group who initially surrounded me. Blondie raised her gun toward Serena, and I tackled her. Bobby was dead. I didn't need to kill anyone else. She fired her gun and took out a lamp. I used the cord to tie her up."

"Zave, what you did in that home was impressive," he repeated. "I barely put down one—you neutralized three. And it wasn't an easy task knocking that post out of place."

"So, what are you going to do with the new information?"

Jon continued to walk for a moment, before sharing, "I'm going to go with the truth. Bobby aimed his rifle at me. Serena nudged him to prevent him from taking a shot. Bobby knocked her to the ground. Serena and you drew simultaneously and fired. Bobby died. And you're not going to tell me you didn't care if Bobby was a threat. He was a threat and that's what matters."

"How do you justify the continuum of force? I didn't see Bobby raise his gun toward you."

Jon explained, "I know there's a process we're taught. But the statute specifically states an officer can use deadly force if, without action, the behavior creates a substantial risk of causing death. There is no doubt in my mind that Bobby would've killed one of us if you hadn't shot him. It probably would have been Serena or me. And then you saved Serena by knocking Dallas Alice off balance and hogtieing her with a lamp cord."

I considered, "By the way—how in the hell did you get Buck to help?"

"When you deal with a gang, do you see guys who can be pulled back out of it?"

"Yeah. Most are, eventually."

"I see the same thing with these militias. Remember, they're all just people. Some can be turned, some can't. I overheard Buck saying they shouldn't have kidnapped Lauren, so I captured him alone and asked him to help her. After I filled him in on the truth about Bobby, he was in. It cost Buck his life. Bobby killed him with the intention of blaming you."

"How do you know it was Bobby?"

"Dr. Ho tested the drops of blood on Lauren. They were Bobby's. He had to be the one standing over her when Buck was shot. How did you draw blood from Bobby?"

"I didn't. Lauren bit him."

Jon smiled. "Good for her. I will be recommending you for a Public Safety Medal of Valor." The highest award given to police officers.

I didn't feel deserving. "I felt like I was angry and out of control."

"Bobby Long murdered Sadie, Dan, Wesley, and Buck. You tried to arrest him peacefully and it almost cost you your life. The medal is deserved. Plus, they'll never find fault with you, with that recommendation in place."

I stopped walking, shook his hand, and gave him a shoulder-to-shoulder, man-hug. "Thank you." Seeking clarification, I asked, "So, it's all good?"

"Yes. We can start walking back and I'll take your official statement—but don't tell me what you didn't see. You didn't see him raise the gun. You also didn't see aliens or six maids a- milking. Just explain what you did, and I'll work it into the chronology of verified events."

I considered, "If it's okay, can I help out with the raid on the rest of the militia?"

Jon laughed, "Now you're pushing your luck. You won't be cleared in time. The FBI's taken over the case, now, anyway. Bobby's group is identified as a terrorist cell. To tell you the truth, I'd be surprised if the group is big. The small groups are the most dangerous. Some crazy guy like Bobby can dominate them without being checked. You're out of this. Enjoy your time off. Anything else you need to address?"

I shook my head, "Nothing you can help me with." As I'd seen him do over and over, Jon remained silent, waiting for me to fill in the dead air. And I did. I said, "My personal life is even more of a mess. Lauren asked me to go north with her, but I told her I had to wrap this up. I should've left the taproom when you and Serena did."

He seemed to understand what that meant, but he said nothing.

I admitted, "I believe that a relationship with Lauren would be the best possible change in my life right now, but I thoroughly screwed that up last night. There's no way I could expect her to understand or forgive me. And I don't want to let her go. Right now, I think I'm the worst version of me and I'm getting accolades. When I was a decent man, people seemed to be convinced I was a piece of shit. Now, my colleagues think I'm a hero and I really am a POS. How can I get Lauren, or anyone, to believe in me, after all this?"

Jon seemed to have a thought, but he looked away and kept it to himself.

I said, "This is not the time to shut off that educational banter. Let's hear it."

"You're confused because you're asking the wrong question."

"Okay-- what's the right question?"

"What kind of man are you? If you want honesty, you have to be an honest man. If you want love, you need to be a loving man. And if you want forgiveness, you've got to be a forgiving man. It's time to put away your pride and put it all out there. If she walks away, you have the satisfaction of being true to your nature. You're not naturally a liar."

He was right. My stupidity was going to cost me the best relationship I'd ever had, but I couldn't hide this and feel good about myself. The old me would have either just abandoned the relationship or acted like nothing happened.

I asked, "Don't you think it's a little weird that she was with Sean and then me?"

Jon shrugged, "No. We all have a type. She likes intelligent black investigators. I like women with dark hair, regardless of race. Serena likes neurotic, obsessive men."

I laughed. "How are you obsessive?"

He smiled. "I noticed that you didn't ask how I'm neurotic. Facts and data run through my brain with the slightest trigger. I feel like I'm providing a public service by sharing it, even though I'm aware the majority of people don't really give a damn."

"So, what am I attracted to?"

"From the little I know of you; I'd say women who know what they want. Lauren loves her work. Jada loves her work. My bet is you'll find the same pattern when you delve into your past."

He was right . . .

8:45 P.M.
STONE ARCH BRIDGE
100 PORTLAND AVENUE, DINKYTOWN, MINNEAPOLIS

LAUREN AND I WALKED THE STONE ARCH BRIDGE over the Mississippi, while bicyclists and skateboarders whooshed by. It was warm but overcast. We had a beautiful view of the Minneapolis skyline. As the sun prepared to set, the Pillsbury Flour Mill and Golden Medal Flour signs lit up. Jon's need for data had infiltrated my brain. I found myself recalling from school that, prior to 1921, Minneapolis was the largest flour producer in the world. The industry was so valued, it received military protection in World War I. Sabotage was suspected when a 1917 fire destroyed two large mills.

Lauren was telling me what a hero I'd been, while I was trying to think of way to tell her what I'd done.

I asked, "Are you doing okay?"

"I think so. I feel terrible that a man died saving my life. I'd like to thank his family. I think I'm still processing it all—that whole situation was insane. Maybe you deal with this all the time, but it chills me to the bone."

"Nobody deals with this all the time."

She studied me carefully. "What's on your mind, Zave? Something's bothering you."

My demons advised, *Give her a reason to break up with you. Then you won't have to even mention it.* I said, "I can't afford to take you to all the places Sean could."

Lauren laughed, "Where do you think we went? Sean told me he liked quaint little places, out of the metro. Now I realize he was trying to avoid being seen with me. And he was *tight*. When I consider he was paying for a wedding, it all makes sense."

We headed down the walk to the ruins below the south end of the bridge and sat.

She wasn't appeased. "What is it? Are you breaking up with me?"

"I hope not." I gave the rubble under my feet a kick. Finally, I looked her in the eyes. "I slept with Jada last night. We were hashing out the case and I was stressed. I'm sorry. I regret it."

She seethed in silence; I felt her fondness for me freezing over.

I told her, "I swear, it won't happen again."

In an icy tone, she asked, "Do you feel better—getting even?"

"No. I don't even know if it was about getting even. I have a way of self-destructing. I want you." I reached for her hand, but she raised it, halting me.

Her beautiful baby blues glossed over with tears that I caused. I forced myself to keep my eyes on her face, my conscience absorbing what I'd done in full force. Lauren's words were seasoned with heartache and a healthy dash of bitterness. "I was worried Jada would come after me, but she did one better, didn't she?"

"I'm sorry. I had so many things piling up in my head with being framed, having killed someone, then being suspended, the deposition—I wasn't thinking clearly."

Lauren stood, "We're destroying each other, aren't we?"

"Not anymore. I promise you; I'm not doing any more damage. I didn't think—and I fell into an old pattern I'm now abandoning."

She was shaking as she laughed softly but without humor. I earned that. She had no reason to believe me.

I asked, "What are you thinking? Tell me."

With her head down, long blonde bangs hanging over her face, she said quietly, "I was reminiscing about your warm breath on my neck when we lay together at the cabin. I was so content. I remember thinking *this is what peace feels like.*" She stepped back, "I started the hurt. Now I'm ending it. I'm sorry, but I can't see you again, Zave."

I urged, "We can work through this, Lauren. Give us sixty days. And if you don't want me, I promise I'll never contact you again."

"We had two great days. Thank you for them. But the rest of our dates didn't work. *We* don't work."

I was too ashamed to face her. What more could I say? *The truth will set you free—what a load of crap.*

She finally said, "My dad thought I never should have left Morrison County. He told me I might find a better job, but not better people." She paused, "I'm not going to resent you for this, Zave. I have no one to blame but myself. Every lie costs somebody something, doesn't it?"

I glanced up and listened.

"I thought I was protecting Sean and, if I'm being honest, myself. But we were burning Jada. She paid the price with her heart and soul. My submission to silence, at Sean's request, made me complicit. And I hurt you. Look at all the carnage. How do we ever create a just world when we lie to each other? Have you ever talked about relationships with Jon?"

"Only minimally. How do you know Jon?"

"They helped me get started in forensic work. Serena and Jon can be pretty damn funny. They pretend to pick each other up in the bar sometimes." She briefly smiled, before getting back to us. "Jon says water always runs to the lowest level—meaning, when you're messing up, you end up in relationships with people who are messed up."

I interrupted, "I'm capable of learning from my mistakes and rising."

Her mind was made up. Lauren sighed, "I'm sorry I brought you down to where I was at. We both can be terrible people but on the bright side, we're still alive to change it. I wish you well, Zave."

"Please—don't go."

With a sad smile, she told me, "You'll find another. There's plenty like me to be found."

I wanted to tell her that wasn't true, but I was afraid of breaking down.

After a couple steps, she turned back, "If you feel a chill in the air, it's me."

64

*"Our glory derives not just from our most obvious
triumphs, but how we've wrestled triumph from
tragedy, and how we've been able to remake
ourselves, again and again and again,
in accordance with our highest ideals."*
—Barak Obama

2021

JON FREDERICK

8:00 A.M., THURSDAY, JUNE 24
SNAKE RIVER DRIVE, PINE CITY

The quaint country farmhouse Bobby planned on escaping to, was close to a waterway. The Anishinaabe people who lived along the river called it the Ginebigo-ziibi, which meant Snake River. It was located in the geographic middle of the state, on the eastern side. Snake River was the main waterway connecting the St. Croix River with Mille Lacs Lake. It was one of the few rivers in Minnesota that had sturgeon.

The two-story farmhouse we were closing in on was well-hidden in a pine forest, which was likely why the closest town was named Pine City. The FBI indicated there had been numerous weapons orders made to the home. Wyatt and Bailey Wilder had installed an advanced security camera system and Bailey was an award-winning shooter. Our RF detectors enabled us to avoid their motion sensitive cameras.

One of the great things about working with the FBI was their toys. With the thermal imaging infrared cameras, they were able to determine there were only two people in the house. While the old thermal cameras you see on detective shows illuminated human-shaped blobs moving around, the new technology was detailed enough for facial recognition. Subsequently, I knew going in the only people present were Wyatt and Bailey—the homeowners.

The couple had Swans ice cream delivered to the home and I agreed to enter the house today as the Swans delivery man, with the hope of ending this investigation without any more deaths. My task was to keep both distracted from checking their security cameras, so the FBI could breach the house without a gunfight. I stood on the country porch, knocking on the door, holding their most recent order of dreamsicle ice cream and a new order form.

Wyatt answered the door in hard-worn overalls and a dirty white t-shirt. Somewhere in his forties, his face was etched with the roadmap of a tough life. He squinted past me, a spray of lines creasing at the sides of his alert eyes, to make sure I was alone, then called back over his shoulder, "Bailey! It's the Schwantz man."

Bailey bustled to the door in ragged, Daisy Dukes and a cropped plaid top, both of which were a size too small and forced her fleshy middle to spill out wherever the fabric ended. It was as if her entrapped figure was trying to make a break for it. She was also in her forties, though appeared to be having some difficulty embracing her age and her considerable weight. I channeled my mother and thought, *God bless her.*

Bailey admonished Wyatt through a mouthful of chewing gum, "I told you to stop calling him that." She turned to me, "Where's Rick?"

"Rick is sick."

"Does he have the 'rona?" She snapped her gum waiting for my response.

I responded, "No. I think he was having some back issues."

Bailey remarked, "Grain Belt Blu flu from his Wednesday night golf league." She led me into the house, and I joined her at the kitchen table.

As she paged through the order magazine, Wyatt looked over her shoulder and commented, "The baby back ribs look good."

Bailey asked me, "Are you vaccinated?"

"Yes."

Her tone changed as she worked her gum to prepare for another snap. "That's a problem."

"Why?"

She said, "I have a website you should look at. The government's putting small micro devices in the serum so they can track you once you're injected. Even the Vikings quarterbacks are avoiding that vaccine."

God bless her, I reminded myself. I told her, "They're paid millions of dollars because they're great athletes, not because they're sojourners of medical wisdom."

Wyatt had stepped away, but now came back and added, "It all started with Reagan. He had drones made to look like crows so they could fly around and spy on us. It was all part of his Star Wars defense program."

Bailey added, "Why do you think crows are always sitting on highline wires? They need to recharge." She nodded at me with big eyes, waiting for me to be shocked.

I rubbed my chin, allowing my fingers to cover my mouth briefly to hide my grimace. "I don't know that the government needs to follow us around or inject things into our body, to know what we're doing. People volunteer this information over the internet all the time."

Wyatt nodded, "Damn straight."

Bailey blew a bubble and eyed me up. "Are you one of them right-wing libtards?"

"I've lost faith in both parties. People like us are paying 30% of our income in taxes, while billionaires pay 1%. The top 1% has more money than the entire middle class—46% of the population. That change in the distribution of wealth occurred in 2010."

Bailey pointed a pudgy finger at me and added, "When we had a *black* president." She pulled a piece of gum out of her mouth and stretched it in front of her. I was momentarily unnerved by the dirt under her unpainted nails.

I explained, "It was headed that direction for thirty years before Obama. It was simply in 2010 when the line was crossed, and it's gotten worse with every president, since. Neither party wants to make billionaires pay their fair share. Last year, while most of us struggled to maintain, the richest billionaires increased their wealth forty percent."

Wyatt added, "And we have to pay out millions of dollars to black families in settlements."

I interjected, "The payouts are the result of bad policy."

Bailey popped the piece of gum back in her mouth and directed, "Explain."

I had their attention, now. "We're letting billionaires slide along tax free and failing to help poor people nationwide. What if we changed our educational system to create the jobs we need in America? We need software engineers, builders, and nurses. We could design schools so people could get computer programming jobs right out of high school. We outsource thousands of those jobs to China. It would give opportunities to people who struggle, rather than turning to crime. It's not just Minneapolis where lack of a livable wage is a problem; it's throughout rural America. The working class is angry—all races. Instead of addressing the problem, we're turning on each other."

Wyatt couldn't walk away from the conversation. He dragged a chair out and plopped down with us at the table. A gust of foul body odor wafted my way with his movement. "The price of lumber went up four hundred percent this summer and has now dropped to two hundred. We're supposed to be happy that were only paying twice as much for lumber now. How can you afford a house when your wages don't change?"

"I agree," I said. "And as a financial superpower, America is better off than it's ever been." I added, "The recovery actually began back in 2010 when Obama was president."

My last addition infuriated both Wyatt and Bailey and they edged closer to me, hackles up. I finished with, "We need to share the wealth with all of America, rather than allowing a select few to live like kings and vacation in space."

The kitchen suddenly filled with FBI agents.

Wyatt and Bailey were arrested without incident, for Aiding and Abetting a Known Felon.

8:30 A.M., FRIDAY, JUNE 25, 2021
BUREAU OF CRIMINAL APPREHENSION, 1430 MARYLAND
AVENUE EAST, ROOSEVELT, ST. PAUL

THE FEDS WERE A LITTLE DISAPPOINTED IN the size of the "terrorist cell." It was basically a small group of people Bobby Long had convinced to protect him. The FBI's need to take credit for shutting down a terrorist cell quickly justified the Nowthen killings. It was finally over.

Sean Reynolds meandered into my office as I was cleaning out my desk. His usual crisp, black suit and white shirt were a little disheveled, which is typical of anyone in this office other than Sean. He looked defeated.

He tiredly told me, "I listened to the recordings of your conversation with the Wilders. You were instructed to go in there and maintain a conversation and instead, you started an argument." He laughed, "I'm not upset. It's your nature. Like asking the fox to protect the henhouse."

I smiled, "Arguing is much more fun and compelling. I was instructed to distract them. We're all a little more distracted when we're irritated."

Sean stared out my office window. "Zave turned out to be a rock star—well deserving of the award."

"I agree. Serena stepped in at the right time. I'm grateful Lauren survived it."

He looked away, electing not to respond.

I continued, "As for me, I had one guy to beat and he damn near killed me."

"I watched your body camera footage. That was a brutal fight. He was trying to gut you out."

"I know." I tamped down an inward shudder; it wasn't something I enjoyed replaying in my mind. *Brutal fights* were not my thing and I hated it had come to that. "I didn't want to push the knife up toward my heart, so I managed to wrench it down—which is a risky task." I thought about how close he came to making me a eunuch.

"We walk a fine line," Sean said. "Everybody watching how that skinhead almost skinned you thinks you should've shot him. But if you would have shot him, you could've been fired." He asked, "Why were you the only one wearing a body camera?"

"Zave was on his way back from vacation when he was lured to Nowthen. He thought he received a directive from you. And Serena couldn't wear a camera—she was still undercover."

"I guess that makes sense."

Sean looked disheartened. I asked, "Are you okay?"

"Yeah. Stupid, but okay. Jada and I are done—at least for now. I don't know what got into me. Maybe I wanted to be twenty-five again. Instead, I had a heart attack and almost died. Like they say, you only realize what you had once it's lost. I complained that Jada was always on my case. She just wanted me to live. And I was acting like I was invincible."

"You can't get married if you don't know what you want."

"You actually *can*. I almost did." He chuckled, "You just shouldn't." With melancholy, he said, "Thanks for asking. Isaiah saves me. Knowing my boy needs me keeps me going." Sean looked me over. "We could still use you in Minneapolis."

"I appreciate the offer, but I can't be away from my kids this long again."

He nodded, "I get it. If you want to stay with the BCA, I have an unsolved murder in your neck of the woods I'd like you to look into."

He had my attention, now. I wanted to ask about the case, but if he started telling me about it, I'd be thinking about it during my time off.

As I folded in the flaps from my cardboard box with finality, I told him, "That has possibilities. Give me a week off with my family and we'll talk."

65

2021

SERENA FREDERICK

9:30 P.M., SATURDAY, JULY 17
LOWELL INN, 102 2ND STREET NORTH, STILLWATER

Jon and I were spending a romantic weekend in Stillwater. We enjoyed Caribbean food at Marx Fusion Bistro, and then relaxed at the historic Lowell Inn. Knowing I didn't kill Bobby made me feel better, even though the reality was I was just a terrible shot. It helped that Jon and I were better than ever.

He opened the curtain of our luxurious suite, and we watched a light rain offering starving foliage a reprieve from the summer's drought. Rivulets of water streamed down the window, and I marveled at the rippling shadows of rain dancing on Jon's bare chest. The drought was broken—for now, anyway. As he picked his shirt up off the floor, I suggested, "Why don't you go across the street and have a glass of beer at the Velveteen Speakeasy while I shower? I'll meet you when I'm done."

The boyish smile that's always stirred my heart spread across his face. "Sounds good."

I could feel his loving on eyes on me as I left the bed and headed to the bathroom.

Jon softly said, "You're beautiful."

I teased, "That's enough of that kind of talk—at least for now. Go have a beer."

He told me, "I'm going to buy the kids a kite. Seeing the girl flying the kite down by the Lift Bridge this afternoon makes me want to fly one with them."

As I turned on the water, I raised my voice from the bathroom. "Do you think Nora can get one off the ground? She'll be frustrated if she can't."

"She will. She has her mother's determination. So, I'll be filling my brain with kite-flying terms until you arrive."

Knowing he wasn't joking made the comment so amusing to me. My handsome, loving, geek of a husband.

THE VELVETEEN SPEAKEASY,
123 2ND STREET NORTH, STILLWATER

I WALKED DOWN THE DARK STEPS INTO THE DIMLY lit, brick basement bar, just in time to see a woman in a black spandex mini dress sidling up to the empty barstool next to Jon.

He leaned back as she perched on the edge of the stool and leaned in. I smiled and decided to observe for a moment, staying directly behind him, but close enough to listen in.

The young woman asked him, "What are you into?"

He took a sip of beer and told her, "Flying kites."

"Is that a metaphor?" She offered him an out, "For the freedom they have when they've reached their pinnacle—flying alone."

He shook his head and flatly told her, "No. I'm very literal." He caught me out of the corner of his eye, as he told her, "Flying kites isn't my favorite thing, but it's right up there. It has its ups and downs."

With an annoying snort she replied, "I get it—ups and downs. Honestly, I'm not a big fan of kite flying."

He remarked, "That's too bad, because it's just what a kite flyer could use."

I did love the man's wordplay.

Jon asked the spandex-clad woman, "What's the worst comment a kite flyer can get from his kite string?"

Puzzled, she asked, "What?"

"I'm a frayed knot." He smiled to himself.

Not picking up on the pun, she asked, "What exactly do you enjoy about flying kites?"

I could see the glimmer he got in his eyes when he was about to spin a tale.

"I like running like a madman trying to get them up in the air. When I'm in public places, I smash into things and people, but it's so worth it."

Confused, she backed away a little. "Okay."

He continued, "Have you ever heard of soul flying?"

Unsure where the conversation was going, she said, "No."

"Soul flying is when you let all of your emotions out flying a kite."

I approached the bar and stepped between them. "I saw a man downtown barreling through the crowd at the lift bridge trying to fly a kite." I ran my hand slowly across my throat and onto my chest, as if I had to wipe the sizzling hot sweat away. "Was that you?"

Jon nodded. "Soul flying. Honestly, I feel I may have revealed too much of myself."

I said to him, "It was so free spirited. I could picture you naked."

Baffled, the woman's head swiveled, staring at the two of us.

He slid off his barstool and stepped toward me. "It's not all fun and games. There's a dark side to kite flying—quad lines, stunt kites, kite cutting."

I said in my most seductive tone, "So dangerous and exhilarating." I placed my finger over his lips. "Say no more. Just take me home."

As he took my hand and led me away, I could hear the woman saying, "Wait—the two of you are together, right?"

Jon grinned and said for my ears only, "A little tail makes for a great flight."

I could have told him to *go fly a kite*, but I didn't . . .

66

"The ultimate measure of a man is not where he stands in moments of comfort and convenience, but where he stands at times of challenge and controversy."
—Martin Luther King Jr.

2021

XAVIER "ZAVE" WILLIAMS

8:00 P.M., SUNDAY, AUGUST 22
STONE ARCH BRIDGE
100 PORTLAND AVENUE,
DINKYTOWN, MINNEAPOLIS

I got my award and was back at work as an investigator. Since I'd focused on being the best man I could be, my demons didn't talk to me anymore.

It was too quiet around my house. I was still single and honestly more miserable for having known Lauren. I was making better choices in my life but being alone was gut-wrenching without her. I hadn't seen her at work, recently. I heard she was spending time with her family up north. She might have taken work elsewhere. I was afraid to ask.

I enjoyed some time with my family, too. Mom and Dad were laughing last night while mom attempted to give dad a haircut. I wished Lauren would have been there to capture that moment in a drawing. Dad sitting back with that sly grin, black muscle shirt and army green work pants, holding a wide-mouth Mickey's Malt. My dad referred to the green bottle as the *grenade*. Mom carefully trimmed while joking with him and the love between them warmed my heart. Every day, I came across a scene Lauren would capture so well.

I was walking the bridge tonight. I had asked Lauren, back on June 16, to give us sixty days. Today was sixty days. I doubted she paid any attention to the comment back then, but I was here anyway, hoping for a miracle.

It was a clear and hot night. There were a lot of people on the bridge, but Lauren wasn't one of them. It was okay. Life lessons were hard. After a couple weeks of not eating some days, then eating so much I could hardly walk, on others, I was back to working out again. I knew every shop in the metro that had mint chocolate chip ice cream. But what good did knowing do, when there was no one to tell it to?

I meandered down to the ruins where we last spoke. No Lauren.

I sat on the concrete ledge overlooking the stream. *What did I learn from this?* The obvious was that I hated being alone. The latent lesson—I would protect time with a loved one in the future, instead of assuming it would always be there for me later.

"Zave," a soft voice called from behind me.

I immediately hopped off the ledge and turned, "Lauren."

Incandescent sapphire blue eyes, black tank top, blue jean shorts. I'd been told that a blue flame is the hottest. Now I knew with certainty. My words awkwardly tumbled out, "I—I was kind of hoping you'd be here."

Almost apologetically, she shared, "I dressed the same, because I wanted you to recognize me."

I would have recognized those blue eyes in a space suit.

She smiled, "Technically, this is the sixtieth day."

I poured out, "I haven't been with anyone since we last spoke. My thinking is clear. I want to start over. Be with just you and see where it lands."

She patted our rock and we sat on it together. "After taking some time off, I realized we were both caught in a hurricane of drama, and it almost destroyed me. But in that whirlwind were two wonderful nights. If there's any chance we could have two more, I'm in—whole heartedly."

"Me, too. I love you, Lauren." I sang, *"You are so beautiful—to me."*

She responded in kind, "This is crazy—but I love you too, Zave."

We kissed . . .

67

For there is always light.
If only we are brave enough to see it.
If only we are brave enough to be it."
—AMANDA GORMAN

2021

JON FREDERICK

9:53 P.M., SEPTEMBER 21
PIERZ

Serena and I sat in the dark in our backyard, rocking on the cushioned swing, with the children's bedroom monitors resting on the outdoor coffee table in front of us. The fall night was still 73 degrees, which was unusually warm for this time of year. We leaned on each other in shorts and t-shirts looking up at the stars. Serena sipped on an Ancient Peaks cabernet, while I took a large swallow of Beaver Island's Octoberfest. I had poured the beer over home grown hops and let it cool before serving it up. The wet hopping turned out even better than I anticipated—so refreshing!

The kids were healthy and finally asleep.

Serena took my hand and rubbed it. "I'm glad this case is over. Since the shooting, I have this incredible need to be close to you."

I understood. "I'm not going anywhere, Serena. I love you." I pulled her closer. "The way you love me makes me feel like I matter. You bring me peace and make me happier than a baby getting that first taste of candy."

Serena kissed me and then snuggled her warm body closer against mine. "How do you fix Minneapolis?"

I kissed the top of her head and thought out loud. "The problem is police officers deny the obvious and accept the improbable, with black men in particular. They pull over a black man and assume he stole the car and used it to rob a gas station at gunpoint—which is highly improbable. This assumption immediately makes it a life-or-death situation. The obvious is he's just on his way home, like everybody else. We need cops policing the neighborhood, who know the people. They need to be part of the community."

Serena continued to challenge me. "What would you do about all the shootings?"

"The problem is multi-faceted. First, it's a pandemic issue. People don't realize that the second year after the Spanish Flu pandemic, in 1919, there was a huge spike in violent crime. When people are scared and distrustful of the government, they lose it. The government lied to Americans, telling people the pandemic started in Spain, when the truth was the first documented case was in Kansas. They lied to us about COVID, too, initially telling people masks wouldn't help in an effort to prevent the general public from buying them all up. Add in the illegal gun problem we have today. Last year, over four thousand illegal weapons were seized by police—double the number confiscated just ten years earlier. You make people tense, give them guns, and they shoot each other."

"It sounds so overwhelming. So, what's the solution?"

"Local policing. My heart breaks for the parents who've lost their kids to these shootings. If it was my kid, I'd detain every person involved in a shooting until I had answers. But that would make me just another white guy unfairly incarcerating people. It has to be done by people who are known and trusted by the local community." I took a sip and gave her some grief, "Woman, you need to learn to chill. Here we are, alone on a peaceful night. This is a daytime conversation."

She laughed, "That sounds like something your dad would say." She nuzzled against me. "When I look at the stars, I worry about the world. You're like an old cowboy who gets so relaxed out here you could fall asleep."

"True." I couldn't argue with that.

She kissed the back of my hand and asked, "Do you think Lauren and Zave will make it?"

I grinned, "I think they already have."

She teasingly poked me, "You know what I mean."

"They're happy and that's perfect. God only knows."

Serena peeked up at me, "What do you think we need?"

"More hops. I didn't grow enough hops this year." I took a sip of my satisfying malt beverage. "I'll only be able to enjoy this concoction a couple times."

She nudged me again, "I'm serious."

So was I. But I responded, "I will love you until these stars go out." I hesitated, "And after. I love moments like this. I don't even feel we need to say anything. I can feel your love through your warmth and I'm content. Life is wonderful."

Serena's voice was soothing and her gaze tranquil when she turned to me and said, "I think I'd like to stay home for a bit again. Nora and Jackson are growing so fast."

I set my glass down and relaxed against her. I could feel her heart beating harmoniously with mine. "I can transfer back to St. Cloud with the BCA and work an unresolved homicide here. You can help me, as you have in the past, and we'll get our private practice rolling when you're ready. Nora and I will get Jackson enlisted in our warrior training and we'll be chopping wood with our bare hands like a family of ninjas back here."

Serena raised an eyebrow. "I can't believe the way Nora can sound out words. She asked me today what *irections* were."

"Where did she hear someone talking about erections?"

"That's what I asked. Nora told me, *in school.* Then she walked to the table and showed me her handout. It had been three-hole punched, and the punch hole eliminated the *D* in *Directions.* It ended up being a much easier conversation than I anticipated."

I laughed, "We'll be okay. With all the love in this household, we're going to have some great stories yet.'"

Serena kissed me, "I agree . . . "

About the Author

F RANK WEBER is a forensic psychologist who has completed assessments for homicide, sexual assault, and physical assault cases. He has received the President's Award from the Minnesota Correctional Association for his forensic work. Frank has presented at state and national conventions and teaches college courses in psychology and social problems. Raised in the small rural community of Pierz, Minnesota, Frank is one of ten children (yes Catholic), named in alphabetical order. Despite the hand-me-downs, hard work, and excessive consumption of potatoes (because they were cheap), there was always music and humor. Frank has been blessed to share his life with his wife Brenda, since they were teenagers.